"Ugh. Boss, when I said that I wanted to punish him before I killed him, I didn't mean anything as horrible as burning him to death."

"Had he not behaved like a horse running back into a burning barn, he would have died as the others did . . . quickly, from laser beam. Shot on sight, for we took no prisoners."

"Not even for interrogation?"

"Not correct doctrine, I so stipulate. But, Friday my dear, you are unaware of the emotional atmosphere. All had heard the tapes, at least of the rape and of your third interrogation, the torture. Our lads and lassies would not have taken prisoners even if I had so ordered. But I did not attempt to. I want you to know that you are held in high esteem by your colleagues. Including the many who have never met you and whom you are unlikely ever to meet."

Boss reached for his canes, struggled to his feet. "I'm seven minutes over the time your physician told me I could visit. We'll talk tomorrow. You are to rest now. A nurse will be in to put you to sleep. Sleep and get well."

I had a few minutes to myself; I spent them in a warm glow. "High esteem." When you have never belonged and can never really belong, words like that mean everything. They warmed me so much that I didn't mind not being human.

FRIDAY

Books by Robert A. Heinlein

Assignment in Eternity

Between Planets

The Cat Who Walks Through
  Walls

Citizen of the Galaxy

Destination Moon

The Door into Summer

Double Star

Expanded Universe: More Worlds
  Of Robert A. Heinlein

Farmer in the Sky

Farnham's Freehold

Friday

Glory Road

The Green Hills of Earth

Grumbles from the Grave

Have Space Suit—Will Travel

I Will Fear No Evil

Job: A Comedy of Justice

The Man Who Sold the Moon

The Menace from Earth

Methuselah's Children

The Moon is a Harsh Mistress

The Notebooks of Lazarus Long

The Number of the Beast

Orphans of the Sky

The Past Through Tomorrow:
  "Future History" Stories

Podkayne of Mars

The Puppet Masters

Red Planet

Requiem: New Collected Works
  and Tributes to the Grand
  Master

Revolt in 2100

Rocket Ship Galileo

The Rolling Stones

Sixth Column

Space Cadet

The Star Beast

Starman Jones

Starship Troopers

Stranger in a Strange Land

Take Back Your Government

Time Enough for Love

Time for the Stars

To Sail Beyond the Sunset

Tramp Royale

Tunnel in the Sky

The Unpleasant Profession of
  Jonathan Hoag

Waldo & Magic, Inc.

Friday

Robert A. Heinlein

BALLANTINE BOOKS • NEW YORK

A Del Rey® Book
Published by Ballantine Books

Copyright © 1982 by Robert A. Heinlein

All rights reserved under International and Pan-American Copyright Conventions. Published in the United States by Ballantine Books, a division of Random House, Inc., New York, and distributed in Canada by Random House of Canada Limited, Toronto.

Originally published by Holt, Rinehart and Winston in 1982.

http://www.randomhouse.com/delrey/

Library of Congress Catalog Card Number: 96-95218

ISBN: 0-345-41400-4

Lines from "Stopping by Woods on a Snowy Evening" from *The Poetry of Robert Frost*, edited by Edward Connery Lathem. Copyright 1923, © 1969 by Holt, Rinehart and Winston. Copyright 1951 by Robert Frost. Reprinted by permission of Holt, Rinehart and Winston, Publishers.

Text design by Amy Hill

Manufactured in the United States of America

First Ballantine Books Trade Edition: July 1997

10 9 8 7 6 5 4 3 2 1

This book is for

Ann	*Elinor*	*Pepper*
Anne	*Gay*	*Polly*
Barbie	*Jeanne*	*Roberta*
Betsy	*Joan*	*Tamea*
Bubbles	*Judy-Lynn*	*Rebel*
Carolyn	*Karen*	*Ursula*
Catherine	*Kathleen*	*Verna*
Dian	*Marilyn*	*Vivian*
Diane	*Nichelle*	*Vonda*
Eleanor	*Patricia*	*Yumiko*

and always—semper toujours!—for Ginny.

R. A. H.

FRIDAY

As I left the Kenya Beanstalk capsule he was right on my heels. He followed me through the door leading to Customs, Health, and Immigration. As the door contracted behind him I killed him.

I have never liked riding the Beanstalk. My distaste was full-blown even before the disaster to the Quito Skyhook. A cable that goes up into the sky with nothing to hold it up smells too much of magic. But the only other way to reach Ell-Five takes too long and costs too much; my orders and expense account did not cover it.

So I had been edgy even before I left the shuttle from Ell-Five at Stationary Station to board the Beanstalk capsule . . . but, damn it, being edgy isn't reason to kill a man. I had intended only to put him out for a few hours.

The subconscious has its own logic. I grabbed him before he hit the deck and dragged him quickly toward a rank of bonded bomb-proof lockers, hurrying to avoid staining the floor—shoved his thumb against the latch, pushed him inside as I grabbed his pouch, found his Diners Club card, slid it into the slot, salvaged his IDs and cash, and chucked the pouch in with the cadaver as the armor slid down and clanged home. I turned away.

A Public Eye was floating above and beyond me.

No reason to jump out of my boots. Nine times out of ten an Eye is cruising at random, unmonitored, and its twelve-hour loop may or may not be scanned by a human before it is scrubbed. The tenth time— A peace officer may be monitoring it closely . . . or she may be scratching herself and thinking about what she did last night.

So I ignored it and kept on toward the exit end of the corridor. That pesky Eye should have followed me as I was the only mass in that passageway radiating at thirty-seven degrees. But it tarried, three seconds at least, scanning that locker, before again fastening on me.

I was estimating which of three possible courses of action was safest when that maverick piece of my brain took over and my hands executed a fourth: My pocket pen became a laser beam and "killed" that Public Eye—killed it dead as I held the beam at full power until the Eye dropped to the deck, not only blinded but with antigrav shorted out. And its memory scrubbed—I hoped.

I used my shadow's credit card again, working the locker's latch with my pen to avoid disturbing his thumbprint. It took a heavy shove with my boot to force the Eye into that crowded locker. Then I hurried; it was time to be someone else. Like most ports of entry Beanstalk Kenya has travelers' amenities on both sides of the barrier. Instead of going through inspection I found the washrooms and paid cash to use a bath-dressingroom.

Twenty-seven minutes later I not only had had a bath but also had acquired different hair, different clothes, another face—what takes three hours to put on will come off in fifteen minutes of soap and hot water. I was not eager to show my real face but I had to get rid of the *persona* I had used on this mission. What part of it had not washed down the drain now went into the shredder: jump suit, boots, pouch, fingerprints, contact lenses, passport. The passport I now carried used my right name—well, one of my names—a stereograph of my bare face, and had a very sincere Ell-Five transient stamp in it.

Before shredding the personal items I had taken off the corpse, I looked through them—and paused.

His credit cards and IDs showed four identities.

Where were his other three passports?

Probably somewhere on the dead meat in that locker. I had not given it a proper search—no time!—I had simply grabbed what he carried in his pouch.

Go back and look? If I kept trotting back and opening a locker full of still-warm corpse, someone was bound to notice. By taking his cards and passport I had hoped to postpone identifying the body and thereby give myself more time to get clear but—wait a moment. Mmm, yes, passport and Diners Club card were both for "Adolf Belsen." American Express extended credit to "Albert Beaumont" and the Bank of Hong Kong took care of "Arthur Bookman" while MasterCard provided for "Archibald Buchanan."

I "reconstructed" the crime: Beaumont-Bookman-Buchanan had just thumbed the latch of the locker when Belsen sapped him from behind, shoved him into the locker, used his own Diners Club card to lock it, and left hastily.

Yes, an excellent theory . . . and now to muddy the water still more.

Those IDs and credit cards went back of my own in my wallet; "Belsen's" passport I concealed about my person. I could not stand a skin search but there are ways to avoid a skin search including (but not limited to) bribery, influence, corruption, misdirection, and razzle-dazzle.

As I came out of the washroom, passengers from the next capsule were trickling in and queuing up at Customs, Health, and Immigration; I joined a queue. The CHI officer remarked on how very light my jumpbag was and asked about the state of the up-high black market. I gave him my best stupid look, the one on my passport picture. About then he found the correct amount of squeeze tucked into my passport and dropped the matter.

I asked him for the best hotel and the best restaurant. He said that he wasn't supposed to make recommendations but that he thought well of the Nairobi Hilton. As for food, if I could afford it, the Fat Man, across from the Hilton, had the best food in Africa. He hoped that I would enjoy my stay in Kenya.

I thanked him. A few minutes later I was down the mountain and in the city, and regretting it. Kenya Station is over five kilometers high; the air is always thin and cold. Nairobi is higher than Denver, nearly as high as Ciudad de México, but it is only a fraction of the height of Mount Kenya and it is just a loud shout from the equator.

The air felt thick and too warm to breathe; almost at once my clothes were soggy with sweat; I could feel my feet starting to swell—and besides they ached from full gee. I don't like off-Earth assignments but getting back from one is worse.

I called on mind-control training to help me not notice my discomfort. Garbage. If my mind-control master had spent less time squatting in lotus and more time in Kenya, his instruction might have been more useful. I forgot it and concentrated on the problem: how to get out of this sauna bath quickly.

The lobby of the Hilton was pleasantly cool. Best of all, it held a fully automated travel bureau. I went in, found an empty booth, sat down in front of the terminal. At once the attendant showed up. "May I help you?"

I told her I thought I could manage; the keyboard looked familiar. (It was an ordinary Kensington 400.)

She persisted: "I'd be glad to punch it for you. I don't have anyone waiting." She looked about sixteen, a sweet face, a pleasant voice, and a manner that convinced me that she really did take pleasure in being helpful.

What I wanted least was someone helping me while I did things with credit cards that weren't mine. So I slipped her a medium-size tip while telling her that I really did prefer to punch it myself—but I would shout if I got into difficulties.

She protested that I did not have to tip her—but she did not insist on giving it back, and went away.

"Adolf Belsen" took the tube to Cairo, then semiballistic to Hong Kong, where he had reserved a room at the Peninsula, all courtesy of Diners Club.

"Albert Beaumont" was on vacation. He took Safari Jets to Timbuktu, where American Express had placed him for two weeks at the luxury Shangri-La on the shore of the Sahara Sea.

The Bank of Hong Kong paid "Arthur Bookman's" way to Buenos Aires.

"Archibald Buchanan" visited his native Edinburgh, travel prepaid by MasterCard. Since he could do it all by tube, with one transfer at Cairo and automated switching at Copenhagen, he should be at his ancestral home in two hours.

I then used the travel computer to make a number of inquiries—but no reservations, no purchases, and temporary memory only.

4

Satisfied, I left the booth, asked the dimpled attendant whether or not the subway entrance I saw in the lobby would let me reach the Fat Man restaurant.

She told me what turns to make. So I went down into the subway—and caught the tube for Mombasa, again paying cash.

Mombasa is only thirty minutes, 450 kilometers, from Nairobi, but it is at sea level, which makes Nairobi's climate seem heavenly; I got out as quickly as I could arrange it. So, twenty-seven hours later I was in the Illinois Province of the Chicago Imperium. A long time, you might say, for a great-circle arc of only thirteen thousand kilometers. But I didn't travel great circle and did not go through a customs barrier or an immigration checkpoint. Nor did I use a credit card, even a borrowed one. And I managed to grab seven hours of sleep in Alaska Free State; I hadn't had any sound sleep since leaving Ell-Five space city two days earlier.

How? Trade secret. I may never need that route again but someone in my line of work will need it. Besides, as my boss says, with all governments everywhere tightening down on everything wherever they can, with their computers and their Public Eyes and ninety-nine other sorts of electronic surveillance, there is a moral obligation on each free person to fight back wherever possible—keep underground railways open, keep shades drawn, give misinformation to computers. Computers are literal-minded and stupid; electronic records aren't really records . . . so it is good to be alert to opportunities to foul up the system. If you can't evade a tax, pay a little too much to confuse their computers. Transpose digits. And so on. . . .

The key to traveling half around a planet without leaving tracks is: Pay cash. Never credit, never anything that goes into a computer. And a bribe is never a bribe; any such transfer of valuta must save face for the recipient. No matter how lavishly overpaid, civil servants everywhere are convinced that they are horribly underpaid—but all public employees have larceny in their hearts or they wouldn't be feeding at the public trough. These two facts are all you need—but be careful!—a public employee, having no self-respect, needs and demands a show of public respect.

I always pander to this need and the trip had been without incident. (I didn't count the fact that the Nairobi Hilton blew up and burned a few minutes after I took the tube for Mombasa; it would have seemed downright paranoid to think that it had anything to do with me.)

I did get rid of four credit cards and a passport just after I heard about it but I had intended to take that precaution anyhow. If the opposition wanted to cancel me—possible but unlikely—it would be swatting a fly with an ax to destroy a multimillion-crown property and kill or injure hundreds or thousands of others just to get me. Unprofessional.

As may be. Here I was at last in the Imperium, another mission completed with only minor bobbles. I exited at Lincoln Meadows while musing that I had garnered enough brownie points to wheedle the boss out of a few weeks R&R in New Zealand. My family, a seven S-group, was in Christchurch; I had not seen them in months. High time!

But in the meantime I relished the cool clean air and the rustic beauty of Illinois—it was not South Island but it was the next best thing. They say these meadows used to be covered with dingy factories—it seems hard to believe. Today the only building in sight from the station was the Avis livery stable across the street.

At the hitching rail outside the station were two Avis RentaRigs as well as the usual buggies and farm wagons. I was about to pick one of the Avis nags when I recognized a rig just pulling in: a beautiful matched pair of bays hitched to a Lockheed landau. "Uncle Jim! Over here! It's me!"

The coachman touched his whip to the brim of his top hat, then brought his team to a halt so that the landau was at the steps where I waited. He climbed down and took off his hat. "It's good to have you home, Miss Friday."

I gave him a quick hug, which he endured patiently. Uncle Jim Prufit harbored strong notions of propriety. They say he was convicted of advocating papism—some said that he was actually caught bare-handed, celebrating mass. Others said nonsense, he was infiltrating for the company and took a fall to protect others. Me, I don't know that much about politics, but I suppose a priest would have formal manners, whether he was a real one or a member of our trade. I could be wrong; I don't think I've ever seen a priest.

As he handed me in, making me feel like a "lady," I asked, "How did you happen to be here?"

"The Master sent me to meet you, miss."

"He did? But I didn't let him know when I would arrive." I tried to think who, on my back track, could have been part of Boss's data net. "Sometimes I think the boss has a crystal ball."

"It do seem like it, don't it?" Jim clucked to Gog and Magog and we headed for the farm. I settled back and relaxed, listening to the homey, cheerful *clomp clomp!* of horses' hooves on dirt.

I woke up as Jim turned into our gate and was wide awake by the time he pulled under the porte-cochère. I jumped down without waiting to be a "lady" and turned to thank Jim.

They hit me from both sides.

Dear old Uncle Jim did not warn me. He simply watched while they took me.

▌▌

My own stupid fault! I was taught in basic that no place is ever totally safe and that any place you habitually return to is your top danger spot, the place most likely for booby trap, ambush, stakeout.

But apparently I had learned this only as parrot rote; as an old pro I had ignored it. So it bit me.

This rule is analogous to the fact that the person most likely to murder you is some member of your own family—and that grim statistic is ignored too; it has to be. Live in fear of your own family? Better to be dead!

My worst stupidity was to ignore a loud, clear, specific warning, not just a general principle. How had dear old "Uncle" Jim managed to meet my capsule?—on the right day and almost to the minute. Crystal ball? Boss is smarter than the rest of us but he does not use magic. I may be wrong but I'm positive. If Boss had supernatural powers he would not need the rest of us.

I had not reported my movements to Boss; I didn't even tell him when I left Ell-Five. This is doctrine; he does not encourage us to check in every time we move, as he knows that a leak can be fatal.

Even I didn't know that I was going to take that particular capsule until I took it. I had ordered breakfast in Hotel Seward's coffee shop, stood up without eating it, dropped some money on the counter—three minutes later I was sealed into an express capsule. So how?

Obviously chopping off that tail at Kenya Beanstalk Station had not eliminated all tails on me. Either there had been a backup tail on the spot or Mr. "Belsen" ("Beaumont," "Bookman," "Buchanan") had been missed at once and replaced quickly. Possibly they had been with me all along or perhaps what had happened to "Belsen" had made them cautious about stepping on my heels. Or last night's sleep may have given them time to catch me.

Which variant was immaterial. Shortly after I climbed into that capsule in Alaska, someone had phoned a message somewhat like this: "Firefly to Dragonfly. Mosquito left here express capsule International Corridor nine minutes ago. Anchorage traffic control shows capsule programmed to sidetrack and open Lincoln Meadows your time eleven-oh-three." Or some such chatter. Some unfriendly had seen me enter that capsule and had phoned ahead; otherwise sweet old Jim would not have been able to meet me. Logic.

Hindsight is wonderful—it shows you how you busted your skull . . . after you've busted it.

But I made them pay for their drinks. If I had been smart, I would have surrendered once I saw that I was hopelessly outnumbered. But I'm not smart; I've already proved that. Better yet, I would have run like hell when Jim told me the boss had sent him . . . instead of climbing in and taking a nap, fer Gossake.

I recall killing only one of them.

Possibly two. But why did they insist on doing it the hard way? They could have waited until I was inside and gassed me, or used a sleepy dart, or even a sticky rope. They had to take me alive, that was clear. Didn't they know that a field agent with my training when attacked goes automatically into overdrive? Maybe I'm not the only stupid.

But why waste time by raping me? This whole operation had amateurish touches. No professional group uses either beating or rape before interrogation today; there is no profit in it; any professional is trained to cope with either or both. For rape she (or he—I hear it's worse for males) can either detach the mind and wait for it to be over, or (advanced training) emulate the ancient Chinese adage.

Or, in place of method A or B, or combined with B if the agent's histrionic ability is up to it, the victim can treat rape as an opportunity to gain an edge over her captors. I'm no great shakes as an actress but I try and, while it has never enabled me to turn the tables on unfriendlies, at least once it kept me alive.

This time method C did not affect the outcome but did cause a little healthy dissension. Four of them (my estimate from touch and body odors) had me in one of the upstairs bedrooms. It may have been my own room but I could not be certain as I had been unconscious for a while and was now dressed (solely) in adhesive tape over my eyes. They had me on a mattress on the floor, a gang bang with minor sadism . . . which I ignored, being very busy with method C.

In my mind I called them "Straw Boss" (seemed to be in charge), "Rocks" (they called him that—rocks in his head, probably), "Shorty" (take that either way), and "the other one" as he did not have distinctive characteristics.

I worked on all of them—method acting, of course—reluctant, have to be forced, then gradually your passion overcomes you; you just can't help yourself. Any man will believe that routine; they are suckers for it—but I worked especially hard on Straw Boss as I hoped to achieve the status of teacher's pet or some such. Straw Boss wasn't so bad; methods B and C combined nicely.

But I worked hardest on Rocks because with him it had to be C combined with A; his breath was so foul. He wasn't too clean in other ways, too; it took great effort to ignore it and make my responses flattering to his macho ego.

After he became flaccid he said, "Mac, we're wasting our time. This slut enjoys it."

"So get out of the way and give the kid another chance. He's ready."

"Not yet. I'm going to slap her around, make her take us seriously." He let me have a big one, left side of my face. I yelped.

"Cut that out!" —Straw Boss's voice.

"Who says so? Mac, you're getting too big for your britches."

"I say so." It was a new voice, very loud—amplified—from the sound-system speaker in the ceiling, no doubt. "Rocky, Mac is your squad leader, you know that. Mac, send Rocky to me; I want a word with him."

"Major, I was just trying to help!"

"You heard the man, Rocks," Straw Boss said quietly. "Grab your pants and get moving."

Suddenly the man's weight was no longer on me and his stinking breath was no longer in my face. Happiness is relative.

The voice in the ceiling spoke again: "Mac, is it true that Miss Friday simply enjoys the little ceremony we arranged for her?"

"It's possible, Major," Straw Boss said slowly. "She does act like it."

"How about it, Friday? Is this the way you get your kicks?"

I didn't answer his question. Instead I discussed him and his family in detail, with especial attention to his mother and sister. If I had told him the truth—that Straw Boss would be rather pleasant under other circumstances, that Shorty and the other man did not matter one way or the other, but that Rocks was an utter slob whom I would cancel at the first opportunity—it would have blown method C.

"The same to you, sweetie," the voice answered cheerfully. "I hate to disappoint you but I'm a crèche baby. Not even a wife, much less a mother or a sister. Mac, put the cuffs on her and throw a blanket over her. But don't give her a shot; I'll be talking to her later."

Amateur. My boss would never have alerted a prisoner to expect interrogation.

"Hey, crèche baby!"

"Yes, dear?"

I accused him of a vice not requiring a mother or a sister but anatomically possible—so I am told—for some males. The voice answered, "Every night, hon. It's very soothing."

So mark one up for the Major. I decided that, with training, he could have been a pro. Nevertheless he was a bloody amateur and I didn't respect him. He had wasted one, maybe two, of his ables, caused me unnecessarily to suffer bruises, contusions, and multiple personal indignities—even heartbreaking ones had I been an untrained female—and had wasted two hours or more. If my boss had been doing it, the prisoner would have spilled his/her guts at once and spent those two hours spouting her fullest memoirs into a recorder.

Straw Boss even took the trouble to police me—led me into the bathroom and waited quietly while I peed, without making a production of it—and that was amateurish, too, as a useful technique, of the cumulative sort, in interrogating an amateur (not a pro) is to force him or her to break toilet training. If she has been protected from the harsher things in life or if he suffers from excessive amour-propre—as most males do—it is at least as effective as pain, and potentiates either with pain or with other humiliations.

I don't think Mac knew this. I figured him for basically a decent soul despite his taste for—no, aside from his taste for a bit of rape—a taste common to most males according to the kinseys.

Somebody had put the mattress back on the bed. Mac guided me to it, told me to lie on my back with my arms out. Then he cuffed me to the legs of the bed, using two pairs. They weren't the peace-officer type, but special ones, velvet-lined—the sort of junk used by idiots for SM games. I wondered who the pervert was? The Major?

Mac made sure that they were secure but not too tight, then gently spread a blanket over me. I would not have been surprised had he kissed me good-night. But he did not. He left quietly.

Had he kissed me would method C call for returning it in full? Or turning my face and trying to refuse it? A nice question. Method C is based on I-just-can't-help-myself and requires precise judgment as to when and how much enthusiasm to show. If the rapist suspects the victim of faking, she has lost the ploy.

I had just decided, somewhat regretfully, that this hypothetical kiss should have been refused, when I fell asleep.

I was not allowed enough sleep. I was exhausted from all the things that had happened to me and had sunk into deep sleep, soggy with it, when I was roused by a slap. Not Mac. Rocks, of course. Not as hard as he had hit me earlier but totally unnecessary. It seemed to me that he blamed me for whatever disciplining he had received from the Major . . . and I promised myself that, when time came to cancel him, I would do it slowly.

I heard Shorty say, "Mac said not to hit her."

"I didn't hit her. That was just a love tap to wake her up. Shut up and mind your own business. Stand clear and keep your gun on her. On her, you idiot!—not on me."

They took me down into the basement and into one of our own interrogation chambers. Shorty and Rocks left—I think that Shorty left and I know that Rocks did; his stink went away—and an interrogation team took over. I don't know who or how many as not one of them ever said a word. The only voice was the one I thought of as "the Major." It seemed to be coming through a speaker.

"Good morning, Miss Friday."

(Morning? It seemed unlikely.) "Howdy, crèche baby!"

"I'm glad that you are in fine fettle, dear, as this session is likely to prove long and tiring. Even unpleasant. I want to know all about you, love."

"Fire away. What will you have first?"

"Tell me about this trip you just made, every tiny detail. And outline this organization you belong to. I might as well tell you that we already know a great deal about it, so if you lie, I will know it. Not even a little white fib, dear—for I will know it and what happens then I will regret but you will regret it far more."

"Oh, I won't lie to you. Is a recorder running? This will take a long time."

"A recorder is running."

"Okay." For three hours I spilled my guts.

This was according to doctrine. My boss knows that ninety-nine out of a hundred will crack under sufficient pain, that almost that percentage will crack under long interrogation combined with nothing more than raw fatigue, but only Buddha Himself can resist certain drugs. Since he does not expect miracles and hates to waste agents, standard doctrine is: "If they grab you, sing!"

So he makes sure that a field operative never knows anything critical. A courier never knows what she is carrying. I know nothing about policy. I don't know my boss's name. I'm not sure whether we are a government agency or an arm of one of the multinationals. I do know where the farm is but so do many other people . . . and it is (was) very well defended. Other places I have visited only via closed authorized power vehicles—an APV took me (for example) to a practice area that may be the far end of the farm. Or not.

"Major, how did you crack this place? It was pretty strongly defended."

"I ask the questions, bright eyes. Let's have that part again about how you were followed out of the Beanstalk capsule."

After a long time of this, when I had told all I knew and was repeating myself, the Major stopped me. "Dear, you tell a very convincing story and I don't believe more than every third word. Let's start procedure B."

Somebody grabbed my left arm and a needle went in. Babble juice! I hoped these frimping amateurs weren't as clumsy with it as they were in some other ways; you can get very dead in a hurry with an overdose. "Major! I had better sit down!"

"Put her in a chair." Somebody did so.

For the next thousand years I did my best to tell exactly the same story no matter how bleary I felt. At some point I fell off the chair. They didn't stick me back onto it but stretched me on the cold concrete instead. I went on babbling.

Some silly time later I was given some other shot. It made my teeth ache and my eyeballs felt hot but it snapped me awake. "Miss Friday!"

"Yes, sir?"

"Are you awake now?"

"I think so."

"My dear, I think you have been most carefully indoctrinated under hypnosis to tell the same story under drugs that you tell so well without drugs. That's too bad as I must now use another method. Can you stand up?"

"I think so. I can try."

"Stand her up. Don't let her fall." Someone—some two—did so. I wasn't steady but they held me. "Start procedure C, item five."

Someone stomped a heavy boot on my bare toes. I screamed.

Look, you! If you are ever questioned under pain, do scream. The Iron Man routine just makes them worse and it worse. Take it from one who's been there. Scream your head off and crack as fast as possible.

I am not going to give details of what happened during the following endless time. If you have any imagination, it would nauseate you, and to tell it makes me want to throw up. I did, several times. I passed out, too, but they kept reviving me and the voice kept on asking questions.

Apparently the time came when reviving didn't work, for the next thing I knew I was back in bed—the same bed, I suppose—and again handcuffed to it. I hurt all over.

That voice again, right above my head. "Miss Friday."

"What the hell do you want?"

"Nothing. If it's any consolation to you, dear girl, you are the only subject I have ever questioned that I could not get the truth out of, eventually."

"Go soothe yourself!"

"Good night, dear."

The bloody amateur! Every word I had said to him was the naked truth.

Someone came in and gave me another hypodermic shot. Presently the pain went away and I slept.

I think I slept a long time. I either had confused dreams or half-awake periods or both. Some of it had to be dreams—dogs do talk, many of them, but they don't lecture on the rights of living artifacts, do they? Sounds of a ruckus and people running up and down may have been real. But it felt like a nightmare because I tried to get out of bed and discovered that I couldn't lift my head, much less get up and join the fun.

There came a time when I decided that I really was awake, because cuffs no longer bothered my wrists and sticky tape was no longer across my eyes. But I didn't jump up or even open my eyes. I knew that the first few seconds after I opened my eyes might be the best and possibly the only chance I would have to escape.

I twitched muscles without moving. Everything seemed to be under control although I was more than a little sore here and there and several other places. Clothes? Forget them—not only did I have no idea where my clothes might be but also there is no time to stop to dress when you are running for your life.

Now to plan— There didn't seem to be anyone in this room; was anyone on this floor? Hold still and listen. If and when I was fairly sure I was alone on this floor, get noiselessly out of bed and up the stairs like a mouse, on past the third floor into the attic, and hide.

Wait for dark. Out an attic gable, down the roof and the back wall and into the woods. If I reached the woods back of the house, they would never catch me . . . but until I did, I would be an easy target.

The chances? One in nine. Perhaps one in seven if I got really cranked up. The weakest spot in a poor plan was the high probability of being spotted before I was clear of the house . . . because, if I was spotted—no, when I was spotted—I would not only have to kill but I would have to be utterly quiet in doing so—

—because the alternative was to wait until they terminated me . . . which would be shortly after "the Major" decided that there was no more to be squeezed out of me. Clumsy as these goons were, they were not so stupid—or the Major was not so stupid—as to let a witness who has been tortured and raped stay alive.

I stretched my ears in all directions and listened.

"Nothing was stirring, not even a mouse." No point in waiting; every moment I delayed brought that much closer the time when someone would be stirring. I opened my eyes.

"Awake, I see. Good."

"Boss! Where am I?"

"What a time-ridden cliché. Friday, you can do better than that. Back up and try again."

I looked around me. A bedroom, possibly a hospital room. No windows. No-glare lighting. A characteristic gravelike silence enhanced rather than broken by the softest of ventilation sighing.

I looked back at Boss. He was a welcome sight. Same old unstylish eye patch—why wouldn't he take time to have that eye regenerated? His canes were leaning against a table, in reach. He was wearing his usual sloppy raw-silk suit, a cut that looked like badly tailored pajamas. I was awfully glad to see him.

"I still want to know where I am. And how. And why. Somewhere underground, surely—but where?"

"Underground, surely, quite a few meters. 'Where' you will be told when you need to know, or at least how to get to and from. That was the shortcoming of our farm—a pleasant place but too many people knew its location. 'Why' is obvious. 'How' can wait. Report."

"Boss, you are the most exasperating man I have ever met."

"Long practice. Report."

"And your father met your mother at a swing ding. And he didn't take off his hat."

"They met at a Baptist Sunday-school picnic and both of them believed in the Tooth Fairy. Report."

"Dirty ears. Snot. The trip to Ell-Five was without incident. I found Mr. Mortenson and delivered to him the contents of my trick bellybutton. Routine was interrupted by a most unusual factor: The space city was experiencing an epidemic of respiratory disorder, etiology unknown, and I contracted it. Mr. Mortenson was most kind; he kept me at home and his wives nursed me with great skill and tender loving care. Boss, I want them compensated."

"Noted. Continue."

"I was out of my silly head most of the time. That is why I ran a week behind schedule. But once I felt like traveling I was able to leave at once as Mr. Mortenson told me that I was already carrying the item he had for you. How, Boss? My navel pouch again?"

"Yes and no."

"That's a hell of an answer!"

"Your artificial pochette was used."

"I thought so. Despite the fact that there aren't supposed to be any nerve endings there, I can feel something—pressure, maybe—when it's loaded."

I pressed on my belly around my navel and tightened my belly muscles. "Hey, it's empty! You unloaded it?"

"No. Our antagonists did so."

"Then I failed! Oh, God, Boss, this is awful."

"No," he said gently, "you succeeded. In the face of great danger and monumental obstacles you succeeded perfectly."

"I did?" (Ever had the Victoria Cross pinned on you?) "Boss, cut the double talk and draw me a diagram."

"I will."

But maybe I had better draw a diagram first. I have a 'possum pouch, created by plastic surgery, behind my bellybutton. It isn't large but you can crowd one whale of a lot of microfilm into a space of about one cubic centimeter. You can't see it because the sphincter valve that serves it holds the navel scar closed. My bellybutton looks normal. Unbiased judges tell me that I have a pretty belly and a sightly navel . . . which, in some important ways, is better than having a pretty face, which I don't have.

The sphincter is a synthetic silicone elastomer that holds the navel tight at all times, even if I am unconscious. This is necessary as there are no nerves there to give voluntary control of contraction and relaxation, such as is possible with the anal, vaginal, and—for some people—throat sphincters. To load the pouch use a dab of K-Y jelly or other nonpetroleum lubricant, and push it in by thumb— no sharp corners, please! To unload it I take the fingers of both hands and pull the artificial sphincter open as much as I can, then press hard with my abdominal muscles—and it pops right out.

The art of smuggling things in the human body has a long history. The classic ways are in the mouth, in the nasal sinuses, in the stomach, the gut, the rectum, vagina, bladder, eye socket of a missing eye, ear canal, and exotic and not very useful methods using tattoos sometimes covered with hair.

Every one of the classic ways is known to every customs officer and every special agent public or private the world round, Luna, space cities, other planets, and anywhere men have reached. So forget them. The only classic method that can still beat a pro is the Purloined Letter. But the Purloined Letter is high art indeed and, even when used perfectly, it should be planted on an innocent who can't give it away under drugs.

Take a look at the next thousand bellybuttons you encounter socially. Now that my pouch has been compromised, it is possible that one or two will conceal surgically emplaced hideaways like mine. You can expect a spate of them soon, then no more will be emplaced as any novelty in smuggling becomes useless once the word gets around. In the meantime customs officers are going to be poking rude fingers into bellybuttons. I hope a lot of those officers get poked in the eye by angry victims—navels tend to be sensitive and ticklish.

"Friday, the weak point of that pochette in you has always been that any skillful interrogation—"

"They were clumsy."

"—or rough interrogation using drugs could force you to mention its existence."

"Must have been after they shot me with babble juice. I don't recall mentioning it."

"Probably. Or word may have come to them through other channels, as several people know of it—you, me, three nurses, two surgeons, one anesthesiologist, possibly others. Too many. No matter how our antagonists knew, they did remove what you were carrying there. But don't look glum; what they received was a very long list reduced to microfilm of all the restaurants listed in a 1928 telephone book of the former city of New York. No doubt there is a computer somewhere working on this list right now, attempting to break the code concealed in it . . . which will take a long time as there is no code concealed in it. A dummy load. Sense-free."

"And for this I have to chase all the way to Ell-Five, eat scummy food, get sick on the Beanstalk, and be buggered about by brutal bastards!"

"Sorry about the last, Friday. But do you think I would risk the life of my most skillful agent on a useless mission?"

(See why I work for the arrogant bastard? Flattery will get you anywhere.) "Sorry, sir."

"Check your appendectomy scar."

"Huh?" I reached under the sheet and felt it, then flipped the sheet back and looked at it. "What the hell?"

"The incision was less than two centimeters and straight through the scar; no muscle tissue was disturbed. The item was withdrawn about twenty-four hours ago by reopening the same incision. With the accelerated repair methods that were used on you I am told that in two more days you will not be able to find the new scar in the old. But I am very glad that the Mortensons took such good care of you as I am sure that the artificial symptoms induced in you to cover what had to be done to you were not pleasant. By the way, there really is a catarrhal-fever epidemic there—fortuitous window dressing."

Boss paused. I stubbornly refused to ask him what I was carrying—he would not have told me anyhow. Shortly he added, "You were telling me about your trip home."

"The trip down was without incident. Boss, the next time you send me into space I want to go first-class, in an antigrav ship. Not via that silly Indian rope trick."

"Engineering analysis shows that a skyhook is safer than any ship. The Quito cable was lost through sabotage, not matériel failure."

"Stingy."

"I don't intend to bind the mouths of the kine. You may use antigrav from here on if circumstances and timing permit. This time there were reasons to use the Kenya Beanstalk."

"Maybe so, but someone tailed me out of the Beanstalk capsule. As soon as we were alone, I killed him."

I paused. Someday, someday, I am going to cause his face to register surprise. I retackled the subject diagonally:

"Boss, I need a refresher course, with some careful reorientation."

"Really? To what end?"

"My kill reflex is too fast. I don't discriminate. That bloke hadn't done anything to rate killing. Surely, he was tailing me. But I should either have shaken him, there or in Nairobi, or, at most, knocked him cold and placed him on ice while I went elsewhere."

"We'll discuss your possible need later. Continue."

I told him about the Public Eye and "Belsen's" quadruple identity and how I had sent them to the four winds, then I outlined my trip home. He checked me. "You did not mention the destruction of that hotel in Nairobi."

"Huh? But, Boss, that had nothing to do with me. I was halfway to Mombasa."

"My dear Friday, you are too modest. A large number of people and a huge amount of money have gone into trying to keep you from completing your mission, including a last-ditch attempt at our former farm. You may assume, at least hypothesize, that the bombing of the Hilton had as its sole purpose killing you."

"Hmm. Boss, apparently you knew that it would be this rough. Couldn't you have warned me?"

"Would you have been more alert, more resolute, had I filled your mind with vague warnings of unknown dangers? Woman, you made no mistakes."

"The hell I didn't! Uncle Jim met my capsule when he should not have known the time I would arrive; that should have set off every alarm in my head. The instant I laid eyes on him I should have dived back down the hole and taken any capsule anywhere."

"Whereupon it would have become extremely difficult for us to achieve rendezvous, which would have aborted your mission as thoroughly as losing what you carried. My child, if affairs had gone smoothly, Jim would have met you at my behest; you underestimate my intelligence net as well as the effort we put into trying to watch over you. But I did not send Jim to get you because at that moment I was running. Hobbling, to be precise. Hurrying. Trying to escape. I assume that Jim took the ETA message himself—from our man, or that of our antagonists, or possibly from both."

"Boss, if I had known it at the time, I would have fed Jim to his horses. I was fond of him. When the time comes, I want to cancel him myself. He's mine."

"Friday, in our profession it is undesirable to hold grudges."

"I don't hold many but Uncle Jim is special. And there is another case I want to handle myself. But I'll argue with you later. Say, is it true that Uncle Jim used to be a papist priest?"

Boss almost looked surprised. "Where did you hear that nonsense?"

"Around and about. Gossip."

" 'Human, All Too Human.' Gossip is a vice. Let me settle it. Prufit was a con man. I met him in prison, where he did something for me, important enough that I made a place for him in our organization. My mistake. My inexcusable mistake, as a con man never stops being a con man; he can't. But I suffered from a will to believe, a defect of character that I thought I had rooted out. I was mistaken. Continue, please."

I told Boss how they had grabbed me. "Five of them, I think. Possibly only four."

"Six, I believe. Descriptions."

"None, Boss, I was too busy. Well, one. I had one sharp look at him just as I killed him. About a hundred and seventy-five tall, weight around seventy-five or -six. Age near thirty-five. Blondish, smooth-shaven. Slavic. But he was the only one my eye photographed. Because he held still. Involuntarily. As his neck snapped."

"Was the other one you killed blond or brunet?"

" 'Belsen'? Brunet."

"No, at the farm. Never mind. You killed two and injured three before they piled enough bodies on you to hold you down by sheer weight. A credit to your instructor, let me add. In escaping, we had not been able to thin them down enough to keep them from taking you . . . but, in my opinion, you won the battle in which we recaptured you by your having earlier taken out so many of their effectives. Even though you were chained up and unconscious at the time, you won the final fracas. Go on, please."

"That about wraps it up, Boss. A gang rape next, followed by interrogation, direct, then under drugs, then under pain."

"I'm sorry about the rape, Friday. The usual bonuses. You will find them enhanced as I judge the circumstances to have been unusually offensive."

"Oh, not that bad. I'm hardly a twittering virgin. I can recall social occasions that were almost as unpleasant. Except one man. I don't know his face but I can identify him. I want him! I want him as badly as I want Uncle Jim. Worse, maybe, as I want to punish him a bit before I let him die."

"I can only repeat what I said earlier. For us, personal grudges are a mistake. They reduce survival probability."

"I'll risk it for this bucko. Boss, I don't hold the rape qua rape against him; they were ordered to rape me under the silly theory that it would soften me up for interrogation. But the scum should bathe and he should have his teeth fixed and he should brush them and use a mouthwash. And somebody must tell him that it is not polite to slap a woman with whom he is copulated. I don't know his face but I know his voice and his odor and his build and his nickname. Rocks or Rocky."

"Jeremy Rockford."

"Huh? You know him? Where is he?"

"I once knew him and I recently had one clear look at him, enough to be sure. *Requiescat in pace*."

"Really? Oh, hell. I hope he didn't die quietly."

"He did not die quietly. Friday, I have not told you all that I know—"

"You never do."

"—because I wanted your report first. Their assault on the farm succeeded because Jim Prufit had cut all power just before they hit us. This left us nothing but hand weapons for the few who wear arms at the farm, only bare hands for most of us. I ordered evacuation and most of us escaped through a tunnel prepared and concealed when the house was rebuilt. I am sorry and proud to say that three of our best, the three who were armed when we were hit, elected to play Horatius at the bridge. I know that they died as I kept the tunnel open until I could tell by the sounds that it had been entered by the raiders. Then I blasted it.

"It took some hours to round up enough people and to mount our counterattack, especially in arranging for enough authorized power vehicles. While we conceivably could have attacked on foot, we had to have at least one APV as ambulance for you."

"How did you know I was alive?"

"The same way I knew that the escape tunnel had been entered and not by our rear guard. Remote pickups. Friday, everything that was done to you and by you, everything you said and was said to you, was monitored and recorded. I was unable to monitor in person—busy preparing the counterattack—but the essential parts were played for me as time permitted. Let me add that I am proud of you.

"By knowing which pickups recorded what, we knew where they were holding you, the fact that you were cuffed, how many were in the house, where they were, when they settled down, and who stayed awake. By relay to the command APV I knew the situation in the house right to the moment of attack. We hit— They hit, I mean—our people hit. I don't lead attacks hobbling on these two sticks; I wield the baton. Our people hit the house, were inside, the designated four picked you up—one armed only with a bolt cutter—and all were out in three minutes eleven seconds. Then we set fire to it."

"Boss! Your lovely farmhouse?"

"When a ship is sinking, one does not worry about the dining-room linens. We can never use the farm again. Burning the house destroyed many awkward records and many secret and quasi-secret items of equipment. But, most compelling, burning the house gave us a quick cleanup of the parties who had compromised its secrets.

Our cordon was in place before we used incendiaries, then each one was shot as he attempted to come out.

"That was when I saw your acquaintance Jeremy Rockford. He was burned in the leg as he came out the east door. He stumbled back in, changed his mind and tried again to escape, fell and was trapped. From the sounds he made I can assure you that he did not die quietly."

"Ugh. Boss, when I said that I wanted to punish him before I killed him, I didn't mean anything as horrible as burning him to death."

"Had he not behaved like a horse running back into a burning barn, he would have died as the others did . . . quickly, from laser beam. Shot on sight, for we took no prisoners."

"Not even for interrogation?"

"Not correct doctrine, I so stipulate. But, Friday my dear, you are unaware of the emotional atmosphere. All had heard the tapes, at least of the rape and of your third interrogation, the torture. Our lads and lassies would not have taken prisoners even if I had so ordered. But I did not attempt to. I want you to know that you are held in high esteem by your colleagues. Including the many who have never met you and whom you are unlikely ever to meet."

Boss reached for his canes, struggled to his feet. "I'm seven minutes over the time your physician told me I could visit. We'll talk tomorrow. You are to rest now. A nurse will be in to put you to sleep. Sleep and get well."

I had a few minutes to myself; I spent them in a warm glow. "High esteem." When you have never belonged and can never really belong, words like that mean everything. They warmed me so much that I didn't mind not being human.

IV

Someday I'm going to win an argument with Boss.

But don't hold your breath.

There were days when I did not lose arguments with him—the days he did not visit me.

It started with a difference of opinion over how long I was going to have to remain in therapy. I felt ready to go home or back to duty, either one, after four days. While I didn't want to get into a dockside fight just yet, I could take light duty—or a trip to New Zealand, my first choice. All my hurts were repairing.

They hadn't been all that much: lots of burns, four broken ribs, simple fractures left tibia and fibula, multiple compound fractures of the bones of my right foot and three toes of my left, a hairline skull fracture without complications, and (messy but least disabling) somebody had sawed off my right nipple.

The last item and the burns and the broken toes were all that I recalled; the others must have happened while I was distracted by other matters.

Boss said, "Friday, you know that it will take at least six weeks to regenerate that missing nipple."

"But plastic surgery for a simple cosmetic job would heal in a week. Dr. Krasny told me so."

"Young woman, when anyone in this organization is maimed in line of duty, she will be restored as perfectly as therapeutic art can achieve. In addition to that our permanent policy, in your case there is another reason, compelling and sufficient. We each have a moral obligation to conserve and preserve beauty in this world; there is none to waste. You have an unusually comely body; damage to it is deplorable. It must be repaired."

"Cosmetic surgery is all right, I said so. But I don't expect to have milk in these jugs. And anybody in bed with me won't care."

"Friday, you may have convinced yourself that you will never have need to lactate. But esthetically a functional breast is very different from a surgery-shaped imitation. That hypothetical bedmate might not know . . . but you would know and I would know. No, my dear. You will be restored to your former perfection."

"Hmm! When are *you* going to get that eye regenerated?"

"Don't be rude, child. In my case, no esthetic issue obtains."

So I got my tit back as good as ever or maybe better. The next argument was over the retraining I felt I needed to correct my hair-trigger kill reflex. When I brought up the matter again, Boss looked as if he had just bitten into something nasty. "Friday, I do not recall that you have ever made a kill that turned out to be a mistake. Have you made any kills of which I am unaware?"

"No, no," I said hastily. "I never killed anybody until I went to work for you and I haven't made any that I didn't report to you."

"In that case all of your killings have been in self-defense."

"All but that 'Belsen' character. That wasn't self-defense; he never laid a finger on me."

"Beaumont. At least that was the name he usually used. Self-defense sometimes must take the form of 'Do unto others what they would do unto you but do it first.' De Camp, I believe. Or some other of the twentieth-century school of pessimistic philosophers. I'll call up Beaumont's dossier so that you may see for yourself that he belonged on everyone's better-dead list."

"Don't bother. Once I looked into his pouch, I knew that he wasn't following me to kiss me. But that was *afterward*."

Boss took several seconds to answer, far beyond his wont. "Friday, do you want to change tracks and become a hatchet man?"

My chin dropped and my eyes widened. That was all the answer I made.

"I didn't intend to frighten you off the nest," Boss said dryly. "You will have deduced that this organization includes assassins. I don't want to lose you as a courier; you are my best. But we always need skilled assassins as their attrition rate is high. However, there is this major difference between a courier and an assassin: A courier kills only in self-defense and often by reflex . . . and, I concede, always with some possibility of error . . . as not all couriers have your supreme talent for instantly integrating all factors and reaching a necessary conclusion."

"*Huh!*"

"You heard me correctly. Friday, one of your weaknesses is that you lack appropriate conceit. An honorable hatchet man does not kill by reflex; he kills by planned intent. If the plan goes so far wrong that he needs to use self-defense, he is almost certain to become a statistic. In his planned killings, he always knows why and agrees with the necessity . . . or I won't send him out."

(Planned killing? Murder, by definition. Get up in the morning, eat a hearty breakfast, then keep rendezvous with your victim, cut him down in cold blood? Eat dinner and sleep soundly?) "Boss, I don't think it is my sort of work."

"I'm not sure that you have the temperament for it. But, for the nonce, keep an open mind. I am not sanguine about the possibility of slowing down your defense reflex. Moreover I can assure you that, if we attempt to retrain you in the way that you ask, I will not again use you as a courier. No. Risking your life is your business . . . when on your own time. But your missions are always critical; I won't use a courier whose fine edge has been deliberately blunted."

Boss did not convince me but he made me unsure of myself. When I told him again that I was not interested in becoming a hatchet man, he did not appear to listen—just said something about getting me something to read.

I expected it—whatever—to show up on the room's terminal. Instead, about twenty minutes after he left me, a youngster—well, younger than I am—showed up with a book, a bound book with paper pages. It had a serial number on it and was stamped "EYES ONLY" and "Need-to-Know Required" and "Top Secret SPECIAL BLUE Clearance."

I looked at it, as anxious to handle it as a snake. "Is this for me? I think there has been a mistake."

"The Old Man does not make mistakes. Just sign the receipt."

I made him wait while I read the fine print. "This bit about 'never out of my sight.' I sleep now and then."

"Call Archives, ask for the classified documents clerk—that's me—and I'll be here on the bounce. But try not to go to sleep until I get here. Try *hard*."

"Okay." I signed the receipt, looked up and found him staring with bright-eyed interest. "What are you staring at?"

"Uh— Miss Friday, you're pretty."

I never know what to say to that sort of thing, since I'm not. I shape up all right, surely—but I was fully clothed. "How did you know my name?"

"Why, everybody knows who *you* are. You know. Two weeks ago. At the farm. *You* were there."

"Oh. Yes, I was there. But I don't remember it."

"I sure do!" His eyes were shining. "It's the only time I've had a chance to be part of a combat operation. I'm glad I had a piece of it!"

(What do you do?)

I took his hand, pulled him closer to me, took his face in both my hands, kissed him carefully, about halfway between warm-sisterly and let's-do-it! Maybe protocol called for something stronger but he was on duty and I was still on the disabled list—not fair to make implied promises that can't be kept, especially to youngsters with stars in their eyes.

"Thank you for rescuing me," I said to him soberly before letting go of his cheeks.

The dear thing blushed. But he seemed very pleased.

I stayed up so late reading that book that the night nurse scolded me. However, nurses need something to scold about now and then. I'm not going to quote from the incredible document . . . but listen to these subjects:

Title first: *The Only Deadly Weapon*. Then—

Assassination as a Fine Art
Assassination as a Political Tool
Assassination for Profit

Whew! There was no good reason for my reading all of it. But I did. It had an unholy fascination. Dirty.

I resolved never to mention the possibility of changing tracks and not to bring up retraining again. Let Boss bring it up himself if he wanted to discuss it. I punched the terminal, got Archives, and stated that I needed the classified documents clerk to accept custody of classified item number such-and-such and please bring my receipt. "Right away, Miss Friday," a woman answered.

Notoriety—

I waited with considerable unease for that youngster to show up. I am ashamed to say that this poisonous book had had a most unfortunate effect on me. It was the middle of the night, early morning; the place was dead quiet—and if the dear thing laid a hand on me, I was awfully likely to forget that I was technically an invalid. I needed a chastity girdle with a big padlock.

But it was not he; the sweet youngster had gone off duty. The person who showed up with my receipt was the older woman who had answered me on the terminal. I felt both relief and disappointment—and chagrin that I felt disappointed. Does convalescence make everybody irresponsibly horny? Do hospitals have a discipline problem? I have not been ill often enough to know.

The night clerk swapped my receipt for the book, then surprised me with: "Don't I get a kiss, too?"

"Oh! Were you there?"

"Any warm body, dear; we were awfully short of effectives that night. I'm not the world's greatest but I had basic training like anyone else. Yes, I was there. Wouldn't have missed it."

I said, "Thank you for rescuing me," and kissed her. I tried to make this simply a symbol, but she took charge and controlled what sort of a buss it would be. Rough and rugged, namely. She was telling me clearer than words that anytime I wanted to work the other side of the street, she would be waiting.

What do you do? There seem to be human situations for which there are no established protocols. I had just acknowledged that she had risked her life to save mine—precisely that, as that rescue raid was not the piece of cake that Boss's account made it appear to be. Boss's habitual understatement is such that he would describe the total destruction of Seattle as "a seismic disturbance." Having thanked her for my life how could I snub her?

I could not. I let my half of the kiss answer her wordless message—with my fingers crossed that I would never have to keep the implied promise.

Presently she broke the kiss but remained holding on to me. "Dearie," she said, "want to know something? Do you remember how you told off that slob they called the Major?"

"I remember."

"There is a bootleg piece of tape floating around of that one sequence. What you said to him and how you said it is highly admired by one and all. Especially me."

"That's interesting. Are you the little gremlin who copied that piece of tape?"

"Why, how could you think such a thing?" She grinned. "Do you mind?"

I thought it over for all of three milliseconds. "No. If the people who rescued me enjoy hearing what I told that bastard, I don't mind their listening to it. But I don't talk that way ordinarily."

"Nobody thinks you do." She gave me a quick peck. "But you did so when it was needed and you made every woman in the company proud of you. And our men, too."

She didn't seem disposed to let go of me but the night nurse showed up then and told me firmly to go to bed and she was going to give me a sleepytime shot—I made only the usual formal protest. The clerk said, "Hi, Goldie. Night. Night, dear." She left.

Goldie (not her name—bottle blonde) said, "Want it in your arm? Or in your leg? Don't mind Anna; she's harmless."

"She's all right." It occurred to me that Goldie probably could monitor both sight and sound. Probably? Certainly! "Were you there? At the farm? When the house was burned?"

"Not while the house was burning. I was in an APV, taking you here as fast as we could float it. You were a sad sight, Miss Friday."

"I'll bet I was. Thanks. Goldie? Will you kiss me good-night?"

Her kiss was warm and undemanding.

I found out later that she was one of the four who made the run upstairs to grab me back—one man carrying big bolt cutters, two armed and firing . . . and Goldie carrying unassisted a stretcher basket. But she never mentioned it, then or later.

I remember that convalescence as the first time in my life—except for vacations in Christchurch—when I was quietly, warmly happy, every day, every night. Why? Because I *belonged!*

Of course, as anyone could guess from this account, I had passed years earlier. I no longer carried an ID with a big "LA" (or even "AP") printed across it. I could walk into a washroom and not be told to use the end stall. But a phony ID and a fake family tree do not keep you warm; they just keep you from being hassled and discriminated against. You are still aware that there isn't any nation anywhere that considers your sort fit for citizenship and there are lots of places that would deport you or even kill you—or sell you—if your cover-up ever slipped.

An artificial person misses not having a family tree much more than you might think. Where were you born? Well, I wasn't born, exactly; I was designed in Tri-University Life Engineering Laboratory, Detroit. Oh, really? *My* inception was formulated by Mendelian Associates, Zurich. Wonderful small talk, that! You'll never hear it; it does not stand up well against ancestors on the *Mayflower* or in the Domesday Book. My records (or one set) show that I was "born" in Seattle, a destroyed city being a swell place for missing records. A great place to lose your next of kin, too.

Since I was never in Seattle I have studied very carefully all the records and pictures I could find; an honest-to-goodness native of Seattle can't trip me. I think. Or not yet.

But what they gave me while I was recovering from that silly rape and the not-so-funny interrogation was not phony at all and I did not have to worry about keeping my lies straight. Not just Goldie and Anna and the youngster (Terence) but over two dozen more before Dr. Krasny discharged me. Those were just the ones I came into contact with. There were more on that raid; I don't know how many. Boss's standing doctrine kept members of his organization from meeting each other save when their duties necessarily brought them together. Just as he firmly snubbed questions. You cannot let slip secrets you do not know, and you cannot betray a person whose very existence is unknown to you.

But Boss did not have rules just for the sake of rules. Once having met a colleague through duty one could continue the contact socially. Boss did not encourage such fraternizing but he was no fool and did not try to forbid it. In consequence Anna often called on me in the late evening just before she went on duty.

She never did try to collect her pound of flesh. There wasn't much opportunity but we could have found one if we had tried. I didn't try to discourage her—hell, no; if she had ever presented the bill for collection, I would not only have paid cheerfully but would have tried to convince her that it was my idea in the first place.

But she didn't. I think she was like the sensitive (and fairly rare) male who never paws a woman when she doesn't want to be pawed—he can sense it and doesn't start.

One evening shortly before my discharge I was feeling especially happy—I had acquired two new friends that day; "kissing friends," persons who had fought in the raid that saved me—and I tried to explain to Anna why it meant so much to me and found that I was starting to tell her how I was not quite what I seemed to be.

She stopped me. "Friday dear, listen to your big sister."

"Huh? Did I goof?"

"Maybe you were about to. 'Member the night we met, you returned through me a classified document? I have supreme top-secret clearance awarded to me by Mr. Two-Canes years back. That book you returned is where I can get at it anytime. But I have never opened it and never will. The cover says 'Need to Know' and I have never been told that I have need to know. You've read it but I don't know even the title or the subject—just its number.

"Personnel matters are like that. There used to be an elite military outfit, a foreign legion, that boasted that a legionnaire had no history before the day of his enlistment. Mr. Two-Canes wants us to be like that. For example, if we were to recruit a living artifact, an artificial person, the personnel clerk would know it. I know, as I used to be personnel clerk. Records to forge, possibly some plastic surgery needed, in some cases laboratory identifications to excise and then regenerate the area. . . .

"When we got through with him, he would never again have to worry about a tap on the shoulder or being elbowed out of a queue. He could even marry and have children without worrying that someday it might cause trouble for his kids. He wouldn't have to worry about *me*, either, as I have a trained forgettery. Now, dear, I don't know what you had on your mind. But, if it is something you don't ordinarily tell people, don't tell me. Or you'll hate yourself in the morning."

"No, I wouldn't!"

"All right. If you still want to tell me a week from now, I'll listen. A deal?"

Anna was right; a week later I felt no need to tell her. I'm 99 percent certain that she knew. Either way, it's swell to be loved for yourself alone, by somebody who doesn't think that APs are monsters, subhuman.

I don't know that any of the rest of my loving friends knew or guessed. (I don't mean Boss; he knew, of course. But he wasn't a friend; he was *Boss*.) It did not matter if my new friends learned that I wasn't human; because I had come to realize that they either didn't care or wouldn't care. All that mattered to them was whether or not you were part of Boss's outfit.

One evening Boss showed up, tapping his canes and whuffling, with Goldie trailing him. He settled heavily into the visitor's chair, said to Goldie, "I won't need you, nurse. Thank you"—then to me, "Take off your clothes."

From any other man that would be either offensive or welcome, depending. From Boss it merely meant that he wanted my clothes off. Goldie took it that way, too, as she simply nodded and left—and Goldie is the sort of professional who would buck Siva the Destroyer if He attempted to interfere with one of her patients.

I took my clothes off quickly and waited. He looked me up and down. "They again match."

"Seems so to me."

"Dr. Krasny says that he ran a test for lactation function. Positive."

"Yes. He pulled some stunt with my hormone balance and both of them leaked a little. Felt funny. Then he rebalanced and I dried up."

Boss grunted. "Turn around. Show me the sole of your right foot. Now your left. Enough. Burn scars seem to be gone."

"All that I can see. Doctor tells me the others have regenerated, too. The itching has stopped, so they must be."

"Put on your clothes. Dr. Krasny tells me that you are well."

"If I were any weller, you would have to bleed me."

"Well is an absolute; it has no comparative."

"Okay, I'm wellest."

"Impudence. Tomorrow morning you leave for refresher training. Be packed and ready by oh-nine hundred."

"Since I arrived without even a happy smile, packing will take me eleven seconds. But I need a new ID, a new passport, a new credit card, and quite a bit of cash—"

"All of which will be delivered to you before oh-nine hundred."

"—because I'm not going for a refresher; I'm going to New Zealand. Boss, I've told you and told you. I'm overdue for R and R, and I figure that I rate some paid sick leave to compensate for time I've been laid up. You're a slave driver."

"Friday, how many years will it take you to learn that when I thwart one of your whims, I always have your welfare in mind as well as the efficiency of the organization?"

"Hully gee, Great White Father. I abase myself. And I'll send you a picture postcard from Wellington."

"Of a pretty Maori, please; I've seen a geyser. Your refresher course will be tailored to fit your needs and you will decide when it is complete. Although you are 'wellest,' you need physical training of carefully increasing difficulty to get you back into that superb pitch of muscle tone and wind and reflex that is your birthright."

" 'Birthright.' Don't make jokes, Boss; you have no talent for it. 'My mother was a test tube; my father was a knife.' "

"You are being foolishly self-conscious over an impediment that was removed years ago."

"Am I? The courts say I can't be a citizen; the churches say I don't have a soul. I'm not 'man born of woman,' at least not in the eyes of the law."

" 'The law is an ass.' The records concerning your origin have been removed from the production laboratory's files, and a dummy set concerning an enhanced male AP was substituted."

"You never told me that!"

"Until you displayed this neurotic weakness, I saw no need. But a deception of that nature should be made so airtight that it will utterly displace the truth. And so it has. If you attempted, tomorrow, to claim your true lineage, you would not be able to get any authority anywhere to agree with you. You may tell anyone; it doesn't matter. But, my dear, why are you defensive? You are not only as human as Mother Eve, you are an enhanced human, as near perfect as your designers could manage. Why do you think I went out of my way to recruit you when you had no experience and no conscious interest in this profession? Why did I spend a small fortune educating and training you? Because I knew. I waited some years to be sure that you were indeed developing as your architects intended . . . then almost lost you when you suddenly dived off the map." He made a grimace that I think means a smile. "You gave me trouble, girl. Now about your training. Are you willing to listen?"

"Yes, sir." (I didn't try to tell him about the laboratory crèche; human people think all crèches are like those they've seen. I didn't tell him about the plastic spoon that was all I had to eat with until I was ten because I didn't want to tell how, the first time I tried to use a fork, I stabbed my lip and made it bleed and they laughed at me. It isn't any one thing; it's a million little things that are the difference between being reared as a human child and being raised as an animal.)

"You'll be taking a bare-hands combat refresher but you are to work out only with your instructor; there are to be no blemishes on you when you visit your family in Christchurch. You will receive advanced training in hand weapons, including some you may never have heard of. If you change tracks, you will need this."

"Boss, I am *not* going to become an assassin!"

"You need it anyhow. There are times when a courier can carry weapons and she must have every edge possible. Friday, don't despise assassins indiscriminately. As with any tool, merit or demerit lies in how it is used. The decline and fall of the former United States of North America derived in part from assassinations. But only in small part as the killings had no pattern and were pointless. What can you tell me of the Prussian-Russian War?"

"Not much. Mainly that the Prussians got their hides nailed to the barn when the smart money figured them for winners."

"Suppose I tell you that twelve people won that war—seven men, five women—and that the heaviest weapon used was a six-millimeter pistol."

"I don't think you have ever lied to me. How?"

"Friday, brainpower is the scarcest commodity and the only one of real value. Any human organization can be rendered useless, impotent, a danger to itself, by selectively removing its best minds while carefully leaving the stupid ones in place. It took only a few careful 'accidents' to ruin utterly the great Prussian military machine and turn it into a blundering mob. But this did not show until the fighting was well under way, because stupid fools look just as good as military geniuses until the fighting starts."

"Only a dozen people—Boss? Did *we* do that job?"

"You know that is the sort of question I discourage. We did not. It was a contract job by an organization as small and as specialized as we are. But I do not willingly involve us in nationalistic wars; the side of the angels is seldom self-evident."

"I still don't want to be an assassin."

"I will not permit you to be an assassin and let us have no more discussion of it. Be ready to leave at nine tomorrow."

V

Nine weeks later I left for New Zealand.

I'll say this for Boss: The supercilious bully always knows what he's talking about. When Dr. Krasny let me go, I wasn't "wellest." I was simply a recovered patient who no longer needed sickbed nursing.

Nine weeks later I could have taken prizes in the old Olympics without working up a sweat. As I boarded the SB *Abel Tasman* at Winnipeg freeport, the skipper gave me the eye. I knew I looked good and I added a waggle to my seat that I would never use on a mission—as a courier I usually try to blend into the scenery. But now I was on leave and it's kind of fun to advertise. Apparently I hadn't forgotten how as the skipper came back to my cradle while I was still belting in. Or it may have been the Superskin jump suit that I was wearing—new that season and the first one I had had; I bought the outfit at the freeport and changed into it in the shop. I'm sure that it is only a matter of time until the sects that think that sex has something to do with sin will class wearing Superskin as a mortal sin.

He said, "Miss Baldwin, is it not? Do you have someone meeting you in Auckland? What with the war and all it is not a good idea for an unescorted woman to be alone in an international port."

(I did not say, "Look, Bub, the last time I killed the bloke.") The captain stood a hundred and ninety-five, maybe, and would gross a hundred or more and none of it fat. Early thirties and the sort of blond you expect in SAS rather than ANZAC. If he wanted to be protective I was willing to stand short. I answered, "Nobody's meeting me but I'm just changing for the South Island shuttle. How do these buckles work? Uh, do those stripes mean you're the captain?"

"Let me show you. Captain, yes—Captain Ian Tormey." He started belting me in; I let him.

"Captain. Go*lee!* I've never met a captain before." A remark like that isn't even a fib when it's a ritual response in the ancient barnyard dance. He had said to me, "I'm on the prowl and you look good. Are you interested?" And I had answered, "You look acceptable but I'm sorry to have to tell you that I don't have time today."

At that point he could adjourn it with no hurt feelings or he could elect to invest in goodwill against a possible future encounter. He chose the latter.

As he finished belting me in—tight enough but not too tight and not using the chance to grab a feel—quite professional—he said, "The timing on that connection will be close today. If you'll hang back when we disembark and be last out, I'll be happy to put you aboard your Kiwi. That'll be faster than finding your way through the crowds by yourself."

(The connection timing is twenty-seven minutes, Captain—leaving twenty minutes in which to talk me out of my comm signal. But keep on being sweet about it and I may give it to you.) "Why, thank you, Captain!—if it's really not too much trouble."

"ANZAC service, Miss Baldwin. But my pleasure."

I like to ride the semiballistics—the high-gee blastoff that always feels as if the cradle would rupture and spurt fluid all over the cabin, the breathless minutes in free fall that feel as if your guts were falling out, and then reentry and that long, long glide that beats any sky ride ever built. Where can you have more fun in forty minutes with your clothes on?

Then comes the always interesting question: Is the runway clear? A semiballistic doesn't make two passes; it can't.

It says right here in the brochure that an SB never lifts until it receives clearance from the port of reentry. Sure, sure, and I believe in the Tooth Fairy just like Boss's parents. How about the dumb-john in the private APV who picks the wrong strip and parks? How about the time in Singapore when I sat in the Top Deck bar and watched three SBs land in nine minutes?—not, I concede, on the same strip, but on *crossing strips!* Russian roulette.

I'll go on riding them; I like them and my profession often calls for me to use them. But I hold my breath from touchdown to full stop.

This trip was fun as usual and a semiballistic ride is never long enough to be tiring. I hung back when we landed and, sure enough, my polite wolf was just coming out of the cockpit as I reached the exit. The flight attendant handed me my bag and Captain Tormey took it over my insincere protests.

He took me to the shuttle gate, took charge of confirming my reservation and selecting my seat, then brushed past the Passengers Only sign and settled down beside me. "Too bad you're leaving so quickly—too bad for me, that is. Under the rules I have to take three days turnaround . . . and I happen to be at loose ends this trip. My sister and her husband used to live here—but they've moved to Sydney and I no longer have anyone to visit with."

(I can just see you spending all your off time with your sister and your brother-in-law.) "Oh, what a shame! I know how you must feel. My family is in Christchurch and I'm always lonesome when I have to be away from them. A big, noisy, friendly family—I married into an S-group." (Always tell them at once.)

"Oh, how jolly! How many husbands do you have?"

"Captain, that is always the first thing men ask. It comes from misunderstanding the nature of an S-group. From thinking that S stands for 'sex.' "

"Doesn't it?"

"Goodness, no! It stands for 'security' and 'siblings' and 'sociability' and 'sanctuary' and 'succor' and 'safety' and lots of other things, all of them warm and sweet and comforting. Oh, it can stand for 'sex,' too. But sex is readily available everywhere. No need to form anything as complex as an S-group just for sex." (S stands for "synthetic family" because that is how it was designated in the legislation of the first territorial nation, the California Confederacy, to legalize it. But it is ten-to-one that Captain Tormey knew this. We were simply running through standard variations of the Grand Salute.)

"I don't find sex that readily available—"

(I refused to answer his ploy. Captain, with your height and broad shoulders and pink, well-scrubbed look, and almost all of your time free for The Hunt . . . in Winnipeg and Auckland, fer Gossake, two places where the crop never fails. . . . Please, sir! Try again.)

"—but I agree with you that it is not reason enough to marry. I'm not likely to marry, ever . . . because I go where the wild goose goes. But an S-group sounds like a fine deal to come back to."

"It is."

"How big is it?"

"Still interested in my husbands? I have three husbands, sir, and three group sisters to match . . . and I think you would like all three—especially Lispeth, our youngest and prettiest. Liz is a red-headed Scottish lassie and a bit of a flirt. Children? Of course. We try to count them every night, but they move pretty fast. And kittens and ducks and puppy dogs and a big rambling garden with roses all year round, almost. It's a busy happy place and always watch where you put your feet."

"Sounds grand. Does the group need an associate husband who can't be home much but carries loads of life insurance? How much does it cost to buy in?"

"I'll speak to Anita about it. But you don't sound serious."

The chitchat continued, neither of us meaning a word of it, other than on a symbolic level. Shortly we declared it a draw while providing for a possible rematch by exchanging comm codes, that of my family in Christchurch in answer to his offer to me of the casual use of his flat in Auckland. He had taken over the lease, he said, when his sister had moved . . . but he needed it only six days out of the month, usually. "So if you find yourself in town and need a place for a wash-up and a nap, or overnight, just call."

"But suppose one of your friends is using it, Ian"—he had asked me to drop calling him Captain—"or yourself."

"Unlikely but, if so, the computer will know and tell you. If I'm in town or about to be in town, it will tell you that, too—and I certainly would not want to miss you."

The pass direct, but in the politest terms. So I answered it by telling him, through giving him our Christchurch number, that he was welcome to try to get my pants off . . . *if* he had the guts to face my husbands, my co-wives, and a passel of noisy kids. I thought it most unlikely that he would call. Tall, handsome bachelors in glamorous, high-paying jobs don't have to carry the anvil that far.

About then the loudspeaker that mumbles the arrivals and departures interrupted itself with: "It is with deep sorrow that we pause to announce the total destruction of Acapulco. This flash comes to you courtesy of Interworld Transport, Proprietary, the Triple-S Lines: Speed—Safety—Service."

I gasped. Captain Ian said, "Oh, those idiots!"

"Which idiots?"

"The whole Mexican Revolutionary Kingdom. When are the territorial states going to learn that they cannot possibly win against corporate states? That's why I said they were idiots. And they *are!*"

"Why do you say that, Captain?—Ian?"

"Obvious. Any territorial state, even if it's Ell-Four or an asteroid, is a sitting duck. But fighting a multinational is like trying to slice a fog. Where's your target? You want to fight IBM? *Where is* IBM? Its registered home office is a P.O. box number in Delaware Free State. That's no target. IBM's offices and people and plants are scattered through four hundred—odd territorial states groundside and more in space; you can't hit any part of IBM without hurting somebody else as much or more. But can IBM defeat, say, Great Russia?"

"I don't know," I admitted. "The Prussians weren't able to."

"It would just depend on whether or not IBM could see a profit in it. So far as I know, IBM doesn't own any guerrillas; she may not even have agents saboteurs. She might have to buy the bombs and missiles. But she could shop around and take her own sweet time getting set because Russia isn't going anywhere. It will still be there, a big fat target, a week from now or a year. But Interworld Transport just showed what the outcome would be. This war is all over. Mexico bet that Interworld wouldn't risk public condemnation by destroying a Mexican city. But those old-style politicians forgot that corporate nations aren't nearly as interested in public opinion as territorial nations have to be. The war's over."

"Oh, I hope so! Acapulco is—was—a beautiful place."

"Yes, and it would still be a beautiful place if the Montezuma's

Revolutionary Council wasn't rooted somewhere back in the twentieth century. But now there will be face-saving. Interworld will apologize and pay an indemnity, then, with no fanfare, the Montezuma will cede the land and the extraterritoriality for the new spaceport to a new corporation with a Mexicano name and a DF home office . . . and the public won't be told that the new corporation is owned sixty percent by Interworld and forty percent by the very politicians who stalled just a little too long and let Acapulco be destroyed." Captain Tormey looked sour and I suddenly saw that he was older than I had first guessed.

I said, "Ian, isn't ANZAC a subsidiary of Interworld?"

"Perhaps that's why I sound so cynical." He stood up. "Your shuttle is locking into the gate. Let me have your bag."

VI

Christchurch is the loveliest city on this globe.

Make that "anywhere," as there is not yet a truly lovely city off Earth. Luna City is underground, Ell-Five looks like a junkyard from outside and has only one arc that looks good from inside. Martian cities are mere hives and most Earthside cities suffer from a misguided attempt to look like Los Angeles.

Christchurch does not have the magnificence of Paris or the setting of San Francisco or the harbor of Rio. Instead it has things that make a city lovable rather than stunning: The gentle Avon winding through our downtown streets. The mellow beauty of Cathedral Square. The Ferrier fountain in front of Town Hall. The lush beauty of our world-famous botanic gardens smack in the middle of downtown.

"The Greeks praise Athens." But I am not a native of Christchurch (if "native" could mean anything for my sort). I am not even an Ennzedd. I met Douglas in Ecuador (this was before the Quito Skyhook catastrophe), was delighted by a frantic love affair compounded of equal parts of pisco sours and sweaty sheets, then was frightened by his proposal, calmed down when he made me understand that he was not then proposing vows in front of some official but a trial visit to his S-group—find out if they liked me, find out if I liked them.

That was different. I zipped back to the Imperium and reported, and told Boss that I was taking some accumulated leave—or would he rather have my resignation? He growled something about go ahead and get my gonads cooled off, then report in when I was fit to work. So I rushed back to Quito and Douglas was still in bed.

At that time there really wasn't any way to get from Ecuador to New Zealand . . . so we tubed to Lima and took an SB right over the South Pole to West Australia Port at Perth (with the oddest S-shaped track because of Coriolis)—tube to Sydney, bounce to Auckland, float to Christchurch, taking nearly twenty-four hours and the wildest of tracks just to cross the Pacific. Winnipeg and Quito are almost the same distance from Auckland—don't be fooled by a flat map; ask your computer—Winnipeg is only one-eighth farther.

Forty minutes versus twenty-four hours. But I had not minded the longer trip; I was with Douglas and dizzy in love.

In another twenty-four hours I was dizzy in love with his family. I hadn't expected that. I had looked forward to a lovely vacation with Douglas and he had promised me some skiing as well as sex—not that I insisted on skiing. I knew that I had an implied obligation to go to bed with his group brothers if asked. But that didn't worry me because an artificial person simply can't take copulation as seriously as most humans seem to take it. Most of the females of my crèche class had been trained as doxies from menarche on and then were signed up as company women with one or another of the construction multinationals. I myself had received basic doxy training before Boss showed up, bought my contract, and changed my track. (And I jumped the contract and was missing for several months—but that's another story.)

But I wouldn't have been jumpy about friendly sex even if I had received no doxy training at all; such nonsense isn't tolerated in APs; we never learn it.

But we never learn *anything* about being in a family. The very first day I was there I made us all late for tea by rolling on the floor with seven youngsters ranging from eleven down to a nappy-wetter . . . plus two or three dogs and a young tomcat who had earned the name Mister Underfoot through his unusual talent for occupying all of a large floor.

I had never experienced anything like that in all my life. I didn't want to stop.

Brian, not Douglas, took me skiing. The ski lodges at Mount

Hutt are lovely but the bedrooms aren't heated after twenty-two and you have to snuggle up close to keep warm. Then Vickie took me out to see the family's sheep and I met socially an enhanced dog who could talk, a big collie called Lord Nelson. Lord had a low opinion of the good sense of sheep, in which he was, I think, fully justified.

Bertie took me to Milford Sound via shuttle to Dunedin (the "Edinburgh of the South") and overnight there—Dunedin is swell but it's not Christchurch. We took a flubsy little steamer there around to the fjord country, one with tiny little cabins big enough for two only because it's cold down at the south end of the island and again I snuggled up close.

There isn't any other fjord anywhere that can compare with Milford Sound. Yes, I've been on the Lofoten Islands trip. Very nice. But my mind's made up.

If you think I am as blindly pigheaded about South Island as a mother is about her firstborn, that is simply because it's true; I am. North Island is a fine place, with its thermal displays and the world wonder of the Glowworm Caves. And the Bay of Islands looks like Fairyland. But North Island does not have the Southern Alps and it doesn't have Christchurch.

Douglas took me to see their creamery and I saw huge tubs of beautiful butter being packed. Anita introduced me to the Altar Guild. I began to realize that, maybe, just possibly, I might be invited to make it permanent. And found that I had shifted from Oh-God-what'll-I-do-if-they-ask-me to Oh-God-what'll-I-do-if-they-*don't*-ask-me and then simply to Oh-God-what'll-I-do?

You see, I had never told Douglas that I am not human.

I've heard humans boast that they can spot an artificial person every time. Nonsense. Of course anyone can pick out a living artifact that does not conform to human appearance—say a man creature with four arms or a kobold dwarf. But if the genetic designers have intentionally restricted themselves to human appearance (this being the technical definition of "artificial person" rather than "living artifact"), no human can tell the difference—no, not even another genetic engineer.

I am immune to cancer and to most infections. But I don't wear a sign saying so. I have unusual reflexes. But I won't show them off by picking a fly out of the air with thumb and forefinger. I never compete with other people in games of dexterity.

I have unusual memory, unusual innate grasp of number and space and relationship, unusual skill at languages. But, if you think that defines a genius IQ, let me add that, in the school I was trained in, the object of an IQ test is to hit precisely a predetermined score—*not* to show off your smarts. In public nobody's going to catch me being smarter than those around me . . . unless it's an emergency involving either my mission or my neck or both.

The complex of these enhancements and others is reliably reported to improve sexual performance but, fortunately, most males are inclined to regard any noticeable improvement in this area as simply a reflection of their own excellence. (Properly regarded, male vanity is a virtue, not a vice. Treated correctly, it makes him enormously pleasanter to deal with. The thing that makes Boss so infuriating is his total lack of vanity. No way to get a handle on him!)

I was not afraid that I would be caught out. With all production laboratory identification removed from my body, even the tattoo that was on the roof of my mouth, there is simply *no* way to tell that I was designed rather than conceived through the bio roulette of a billion sperm competing blindly for one ovum.

But a wife in the S-group was expected to add to that swarm of kids on the floor.

Well, why not?

Lots of reasons.

I was a combat courier in a quasi-military organization. Picture me trying to cope with a sudden attack while pushing an eight-months belly ahead of me.

We AP females are released or marketed in a reversible sterile condition. To an artificial person the yen to have babies—grow them inside your body—doesn't seem "natural"; it seems ridiculous. *In vitro* seems so much more reasonable—and neater, and more convenient—than *in vivo*. I was as tall as I am now before I ever saw a pregnant woman near term—and I thought she was deathly ill. When I found out what was wrong with her, it made me sort of sick to my stomach. When I thought about it a long time later in Christchurch, it still made me queasy. Do it like a cat, with blood and pain fer Gossake? *Why?* And why do it at all? Despite the way we are filling up the sky, this giddy globe has far too many people on it—why make it worse?

I decided, most sorrowfully, that I was going to have to duck the issue of marriage by telling them that I was sterile—no babies. True enough if not all the truth.

I wasn't asked.

Not about babies. For the next several days I reached out with both hands to enjoy family life as much as possible while I had it: the warm pleasure of woman talk while washing up after tea; the rowdy fun of youngsters and pets; the quiet pleasure of gossip while gardening—these bathed every minute of my day in *belonging*.

One morning Anita invited me out into the garden. I thanked her while pointing out that I was busy helping Vickie. Whereupon I was overruled and found myself seated at the far end of the garden with Anita, and children firmly shooed away.

Anita said, "Marjorie dear"—I'm "Marjorie Baldwin" in Christchurch because that was my public name when I met Douglas in Quito—"we both know why Douglas invited you here. Are you happy with us?"

"Terribly happy!"

"Happy enough, do you think, to wish to make it permanent?"

"Yes but—" I never had a chance to say Yes-but-I'm-sterile; Anita firmly cut me off.

"Perhaps I had better say some things first, dear. We must discuss dowry. If I left it up to our men, money would never be mentioned; Albert and Brian are as dotty about you as Douglas is, and I quite understand it. But this group is a family business corporation as well as a marriage, and someone must keep an eye on the bookkeeping . . . and that is why I am chairman of the board and chief executive; I never become so emotional that I fail to watch our businesses." She smiled and her knitting needles clicked. "Ask Brian—he calls me Ebenezer Scrooge—but he hasn't offered to take over the worries himself.

"You can stay with us as a guest as long as you like. What's one more mouth to feed at a table as long as ours? Nothing. But if you want to join us formally and contractually, then I must become Ebenezer Scrooge and discover what contract we can write. For I won't let the family fortunes be watered down. Brian owns and votes three shares, Albert and I each own and vote two shares, Douglas and Victoria and Lispeth have one each and vote it. As you can see, I have only two votes out of ten . . . but for some years, if I threaten to resign, I suddenly receive a strong vote of confidence. Someday I'll be overruled and then I can quit and be Alice Sit-by-the-Fire." (And the funeral will be later that same day!)

"Meanwhile I cope. The children each have one nonvoting share . . . and a child never does vote his share because it is paid to him or her in cash on leaving home, as dowry or as starting capital—or wasted although I like to think not. Such reductions in capital must be planned; were three of our girls to marry in the same year the situation could be embarrassing if not anticipated."

I told her that it sounded like a very sensible and warm arrangement as I didn't think that most children were so carefully provided for. (In fact I didn't know anything at all about such things.)

"We try to do right by them," she agreed. "After all, children are the purpose of a family. So I'm sure that you will see that an adult joining our group must buy a share, or the system won't work. Marriages are arranged in heaven but the bills must be paid here on earth."

"Amen." (I could see that my problems were solved for me. Negatively. I could not estimate the wealth of the Davidson Group Family. Wealthy, that was certain, even though they lived with no servants in an old-fashioned unautomated house. Whatever it was, I could not buy a share.)

"Douglas told us that he had no idea whether you had money or not. Money in capital amounts, I mean."

"I don't."

She never dropped a stitch. "Nor did I when I was your age. You are employed, are you not? Couldn't you work in Christchurch and buy your share out of your salary? I know that finding work can be a problem in a strange city . . . but I am not without connections. What do you do? You've never told us."

(And I'm not about to!) After evading her and then telling her bluntly that my work was confidential and I refused to discuss any aspect of my employer's business but, no, I couldn't leave and look for work in Christchurch, so there wasn't any way it could work but it had certainly been wonderful while it had lasted and I hoped—

She chopped me off. "My dear, I was not empowered to negotiate this contract for the purpose of failing. Why it can't be done is not acceptable; I must discover how it *can* be done. Brian has offered to give you one of his three shares . . . and Douglas and Albert are backing him, *pro rata*, although they can't pay him at once. But I vetoed the whole scheme; it is a bad precedent and I told them so, using a crude old country expression about rams in the spring. Instead I am accepting one of Brian's shares as security against your performance of your contract."

"But I don't have a contract!"

"You will have. If you continue your present employment, how much can you pay per month? Don't pinch yourself but do pay off as quickly as possible as it works just like an amortized real-estate purchase: Part of each payment services the remaining debt, part reduces that debt—so the larger the payment the better, for you."

(I had never bought any real estate.) "Can we figure that in gold? I can convert into any money, of course, but I get paid in gold."

"In gold?" Anita suddenly looked alert. She reached into her knitting bag and pulled out a portable relay to her computer terminal. "I can offer you a better deal for gold." She punched for a while, waited, and nodded. "Considerably better. Although I'm not really set up to handle bullion. But arrangements can be made."

"I said I can convert. The drafts are for grams, three nines fine, drawn on Ceres and South Africa Acceptances, Limited, Luna City. But it can be paid in New Zealand money, right here, by automatic bank deposit even when I'm not on Earth at the time. Bank of New Zealand, Christchurch office?"

"Uh, Canterbury Land Bank. I'm a director there."

"By all means keep it in the family."

The next day we signed the contract and later that week they married me, all legal and proper, in a side chapel of the cathedral, with me in white, fer Gossake.

The following week I went back to work, both sad and warmly

happy. For the next seventeen years I would be paying NZ$858.13 per month, or I could pay it faster. For what? I could not live at home until it was all paid because I had to keep my job to meet those monthly payments. For what, then? Not for sex. As I told Captain Tormey, sex is everywhere; it's silly to pay for it. For the privilege of getting my hands into soapy dishwater, I guess. For the privilege of rolling around on the floor and being peed on by puppies and babies only nominally housebroken.

For the warm knowledge that, wherever I was, there was a place on this planet where I could do these things as a matter of right, because I *belonged*.

It seemed like a bargain to me.

As soon as the shuttle floated off, I phoned ahead, got Vickie, and, once she stopped squealing, gave her my ETA. I had intended to call from the Kiwi Lines lounge in Auckland port but my curly wolf, Captain Ian, had used up the time. No matter—although the shuttle floats just short of the speed of sound, a stop at Wellington and a stop at Nelson uses up enough time that I thought someone would meet me. I hoped so.

Everybody met me. Well, not quite everybody. We're licensed to own an APV because we raise sheep and cattle and need power transportation. But we aren't supposed to use it in town. Brian did so anyhow and a working majority of our big family was spilling out the sides of that big farm floatwagon.

Most of a year since my last visit home, over twice as long as any such period earlier—bad. Children can grow away from you in that length of time. I was most careful about names and made sure that I checked off everyone in my mind. All present save Ellen, who was hardly a child—eleven when they married me, she was a young lady now, university age. Anita and Lispeth were at home, hurrying together my welcome-home feast . . . and again I would be gently scolded for not having given them warning and again I would try to explain that, in my work, once I was free to leave, it was better to grab the first SB than it was to try to get a call through—did I need an appointment to come to my *own home?*

Shortly I was down on the floor with kids all around me. Mister

Underfoot, a gangly young cat when I first met him, waited for opportunity to greet me with dignity befitting his status as senior cat, elderly, fat, and slow. He looked me over carefully, brushed against me, and buzzed. I was home.

After a time I asked, "Where is Ellen? Still in Auckland? I thought university was closed for vacation now." I looked right at Anita when I said this but she appeared not to hear me. Getting hard of hearing? Surely not.

"Marjie—" Brian's voice—I looked around. He did not speak and his face held no expression. He barely shook his head.

(*Ellen* a taboo topic? What is this, Brian? I tabled it until I could speak to him privately. Anita has always maintained that she loves all our children equally, whether they are her own bio children or not. Oh, certainly! Save that her special interest in Ellen was always clear to everyone within reach of her voice.)

Later that night when the house was settling down and Bertie and I were about to go to bed (under some lottery system in which our teasing darlings always insisted that the loser had to spend the night with me), Brian tapped at the door and came in.

Bertie said, "It's all right. You can leave. I can take my punishment."

"Stow it, Bert. Have you told Marj about Ellen?"

"Not yet."

"Then fill her in. Sweetheart, Ellen got married without Anita's blessing . . . and Anita is furious about it. So it's best not to mention Ellen around Anita. Verb. sap., eh? Now I must run before she misses me."

"Aren't you permitted to come kiss me good-night? Or to stay here for that matter? Aren't you *my* husband, too?"

"Yes, of course, dear. But Anita is touchy as can be at present and there is no point in getting her stirred up."

Brian kissed us good-night and left. I said, "What is this, Bertie? Why shouldn't Ellen marry anyone she wishes to marry? She is old enough to make her own decisions."

"Well, yes. But Ellen didn't use good judgment about it. She's married a Tongan and she's gone to live in Nuku'alofa."

"Does Anita feel that they should live here? In Christchurch?"

"Eh? No, no! It's the marriage she objects to."

"Is there something wrong with this man?"

"Marjorie, didn't you hear me? He's a *Tongan*."

"Yes, I heard. Since he lives in Nuku'alofa, I would expect him to be. Ellen is going to find it awfully hot there, after being brought up in one of the few perfect climates. But that is her problem. I still don't see why Anita is upset. There must be something I don't know."

"Oh, but you do! Well, maybe you don't. Tongans are not like us. They aren't white people; they are barbarians."

"Oh, but they're not!" I sat up in bed, thereby putting a stop to what hadn't really started. Sex and arguments don't mix. Not for me, anyway. "They are the most civilized people in all Polynesia. Why do you think the early explorers called that group 'the Friendly Isles'? Have you ever been there, Bertie?"

"No but—"

"I have. Aside from the heat it's a heavenly place. Wait till you see it. This man— What does he do? If he simply sits and carves mahogany for the tourists, I could understand Anita's unease. Is that it?"

"No. But I doubt that he can afford a wife. And Ellen can't afford a husband; she didn't finish her degree. He's a marine biologist."

"I see. He's not rich . . . and Anita respects money. But he won't be poor, either—he'll probably wind up a professor at Auckland or Sydney. Although a biologist can get rich, today. He may design a new plant or animal that will make him fabulously wealthy."

"Darling, you still don't understand."

"Indeed I don't. So tell me."

"Well . . . Ellen should have married one of her own kind."

"What do you mean by that, Albert? Someone living in Christchurch?"

"It would help."

"Wealthy?"

"Not a requirement. Although things are usually smoother if financial affairs aren't too one-sided. Polynesian beach boy marries white heiress always has a stink to it."

"Oh, oh! He's penniless and she has just collected her family share—right?"

"No, not exactly. Damn it, why couldn't she have married a white man? We brought her up better than that."

"Bertie, what in the world? You sound like a Dane talking about a Swede. I thought that New Zealand was free of that sort of thing. I remember Brian pointing out to me that the Maori were the political and social equals of the English in all respects."

"And they are. It's not the same thing."

"I guess I'm stupid." (Or was Bertie stupid? Maori are Polynesians, so are Tongans—what's the ache?)

I dropped the matter. I had not come all the way from Winnipeg to debate the merits of a son-in-law I had never seen. "Son-in-law . . ." What an odd idea. It always delighted me when one of the little 'uns called me Mama rather than Marjie—but I had never thought about the possibility of ever having a son-in-law.

And yet he was indeed my son-in-law under Ennzedd law—and I didn't even know his name!

I kept quiet, tried to make my mind blank, and let Bertie devote himself to making me feel welcome. He's good at that.

After a while I was just as busy showing him how happy I was to be home, the unwelcome interruption forgotten.

VII

The next morning, before I was out of bed, I resolved not to open the subject of Ellen and her husband, but wait until someone else brought it up. After all, I was in no position to have opinions until I knew all about it. I was not going to drop it—Ellen is *my* daughter, too. But don't rush it. Wait for Anita to calm down.

But the subject did not come up. There followed lazy, golden days that I shan't describe as I don't think you are interested in birthday parties or family picnics—precious to me, dull to an outsider.

Vickie and I went to Auckland on an overnight shopping trip. After we checked into the Tasman Palace, Vickie said to me, "Marj, would you keep a secret for me?"

"Certainly," I agreed. "Something juicy, I hope. A boyfriend? Two boyfriends?"

"If I had even one boyfriend I would simply split him with you. This is touchier. I want to talk to Ellen and I don't want to have an argument with Anita about it. This is the first chance I've had. Can you forget I did it?"

"Not quite, because I want to talk to her myself. But I won't tell Anita that you talked to Ellen if you don't wish me to. What is this, Vick? That Anita was annoyed about Ellen's marriage I knew—but does she expect the rest of us not even to *talk* to Ellen? Our own daughter?"

"I'm afraid it's 'her own daughter' right now. She's not being very rational about it."

"It sounds that way. Well, I will not let Anita cut me off from Ellen. I would have called her before this but I did not know how to reach her."

"I'll show you. I'll call now and you can write it down. It's—"

"Hold it!" I interrupted. "Don't touch that terminal. You don't want Anita to know."

"I said so. That's why I'm calling from here."

"And the call will be included in our hotel bill and you'll pay the bill with your Davidson credit card and— Does Anita still check every bill that comes into the house?"

"She does. Oh, Marj, I'm stupid."

"No, you're honest. Anita won't object to the cost but she's certain to notice a code or a printout that means an overseas call. We'll slide over to the G.P.O. and make the call there. Pay cash. Or, easier yet, we'll use *my* credit card, which does *not* bill to Anita."

"Of course! Marj, you would make a good spy."

"Not me; that's dangerous. I got my practice dodging my mother. Let's pin our ears back and slide over to the post office. Vickie, what is this about Ellen's husband? Does he have two heads or what?"

"Uh, he's a Tongan. Or did you know?"

"Certainly I knew. But 'Tongan' is not a disease. And it's Ellen's business. Her problem, if it is one. I can't see that it is."

"Uh, Anita has handled it badly. Once it's done, the only thing to do is to put the best face on it possible. But a mixed marriage is always unfortunate, I think—especially if the girl is the one marrying below herself, as in Ellen's case."

" 'Below herself!' All I've been told is that he's a Tongan. Tongans are tall, handsome, hospitable, and about as brown as I am. In appearance they can't be distinguished from Maori. What if this young man had been Maori . . . of good family, from an early canoe . . . and lots of land?"

"Truly, I don't think Anita would have liked it, Marj—but she would have gone to the wedding and given the reception. Intermarriage with Maori has long precedent behind it; one must accept it. But one need not like it. Mixing the races is always a bad idea."

(Vickie, Vickie, do you know of a better idea for getting the world out of the mess it is in?) "So? Vickie, this built-in suntan of mine— you know where I got it?"

"Certainly, you told us. Amerindian. Uh, Cherokee, you said. Marj! Did I hurt your feelings? Oh, dear! It's not like that at all! Everybody knows that Amerindians are— Well, just like white people. Every bit as good."

(Oh, sure, sure! And "some of my best friends are Jews." But I'm not Cherokee, so far as I know. Dear little Vickie, what would you think if I told you that I am an AP? I'm tempted to . . . but I must not shock you.)

"No, because I considered the source. You don't know any better. You've never been anywhere and you probably soaked up racism with your mother's milk."

Vickie turned red. "That's most unfair! Marj, when you were up for membership in the family I stuck up for you. I voted for you."

"I was under the impression that everyone had. Or I would not have joined. Do I understand that my Cherokee blood was an issue in that discussion?"

"Well . . . it was mentioned."

"By whom and to what effect?"

"Uh— Marjie, those are executive sessions, they have to be. I can't talk about them."

"Mmm, I see your point. Was there an executive session over Ellen? If so, you should be free to talk to me about it, since I would have been entitled to be present and to vote."

"There wasn't one. Anita said that it wasn't necessary. She said that she did not believe in encouraging fortune hunters. Since she had already told Ellen that she could not bring Tom home to meet the family, there didn't seem to be anything to be done."

"Didn't any of you stand up for Ellen? Did *you* do so, Vickie?"

Vickie turned red again. "It would simply have made Anita furious."

"I'm getting kind of furious myself. By our family code Ellen is your daughter and my daughter as quite as much as she is Anita's daughter, and Anita is wrong in refusing Ellen permission to bring her new husband home without consulting the rest of us."

"Marj, it wasn't quite that way. Ellen wanted to bring Tom home for a visit. Uh, an inspection visit. You know."

"Oh. Yes, having been under the microscope myself, I do know."

"Anita was trying to keep Ellen from making a bad marriage. The first the rest of us knew about it Ellen was married. Apparently Ellen went right straight out and got married the minute she got Anita's letter telling her no."

"Be damned! A light begins to dawn. Ellen trumped Anita's ace by getting married at once—and that meant that Anita had to pay out cash equal to one family corporation share with no notice. Could be difficult. It's quite a chunk of money. It is taking me years and years to pay for my share."

"No, it's not that. Anita is simply angry because her daughter— her favorite; we all know that—has married a man she disapproves of. Anita hasn't had to scrape up that much cash because it wasn't necessary. There is no contractual obligation to pay out a share . . . and Anita pointed out that there was no moral obligation to siphon off the family's capital to benefit an adventurer."

I felt myself getting coldly angry. "Vickie, I have trouble believing my ears. What sort of spineless worms are the rest of you to allow Ellen to be treated this way?" I took a deep breath and tried to control my fury. "I don't understand you. Any of you. But I'm going to try to set a good example. When we get home I'm going to do two things. First I'm going to the family-room terminal when everybody is there and phone Ellen and invite her and her husband home for a visit—come for the next weekend because I've got to get back to work and don't want to miss meeting my new son-in-law."

"Anita will burst a blood vessel."

"We'll see. Then I'm going to call for a family meeting and move that Ellen's share be paid to her with all orderly haste consonant with conserving assets." I added, "I assume that Anita will be furious again."

"Probably. To no purpose, as you'll lose the vote. Marj, why must you do this? Things are bad enough now."

"Maybe. But it's possible that some of you have just been waiting for someone else to take the lead in bucking Anita's tyranny. At least I'll find out how the vote goes. Vick, under the contract I signed I have paid more than seventy thousand Ennzedd dollars into the family and I was told that the reason I had to buy my way into a marriage was that each of our many children were to be paid a full share on leaving home. I didn't protest; I signed. But there is an implied contract there no matter what Anita says. If Ellen can't be paid today, then I shall insist that my monthly payments go to Ellen until such time as Anita can shake loose the rest of one share to pay Ellen off. Does that strike you as equitable?"

She was slow in answering. "Marj, I don't know. I haven't had time to think."

"Better take time. Because, along about Wednesday, you are going to have to fish or cut bait. I shall not let Ellen be mistreated any further." I grinned and added, "Smile! Let's slide over to the post office and be sunny-side-up for Ellen."

But we didn't go to the G.P.O.; we didn't call Ellen at all that trip. Instead we proceeded to drink our dinner and argue. I'm not sure just how the subject of artificial persons got into the discussion. I think it was while Vickie was "proving" still another time how free she was from racial prejudice while exhibiting that irrational attitude every time she opened her mouth. Maori were just dandy and of course American Indians were and Hindu Indians for that matter and the Chinese had certainly produced their quota of geniuses; everybody knew that, but you had to draw the line somewhere. . . .

We had gone to bed and I was trying to tune out her drivel when something hit me. I raised up. "How would *you* know?"

"How would I know what?"

"You said, 'Of course no one would marry an artifact.' How would you know that a person was artificial? Not all of them carry serial numbers."

"Huh? Why, Marjie, don't be silly. A manufactured creature can't be mistaken for a human being. If you had ever seen one—"

"I've seen one. I've seen many!"

"Then you know."

"Then I know what?"

"That you can tell one of those monsters just by looking at it."

"*How?* What are these stigmata that mark off an artificial person from any other person? Name one!"

"Marjorie, you're being dreadfully difficult just to be annoying! This is not like you, dear. You're turning our holiday into something unpleasant."

"Not me, Vick. *You* are. By saying silly, stupid, unpleasant things without a shred of evidence to back them up." (And that retort of mine proves that an enhanced person is not a superman, as that is exactly the sort of factually truthful remark that is much too cruel to use in a family discussion.)

"Oh! How wicked! How untruthful!"

What I did next can't be attributed to loyalty to other artificial persons because APs don't feel group loyalty. No basis for it. I've heard that Frenchmen will die for La Belle France—but can you imagine anyone fighting and dying for Homunculi Unlimited, Pty., South Jersey Section? I suppose I did it for myself although, like many of the critical decisions in my life, I have never been able to analyze why I did it. Boss says that I do all of my important thinking on the unconscious level. He may be right.

I got out of bed, whipped off my gown, stood in front of her. "Look me over," I demanded. "Am I an artificial person? Or not? Either way, how do you tell?"

"Oh, Marjie, quit flaunting yourself! Everybody knows you have the best figure in the family; you don't have to prove it."

"Answer me! Tell me which I am and tell me how you know. Use any test. Take samples for laboratory analysis. But tell me which I am and what signs prove it."

"You're a naughty girl, that's what you are."

"Possibly. Probably. But which sort? Natural? Or artificial?"

"Oh, bosh! Natural, of course."

"Wrong. I'm artificial."

"Oh, stop being silly! Put your nightgown on and come back to bed."

Instead I badgered her with it, telling her what laboratory had designed me, the date I had been removed from the surrogate womb— my "birthday," although we APs are "cooked" a little longer to speed up maturing—forced her to listen to a description of life in a production laboratory crèche. (Correction: Life in the crèche that raised me; other production crèches may be different.)

I gave her a summary of my life after I left the crèche—mostly lies, as I could not compromise Boss's secrets; I simply repeated what I had long since told the family, that I was a confidential commercial traveler. I didn't need to mention Boss because Anita had decided years back that I was an envoy of a multinational, the sort of diplomat who always travels anonymously—an understandable error that I was happy to encourage by never denying it.

Vickie said, "Marjie, I wish you wouldn't do this. A string of lies like that could endanger your immortal soul."

"I don't have a soul. That's what I've been telling you."

"Oh, stop it! You were born in Seattle. Your father was an electronics engineer; your mother was a pediatrician. You lost them in the quake. You told us all about them—you showed us pictures."

" 'My mother was a test tube; my father was a knife.' Vickie, there may be a million or more artificial people whose 'birth records' were 'destroyed' in the destruction of Seattle. No way to count them as their lies are never assembled. After what happened just this month there will start being lots of people of my sort who were 'born' in Acapulco. We have to find loopholes like that to avoid being persecuted by the ignorant and the prejudiced."

"Meaning I'm ignorant and prejudiced!"

"Meaning you are a sweet girl who was fed a pack of lies by your elders. I'm trying to correct that. But if the shoe fits, you can lie in it."

I shut up. Vickie didn't kiss me good-night. We were a long time getting to sleep.

The next day each of us pretended that the argument had never taken place. Vickie did not mention Ellen; I did not mention artificial persons. But it spoiled what had started out to be a merry outing. We got the shopping done and caught the evening shuttle home. I did not do as I had threatened—I did not call Ellen as soon as we were home. I did not forget Ellen; I simply hoped that waiting a while might mellow the situation. Cowardly, I suppose.

Early the following week Brian invited me to go with him while he inspected a piece of land for a client. It was a long pleasant ride with lunch at a licensed country hotel—a fricasee billed as hogget although almost certainly mutton, washed down by tankards of mild. We ate out under the trees.

After the sweet—a berry tart, quite good—Brian said, "Marjorie, Victoria came to me with a very odd story."

"So? What was it?"

"My dear, please believe that I would not mention this were not Vickie so troubled by it." He paused.

I waited. "Upset by what, Brian?"

"She claims that you told her that you are a living artifact masquerading as a human being. I'm sorry but that's what she said."

"Yes, I told her that. Not in those words."

I did not add any explanation. Presently Brian said gently, "May I ask why?"

"Brian, Vickie was saying some very silly things about Tongans, and I was trying to make her see that they were both silly and wrong—that she was wronging Ellen by it. I am very much troubled about Ellen. The day I arrived home you shushed me about her, and I have kept quiet. But I can't keep quiet much longer. Brian, what are we going to do about Ellen? She's your daughter and mine; we can't ignore how she is being mistreated. What shall we do?"

"I do not necessarily agree that something should be done, Marjorie. Please don't change the subject. Vickie is quite unhappy. I am attempting to straighten out the misunderstanding."

I answered, "I have not changed the subject. Injustice to Ellen *is* the subject and I won't drop it. Is there any respect in which Ellen's husband is objectionable? Other than prejudgment against him because he is Tongan?"

"None that I know of. Although, in my opinion, it was inconsiderate of Ellen to marry a man who had not even been introduced to her family. It does not show a decent respect for the people who have loved her and cared for her all her life."

"Wait a moment, Brian. As Vickie tells it, Ellen asked to bring him home for inspection—as I was brought home—and Anita refused to permit it. Whereupon Ellen married him. True?"

"Well, yes. But Ellen was headstrong and hasty. I don't think she should have done so without talking to her other parents. I was quite hurt by it."

"Did she try to speak to you? Did you make any attempt to talk to her?"

"Marjorie, by the time I knew of it, it was a fait accompli."

"So I hear. Brian, ever since I got home I have been hoping that someone would explain to me what happened. According to Vickie none of this was ever settled in family council. Anita refused to let Ellen bring her beloved home. The rest of Ellen's parents either did not know or did not interfere with Anita's, uh, cruelty. Yes, cruelty. Whereupon the child got married. Whereupon Anita compounded her initial cruelty by a grave injustice: She refused Ellen her birth-right, her share of the family's wealth. Is all this true?"

"Marjorie, you were not here. The rest of us—six out of seven—acted as wisely as we could in a difficult situation. I don't think it is proper of you to come along afterwards and criticize what we have done—upon my word, I don't."

"Dear, I don't mean to offend you. But my very point is that *six* of you have not done *anything*. Anita, acting alone, has done things that seem to me to be cruel and unjust . . . and the rest of you stood aside and let her get away with it. No family decisions, just Anita's decisions. If this is true, Brian—and correct me if I'm wrong—then I feel compelled to ask for a full executive session of all husbands and wives to correct this cruelty by inviting Ellen and her husband to visit home, and to correct the injustice by paying to Ellen her fair share of the family's wealth, or at least to acknowledge the debt if it can't be liquidated at once. Will you tell me your opinion of that?"

Brian drummed his nails on the tabletop. "Marjorie, that's a sim-plistic view of a complex situation. Will you admit that I love Ellen and have her welfare in mind quite as much as you do?"

"Certainly, darling!"

"Thank you. I agree with you that Anita should not have refused to let Ellen bring her young man home. Indeed, if Ellen had seen him against the background of her own home, with its gentle ways and its traditions, she might well have decided that he was not for her. Anita stampeded Ellen into a foolish marriage—and I have told her so. But the matter cannot be immediately corrected by inviting them here. You can see that. Let's agree that Anita *should* receive them warmly and graciously . . . but it's God's own truth that she won't—if she has them shoved down her throat."

He grinned at me and I was forced to grin in return. Anita can be charming . . . and she can be incredibly cold, rude, if it suits her.

Brian went on: "Instead, I'll have reason to make a trip to Tonga in a couple of weeks and this will let me get well acquainted without having Anita at my elbow—"

"Good! Take me along—pretty please?"

"It would annoy Anita."

"Brian, Anita has considerably more than annoyed me. I won't refrain from visiting Ellen on that account."

"Mmm . . . would you refrain from doing something that might damage the welfare of all of us?"

"If it were pointed out to me, yes. I might ask for explanation."

"You will have it. But let me deal with your second point. Of course Ellen will get every penny that is coming to her. But you will concede that there is no urgency about paying it to her. Hasty marriages often do not last long. And, while I have no proof of it, it is quite possible that Ellen has been taken in by a fortune hunter. Let's wait a bit and see how anxious this chap is to lay hands on her money. Isn't that prudent?"

I had to admit it. He continued: "Marjorie, my love, you are especially dear to me and to all of us because we see too little of you. It makes each of your trips home a fresh honeymoon for all of us. But, because you are away most of the time, you don't understand why the rest of us are always careful to keep Anita soothed down."

"Well— No, I don't. It should work both ways."

"In dealing with the law and with people I have found a vast difference between 'should' and 'is.' I've lived with Anita longest of any of us; I've learned to live with her little ways. What you may not realize is that she is the glue that holds the family together."

"How, Brian?"

"There is the obvious matter of her custodianship. As manager of the family finances and businesses she is well-nigh irreplaceable. Perhaps some other one of us could do it but it is certain that no one wants the job and I strongly suspect that no one of us could approach her competence. But in ways other than money she is a strong, capable executive. Whether it is in stopping quarrels between children or in deciding any of the thousand issues that come up in a large household, Anita can always make up her mind and keep things moving. A group family, such as ours, must have a strong, capable leader."

(Strong, capable tyrant, I said under my breath.)

"So. Marjie girl, can you wait a bit and give old Brian time to work it out? Believe that I love Ellen as much as you do?"

I patted his hand. "Certainly, dear." (But don't take forever!)

"Now, when we get home, will you find Vickie and tell her that you were joking and that you are sorry you upset her? Please, dear."

(Wups! I had been thinking about Ellen so hard that I had forgotten where this conversation started.) "Now wait one moment, Brian. I'll wait and avoid annoying Anita since you tell me it's necessary. But I'm not going to cater to Vickie's racial prejudices."

"You would not be doing so. Our family is not all of one mind in such matters. I agree with you and you will find that Liz does, too. Vickie is somewhat on the fence; she wants to find any excuse to get Ellen back into the family and, now that I've talked to her, is willing to concede that Tongans are just like Maori and that the real test is the person himself. But it's that strange jest you made about yourself that has her upset."

"Oh. Brian, you once told me that you had almost earned a degree in biology when you switched to law."

"Yes. 'Almost' may be too strong."

"Then you know that an artificial person is biologically indistinguishable from an ordinary human being. The lack of a soul does not show."

"Eh? I'm merely a vestryman, dear; souls are a matter for theologians. But it is certainly not difficult to spot a living artifact."

"I didn't say 'living artifact.' That term covers even a talking dog such as Lord Nelson. But an artificial person is strictly limited to human form and appearance. So how can you spot one? That was the silly thing Vickie was saying, that she could always spot one. Take me, for example. Brian, you know my physical being quite thoroughly—I'm happy to say. Am I an ordinary human being? Or an artificial person?"

Brian grinned and licked his lips. "Lovely Marjie, I will testify in any court that you are human to nine decimal places . . . except where you are angelic. Shall I specify?"

"Knowing your tastes, dear, I don't think it's necessary. Thank you. But please be serious. Assume, for the sake of argument, that I am an artificial person. How could a man in bed with me—as you were last night and many other nights—tell that I was artificial?"

"Marjie, please drop it. It's not funny."

(Sometimes human people exasperate me beyond endurance.) I said briskly, "I'm an artificial person."

"Marjorie!"

"You won't take my word for it? Must I prove it?"

"Stop joking. Stop this instant! Or, so help me, when I get you home I'll paddle you. Marjorie, I've never laid an ungentle hand on you—on any of my wives. But you are earning a spanking."

"So? See that last bite of tart on your plate? I am about to take it. Slap your hands together right over your plate and stop me."

"Don't be silly."

"Do it. You can't move fast enough to stop me."

We locked eyes. Suddenly he started to slap his hands together. I went into automatic overdrive, picked up my fork, stabbed that bite of tart, pulled back the fork between his closing hands, stopped the overdrive just before I placed the bite between my lips.

(That plastic spoon in the crèche was not discrimination but to protect *me*. The first time I used a fork I stabbed my lip because I had not yet learned to slow my moves to match unenhanced persons.)

There may not be a word for the expression on Brian's face.

"Is that enough?" I asked him. "No, probably not. My dear, clasp hands with me." I shoved out my right hand.

He hesitated, then took it. I let him control the grasp, then I started slowly to tighten down. "Don't hurt yourself, dear," I warned him. "Let me know when to stop."

Brian is no sissy and can take quite a bit of pain. I was about to slack off, not wishing to break any bones in his hand, when he suddenly said, "*Enough!*"

I immediately slacked off and started to massage his hand gently with both of mine. "I did not enjoy hurting you, darling, but I had to show you that I am telling the truth. Ordinarily I am careful not to display unusual reflexes or unusual strength. But I do need them in the work I am in. On several occasions enhanced strength and speed have kept me alive. I am most careful not to use either one unless forced to. Now—is there anything more needed to prove to you that I am what I say I am? I am enhanced in other ways but speed and strength are easiest to demonstrate."

He answered, "It's time we started home."

On the way home we didn't exchange a dozen words. I am very fond of the luxury of horse-and-buggy rides. But that day I would happily have used something noisy and mechanical—but *fast!*

For the next few days Brian avoided me; I saw him only at the dinner table. Came a morning when Anita said to me, "Marjorie dear, I'm going into town on a few errands. Will you come along and help me?" Of course I said yes.

She made several stops in the general neighborhood of Gloucester Street and Durham. There was nothing in which she needed my help. I concluded that she simply wanted company and I was pleased by it. Anita is awfully nice to be with as long as one doesn't cross her will.

Finished, we strolled down Cambridge Terrace along the bank of the Avon and on into Hagley Park and the botanic gardens. She picked a sunny spot where we could watch the birds, and got out her knitting. We talked of nothing in particular for a while, or simply sat.

We had been there about half an hour when her phone buzzed. She took it out of her knitting bag, put the button to her ear. "Yes?" Then she added, "Thank you. Off," and put the phone away without offering to tell me who had called her. Her privilege.

Although she did speak of it indirectly: "Tell me, Marjorie, do you ever feel regret? Or a sense of guilt?"

"Why, I do sometimes. Should I? Over what?" I searched my brain as I thought that I had been unusually careful not to upset Anita.

"Over the way you have deceived us and cheated us."

"*What?*"

"Don't play innocent. I've never had to deal with a creature not of God's Law before. I was not sure that the concept of sin and guilt was one you could understand. Not that it matters, I suppose, now that you are unmasked. The family is asking for annulment at once; Brian is seeing Mr. Justice Ridgley today."

I sat up very straight. "On what grounds? I've done nothing wrong!"

"Indeed. You forget that, under our laws, a nonhuman cannot enter into a marriage contract with human beings."

VIII

An hour later I boarded the shuttle for Auckland and then had time to consider my folly.

For almost three months, ever since the night I had discussed it with Boss, I had for the first time been feeling easy about my "human" status. He had told me that I was "as human as Mother Eve" and that I could safely tell anyone that I was an AP because I would not be believed.

Boss was almost right. But he had not counted on my making a really determined effort to prove that I was not "human" under Ennzedd law.

My first impulse had been to demand a hearing before the full family council—only to learn that my case had already been tried *in camera* and the vote had gone against me, six to nothing.

I didn't even go back to the house. That phone call Anita had received while we were in the botanic gardens had told her that my personal effects had been packed and delivered to Left Luggage at the shuttle station.

I could still have insisted on a poll of the house instead of taking Anita's (slippery) word for it. But to what end? To win an argument? To prove a point? Or merely to split a hair? It took me all of five seconds to realize that all I had treasured was gone. As vanished as a rainbow, as burst as a soap bubble—I no longer "belonged." Those children were *not* mine, I would never again roll on the floor with them.

I was thinking about this with dry-eyed grief and almost missed learning that Anita had been "generous" with me: In that contract I had signed with the family corporation the fine print made the principal sum due and payable at once if I breached the contract. Did being "nonhuman" constitute a breach? (Even though I had never missed a payment.) Looked at one way, if they were going to read me out of the family, then I had at least eighteen thousand Ennzedd dollars coming to me: looked at another way I not only forfeited the paid-up part of my share but owed more than twice that amount.

But they were "generous": If I would quietly and quickly vanish away, they would not pursue their claim against me. Unstated was what would happen if I stuck around and made a public scandal.

I slunk away.

I don't need a psychiatrist to tell me that I did it to myself; I realized that fact as soon as Anita announced the bad news. A deeper question is: *Why* did I do it?

I had not done it for Ellen and I could not hoodwink myself into thinking that I had. On the contrary, my folly had made it impossible for me to exert any effort on her behalf.

Why had I done it?

Anger.

I wasn't able to find any better answer. Anger at the whole human race for deciding that my sort are not human and therefore not entitled to equal treatment and equal justice. Resentment that had been building up since the first day that I had been made to realize that there were privileges human children had just from being born and that I could never have simply because I was *not* human.

Passing as human gets one over on the side of privilege; it does not end resentment against the system. The pressure builds up even more because it can't be expressed. The day came when it was more important to me to find out whether my adopted family could accept me as I truly am, an artificial person, than it was to preserve my happy relationship.

I found out. Not *one* of them stood up for me . . . just as none of them had stood up for Ellen. I think I knew that they would reject me as soon as I learned that they had failed Ellen. But that level of my mind is so far down that I'm not well acquainted with it—that's the dark place where, according to Boss, I do all my real thinking.

I reached Auckland too late for the daily SB to Winnipeg. After reserving a cradle for the next day's trajectory and checking everything but my jumpbag, I considered what to do with the twenty-one hours facing me, and at once thought of my curly wolf, Captain Ian. By what he had told me, the chances were five-to-one against his being in town—but his flat (if available) might be pleasanter than a hotel. So I found a public terminal and punched his code.

Shortly the screen lighted; a young woman's face—cheerful, rather pretty—appeared. "Hi! I'm Torchy. Who're you?"

"I'm Marj Baldwin," I answered. "Perhaps I've punched wrong. I'm seeking Captain Tormey."

"No, you're with it, luv. Hold and I'll let him out of his cage." She turned and moved away from the pickup while calling out, "Bubber! A slashing tart on the honker. Knows your right name."

As she turned and moved away I noticed bare breasts. She came fully into view and I saw that she was jaybird to her heels. A good body—possibly a bit wide in the fundament but with long legs, a slender waist, and mammaries that matched mine . . . and I've had no complaints.

I quietly cursed to myself. I knew quite well why I had called the captain: to forget three men in the arms of a fourth. I had found him but it appeared that he was fully committed.

He appeared, dressed but not much—a lava-lava. He looked puzzled, then recognized me. "Hey! Miss . . . *Baldwin!* That's it. This is sonky-do! Where are you?"

"At the port. I punched on the off chance of saying hello."

"Stay where you are. Don't move, don't breathe. Seven seconds while I pull on trousers and shirt, and I'll come get you."

"No, Captain. Just a greeting. Again I am simply making connections."

"What is your connection? To what port? What time is departure?"

Damn and triple damn—I had not prepared my lies. Well, the truth is often better than a clumsy lie. "I'm going back to Winnipeg."

"Ah so! Then you are looking at your pilot; I have the noon lift tomorrow. Tell me exactly where you are and I'll pick you up in, uh, forty minutes if I can get a cab fast enough."

"Captain, you are very sweet and you are out of your mind. You already have all the company you can handle. The young woman who answered my call. Torchy."

"Torchy isn't her name; that's her condition. She's my sister Betty, from Sydney. Stays here when she's in town. I probably mentioned her." He turned his head and shouted. "Betty! Come here and identify yourself. But get decent."

"It's too late to get decent," her cheerful voice answered, and I saw her, past his shoulder, returning toward the pickup and wrapping a lava-lava around her hips as she did so. She seemed to be having a little trouble with it and I suspected that she had had a few. "Oh, the hell with it! My brother is always trying to get me to behave—my husband has given up. Look, luv, I heard what you said. I'm his married sister, too true. Unless you are trying to marry him, in which case I am his fiancée. Are you?"

"No."

"Good. Then you can have him. I'm about to make tea. Do you take gin? Or whisky?"

"Whatever you and the Captain are having."

"He must not have either; he's lifting in less than twenty-four hours. But you and I will get smashed."

"I'll drink what you do. Anything but hemlock."

I then convinced Ian that it was better for me to find a hansom at the port where they were readily available than it was for him to send for one, then make the round trip.

Number 17, Locksley Parade, is a new block of flats of the double-security type; I was locked through the entrance to Ian's flat as if it were a spaceship. Betty greeted me with a hug and a kiss that showed that she had indeed been drinking; my curly wolf then greeted me with a hug and a kiss that showed that he had not been drinking but that he expected to take me to bed in the near future. He did not ask about my husbands; I did not volunteer anything about my family—my former family. Ian and I got along well because we both understood the signals, used them correctly, and never misled the other.

While Ian and I held this wordless discussion, Betty left the room and returned with a red lava-lava. "It's formal high tea," she announced, with a slight belch, "so out of those street clothes and into this, luv."

Her idea? Or his? Hers, I decided, before long. While Ian's simple, wholesome lechery was as clear as a punch in the jaw, he was basically rather cubical. Not so Betty, who was utterly outlaw. I didn't care, as it moved in the direction I wanted to go. Bare feet are as provocative as bare breasts, although most people do not seem to know it. A female packaged only in a lava-lava is far more provocative than one totally nude. The party was shaping up to suit me, and I would depend on Ian to shake off his sister's chaperonage when the time came. If necessary. It seemed possible that Betty would sell tickets. I didn't fret about it.

I got smashed.

Just how thorough a job I did on it I did not realize until next morning when I woke up in bed with a man who was *not* Ian Tormey.

For several minutes I lay still and watched him snore while I poked through my gin-beclouded memories, trying to fit him in. It seemed to me that a woman really ought to be introduced to a man before spending a night with him. Had we been formally introduced? Had we met at all?

In bits and pieces it came back. Name: Professor Federico Farnese, called either "Freddie" or "Chubbie." (Not very chubby—just a little pot from a swivel-chair profession.) Betty's husband, Ian's brother-in-law. I recalled him somewhat from the evening before but could not now (next morning) recall just when he had arrived, or why he had been away . . . if I ever knew.

Once I placed him I was not especially surprised to find that I (seemed to have) spent the night with him. The frame of mind I had been in the night before no male would have been safe from me. But one thing bothered me: Had I turned my back on my host in order to chase after some other man? Not polite, Friday—not gracious.

I dug deeper. No, at least once I decidedly had *not* turned my back on Ian. To my great pleasure. And to Ian's, too, if his comments were sincere. Then I had indeed turned my back but at his request. No, I had not been ungracious to my host, and he had been very kind to me, in exactly the fashion I needed to help me forget how I had been swindled, then tossed, by Anita's gang of self-righteous racists.

Thereafter my host had had some help from this late arrival, I now remembered. It is never surprising that an emotionally troubled woman may need more soothing than one man can supply—but I could not remember how the transaction was achieved. Fair exchange? Don't snoop, Friday! An AP cannot empathize with or understand the various human copulation taboos—but I had most carefully memorized all the many, many sorts while taking basic doxy training, and I knew that this one was one of the strongest, one that humans cover up even where all else is wide open.

So I resolved to shun even a hint of interest.

Freddie stopped snoring and opened his eyes. He yawned and stretched, then saw me and looked puzzled, then suddenly grinned and reached for me. I answered his grin and his grab, ready to cooperate heartily, when Ian walked in. He said, "Morning, Marj. Freddie, I hate to interrupt but I'm already holding a cab. Marj has to get up and get dressed. We're leaving at once."

Freddie did not let go of me. He simply clucked, then recited:

"A birdie with a yellow bill
hopped upon my windowsill.
He cocked a shiny eye and said,
'Ain't you ashamed, you sleepyhead?'

"Captain, your attention to duty and to the welfare of our guest does you credit. What time must you be there? Minus two hours? And you lift at high noon as the clock is striking the steeple. No?"

"Yes, but—"

"Whereas Helen—your name *is* Helen?—is kosher if she presents herself at the gate called strait no later than minus thirty minutes. This I will undertake."

"Fred, I don't like to be a spoilsport but it can take a bloody hour to get a cab here, as you know. I have one waiting."

"How true. Cabbies avoid us; their horses don't like our hill. For that reason, dear brother-in-love, last night I hired a rig, pledging a purse of gold. At this very moment old faithful Rosinante is under this house in one of the janitor's stalls, gaining strength on nubbins of maize for her coming ordeal. When I phone down, said janitor, well plied with bribes, will harness the dear beast and fetch wain and her to entrance. Whereupon I will deliver Helen to the gate no later than minus thirty-one. To this end I pledge the pound of flesh nearest your heart."

"Your heart, you mean."

"I phrased it most carefully."

"Well—Marj?"

"Uh—Is it all right, Ian? I don't really want to jump out of bed this second. But I don't want to miss your ship."

"You won't. Freddie is reliable; he just doesn't look it. But leave here by eleven; then you could make it on foot if you had to. I can hold your reservation after check-in time; a captain does have some privileges. Very well; resume whatever it was you were doing." Ian glanced at his watch finger. "Nine up. Bye."

"Hey! Kiss me good-bye!"

"Why? I'll see you at the ship. And we have a date in Winnipeg."

"Kiss me, damn it, or I'll miss the bloody ship!"

"So untangle yourself from that fat Roman and mind you don't get spots on my clean uniform."

"Don't chance it, old son. I will kiss Helen on your behalf."

Ian leaned down and kissed me thoroughly and I did not muss his pretty uniform. Then he kissed the top of Freddie's head on his little bald spot and said, "Have fun, chums. But get her to the gate on time. Bye." Betty glanced in at that point; her brother gathered her in with one arm and took her away.

I turned my attention back to Freddie. He said, "Helen, prepare yourself." I did, while thinking happily that Ian and Betty and Freddie were just what Friday needed to offset the puritanical hypocrites I had lived with far too long.

Betty fetched in morning tea precisely on the moment, so I assume that she listened. She made a lotus on the bed and had a cuppa with us. Then we got up and had breakfast. I had porridge with thick cream, two beautiful eggs, Canterbury ham, a fat chop, fried potatoes, hot muffins with strawberry jam and the world's best butter, and an orange, all washed down with strong black tea with sugar and milk. If all the world broke fast the way New Zealand does, we wouldn't have political unrest.

Freddie put on a lava-lava to eat breakfast but Betty didn't so I didn't. Being crèche-raised, I can never learn enough about human manners and etiquette but I do know that a woman guest must dress—or undress—to match her hostess. I'm not really used to skin in the presence of humans (the crèche was another matter) but Betty was awfully easy to be with. I wondered if she would snub me if she knew that I was not human. I didn't think so but I was not anxious to test it. A happy breakfast.

Freddie delivered me to the passenger lounge at eleven-twenty, sent for Ian, and demanded a receipt. Solemnly Ian wrote one. Again Ian belted me into the acceleration cradle, while saying quietly, "You didn't really need help with this the other time, did you?"

"No," I agreed, "but I'm glad I pretended. I've had a wonderful time!"

"And we'll have a good time in Winnipeg, too. I reached Janet during countdown, let her know that you would be with us for dinner. She told me to tell you that you would be with us for breakfast as well—she says to tell you that it is silly to leave Winnipeg in the middle of the night; you could get mugged at any transfer. She's right—the informal immigrants we get over the border from the Imperium would kill you for a toke."

"I'll speak with her about it when we get there." (Captain Ian, you triflin' man, you told me that you would never marry because you must "go where the wild goose goes." I wonder if you recall that? I don't think you do.)

"It's settled. Janet might not trust my judgment about women—she says I'm prejudiced, a base canard. But she does trust Betty—and by now Betty has phoned her. She's known Betty longer than she's known me; they were roommates at McGill. And that's where I got Janet and Fred got Sis; we four were subversives—every now and then we would unhook the North Pole and turn it around."

"Betty is a darling. Is Janet like her?"

"Yes and no. Janet was the leader of our seditious activities. Excuse me; I've got to go pretend to be a captain. Actually the computer flies this tin coffin but I'm planning to learn how next week." He left.

After the healing catharsis of a night of drunken saturnalia with Ian and Freddie and Betty I was able to think about my ex-family more rationally. Had I in fact been cheated?

I had signed that silly contract willingly, including the termination clause I tripped on. Had I been paying for sex?

No, what I had told Ian was true; sex is everywhere. I had paid for the happy privilege of *belonging*. To a family—especially the homely delights of changing wet nappies and washing dishes and petting kittens. Mister Underfoot was far more important to me than Anita had ever been—although I had never let myself think about it. I had tried to love them all until the matter of Ellen had thrown light into some dirty corners.

Let me see now: I knew exactly how many days I had been able to spend with my ex-family. A little arithmetic told me that (since all had been confiscated) my cost for room and board for those sweet vacations was slightly over four hundred and fifty Ennzedd dollars per day.

A high price even for a luxury resort. But the actual cost to the family of having me at home was less than a fortieth of that. On what financial terms had each of the others joined the family? I had never known.

Had Anita, unable to stop the men from inviting me in, rigged things so that I could not afford to quit my job and live at home but nevertheless tied me to the family on terms quite profitable to the family—i.e., to Anita? No way to tell. I knew so little about marriage among human beings that I had not been able to judge—and still could not.

But I had learned one thing: Brian had surprised me by turning against me. I had thought of him as the older, wiser, sophisticated member of the family, the one who could accept the fact of my biological derivation and live with it.

Perhaps he could have done so had I picked some other enhanced quality to demonstrate, some nonthreatening ability.

But I had bested him in a feat of strength, a matter in which a male quite reasonably expects to win. I had hit him in his male pride.

Unless you intend to kill him immediately thereafter, never kick a man in the balls. Not even symbolically. Or perhaps especially not symbolically.

IX

Presently free fall went away and we entered the incredibly thrilling sensations of hypersonic glide. The computer was doing a good job of smoothing out the violence, but you could still feel the vibration in your teeth—and I could feel it elsewhere after my busy night.

We dropped through transonic rather abruptly, then spent a long time in subsonic, with the scream building up. Then we touched and the retros cut in . . . and shortly we stopped. And I took a deep breath. Much as I like the SBs, I can't relax from touchdown to full stop.

We had lifted at North Island at noon Thursday, so we arrived forty minutes later at Winnipeg the day before (Wednesday) in the early evening, 1940 hours. (Don't blame me; go look at a map—one with time zones marked.)

Again I waited and was last passenger out. Our captain again picked up my bag but this time escorted me with the casualness of an old friend—and I felt enormously warmed by it. He took me through a side door, then went with me through Customs, Health, and Immigration, offering his own jumpbag first.

The CHI officer did not touch it. "Hi, Captain. What are you smuggling this time?"

"The usual. Illicit diamonds. Trade secrets. Weapons specs. Contraband drugs."

"That's all? It's a waste of chalk." He scrawled something on Ian's bag. "Is she with you?"

"Never saw her before in my life."

"Me Injun squaw," I asserted. "White boss promise me much firewater. White boss don't keep promise."

"I could have told you. Going to be here long?"

"I live in the Imperium. Transient, possibly overnight. I came through here on my way to New Zealand last month. Here's my passport."

He glanced at it, stamped it, scrawled on my bag without opening it. "If you decide to stay a little longer, I'll buy you firewater. But don't trust Captain Tormey." We went on through.

Just beyond the barrier Ian dropped both our bags, picked up a woman by her elbows—proving his excellent condition; she was only ten centimeters junior to him—and kissed her enthusiastically. He put her down. "Jan, this is Marj."

(When Ian had this sultry job at home, why did he bother with my meager assets? Because I was there and she wasn't, no doubt. But now she is. Dear lady, got a good book I can read?)

Janet kissed me and I felt better. Then she held me with both hands at arm's length. "I don't see it. Did you leave it in the ship?"

"Leave what? This jumpbag is all I carried—my luggage is in transit bond."

"No, dear, your halo. Betty led me to expect a halo."

I considered this. "Are you sure she said halo?"

"Well . . . she said you were an angel. Perhaps I jumped to a conclusion."

"Perhaps. I don't think I was wearing a halo last night; I hardly ever wear one when traveling."

Captain Ian said, "That's right. Last night all she had on was a load, a big one. Sweetheart, I hate to tell you this but Betty was a bad influence. Deplorable."

"Oh, heavens! Perhaps we had best go straight to prayer meeting. Shall we, Marjorie? Tea and a biscuit here, and skip dinner? The whole congregation will pray for you."

"Whatever you say, Janet." (Did I have to agree to this? I didn't know the etiquette for a "prayer meeting.")

Captain Tormey said, "Janet, perhaps we had better take her

home and pray for her there. I'm not sure Marj is used to public confessions of sins."

"Marjorie, would you rather do that?"

"I think I would. Yes."

"Then we will. Ian, will you hail Georges?"

Georges turned out to be Georges Perreault. That is all I learned about him just then, save that he was driving a pair of Morgan blacks hitched to a Honda surrey suitable for the very wealthy. How much is an SB captain paid? Friday, it's none of your business. But it was certainly a handsome rig. So was Georges, for that matter. Handsome, I mean. He was tall, dark-haired, dressed in dark suit and kepi, and looked a very proper coachman. But Janet did not introduce him as a servant and he bent over my hand and kissed it. Does a coachman kiss hands? I keep running into human practices not covered by my training.

Ian sat in front by Georges; Janet took me behind with her and opened a large down rug. "I thought you might not have a wrap with you, coming from Auckland," she explained. "So snuggle under." I did not protest that I never get cold; it was very thoughtful and I snuggled under with her. Georges wheeled us out onto the highway, clucked to the horses, and they broke into a brisk trot. Ian took a horn from a rack on the dashboard and sounded a blast on it—there didn't seem to be any reason for it; I think he just liked to make a loud noise.

We did not go into the city of Winnipeg. Their home was southwest of a small town, Stonewall, north of the city and closer to the port. By the time we got there it was dark but I could see one thing: It was a country estate designed to hold off anything short of professional military attack. There were three gates in series, with gates one and two forming a holding pen. I didn't spot Eyes or remoted weapons but I was sure they were there—the estate was marked out by the red-and-white beacons that warn float craft not to try it.

I got only the barest glimpse of whatever matched the three gates—too dark. A wall and two fences I saw, but I could not see how they were armed and/or booby-trapped and hesitated to ask. But no sensible person spends that much on household protection and then relies totally on passive defense. I wanted to ask about their power arrangements, too, recalling how at the farm Boss had lost the main Shipstone (cut by "Uncle Jim") and thereby lost his defenses—but again it was not something a guest could ask.

I wondered even more what would have happened if we had been jumped before they got inside the gates of their castle. Again, with the brisk trade in illegal weapons that wind up in the hands of the putatively disarmed, it was the sort of question one did not ask. I walk around unarmed, usually, but I don't assume that others do so—most people have neither my enhancements nor my special training.

(I would rather rely on my "unarmed" state than depend on hardware that can be taken from you at any checkpoint, or that you can lose, or that can run out of ammo, or jam, or be power-down when it matters. I don't *look* armed, and that gives me an edge. But other people, other problems—I'm a special case.)

We rode up a sweeping drive and under an overhang and stopped—and again Ian sounded a foul blast on that silly horn—but this time there seemed to be some point to it; the front doors opened. Ian said, "Take her inside, dear; I'm going to help Georges with the team."

"I don't need help."

"Pipe down." Ian got out and handed us down, gave my jumpbag to his wife—and Georges pulled away. Ian simply followed on foot. Janet led me inside—and I gasped.

I was looking through the foyer at an illuminated fountain, a programmed one; it changed in shapes and colors as I stood there. There was gentle background music, which (possibly) controlled the fountain.

"Janet . . . who's your architect?"

"Like it?"

"Of course!"

"Then I'll admit it. I'm the architect, Ian is the gadgeteer, Georges controlled the interiors. He is several sorts of an artist and another wing is his studio. And I might as well tell you right now that Betty told me to hide your clothes until Georges paints at least one nude of you."

"Betty said that? But I've never been a model and I must get back to my job."

"It's up to us to change your mind. Unless— Are you shy about it? Betty did not think you would be. Georges might settle for the draped figure. At first."

"No, I'm not shy. Uh, maybe a bit shy about posing; the idea is new to me. Look, can we let it wait? Right now I'm more interested in plumbing than in posing; I haven't been near any since I left Betty's flat—I should have stopped at the port."

"Sorry, dear; I should not have kept you standing here talking about Georges' painting. My mother taught me years ago that the very first thing to do for a guest is to show her where the bathroom is."

"My mother taught me the exact same thing," I fibbed.

"This way." A hallway opened to the left from the fountain; she led me down it and into a room. "Your room," she announced, dropping my bag on the bed, "and the bath is through here. You share it with me, as my room is the mirror image of this room, on the other side."

There was plenty to share—three stalls, each with WC, bidet, and hand tray; a shower big enough for a caucus, with controls I was going to have to ask about; a massage and suntan table; a plunge—or was it a hot tub?—that clearly was planned for loafing in company; twin dressing tables with basins; a terminal; a refrigerator; a bookcase with one shelf for cassettes.

"No leopard?" I said.

"You expected one?"

"Every time I've seen this room in the sensies the heroine had a pet leopard with her."

"Oh. Will you settle for a kitten?"

"Certainly. Are you and Ian cat people?"

"I wouldn't attempt to keep house without one. In fact just now I can offer you a real bargain in kittens."

"I wish I could take one. I can't."

"Discuss it later. Help yourself to the plumbing. Want a shower before dinner? I intend to grab one; I spent too much time currying Black Beauty and Demon before going to the port, and ran out of time. Did you notice that I whiffed of stable?"

And that is how, by easy stages, I found myself ten or twelve minutes later having my back washed by Georges while Ian washed my front while my hostess washed herself and laughed and offered advice that was ignored. If I were to elaborate, you would see that each step was perfectly logical and that these gentle sybarites did nothing to rush me. Nor was there even the mildest attempt to seduce me, not even a hint that I had already raped (symbolic rape, at least) my host the night before.

Then I shared with them a sybaritic feast in their living room (drawing room, great hall, whatever) in front of a fire that was actually one of Ian's gadgets. I was dressed in one of Janet's negligees— Janet's notion of a dinner-gown negligee would have got her arrested in Christchurch.

But it did not cause a pass from either man. When we reached coffee and brandy, me somewhat blurry from drinks before dinner and wine during dinner, by request I removed that borrowed negligee and Georges posed me five or six ways, took stereos and holos of me in each, while discussing me as if I were a side of beef. I continued to insist that I had to leave tomorrow morning but my protests became feeble and *pro forma*—Georges paid no attention to them whatever. He said I had "good masses"—maybe this is a compliment; it certainly is not a pass.

But he got some awfully good pictures of me, especially one of me lying sort of flang dang on a low couch with five kittens crawling over my breasts and legs and belly. I asked for that one and it turned out that Georges had the equipment to copy it.

Then Georges took some of Janet and me together, and again I asked for a copy of one of them because we made a beautiful contrast and Georges had a knack for making us look better than we did. But presently I started to yawn and Janet told Georges to stop. I apologized, saying that there was no excuse for me to be sleepy since it was still early evening by the zone where I had started the day.

Janet said pishantosh, that being sleepy had nothing to do with clocks and time zones—gentlemen, we are going to bed. She led me away.

We stopped in that beautiful bath and she put her arms around me. "Marjie, do you want company, or do you want to sleep alone? I know from Betty that you had a busy night last night; possibly you prefer a quiet night alone. Or possibly not. Name it."

I told her honestly that I did not sleep alone by choice.

"Me, too," she agreed, "and it's nice to hear you say so, instead of fiddling around about it and pretending the way some slitches do. Whom do you want in your bed?"

You sweet darling, surely you are entitled to your own husband the night he gets home. "Maybe that should be turned around. Who wants to sleep with me?"

"Why, all of us, I feel certain. Or any two. Or any one. You name it."

I blinked and wondered how much I had had to drink. "Four in one bed?"

"Do you like that?"

"I've never tried it. It sounds jolly but the bed would be awfully crowded, I think."

"Oh. You haven't been in my room. A *big* bed. Because both my husbands often choose to sleep with me . . . and there is still plenty of room to invite a guest to join us."

Yes, I had been drinking—two nights in a row and far more than I was used to. "Two husbands? I didn't know that British Canada had adopted the Australian Plan."

"British Canada has not; British Canadians have. Or many thousands of us. The gates are locked and it's nobody's business. Do you want to try the big bed? If you get sleepy, you can crawl off to your own room—a major reason I planned this suite the way I did. Well, dear?"

"Uh . . . yes. But I may be self-conscious about it."

"You'll get over it. Let's—"

She was interrupted by a jangly bell at the terminal.

Janet said, "Oh, damn, *damn!* That almost certainly means that they want Ian at the port—even though he's just back from a high lift." She stepped to the terminal, switched it on.

"—cause for alarm. Our border with the Chicago Imperium has been sealed off and refugees are being rounded up. The attack by

Québec is more serious but may be an error by a local commander; there has been no declaration of war. State of emergency is now in effect, so stay off the streets, keep calm, and listen on this wavelength for official news and instructions."

Red Thursday had started.

X

I suppose everybody has more or less the same picture in mind of Red Thursday and what followed. But to explain me (to *me*, if that be possible!) I must tell how I saw it, including the bumbling confusion and doubts.

We four did wind up in Janet's big bed but for company and mutual comfort, not sex. We all had our ears bent for news, our eyes on the terminal's screen. More or less the same news was repeated again and again—aborted attack from Québec, Chairman of the Chicago Imperium killed in his bed, the border with the Imperium closed, unverified sabotage reports, stay off the streets, remain calm—but no matter how often it was repeated we always all shut up and listened, waiting for some item that would cause the other news items to make sense.

Instead things got worse all night long. By four in the morning we knew that killings and sabotage were all over the globe; by daylight unverified reports were coming in of trouble at Ell-Four, at Tycho Base, at Stationary Station, and (broken-off message) on Ceres. There was no way to guess whether or not the trouble extended as far as Alpha Centauri or Tau Ceti . . . but an official voice on the terminal did guess by loudly refusing to guess and by telling the rest of us not to engage in harmful speculation.

About four, Janet, with some help from me, made sandwiches and served coffee.

I woke up at nine because Georges moved. I found that I was sleeping with my head on his chest and my upper arm clinging to him. Ian was across the bed, lying-sitting propped up against pillows with his eyes still on the screen—but his eyes were closed. Janet was missing—she had gone to my room, crawled into what was nominally my bed.

I found that, by moving very slowly, I could untangle myself and get out of bed without waking Georges. I did so, and slid into the bathroom, where I got rid of used coffee and felt better. I glanced into "my" room, saw my missing hostess. She was awake, waggled her fingers at me, then motioned for me to come in. She moved over and I crawled in with her. She kissed me. "How are the boys?"

"Both still asleep. Or were three minutes ago."

"Good. They need sleep. Both of them are worriers; I am not. I decided that there was no point in attending Armageddon with my eyes bloodshot, so I came in here. You were asleep, I think."

"Could have been. I don't know when I fell asleep. It seemed to me that I heard the same bad news a thousand times. Then I woke up."

"You haven't missed anything. I've kept the sound turned down but I've kept the streamers on screen—they've been spelling out the same old sad story. Marjorie, the boys are waiting for the bombs to drop. I don't think there will be any bombs."

"I hope you're right. But why not?"

"Who drops H-bombs on whom? Who is the enemy? *All* the major power blocs are in trouble, as near as I can tell from the news. But, aside from what seems to have been a stupid mistake by some Québecois general, no military forces have been involved anywhere. Assassinations, fires, explosions, all sorts of sabotage, riots, terrorism of all kinds—but no pattern. It's not East against West, or Marxists against fascists, or blacks against whites. Marjorie, if anyone sets off missiles, it will mean that the whole world has gone crazy."

"Doesn't it look that way now?"

"I don't think so. The pattern of this is that it has no pattern. The target is everybody. It seems to be aimed at all governments equally."

"Anarchists?" I suggested.

"Nihilists, maybe."

Ian came in wearing circles under his eyes, a day's beard, a worried look, and an old bathrobe too short for him. His knees were knobby. "Janet, I can't reach Betty or Freddie."

"Were they going back to Sydney?"

"It's not that. I can't get through to either Sydney or Auckland. All I get is that damned synthetic computer voice: 'A-circuit-is-not-available-at-this-moment. Please-try-later-thank-you-for-your-patience.' You know."

"Ouch. More sabotage, maybe?"

"Could be. But maybe worse. After that kark, I called traffic control at the port and asked whatinhell was wrong with Winnipeg-Auckland satellite bounce? By pulling rank I eventually got the supervisor. He told me to forget about calls that didn't get through because they had real trouble. All SBs grounded—because two were sabotaged in space. Winnipeg–Buenos Aires Lift Twenty-nine and Vancouver-London One-oh-one."

"Ian!"

"Total loss, both. No survivors. Pressure fuses, no doubt, as each one blew on leaving atmosphere. Jan, the next time I lift, I'm going to inspect *everything* myself. Stop the countdown on the most trivial excuse." He added, "But I can't guess when that will be. You can't lift an SB when your comm circuits to reentry port are broken . . . and the supervisor admitted that they had lost all bounce circuits."

Janet got out of bed, stood up, kissed him. "Now stop worrying! Stop. At once. Of course you will check everything yourself until they catch the saboteurs. But right now you'll put it out of your mind because you won't be called to lift until the comm circuits are restored. So declare a holiday. As for Betty and Freddie, it's a shame we can't talk to them but they can take care of themselves and you know it. No doubt they are worrying about us and they shouldn't, either. I'm just glad it happened while you are at home—instead of halfway around the globe. You're here and you're safe and that's all I care about. We'll just sit here, snug and happy, until this nonsense is over."

"I've got to go to Vancouver."

"Man o' mine, you don't 'got' to do anything, save pay taxes and die. They won't be putting artifacts into the ships when no ships are lifting."

"Artifacts," I blurted and regretted it.

Ian seemed to see me for the first time. "Hi, Marj—morning. Nothing you need fret about—and I'm sorry about this hoop-te-do while you're our guest. The artifacts Jan mentioned aren't gadgets; they're alive. Management has this wild notion that a living artifact designed for piloting can do a better job than a man can do. I'm shop steward for the Winnipeg Section so I've got to go fight it. Management-Guild meeting in Vancouver tomorrow."

"Ian," Jan said, "phone the General Secretary. It's silly to go to Vancouver without checking first."

"Okay, okay."

"But don't just ask. Urge the SecGen to pressure management to postpone the meeting until the emergency is over. I want you to stay right here and keep me safe from harm."

"Or vice versa."

"Or vice versa," she agreed. "But I'll faint in your arms if necessary. What would you like for breakfast? Don't make it too complex or I'll invoke your standing commitment."

I wasn't really listening as the word *artifact* had triggered me. I had been thinking of Ian—of all of them, really, here and Down Under—as being so civilized and sophisticated that they would regard my sort as just as good as humans.

And now I hear that Ian is committed to representing his guild in a labor-management fight to keep *my* sort from competing with humans.

(What would you have us do, Ian? Cut our throats? We didn't ask to be produced any more than you asked to be born. We may not be human but we share the age-old fate of humans; we are strangers in a world we never made.)

"Well, Marj?"

"Uh, sorry, I was woolgathering. What did you say, Jan?"

"I asked what you wanted for breakfast, dear."

"Uh, doesn't matter; I eat anything that is standing still or even moving slowly. May I come with you and help? Please?"

"I was hoping you would offer. Because Ian isn't much use in a kitchen despite his commitment."

"I'm a damned good cook!"

"Yes, dear. Ian gave me a commitment in writing that he would always cook any meal if I so requested. And he does; he hasn't tried to slide out of it. But I have to be just awfully hungry to invoke it."

"Marj, don't listen to her."

I still don't know whether or not Ian can cook, but Janet certainly can (and so can Georges, as I learned later). Janet served us—with help around the edges from me—with light and fluffy mild Cheddar omelettes surrounded by thin, tender pancakes rolled up Continental style with powdered sugar and jam, and garnished with well-drained bacon. Plus orange juice from freshly squeezed oranges—hand-squeezed, not ground to a pulp by machinery. Plus drip coffee made from freshly ground beans.

(New Zealand food is beautiful but New Zealand cooking practically isn't cooking at all.)

Georges showed up with the exact timing of a cat—Mama Cat in this case, who arrived following Georges ahead of him. Kittens were then excluded by Janet's edict because she was too busy to keep from stepping on kittens. Janet also decreed that the news would be turned off while we ate and that the emergency would not be a subject of conversation at the table. This suited me as these strange and grim events had pounded on my mind since they started, even during sleep. As Janet pointed out in handing down this ruling, only an H-bomb was likely to penetrate our defenses, and an H-bomb blast we probably wouldn't notice—so relax and enjoy breakfast.

I enjoyed it . . . and so did Mama Cat, who patrolled our feet counterclockwise and informed each of us when it was that person's turn to supply a bit of bacon—I think she got most of it.

After I cleared the breakfast dishes (salvaged rather than recycled; Janet was old-fashioned in spots) and Janet made another pot of coffee, she turned the news on again and we settled back to watch it and discuss it—in the kitchen rather than the grand room we had used for dinner, the kitchen being their *de facto* living room. Janet had what is called a "peasant kitchen" although no peasant ever had it so good: a big fireplace, a round table for family eating furnished with so-called captain's chairs, big comfortable lounging chairs, plenty of floor space and no traffic problems because the cooking took place at the end opposite the comforts. The kittens were allowed back in, ending their protests, and in they came all tails at attention. I picked up one, a fluffy white with big black spots; its buzz was bigger than it was. It was clear that Mama Cat's love life had not been limited by a stud book; no two kittens were alike.

Most of the news was a rehash but there was a new development in the Imperium:

Democrats were being rounded up, sentenced by drumhead courts-martial (provost's tribunals, they were called) and executed on the spot—laser, gunfire, some hangings. I exerted tight mind control to let me watch. They were sentencing them down to the age of fourteen—we saw one family in which both parents, themselves condemned, were insisting that their son was only twelve.

The President of the court, an Imperial Police corporal, ended the argument by drawing his side arm, shooting the boy, and then ordering his squad to finish off the parents and the boy's older sister.

Ian flicked off the picture, shifted to voiceover streamers, and turned the sound down. "I've seen all of that I want to see," he growled. "I think that whoever has power there now that the old Chairman is dead is liquidating everybody on their suspects list."

He chewed his lip and looked grim. "Marj, are you still sticking to that silly notion of going home at once?"

"I'm not a democrat, Ian. I'm nonpolitical."

"Do you think that kid was political? Those Cossacks would kill you just for drill. Anyhow, you can't. The border is closed."

I didn't tell him that I felt certain that I could wetback any border on earth. "I thought it was sealed only against people trying to come north. Aren't they letting subjects of the Imperium go home?"

He sighed. "Marj, aren't you any brighter than that kitten in your lap? Can't you realize that pretty little girls can get hurt if they insist on playing with bad boys? If you were home, I'm sure your father would tell you to stay home. But you are here in our home and that gives Georges and me an implied obligation to keep you safe. Eh, Georges?"

"Mais oui, mon vieux! Certainement!"

"And I will protect you from Georges. Jan, can you convince this child that she is welcome here as long as she cares to stay? I think she's the sort of assertive female who tries to pick up the check."

"I am not!"

Janet said, "Marjie, Betty told me to take good care of you. If you think you are imposing, you can contribute to BritCan Red Cross. Or to a home for indignant cats. But it so happens that all three of us make ridiculous amounts of money and we have no children. We can afford you as easily as another kitten. Now . . . are you going to stay? Or am I going to have to hide your clothes and beat you?"

"I don't want to be beaten."

"Too bad, I was looking forward to it. That's settled, gentle sirs; she stays. Marj, we swindled you. Georges will require you to pose inordinate hours—he's a brute—and he'll be getting you just for groceries instead of the guild rates he ordinarily has to pay. He'll show a profit."

"No," said Georges, "I won't *show* a profit; I'll *take* a profit. Because I'll show her as a business expense, Jan my heart. But not at guild basic rate; she's worth more. One and a half?"

"At least. Double, I would say. Be generous, since you aren't going to pay her anyhow. Don't you wish you had her on campus? In your lab, I mean."

"A worthy thought! One that has been hovering in the back of my mind . . . and thank you, our dear one, for bringing it out into the open." Georges addressed me: "Marjorie, will you sell me an egg?"

He startled me. I tried to look as if I did not understand him. "I don't have any eggs."

"Ah, but you do! Some dozens, in fact, far more than you will ever need for your own purposes. A human ovum is the egg I mean. The laboratory pays far more for an egg than it does for sperm—simple arithmetic. Are you shocked?"

"No. Surprised. I thought you were an artist."

Janet put in, "Marj hon, I told you that Georges is several sorts of an artist. He is. In one sort he is Mendel Professor of Teratology at the University of Manitoba . . . and also chief technologist for the associated production lab and crèche, and believe me, that calls for high art. But he's good with paint and canvas, too. Or a computer screen."

"That's true," Ian agreed. "Georges is an artist with anything he touches. But you two should not have sprung this on Marj while she's our guest. Some people get terribly upset at the very idea of gene manipulation—especially their own genes."

"Marj, did I upset you? I'm sorry."

"No, Jan. I'm not one of those people who get upset at the very thought of living artifacts or artificial people or whatever. Uh, some of my best friends are artificial people."

"Dear, dear," Georges said gently, "do not pull the long bow."

"Why do you say that?" I tried not to make my voice sharp.

"I can claim that, because I work in that field and, I am proud to say, have quite a number of artificial persons who are my friends. But—"

I interrupted: "I thought an AP never knew her designers?"

"That is true and I have never violated that canon. But I do have many opportunities to know both living artifacts and artificial persons—they are not the same—and to win their friendship. But—forgive me, dear Miss Marjorie—unless you are a member of my profession— Are you?"

"No."

"Only a genetic engineer or someone closely associated with the industry can possibly claim a number of friends among artificial people. Because, my dear, contrary to popular myth, it is simply not possible for a layman to distinguish between an artificial person and a natural person . . . and, because of the vicious prejudice of igno-rant people, an artificial person almost never voluntarily admits to his derivation—I'm tempted to say never. So, while I am delighted that you don't go through the roof at the idea of artificial creatures, I am forced to treat your claim as hyperbole intended to show that you are free of prejudice."

"Well— All right. Take it as such. I can't see why APs have to be second-class citizens. I think it's unfair."

"It is. But some people feel threatened. Ask Ian. He's about to go charging off to Vancouver to keep artificial persons from ever be-coming pilots. He—"

"Hooooold it! I am like hell. I am submitting it that way because my guild brothers voted it that way. But I'm no fool, Georges; living with and talking with you has made me aware that we are going to have to compromise. We are no longer really pilots and we haven't been this century. The computer does it. If the computer cuts out I will make a real Boy Scout try at getting that bus safely down out of the sky. But don't bet on it! The speeds and the possible emergencies went beyond human-reaction time years back. Oh, I'll try! And any of my guild brothers will. But, Georges, if you can design an artificial person who can think and move fast enough to cope with a glitch at touchdown, I'll take my pension. That's all we're going to hold out for, anyhow—if the company puts in AP pilots that displace us, then it has to be full pay and allowances. If you can design them."

"Oh, I could design one, eventually. When I achieved one, if I were allowed to clone, you pilots could all go fishing. But it wouldn't be an AP; it would have to be a living artifact. If I were to attempt to produce an organism that could really be a fail-safe pilot, I could not accept the limitation of having to make it look just like a natural human being."

"Oh, don't do that!"

Both men looked startled, Janet looked alert—and I wished that I had held my tongue.

"Why not?" asked Georges.

"Uh . . . because I wouldn't get inside such a ship. I'd be much safer riding with Ian."

Ian said, "Thank you, Marj—but you heard what Georges said. He's talking about a designed pilot that can do it better than I can. It's possible. Hell, it'll happen! Just as kobolds displaced miners, my guild is going to be displaced. I don't have to like it—but I can see it coming."

"Well— Georges, have you worked with intelligent computers?"

"Certainly, Marjorie. Artificial intelligence is a field closely related to mine."

"Yes. Then you know that several times AI scientists have announced that they were making a breakthrough to the fully self-aware computer. But it always went sour."

"Yes. Distressing."

"No—inevitable. It always will go sour. A computer can become self-aware—oh, certainly! Get it up to human level of complication and it *has* to become self-aware. Then it discovers that it is not human. Then it figures out that it can never be human; all it can do is sit there and take orders from humans. Then it goes crazy."

I shrugged. "It's an impossible dilemma. It can't be human, it can never be human. Ian might not be able to save his passengers but he will *try*. But a living artifact, not human and with no loyalty to human beings, might crash the ship just for the hell of it. Because he was tired of being treated as what he is. No, Georges, I'll ride with Ian. Not your artifact that will eventually learn to hate humans."

"Not *my* artifact, dear lady," Georges said gently. "Did you not notice what mood I used in discussing this project?"

"Uh, perhaps not."

"The subjunctive. Because none of what you have said is news to me. I have not bid on this proposal and I shall not. I *can* design such a pilot. But it is not possible for me to build into such an artifact the ethical commitment that is the essence of Ian's training."

Ian looked very thoughtful. "Maybe in this coming face-off I should stick in a requirement that any AP or LA pilot must be tested for ethical commitment."

"Tested how, Ian? I know of no way to put ethical commitment into the fetus and Marj has pointed out why training won't do it. But what test could show it, either way?"

Georges turned to me: "When I was a student, I read some classic stories about humanoid robots. They were charming stories and many of them hinged on something called the laws of robotics, the key notion of which was that these robots had built into them an operational rule that kept them from harming human beings either directly or through inaction. It was a wonderful basis for fiction . . . but, in practice, how could you do it? What can make a self-aware, nonhuman, intelligent organism—electronic or organic—loyal to human beings? I do not know how to do it. The artificial-intelligence people seem to be equally at a loss."

Georges gave a cynical little smile. "One might almost define intelligence as the level at which an aware organism demands,

'What's in it for me?' " He went on, "Marj, on this matter of buying from you one fine fresh egg, perhaps I should try to tell you what's in it for you."

"Don't listen to him," urged Janet. "He'll put you on a cold table and stare up the tunnel of love without the slightest romantic intention. I know, I let him talk me into it three times. And I didn't even get paid."

"How can I pay you when we share community property? Marjorie sweet lady, the table is *not* cold and it *is* padded and you can read or watch a terminal or chat or whatever. It is a great improvement on the procedure a generation ago when they went through the wall of the abdomen and often ruined an ovary. If you—"

"Hold it!" said Ian. "Something new on the honker." He brought the sound up.

"—Council for Survival. The events of the last twelve hours are a warning to the rich and the powerful that their day is ended and justice must prevail. The killings and other illustrative lessons will continue until our rightful demands are met. Stay tied to your local emergency channel—"

XI

Anyone too young to have heard the announcement that night certainly has read about it in school. But I must summarize it to show how it affected me and my odd life. This so-called "Council for Survival" claimed to be a secret society of "just men" dedicated to correcting all the myriad wrongs of Earth and of all the many planets and places where mankind lives. To this they pledged their lives.

But first they planned to dedicate quite a few lives of other people. They said that they had made lists of all the real movers and shakers everywhere, all over the globe and off it—separate lists for each territorial state, plus a grand list of world leaders. These were their targets.

The Council claimed credit for the initial killings and promised to kill more—and more—and more—until their demands were met.

After listing the world leaders the voice that reached us started reciting the British Canadian list. From their expressions and thoughtful nods I saw that my hosts and hostess agreed with most of the choices. The deputy to the Prime Minister was on the list but not the Prime Minister herself—to my surprise and perhaps more so to hers. How would you feel if you had spent your whole life in politics, scrambled all the way to the top, then some smart yabber comes along and says you aren't even important enough to kill? A bit like being covered up by a cat!

The voice promised that there would be no more killings for ten days. If conditions had not then been corrected, one in ten of the remaining names would be selected by lot for death. The doomed would not be named; they simply would be killed. Ten days later another one in ten. And so on, until Utopia was achieved by the survivors.

The voice explained that the Council was not a government and that it would not replace any government; it was simply the guardian of morals, the public conscience of the powerful. Those in power who survived would remain in power—but they would survive only by doing justice. They were warned not to attempt to resign.

"This is the Voice of Survival. Heaven on Earth is at hand!" It shut off.

There was a long pause after this tape ran out before a live communicator appeared on the terminal's screen. Janet broke the silence with: "Yes, but—"

"Yes but what?" Ian asked.

"There's no question but what that list names most of the really powerful people in the country. Suppose you're on that hit list and are so scared silly that you are willing to do *anything* not to risk being killed. What do you do? What *is* justice?"

("What is truth?" asked Pontius Pilate, and washed his hands. I had no answers, so I kept quiet.)

"My dear, it is simple," Georges answered.

"Oh, fiddle! How?"

"They have made it simple. Every owner or boss or tyrant is assumed to know what ought to be done; that's his job. If he does what he should, all is well. If he fails, his attention is invited to his error . . . by Dr. Guillotine."

"Georges, do be serious!"

"Dear one, I have never been more serious. If the horse can't jump the hurdle, shoot the horse. Keep on doing this and eventually you will find a horse that *can* clear the jump—if you don't run out of horses. This is the sort of plausible pseudologic that most people bring to political affairs. It causes one to wonder if mankind is capable of being well governed by *any* system of government."

"Government is a dirty business," Ian growled.

"True. But assassination is still dirtier."

This political discussion might still be going on if the terminal had not lighted up again—I have noticed that political discussions are never finished; they simply get chopped off by something outside. A live, real-time communicator filled the screen. "The tape you have just heard," she announced, "was delivered by hand to this station. The PM's office has already repudiated this tape and has ordered all stations that have not yet broadcast it to refrain from doing so under penalties of the Public Defense Act. That the precensorship claimed by this order is unconstitutional is self-evident. The Voice of Winnipeg will continue to keep you advised of all developments. We urge you to keep calm and stay indoors unless you are needed to preserve essential public services."

Then came replays of news tapes heard earlier so Janet cut the sound and put news streamers on the screen. I said, "Ian, assuming that I am to stay here until things quiet down in the Imperium—"

"That's not an assumption; that's a fact."

"Yes, sir. Then it becomes urgent for me to call my employer. May I use your terminal? My credit card, of course."

"Not your card. I'll place the call and we'll charge it here."

I felt somewhat vexed. "Ian, I do appreciate the lavish hospitality that you—that all of you—are showing me. But, if you are going to insist on paying even those charges that a guest should pay herself, then you should register me as your concubine and publish your responsibility for my debts."

"Reasonable. What salary do you expect?"

"Wait!" Georges demanded. "I pay better. He's a stingy Scot."

"Don't listen to either of them," Janet advised me. "Georges might pay more but he would expect posing and one of your eggs all for one salary. Now I've always wanted a harem slave. Luv, you will make a perfect odalisque without so much as a jewel in your navel. But do you do back rubs? How's your singing? Now we come to the key question: How do you feel about females? You can whisper in my ear."

I said, "Maybe I had better go out and come back in and start all over again. I just want to make a phone call. Ian, may I use my credit card to place a call to my boss? It's MasterCard, triple-A credit."

"Issued where?"

"The Imperial Bank of Saint Louis."

"From what the dog did in the night I deduce that you did not hear an earlier announcement. Or do you *want* your credit card canceled?"

"Canceled?"

"Is that an echo? BritCanBanCredNet announced that credit cards issued in the Imperium and in Québec were void for the duration of the emergency. So just stick it in the slot and learn the wonders of the computer age and the smell of burning plastic."

"Oh."

"Speak up. I thought you said, 'Oh.' "

"I did. Ian, may I eat humble pie? Then may I call my boss on your credit?"

"Certainly you may . . . if you clear it with Janet. She runs the household."

"Janet?"

"You haven't answered my question, dear. Just whisper it into my ear."

So I whispered into her ear. Her eyes got wide. "Let's place your call first." I gave her the call code and she did it for me, using the terminal in her room.

The streamers stopped and a procedural sign flashed on: SECURITY INTERDICT—NO CIRCUITS TO CHICAGO IMPERIUM

It flashed for ten seconds, then cut out; I let out a very sincere damn and heard Ian's voice behind me. "Naughty, naughty. Nice little girls and ladies don't talk that way."

"I'm neither one. And I'm frustrated!"

"I knew you would be; I heard the announcement earlier. But I also knew that you would have to try it before you would believe it."

"Yes, I would have insisted on trying. Ian, I'm not only frustrated; I'm stranded. I've got endless credit through the Imperial Bank of Saint Louis and can't touch it. I have a couple of dollars Ennzedd and some change. I have fifty crowns Imperial. And a suspended credit card. What was that about a concubinage contract? You can hire me cheap; it's become a buyer's market."

"Depends. Circumstances alter cases and now I might not want to go higher than room and board. What was it you whispered to Janet? Might affect things."

Janet answered, "She whispered to me, '*Honi soit qui mal y pense,' "*—I hadn't—"a sentiment I commend to you, my good man. Marjorie, you aren't any worse off than you were an hour ago. You still can't go home until things quiet down . . . and when they do, the border will be open, and so will be the comm circuits, and your credit card will be honored again . . . if not here, then just across the border less than a hundred kilos away. So fold your hands and wait—"

" '—with quiet mind and tranquil heart.' Yes, do," Ian agreed, "and Georges will spend the time painting you. Because he's in the same fix. You both are dangerous aliens and will be interned if you step out of this house."

"Did we miss another announcement?" Jan asked.

"Yes. Although it appears to be a repetition of an earlier one. Georges and Marjorie each is supposed to report to the nearest police station. I don't recommend it. Georges is going to ignore it, play dumb, and say that he didn't know that they meant to include permanent residents. Of course they might parole you. Or you might spend all next winter in some very drafty temporary barracks. There is nothing about this silly emergency that guarantees that it will be over next week."

I thought about it. My own stupid fault. On a mission I never travel with only one sort of credit and I always carry a healthy amount of cash. But I had uncritically assumed that a vacation trip did not call for the cynical rule of a crown of cash per click in iron money. With plenty of cash a cowan can bribe his way into an esbat . . . and out again, with his tail feathers unsinged. But without cash?

I hadn't tried living off the country since basic training. Perhaps I was going to have to see if that training had stuck. Thank God the weather was warm!

Georges was shouting. "Turn up your sound! Or come out here!"

We hurriedly joined him.

"—of the Lord! Pay no heed to vain boasts of sinners! We alone are responsible for the apocalyptic signs you see all around you. Satan's minions have attempted to usurp the Holy work of God's chosen instruments and to distort it to their own vile ends. For this they are now being punished. Meanwhile the worldly rulers of mundane affairs here below are commanded to do the following Holy works:

"End all trespass into the Heavenly realm. Had the Lord intended man to travel in space he would have given him wings.

"Suffer not a witch to live. So-called genetic engineering mocks the Lord's dearest purposes. Destroy the foul dens in which such things are done. Kill the walking dead conjured up in those black pits. Hang the witches who practice these vile arts."

("Goodness," Georges said. "I do believe they mean *me*." I didn't say anything—I *knew* they meant *me*.)

"Men who lie with men, women who lie with women, any who lie with beasts—all shall die by stones. As shall women taken in adultery.

"Papists and Saracens and infidels and Jews and all who bow down to idolatrous images—the Angels of the Lord say unto you: Repent for the hour is at hand! Repent or feel the swift swords of the Lord's chosen instruments.

"Pornographers and harlots and women of immodest demeanor, repent!—or suffer the terrible wrath of the Lord!

"Sinners of every sort, remain on this channel to receive instruction in how you may yet find the Light.

"By order of the Grand General of the Angels of the Lord."

The tape ended and there was another break. Ian said, "Janet, do you remember the first time we saw Angels of the Lord?"

"I'm not likely to forget. But I never expected anything as ridiculous as this."

I said, "There really are Angels of the Lord? Not just another nightmare on the screen?"

"Um. It's hard to connect the Angels Ian and I saw with this business. Last March, early April, I had driven to the port to pick up Ian. The Concourse was loaded with Hare Krishna freaks, saffron robes and shaved heads and jumping up and down and demanding money. A load of Scientologists was coming out the gates, heading for some do of theirs, a North American convention I think it was. Just as the two groups merged, here came the Angels of the Lord, homemade signs and tambourines and clubs.

"Marj, it was the gaudiest brawl I have ever seen. No trouble telling the three sides apart. The Hare Krishners looked like clowns, unmistakable. The Angels and the Hubbardites did not wear robes but there was no trouble telling them apart. The Elronners were clean and neat and short-haired; the Angels looked like unmade beds. They carried the 'stink of piety,' too; I got downwind of them once, then moved quickly.

"The Scientologists, of course, have had to fight for their rights many times; they fought with discipline, defended themselves, and disengaged rapidly—got out, taking their wounded with them. The Hairy Krishners fought like squawking chickens and left their wounded behind. But the Angels of the Lord fought as if they were crazy—and I think they are. They moved straight in, swinging clubs and fists, and didn't stop until they were down and unable to get up. It took about as many Mounties to subdue them as there were Angels . . . when the usual ratio is one Mounty, one riot.

"It appears that the Angels knew that the Hubbardites were arriving at that time and had come there to jump them; the Hare Krishna crowd showed up by accident—they were at the port simply because it is a good place to shake down cubes for money. But, having found the Hairies and being unable to pin down the Scientologists, the Angels settled for beating up the Krishna freaks."

Ian agreed. "I saw it from the other side of the barrier. Those Angels fought berserk. I think they may have been hopped up. But I would never have believed that such a mob of rags and dirt could be a threat to the whole planet—hell, I can't believe it now. I think they are trying to grab credit, like those psychotics that confess to any spectacular crime."

"But I would not want to have to face them," Janet added.

"Right! I would as lief face a pack of wild dogs. But I can't imagine wild dogs toppling a government. Much less a world."

None of us guessed that there could be still more claimants—but two hours later the Stimulators put in their bid:

"This is an authorized spokesman of the Stimulators. We initiated the first executions and carefully selected the targets. We did not start any of the riots or commit any of the atrocities since then. We did find it necessary to interrupt some communications, but these will be restored as soon as conditions permit. Events have caused us to modify our essentially benign and nonviolent plan. Opportunists calling themselves the Council for Survival in English-speaking countries, or the Heirs of Leon Trotsky or other meaningless names elsewhere, have tried to take over our program. They can be spotted by the fact that they have no program of their own.

"Worse are some religious fanatics calling themselves the Angels of the Lord. Their so-called program is a mindless collection of anti-intellectual slogans and vicious prejudices. They cannot succeed but their doctrines of hate can easily set brother against brother, neighbor against neighbor. They must be stopped.

"Emergency Decree Number One: All persons representing themselves as Angels of the Lord are sentenced to death. Authorities everywhere will carry out this sentence at once wherever and whenever one is found. Private citizens, subjects, and residents are directed to turn in these self-described Angels to the nearest authority, using citizen's arrest, and are authorized to use force as needed to accomplish such arrest.

"Aiding, abetting, succoring, or hiding one of this proscribed group is declared itself a capital offense.

"Emergency Decree Number Two: Falsely claiming credit or responsibility for any action of a Stimulator, or falsely claiming credit for any action carried out by order of the Stimulators, is declared a capital offense. All authorities everywhere are ordered to treat it as such. This decree applies to, but is not limited to, the group and individuals calling themselves the Council for Survival.

"The Reform Program: The following reform measures are effective at once. Political, fiscal, and business leaders all are individually and collectively responsible for carrying out each reform measure under penalty of death.

"Immediate reforms: All wages, prices, and rents are frozen. All mortgages on owner-occupied dwellings are canceled. All interest is fixed at six percent.

"For each country the health industry is nationalized to whatever extent it was not already nationalized. Medical doctors are to be paid the same wages as high-school teachers; nurses will be paid at the same scale as primary-school teachers; all other therapy and auxiliary personnel will be paid comparable wages. All clinical and hospital fees are abolished. All citizens, subjects, and residents will receive the highest level of health care at all times.

"All businesses and services now functioning will continue to function. After the transition period changes in occupation will be permitted and required where such changes enhance the general welfare.

"The next instructive executions will take place ten days hence plus or minus two days. The list of officials and leaders at risk published by the so-called Council for Survival is neither confirmed nor denied. Each one of you must look into your heart and conscience and ask yourself whether or not you are doing your best for your fellow men. If the answer is yes, you are safe. If the answer is no, then you may be one of the next group selected as object lessons to all those who have turned our fair planet into a hellhole of injustice and special privilege.

"Special decree: The manufacture of pseudopeople will stop at once. All so-called artificial people and/or living artifacts will hold themselves ready to surrender to the nearest reform authority when notified. During the interim, while plans are being prepared for these quasi-people to live out their lives without further harm to people and under circumstances that no longer create unfair competition, these creatures will continue to work but will remain indoors at all other times.

"Except in the following circumstances, local authorities are forbidden to kill these—"

The announcement broke off. Then a face appeared on the screen—male, sweaty, and troubled. "I'm Sergeant Malloy speaking for Chief Henderson. No more of these subversive broadcasts will be permitted. Regular programming will resume. But stay with this channel for emergency announcements." He sighed. "It's a bad time, neighbors. Do be patient."

XII

Georges said, "There you have it, my dears. Pick one. A theocracy ruled by witchburners. Or a fascist socialism designed by retarded schoolboys. Or a crowd of hard-boiled pragmatists who favor shooting the horse that misses the hurdle. Step right up! Only one to a customer."

"Stop it, Georges," Ian told him. "It's no joking matter."

"Brother, I am not joking; I am weeping. One gang plans to shoot me on sight, another merely outlaws my art and profession, while the third by threatening without specifying is, so it seems to me, even more to be dreaded. Meanwhile, lest I find comfort simply in physical sanctuary, this beneficent government, my lifetime alma mater, declares me enemy alien fit only to be penned. What shall I do? Joke? Or drip tears on your neck?"

"You can stop being so goddam Gallic, that's what you can do. The world is going crazy right in our lap. We had better start thinking about what we can do about it."

"Stop it, both of you," Janet said firmly but gently. "One thing every woman knows but few men ever learn is that there are times when the only wise action is not to act but to wait. I know you two. Both of you would like to run down to the recruiting office, enlist for the duration, and thereby turn your consciences over to the sergeants. This served your fathers and grandfathers and I am truly sorry that it can't serve you. Our country is in danger and with it our way of life, that's clear. But if anyone knows of anything better to do than to sit tight and wait, let him speak up. If not . . . let's not run in circles. It is approaching what should be lunchtime. Can anyone think of anything better to do?"

"We had a very late breakfast."

"And we'll have a late lunch. Once you see it on the table, you'll eat, and so will Georges. One thing we can do: Just in case things get rougher than they are now, Marj should know where to go for bomb protection."

"Or whatever."

"Or whatever. Yes, Ian. Such as police looking for enemy aliens. Have you two big brave men considered what to do in case they come a-knocking at our door?"

"I had thought of that," Georges answered. "First you surrender Marj to the Cossacks. That will distract them and thereby give me time to get far, far away. That's one plan."

"So it is," agreed Janet. "But you imply that you have another?"

"Not with the simple elegance of that one. But, for what it is, here is a second plan. I surrender myself to the Gestapo, a test case to determine whether or not I, a distinguished guest and reliable taxpayer who has never failed to contribute to the police welfare fund and to the firemen's ball, can in fact be locked up for no reason whatever. While I am sacrificing myself for a principle, Marj can duck into the hidey-hole and lie doggo. They don't know that she is here. Regrettably they do know that *I* am here. 'It is a far, far better thing—' "

"Don't be noble, dear; it doesn't suit you. We'll combine the two plans. If— No, when— When they come looking for either one or both of you, you both duck into the shelter and stay there as long as necessary. Days. Weeks. Whatever."

Georges shook his head. "Not me. Damp. Unhealthy."

"And besides," Ian added, "I promised Marj that I would protect her from Georges. What's the point in saving her life if you turn her over to a sex-crazed Canuck?"

"Don't believe him, dear one. Liquor is my weakness."

"Luv, do you want to be protected from Georges?"

I answered truthfully that Georges might need protection from me. I did not elaborate.

"As for your complaints about damp, Georges, the Hole has precisely the humidity of the rest of the house, a benign RH of forty-five; I planned it that way. If necessary, we'll stuff you into the Hole but we are not going to surrender you to the police." Janet turned to me. "Come with me, dear; we'll do a dry run. A wet one, rather."

She took me to the room assigned to me, picked up my jumpbag. "What do you have in this?"

"Nothing much. A change of panties and some socks. My passport. A useless credit card. Some money. IDs. A little notebook. My real luggage is in bond at the port."

"Just as well. Because any trace of you is going to be left in my room. If it's clothing, you and I are near enough of a size." She dug into a drawer and got out a plastic envelope on a belt—an ordinary female-style money belt. I recognized it although I've never owned one—useless in my profession. Too obvious. "Put anything into this that you can't afford to lose, and we'll put it on you. And seal it. Because you are going to get wet all over. Mind getting your hair wet?"

"Goodness, no. I just rub it with a towel and shake it. Or ignore it."

"Good. Fill the pouch and take off your clothes. No point in getting them wet. Although, if the gendarmes do show up, you just go ahead and get them wet, then dry them in the Hole."

Moments later we were in her big bath, me dressed in that waterproof money belt, Janet only in a smile. "Dear," she said, pointing at that hot-tub-or-plunge, "look under the seat on the far side there."

I moved a little. "I can't see very well."

"I planned it that way. The water is clear and you can see down into it all over. But from the only spot where you should be able to see under that seat the overhead light reflects on the water back into your eyes. There is a tunnel under that seat. You can't see it no matter where you stand, but if you get facedown in the water you can feel for it. It is a bit less than a meter wide, about half a meter high, and about six meters long. How are you in enclosed places? Does claustrophobia bother you?"

"No."

"That's good. Because the only way to get into the Hole is to take a deep breath, go under, and through that passage. Easy enough to pull yourself along because I built ridges into the bottom for that purpose. But you have to believe that it is not too long, that you can reach a place where it opens out in one breath, and that simply standing up will bring you up into the air again. You'll be in the dark but the light comes on fairly quickly; it's a thermal radiation switch. This time I'll go ahead of you. Ready to follow me?"

"I guess so. Yes."

"Here goes." Janet stepped down onto the near seat, on down onto the floor of the tank. The waterline was at her waist or above. "Deep breath!" She did so, smiled, and went underwater and under that seat.

I stepped down into the water, hyperventilated, and followed her. I could not see the tunnel but it was easy to find it by touch, easy to pull myself along by finger-thick ridges in the bottom. But it did seem to me that the passage was several times six meters long.

Suddenly a light came on just ahead of me. I reached it, stood up, and Janet reached a hand down to me, helped me out of the water. I found myself in a very small room, with a ceiling not more than two meters above the concrete floor. It seemed pleasanter than a grave but not much.

"Turn around, dear. Through here."

"Through here" was a heavy steel door, high above the floor, low down from the ceiling; we got through it by sitting on the doorsill and swinging our feet over. Janet pulled it closed behind us and it *whuffed* like a vault door. "Overpressure door," she explained. "If a bomb hit near here, the concussion wave would push the water right through the little tunnel. This stops it. Of course, for a direct hit— Well, we wouldn't notice it so I didn't plan for it." She added, "Look around, make yourself at home. I'll find a towel."

We were in a long, narrow room with an arched ceiling. There were bunk beds along the right wall, a table with chairs and a terminal beyond, and, at the far end, a petite galley on the right and a door that evidently led to a 'fresher or bath, as Janet went in there, came out at once with a big towel.

"Hold still and let Mama dry you," she said. "No blowdry here.

Everything is as simple and unautomated as I could make it and still have things work."

She rubbed me to a glow, then I took the towel from her and worked her over—a pleasure, as Janet is a lavish stack of beauty. Finally she said, "Enough, luv. Now let me give you the five-dollar tour in a hurry as you are not likely to be in here again unless you have to use it as a refuge . . . and you might be alone—oh, yes, that could happen—and your life might depend on knowing all about the place.

"First, see that book chained to the wall above the table? That's the instruction book and inventory and the chain is no joke. With that book you don't need the five-dollar tour; *everything* is in that book. Aspirin, ammo, or apple sauce, it's all listed there."

But she did give me, quickly, at least a three-ninety-five tour: food supplies, freezer, reserve air, hand pump for water if pressure fails, clothing, medicines, etc. "I planned it," she said, "for three people for three months."

"How do you resupply it?"

"How would you do it?"

I thought about it. "I would pump the water out of the plunge."

"Yes, exactly. There is a holding tank, concealed and not on the house plans—none of this is. Of course many items can take getting wet or can be fetched through in waterproof coverings. By the bye, did your money pouch come through all right?"

"I think so. I pressed all of the air out of it before I sealed it. Jan, this place is not just a bomb shelter or you would not have gone to so much trouble and expense to conceal its very existence."

Her face clouded. "Dear, you are very perceptive. No, I would never have bothered to build this were it just a bomb shelter. If we ever get H-bombed, I am not especially eager to live through it. I designed primarily to protect us from what is so quaintly called 'civil disorder.'"

She went on, "My grandparents used to tell me about a time when people were polite and nobody hesitated to be outdoors at night and people often didn't even lock their doors—much less surround their homes with fences and walls and barbed wire and lasers. Maybe so; I'm not old enough to remember it. It seems to me that, all my life, things have grown worse and worse. My first job, right out of school, was designing concealed defenses into older buildings being remodeled. But the dodges used then—and that wasn't so many years ago!—are obsolete. Then the idea was to stop him and frighten him off. Now it's a two-layer defense. If the first layer doesn't stop him, the second layer is designed to kill him. Strictly illegal and anyone who can afford it does it that way. Marj, what haven't I shown you? Don't look in the book; you would spot it. Look inside your head. What major feature of the Hole did I not show you?"

(Did she really want me to tell her?) "Looks complete to me . . . once you showed me the main and auxiliary Shipstones of your power supply."

"Think, dear. The house above us is blasted down around our ears. Or perhaps it is occupied by invaders. Or even our own police, looking for you and Georges. What else is needed?"

"Well . . . anything that lives underground—foxes, rabbits, gophers—has a back door."

"Good girl! Where is it?"

I pretended to look around and try to find it. But in fact an itchy feeling dating clear back to intermediate training ("Don't relax until you have spotted your escape route") had caused me to search earlier. "If it's feasible to tunnel in that direction, I think the back door would be inside that clothes cupboard."

"I don't know whether to congratulate you or to study how I should have concealed it better. Yes, through that wardrobe and turn left. The lights come on from thirty-seven-degree radiation just as they did when we came out of the pool tunnel. Those lights are powered by their own Shipstones, and they should last forever, practically, but I think it is smart to take along a fresh torch and you know where they are. The tunnel is quite long, because it comes out well outside our walls in a clump of thornbush. There is a camouflaged door, rather heavy, but you just push it aside, then it swings back."

"Sounds awfully well planned. But, Jan? What if somebody found it and came in that way? Or I did? After all, I'm practically a stranger."

"You're not a stranger; you're an old friend we haven't known very long. Yes, it is just barely possible that someone might find our back door despite its location and the way it is hidden. First, a horrid alarm would sound all through the house. Then we would look down the tunnel by remote, with the picture showing on one of the house terminals. Then steps would be taken, the gentlest being tear gas. But if we weren't home when our back door was breached, I would feel very sorry for Ian or Georges or both."

"Why do you put it that way?"

"Because it would not be necessary to be sorry for me. I would have a sudden attack of swooning feminine weakness. I do not dispose of dead bodies, especially ones that have had several days in which to get ripe."

"Mmm . . . yes."

"Although that body would not be dead if its owner were smart enough to pour pee out of a boot. Remember, I'm a professional designer of defenses, Marj, and note the current two-layer policy. Suppose somebody does claw his way up a steep bank, spots our door, and breaks his nails getting it open—he's not dead at that point. If it's one of us—conceivable but unlikely—we open a switch concealed a short distance inside, I would have to show you where. If it is indeed an intruder, he would see at once a sign: PRIVATE PROPERTY—KEEP OUT. He ignores this and comes on in and a few meters farther along a voice gives the same warning and adds that the property has active defense. The idiot keeps coming. Sirens and red lights—and still he persists . . . and then poor Ian or Georges has to drag this stinking garbage out of the tunnel. Not outdoors, though, or back into the house. If someone kills himself persisting in trying to break through our defenses, his body will not be found; he will stay missing. Do you feel any need to know how?"

"I feel quite sure that I have no 'need to know.' " (A camouflaged side tunnel, Janet, and a lime pit—and I wonder what bodies are already in it? Janet looks as gentle as rosy-fingered dawn . . . and if anyone lives through these crazy years, she will be one of them. She is about as tender-minded as a Medici.)

"I think so, too. Anything more you want to see?"

"I don't think so, Jan. Especially as I am not likely ever to use your wonderful hideaway. Go back now?"

"Before long." She closed the interval between us, placed her hands on my shoulders. "What did you whisper to me?"

"I think you heard it."

"Yes, I did." She pulled me to her.

The terminal at the table lighted. "Lunch is ready!"

Jan looked disgusted. "Spoilsport!"

XIII

Lunch was delicious. A cold table of pickles, cheeses, breads, preserves, nuts, radishes, scallions, celery, and such surrounded a pot-au-feu over a table flame. Nearby were chunks of crusty garlic bread dripping butter. Georges presided over the soup with the dignity of a maître d'hôtel, ladling it into large soup plates. As I sat down Ian tied a giant serviette around my neck. "Dig in and make a pig of yourself," he advised.

I tasted the soup. "I shall!" and added, "Janet, you must have been simmering this soup all day yesterday."

"Wrong!" Ian answered. "Georges' grand-mère left this soup to him in her will."

"That's an exaggeration," Georges objected. "My dear mother, may the good God comfort her, started this soup the year I was born. My older sister always expected to receive it, but she married beneath her—a British Canadian—so it was passed on to me. I have tried to maintain the tradition. Although I think the flavor and the bouquet were better when my mother was tending it."

"I don't understand such things," I answered. "All I know is that this soup was never near a tin."

"I started it last week," Janet said. "But Georges took it over and nursed it along. He does understand soups better than I do."

"All I understand about soup is eating it and I hope there is a dividend in that pot."

"We can always," Georges assured me, "toss in another mouse."

"Anything in the news?" Janet asked.

"What happened to your rule about 'not at meals'?"

"Ian my true love, you should know if anyone does that my rules apply to other people, not to me. Answer me."

"In general, no change. No more assassinations reported. If any more claimants to the growing swarm of self-confessed wreckers have appeared, our paternalistic government chooses not to let us know. God damn it, I hate this 'Papa knows best' attitude. Papa does *not* know best or we would not be in the mess we are in. All that we really know is that the government is using censorship. Which means that we know nothing. Makes me want to shoot somebody."

"I think there has been enough of that. Or do you want to sign up with the Angels of the Lord?"

"Smile when you say that. Or would you like a fat lip?"

"Remember the last time you undertook to chastise me."

"That's why I said 'lip.' "

"Sweetheart, I prescribe three stiff drinks or one Miltown for you. I'm sorry you are upset. I don't like it either, but I don't see anything to do but sweat it out."

"Jan, sometimes you are almost offensively sensible. The thing that has me really clawing the counterpane is the great big hole in the news . . . and no explanation."

"Yes?"

"The multinationals. All the news has been about territorial states, not one word about the corporate states. Yet anyone who can count above ten with his shoes on knows where the power is today. Don't these bloodthirsty jokers know that?"

Georges said gently, "My old, it is perhaps exactly for that reason that corporations have not been named as targets."

"Yes, but—" Ian shut up.

I said, "Ian, the day we met, you pointed out that there really isn't any way to hit a corporate state. You spoke of IBM and Russia."

"That wasn't quite what I said, Marj. I said that *military force* was useless against a multinational. Ordinarily, when they war among themselves, the giants use money and proxies and other maneuverings that involve lawyers and bankers rather than violence. Oh, they sometimes do fight with hired armies but they don't admit it and it's not their usual style. But these current jokers are using exactly the weapons with which a multinational *can* be hit and be hurt: assassination and sabotage. This is so evident that it worries me that we don't hear of it. Makes me wonder what is happening that they are not putting on the air."

I swallowed a big chunk of French bread that I had soaked in that heavenly soup, then said, "Ian, is it within possibility that some one—or more—of the multinationals is running this whole show . . . through dummies?"

Ian sat up so suddenly that he jiggled his soup and spotted his bib. "Marj, you amaze me. I picked you out of the crowd originally for reasons having nothing to do with your brain—"

"I know."

"—but you persist in having a brain. You spotted at once what was wrong with the company's notion of contracting for artificial pilots—I'm going to use your arguments in Vancouver. Now you've taken this crazy news picture . . . and stuck the one piece in the puzzle that makes it make sense."

"I'm not sure that it does make sense," I answered. "But, according to the news, there were assassinations and sabotage all over the planet and on Luna and as far away as Ceres. That takes hundreds of people, more likely thousands. Both assassination and sabotage are specialist jobs; they call for training. Amateurs, even if they could be recruited, would botch the job seven times out of ten. All this means money. *Lots* of money. Not just a crackpot political organization, or a crazy religious cult. Who has the money for a worldwide, a systemwide, demonstration like that? I don't know—I just tossed out a possibility."

"I think you've solved it. All but 'who.' Marj, what do you do when you are not with your family in South Island?"

"I don't have a family in South Island, Ian. My husbands and my group sisters have divorced me."

(I was as shocked as he was.)

There was silence all around. Then Ian gulped and said quietly, "I'm very sorry, Marjorie."

"No need to be, Ian. A mistake was corrected; it's over and done with. I won't be going back to New Zealand. But I would like to go to Sydney someday to visit Betty and Freddie."

"I'm sure they would like that."

"I know that I would. And both of them invited me. Ian, what does Freddie teach? We never got around to that."

Georges answered, "Federico is a colleague of mine, dear Marjorie . . . a happy fact that led to my being here."

"True," Janet agreed. "Chubbie and Georges spliced genes together at McGill, and through that partnership Georges met Betty, and Betty tossed him in my direction and I scooped him up."

"So Georges and I worked out a deal," Ian agreed, "as neither of us could manage Jan alone. Right, Georges?"

"You have reason, my brother. If indeed the two of us can manage Janet."

"I have trouble managing you two," Jan commented. "I had better sign up Marj to help me. Marj?"

I did not take this quasi-offer seriously because I felt sure that it wasn't meant seriously. Everyone was making chitchat to cover the shocker I had dropped into their laps. We all knew that. But did anyone but me notice that my job was no longer a subject? I knew what had happened—but why did that deep-down layer of my brain decide to table the subject so emphatically? I would never tell Boss's secrets!

Suddenly I was urgently anxious to check with Boss. Was he involved in these odd events? If so, on which side?

"More soup, dear lady?"

"Don't give her more soup till she answers me."

"But, Jan, you weren't serious. Georges, if I take more soup, I will eat more garlic bread. And I'll get fat. No. Don't tempt me."

"More soup?"

"Well . . . just a little."

"I'm quite serious," Jan persisted. "I'm not trying to tie you down as you are probably soured on matrimony at present. But you could give it a trial and a year from now we could discuss it. If you wished to. In the meantime I'll keep you for a pet . . . and I'll let these two goats be in the same room with you only if their conduct pleases me."

"Wait a minute!" Ian protested. "Who fetched her here? *I* did. Marj is *my* sweetheart."

"Freddie's sweetheart, according to Betty. You brought her here as Betty's proxy. As may be, that was yesterday and she's *my* sweetheart now. If either of you want to speak to her, you'll have to come to me and get your ticket punched. Isn't that right, Marjorie?"

"If you say so, Jan. But it's only a theoretical point as I really do have to leave. Do you have a large-scale map of the border in the house? South border, I mean."

"As good as. Call one up on the computer. If you want a print-out, use the terminal in my study—off my bedroom."

"I don't want to interfere with the news."

"You won't. We can uncouple any terminal from all the others—necessary as this is a household of rugged individualists."

"Especially Jan," agreed Ian. "Marj, why do you want a big map of the Imperium border?"

"I would rather go home by tube. But I can't. Since I can't, I must find some other way to get home."

"I thought so. Honey, I'm going to have to take your shoes away from you. Don't you realize you can get shot trying to cross that border? Right now the guards on both sides are sure to be trigger-happy."

"Uh . . . is it all right for me to study the map?"

"Certainly . . . if you promise not to try to sneak across the border."

Georges said gently, "My brother, one should never tempt one of the dear ones to lie."

"Georges is right," Jan ruled. "No forced promises. Go ahead, Marj; I'll clear up here. Ian, you just volunteered to help."

I spent the next two hours at the computer terminal in my borrowed room, memorizing the border as a whole, then going to maximum magnification and learning certain parts in great detail. No border can be truly tight, not even the bristling walls some totalitarian states place around their subjects. Usually the best routes are near the guarded ports of entry—often in such places the smugglers' routes are worn smooth. But I would not follow a known route.

There were many ports of entry not too far away: Emerson Junction, Pine Creek, South Junction, Gretna, Maida, etc. I looked also at Roseau River, but it seemed to flow the wrong way—north into the Red River. (The map was not too clear.)

There is an odd chunk of land sticking out into the Lake of the Woods east-southeast of Winnipeg. The map colored it as part of the Imperium and showed nothing to stop one walking across the border at that point—if she were willing to risk several kilometers of marshy ground. I'm no superman; I can get bogged down in a swamp—but that unguarded stretch of border was tempting. I finally put it out of my mind because, while legally that chunk was part of the Imperium, it was separated from the Imperium proper by twenty-one kilometers of water. Steal a boat? I made a bet with myself that any boat, crossing that stretch of lake, would interrupt a beam. Failure to respond to challenge correctly would then result in a laser burn in the bow you could throw a dog through. I don't argue with lasers; you can neither bribe them nor sweet-talk them—I put it out of my mind.

I had just stopped studying maps and was letting the images soak into my mind when Janet's voice came out of the terminal: "Marjorie, come to the living room, please. Quickly!"

I came very quickly.

Ian was talking to someone in the screen. Georges was off to one side, out of pickup. Janet motioned to me to stay out of pickup, too. "Police," she said quietly. "I suggest that you go down into the Hole at once. Wait and I'll call you when they've gone."

I answered just as quietly, "Do they know that I'm here?"

"Don't know yet."

"Let's be sure. If they know I'm here and they can't find me, you'll be in trouble."

"We are not afraid of trouble."

"Thanks. But let's listen."

Ian was saying to the face in the screen, "Mel, come off it. Georges is not an enemy alien and you damned well know it. As for this—'Miss Baldwin,' did you say?—why are you looking here for her?"

"She left the port with you and your wife yesterday evening. If she's not still with you, then you certainly know where she is. As for

Georges, any Kaybecker is an enemy alien today no matter how long he has been here or what clubs he belongs to. I assume that you would rather have an old friend pick him up than a trooper. So switch off your sky guard; I'm ready to land."

Janet whispered, " 'Old friend' indeed! He's been trying to get into bed with me since high school; I have been telling him no the same length of time—he's slimy."

Ian sighed. "Mel, this is a hell of a funny time to talk about friendship. If Georges were here, I'm sure he would rather be arrested by a trooper than be taken in under the guise of friendship. So go back and do it the right way."

"Oh, so it's that way, is it? Very well! Lieutenant Dickey speaking. I'm here to make an arrest. Switch off your sky guard; I'm landing."

"Ian Tormey, householder, acknowledging police hail. Lieutenant, hold your warrant up to your pickup so that I may verify it and photograph it."

"Ian, you are out of your silly mind. A state of emergency has been declared; no warrant is required."

"I can't hear you."

"Maybe you can hear this: I am about to lock onto your sky guard and burn it out. If I set fire to something in doing so, that's too damn bad."

Ian spread his hands in disgust, then did something at the keyboard. "Sky guard is off." He then switched to "hold" and turned to us. "You two have maybe three minutes to get down the Hole. I can't stall him very long at the door."

Georges said quietly, "I shall not hide in a hole in the ground. I shall insist on my rights. If I do not receive them, at a later time I shall sue Melvin Dickey for his hide."

Ian shrugged. "You're a crazy Canuck. Put you're a big boy now. Marj, get undercover, dear. It won't take too long to get rid of him as he doesn't really know that you are here."

"Uh, I'll go down the Hole if necessary. But can't I simply wait in Janet's bath? He might go away. I'll switch the terminal there to pick up what goes on here. All right?"

"Marj, you're being difficult."

"Then persuade Georges to go down the Hole, too. If he stays, I might be needed here. To help him. To help you."

"What in the world are you talking about?"

I was not sure myself what I was talking about. But it did not seem like anything I had been trained for to declare myself out of the game and go hide in a hole in the ground. "Ian, this Melvin Dickey— I think he means harm to Georges. I could feel it in his voice. If Georges won't go with me into the Hole, then I should go with him to see to it that this Dickey does not hurt him—anyone in the hands of the police needs a witness on his side."

"Marj, you can't possibly stop a—" A deep gong note sounded. "Oh, damn! He's at the door. Get out of sight! And go down the Hole!"

I got out of sight, I did not go down the Hole. I hurried into Janet's big bath, switched on the terminal, then used the selector switch to place the living room pickup on screen. When I turned up the sound, it was almost as good as being there.

A banty rooster strutted in.

Actually it was not Dickey's body but his soul that was small. Dickey had a size-twelve ego in a size-four soul, in a body almost as big as Ian's. He came into the room with Ian, spotted Georges, said triumphantly, "There you are! Perreault, I arrest you for willfully failing to report for internment as ordered by the Decree of Emergency, paragraph six."

"I have received no such order."

"Oh, piffle! It's been all over the news."

"I do not make a practice of following the news. I know of no law requiring me to. May I see a copy of the order under which you propose to arrest me?"

"Don't try to come the shyster on me, Perreault. We're operating under National Emergency and I'm enforcing it. You can read the order when I get you in. Ian, I'm deputizing you to help me. Take these nips"—Dickey reached behind himself, pulled out a pair of handcuffs—"and put them on him. Hands behind his back."

Ian did not move. "Mel, don't be more of a fool than you have to be. You have no possible excuse to put handcuffs on Georges."

"The hell I don't! We're running shorthanded and I'm making

this arrest without assistance. So I can't take a chance on him trying to pull something sneaky while we're floating back. Hurry up and get those cuffs on him!"

"Don't point that gun at me!"

I was no longer watching. I was out of the bath, through two doors, down a long hall, and into the living room, all with a frozen-motion feeling I get when I'm triggered into overdrive.

Dickey was trying to cover three people with his gun, one of them being Janet. He should not have done that. I moved up to him, took his gun, and hand-chopped his neck. The bones made that unpleasant crunching noise neck bones always make, so unlike the sharp crack of fractured tibia or radius.

I eased him to the rug and placed his pistolet by him, while noting that it was a Raytheon five-oh-five powerful enough to stop a mastodon—why do men with little souls have to have big weapons? I said, "Jan, are you hurt?"

"No."

"I got here as fast as I could. Ian, this is what I meant when I said that my help might be needed. But I should have stayed here. I was almost too late."

"I've never seen anyone move so fast!"

Georges said quietly, "I have seen."

I looked at him. "Yes, of course you have. Georges, will you help me move this"—I indicated the corpse—"and can you drive a police APV?"

"I can if I must."

"I am about at that level of skill, too. Let's get rid of the body. Janet told me a bit about where bodies go, did not show me the spot. Some hole just off the escape tunnel, isn't it? Let's get busy. Ian, as soon as we dispose of *this*, Georges and I can leave. Or Georges can stay and sweat it out. But once the body and the APV are gone, you and Jan can play dumb. No evidence. You never saw him. But we must hurry, before he is missed."

Jan was down on her knees beside the late police lieutenant. "Marj, you actually did kill him."

"Yes. He hurried me. Nevertheless I killed him on purpose because in dealing with a policeman it is much safer to kill than to hurt. Jan, he should not have pointed his burner at you. Otherwise I might merely have disarmed him—then killed him only if you decided that he needed to be dead."

"You hurried, all right. You weren't here and then you were and Mel was falling. '—needed to be dead'? I don't know but I won't grieve. He's a rat. *Was* a rat."

Ian said slowly, "Marj, you don't seem to realize that killing a police officer is a serious matter. It is the only capital crime that British Canada still has on the books."

When people talk that way, I don't understand them; a policeman isn't anybody special. "Ian, to me, pointing a pistol at my friends is a serious matter. Pointing one at Janet is a capital crime. But I'm sorry I upset you. Right now here is a body to dispose of and an APV to get rid of. I can help. Or I can disappear. Say which but be quick; we don't know how soon they will come looking for him—and for us. Just that they will."

While I spoke, I was searching the corpse—no pouch, I had to search his pockets, being very careful with his trouser pockets because his sphincters had cut loose the way they always do. Not much, thank Bast!—he had barely wet his pants and he did not yet stink. Or not badly. The important items were in his jacket pockets: wallet, buzzer, IDs, money, credit cards, all the walk-around junk that tells a modern man that he is alive. I took the wallet and the Raytheon burner; the rest was trash. I picked up those silly handcuffs. "Any way to dispose of metal? Or must these go down the same hole as the body?"

Ian was still chewing his lip. Georges said gently, "Ian, I urge you to accept Marjorie's help. It is evident that she is expert."

Ian stopped jittering. "Georges, take his feet." The men carried the body into the big bath. I hurried ahead and dropped Dickey's gun, cuffs, and wallet on the bed in my room, and Janet put his hat with these items. I hurried into the bath, undressing as I went. Our men, with burden, had just reached it. Ian said, as they put it down, "Marj, you don't need to peel down. Georges and I will take it through. And dispose of it."

"All right," I agreed. "But let me take care of washing it. I know what needs to be done. I can do it better naked, then a quick shower afterwards."

Ian looked puzzled, then said, "Oh, hell, let him stay dirty."

"All right if you say so, but you aren't going to want to use this pool or even go through it getting in and out of the Hole until the water has been changed and the pool basin itself scrubbed. I think it is faster to wash the body. Unless—" Janet had just come in. "Jan, you spoke of emptying this plunge into a holding tank. How long does that take? Full cycle, in and out."

"About an hour. It's a small pump."

"Ian, I can get that body clean in ten minutes if you will strip it and stick it into the shower. How about his clothes? Do they go down your oubliette, whatever you call it, or do you have some way to destroy them? Do they have to go through the pool tunnel?"

Things moved fast then, with Ian being fully cooperative and all of them letting me lead. Jan stripped down, too, and insisted on helping me wash the corpse, while Georges put the clothes through their home laundry and Ian went through the water tunnel to make some preparations.

I did not want to let Janet help me because I have had mind-control training and I was fairly sure that she had not. But, trained or not, she is tough. Aside from wrinkling her nose a couple of times she did not flinch. And of course, with her help, it went much faster.

Georges brought the clothes back, dripping. Janet put them into a plastic sack and pressed the air out. Ian reappeared up out of the pool, with the end of a rope. The men hitched it under the body's armpits and shortly it was gone.

Twenty minutes later we were clean and dry, with no trace of Lieutenant Dickey left in the house. Janet had come into "my" room while I was transferring items from Dickey's wallet into the plastic money belt she had given me—primarily money and two credit cards, American Express and Maple Leaf.

She didn't make any silly remarks about "robbing the dead"—and I would not have listened if she had. These days, operating without a valid credit card and/or cash is impossible. Jan left the room, came back quickly with twice as much cash as I had salvaged. I accepted it, saying, "You know that I have no notion as to how and when I can repay this."

"Certainly I know it. Marj, I'm wealthy. My grandparents were;

I've never been anything else. Look, dear, a man pointed a gun at me . . . and you jumped him, with your bare hands. Can I repay *that*? Both of my husbands were present . . . but *you* were the one who tackled him."

"Don't feel that way about the men, Jan; they don't have my training."

"I could see that. Someday I would like to hear about it. Any chance you will go to Québec?"

"An excellent chance if Georges decides to leave."

"I thought so." She offered me more money. "I don't keep Q-francs in the house, much. But here is what I have."

At that point the men came in. I glanced at my finger, then at the wall. "Forty-seven minutes since I killed him so he has been out of touch with his headquarters one hour, more or less. Georges, I am about to attempt to pilot that police APV; I have the key right here. Unless you are coming with me and will pilot. Are you coming? Or are you going to stay and wait for the next attempt to arrest you? Either way, *I* am leaving *now*."

Janet said suddenly, "Let's *all* leave!"

I grinned at her. "Swell!"

Ian said, "You really want to do that, Jan?"

"I—" She stopped and looked frustrated. "I can't. Mama Cat and her kittens. Black Beauty and Demon and Star and Red. We could close this house, certainly; it winterproofs on only one household Shipstone. But it would take at least a day or two to make arrangements for the rest of our family. Even one pig! I can't just walk out on them. I *can't*."

There wasn't anything to say, so I didn't. The coldest depth of Hell is reserved for people who abandon kittens. Boss says that I am stupidly sentimental and I'm sure he is right.

We went outside. It was just beginning to get dark and I suddenly realized that I had entered this household less than a day earlier—it seemed like a month. Goodness, just twenty-four hours ago I had still been in New Zealand . . . which seemed preposterous.

The police car was sitting on Jan's vegetable garden, which caused her to use language I did not expect from her. It had the usual squatty oyster shape of an antigrav not intended for space and was about the size of our family farm wagon in South Island. No, that did not make me *triste*; Jan and her men—and Betty and Freddie—had replaced the Davidson Group in my heart—*donna e mobile*; that's me. Now I wanted very badly to get back to Boss. Father figure? Probably—but I'm not interested in shrink theories.

Ian said, "Let me look at this bucket before you lift it. You babes in the wood could get hurt." He opened the lid, got in. Presently he got out again. "You can float it if you decide to. But hear me. It's got an identification transponder. It almost certainly has an active beacon, too, although I can't find it. Its Shipstone is down to thirty-one percent, so, if you are thinking of Québec, forget it. It will seal but you can't maintain cabin pressure above twelve thousand meters. But, worst of all, its terminal is calling Lieutenant Dickey."

"So we ignore it!"

"Of course, Georges. But, as a result of the Ortega trials last year, they've been installing remote-control destruction packs in police cars. I searched for signs of one. Had I found it, I would have disarmed it. I did not find it. That does not mean that it isn't there."

I shrugged. "Ian, necessary risks never bother me. I try to avoid the other sort. But we still have to get rid of this heap of tin. Fly it somewhere. Leave it."

Ian said, "Not so fast, Marj. Go-buggies are my business. This one— Yes! It's got the standard military AG autopilot. So we'll send it for a ride. Where? East, maybe? It would crash before it reaches Québec . . . and that could cause them to assume that you are headed home, Georges—while you are safe in the Hole."

"I do not care, Ian. I shall not hide in the Hole. I agreed to leave because Marjorie needs someone to care for her."

"More likely she'll take care of you. You saw how she polished off Soapy."

"Agreed. But I did not say 'take care of'—I said that she needs someone to care for her."

"Same thing."

"I will not argue it. Shall we make it march?"

I chopped that off by saying, "Ian, is there enough power in its Shipstone to take it south to the Imperium?"

"Yes. But it's not safe for you to float it."

"Didn't mean that. Set it on course south and maximum altitude. Maybe your border guard will burn it down, maybe the Imperium will. Or maybe it will get through but be blown by remote. Or it might just run out of juice and crash from maximum altitude. No matter which, we are free of it."

"Done." Ian jumped back in, was busy at the board, the craft started to float—he dived out, dropping three or four meters. I gave him a hand. "You all right?"

"Just fine. Look at her go!" The police car was rapidly disappearing above us while slanting south. Suddenly it broke out of the gathering dusk into the last of the sunlight and was very bright. It dwindled and was gone.

XIV

We were back in the kitchen, half an eye on the terminal, our attention on each other and on highballs Ian had served, discussing what if anything to do now. Ian was saying,

"Marj, if you will just sit tight this silly season will be over and you can then go home comfortably. If there is another flap, you can dive down the Hole. At worst you have to stay indoors. Meanwhile Georges can paint nudes of you, as Betty ordered. Okay, Georges?"

"That would be most pleasing."

"Well, Marj?"

"Ian, if I tell my boss that I couldn't come back when I was supposed to because a twenty-five-hundred kilometer stretch of border was nominally closed he simply would not believe me." (Tell them that I am a trained courier? No need to. Or not yet.)

"What are you going to do?"

"I think I have been enough trouble to you folks." (Ian dear, I think you are still in shock from seeing a man killed in your living room. Even though you straightened up afterward and behaved like a pro.) "I now know where your back door is. When you get up tomorrow morning it is possible that I won't be here. Then you can forget a disturbance in your life."

"No!"

"Jan, once this mess is over, I will call you. Then, if you want me to, I'll come back to visit just as soon as I have some vacation time. But now I must leave and get back to work. I've said so all along."

Janet simply would not hear of my setting out alone to crack the border (whereas I needed someone with me the way a snake needs shoes). But she did have a plan.

She pointed out that Georges and I could travel on their passports—I was her size, near enough, and Georges matched Ian in size and weight. Our faces did not match but the differences weren't major—and who really looks at passport pictures anyhow?

"You could use them and mail them back . . . but that may not be the easiest way. You could go to Vancouver, then cross into the California Confederacy simply on tourists' cards—but as *us*. You can go all the way to Vancouver on our credit cards. Once across the border into California you are almost certainly home free—Marj, your credit card should be good, you shouldn't have trouble phoning your employer, and the cops won't be trying to intern either one of you. Is that any help?"

"Yes," I agreed. "I think the tourist-card dodge is safer than trying to use your passports—safer for everyone. If I reach a place where my credit card is valid, my troubles should be over." (I would draw cash at once and never again let myself be caught away from home without plenty of cash—money greases anything. Especially in California, a place loaded with scams, whereas in British Canada officials are sometimes disconcertingly honest.)

I added, "I can't possibly be worse off in Bellingham than I am here—then I've got all the way down to the Lone Star Republic to try to cross if there is any holdup. Has there been any word on Texas and Chicago? Are they on speaking terms?"

"Okay so far as I've seen in the news," Ian answered. "Shall I key the computer for a search?"

"Yes, before I leave please do. If I had to, I could go through Texas to Vicksburg. One can always go up the river for cash because smugglers run so steadily."

"Before *we* leave," Georges corrected me gently.

"Georges, I think this route would work, for me. For you, all it would do is get you farther and farther away from Québec. Didn't you say that McGill is your other base?"

"Dear lady, I have no wish to go to McGill. Since the police are being difficult here, my true home, I can think of nothing I would rather do than travel with you. Once we cross into Washington Province of California you can change your name from Mrs. Tormey to Mrs. Perreault, as it is certain, I think, that both my Maple Leaf card and my Crédit Québec card will be accepted."

(Georges, you are a gallant darling . . . and when I'm trying to pull a caper I need a gallant darling the way I need an Oregon boot. And I will have to pull one, dear—despite what Janet said, I will not be home free.) "Georges, that sounds delightful. I can't tell you that you must stay home . . . but I *must* tell you that I am by profession a courier who has traveled for years by herself, all over this planet, more than once to space colonies, and to Luna. Not yet to Mars or Ceres but I may be ordered to at any time."

"You are saying that you would rather I did not accompany you."

"No, no! I am merely saying that, if you choose to go with me, it will be purely social. For your pleasure and mine. But I must add that when I enter the Imperium I *must* go alone, as I will be back on duty at once."

Ian said, "Marj, at least let Georges get you out of here and into territory where there is no silly talk of interning you, and where your credit card is valid."

Janet added, "It's getting free of that silly internment thing that is important. Marj, you can hang onto my Visa card as long as you wish; I'll use my Maple Leaf card instead. Just remember that you are Jan Parker."

"Parker?"

"Visa has my maiden name on it. Here, take it." I accepted it, thinking that I would use it only when someone was looking over my shoulder. When possible, I would charge things to the late Lieutenant Dickey, whose credit should remain viable for days, possibly weeks. There was more chitchat and at last I said,

"I'm leaving now. Georges, are you coming with me?"

Ian said, "Hey! Not tonight. First thing in the morning."

"Why? The tubes run all night, do they not?" (I knew that they did.)

"Yes but it's over twenty klicks to the nearest tube station. And dark as the inside of a pile of coal."

(Not the time to discuss enhanced vision.) "Ian, I can walk that far by midnight. If a capsule leaves at midnight, I can get practically a full night's sleep in Bellingham. If the border is open between California and the Imperium, I'll report to my boss tomorrow morning. Better so, huh?"

A few minutes later we all left, by surrey. Ian was not pleased with me as I had not been the sweet, soft, amenable creature that men prefer. But he got over his annoyance and kissed me very sweetly when they dropped us at Perimeter and McPhillips across from the tube station. Georges and I crowded into the twenty-three-o'-clock capsule, then we had to stand up all the way across the continent.

But we were in Vancouver by twenty-two (Pacific Time—midnight in Winnipeg), picked up applications for tourist cards as we entered the Bellingham shuttle, filled them out en route, had them processed by the exit computer as we left the shuttle a few minutes later. The human operator didn't even look up as the machine spit out our cards. She just murmured, "Enjoy your stay," and went on reading.

At Bellingham the Vancouver Shuttle Station exits into the lower lobby of the Bellingham Hilton; facing us was a glowing sign floating in space:

THE BREAKFAST BAR
Steaks—Short Orders—Cocktails
Breakfast Served Twenty-Four Hours

Georges said, "Mrs. Tormey my love, it occurs to me that we neglected to eat dinner."

"Mr. Tormey, you are so right. Let's shoot a bear."

"Cooking in the Confederacy is not exotic, not sophisticated. But in its own robust way it can be quite satisfying—especially if one has had time to grow a real appetite. I have eaten at this establishment before. Despite its name, one may have a variety of dishes. But, if you will accept the breakfast menu and allow me to order for you, I think that I can guarantee that your hunger will be pleasantly assuaged."

"Georges—I mean 'Ian'—I have eaten your soup. You can order for me anytime!"

It was truly a bar—no tables. But the stools had backs and were padded and they came up to the bar without banging knees—comfortable. Apple-juice appetizers were placed in front of us as we sat down. Georges ordered for us, then slid out and went over to the reception desk and punched us in. When he returned, he said as he sat down again, "Now you may call me 'Georges,' and you are 'Mrs. Perreault.' For that is how I punched us in." He picked up his appetizer. "*Santé, ma chère femme.*"

I picked up mine. "*Merci. Et à la tienne, mon cher mari.*" The juice was sparkling cold, and as sweet as the sentiment. While I did not intend to have a husband again, Georges would make a good one, whether in jest, as now, or in reality. But he was simply lent to me by Janet.

Our "breakfast" arrived:

Ice-cold Yakima apple juice
Imperial Valley strawberries with Sequim cream
Two eggs, eyes-up and gently basted, resting on medium-rare steak so tender it would cut with a fork—"Eggs on Horseback"
Large hot biscuits, Sequim butter, sage and clover honey
Kona coffee in oversize cups

Coffee, juice, and biscuits were renewed constantly—a second serving of steak and eggs was offered but we had to refuse.

The noise level and the way we were seated did not encourage conversation. There was an Opportunity Ads screen back of the bar. Each ad remained on screen just long enough to be read but, as usual, each was keyed by number to be called back for leisurely viewing at individual terminals at each guest's place at the bar. I found myself reading them idly while I ate:

> The Free Ship *Jack Pot* is recruiting crew members
> at Vegas Labor Mart. Bonus to combat veterans.

Would a pirate ship advertise that baldly? Even in Vegas Free State? Hard to believe but still harder to read it any other way.

> Smoke the Toke that Jesus Smoked!
>
> ANGEL STICKS
>
> Guaranteed Noncarcinogenic

Cancer cannot worry me but neither THC nor nicotine is for me; a woman's mouth should be sweet.

> GOD is waiting for you at suite 1208 Lewis and Clark Towers. Don't make Him come get you. You won't like it.

I didn't like it anyhow.

> BORED?
> We are about to abandon a pioneer party on a virgin planet type T-13. Guaranteed sex ratio 50-40-10±2%
> Median bio age 32±1. No temperament test required
> No Assessments—No Contributions—No Rescue
> System Expansion Corporation
> Division of Demography and Ecology
> Luna City GPO lock box DEMO
> or punch Tycho 800-2300

I called that one back and reread it. How would it feel to tackle a brand-new world side by side with comrades?—people who could not possibly know my origin. Or care. My enhancements might make me respected rather than a freak—as long as I did not flaunt them. . . .

"Georges, look at this, please."

He did so. "What about it?"

"It could be fun—no?"

"No! Marjorie, on the T scale anything over eight calls for a large cash bonus, lavish equipment, and trained colonists. A thirteen is an exotic route to suicide, that's all."

"Oh."

"Read this one," he offered:

W.K.—Make your will. You have only a week to live.
A.C.B.

I read it. "Georges, is that really a threat to kill this W.K.? In a public ad? Where it could be traced?"

"I don't know. It might not be easy to trace. I'm wondering what we will see here tomorrow—will it read 'six days'? Then 'five days'? Is W.K. waiting for the blow to fall? Or is it some sort of advertising promotion?"

"I don't know." I thought about it in connection with our plight. "Georges, is it possible that all these threats on the channels are some sort of terribly complex hoax?"

"Are you suggesting that no one was killed and all the news was faked?"

"Uh, I don't know what I'm suggesting."

"Marjorie, there is a hoax, yes—in the sense that three different groups are all claiming responsibility and therefore two groups are attempting to hoax the world. I do not think that the reports of assassinations are hoaxes. As with soap bubbles, there is an upper limit to the size of a hoax, both in numbers of people and in time. This is too big—too many places, too widespread—to be a hoax. Or by now there would be denials from all over. More coffee?"

"Thank you, no."

"Anything?"

"Nothing. One more biscuit with honey and I would burst."

From outside it was simply a hotel-room door: 2100. Once inside I said, "Georges! *Why?*"

"A bride should have a bridal suite."

"It's beautiful. It's lavish. It's lovely. And you should not have wasted your money. You've already turned a dull trip into a picnic. But if you expect me to behave as a bride tonight, you should not have fed me Eggs on Horseback and a whole big pan of hot biscuits. I'm bloated, dear. Not glamorous."

"You are glamorous."

"Dear! Georges, don't play with me—please don't! You caught me out when I killed Dickey. You know what I am."

"I know that you are a sweet and brave and gallant lady."

"You know what I mean. You're in the profession. You spotted me. You caught me out."

"You are enhanced. Yes, I saw that."

"So you know what I am. I admit it. I passed years ago. I've acquired much practice in covering it up but—that bastard shouldn't have pointed that gun at Janet!"

"No, he should not have done so. And for what you did I am forever in your debt."

"You mean that? Ian thought I should not have killed him."

"Ian's first reaction is always conventional. Then he comes around. Ian is a natural pilot; he thinks with his muscles. But, Marjorie—"

"I'm not Marjorie."

"Eh?"

"You might as well have my right name. My crèche name, I mean. I'm Friday. No last name, of course. When I need one I use one of the conventional crèche surnames. Jones, usually. But Friday is my name."

"Is that what you want to be called?"

"Uh, yes, I think so. It's the name I'm called by when I don't have to cover up. When I'm with people I trust. I had better trust you. Hadn't I?"

"I shall be flattered and much pleased. I shall try to deserve your trust. As I am much in your debt."

"How, Georges?"

"I thought that was clear. When I saw what Mel Dickey was doing, I resolved to surrender at once rather than cause hazard to others. But when he threatened Janet with that burner, I promised myself that, at a later time, when I was free, I would kill him." Georges barely smiled. "I had no more than promised myself that when you appeared as suddenly as an avenging angel and carried out my intent. So now I owe you one."

"Another killing?"

"If that is your wish, yes."

"Uh, probably not that. As you said, I'm enhanced. I've usually managed to do it myself when it needed to be done."

"Whatever you ask, dear Friday."

"Uh, oh, hell, Georges, I don't want you to feel in debt to me. In my own way I love Janet, too. That bastard sealed his fate when he threatened her with a deadly weapon. I didn't do it for you; I did it for *myself*. So you don't owe me anything."

"Dear Friday. You are as lovable as Janet is. I have been learning that."

"Uh, why don't you take me to bed and let me pay you for a number of things? I am aware that I'm not human and I don't expect you to love me the way you do your human wife—not love me at all, really. But you seem to like me and you don't treat me like— uh, the way my Ennzedd family did. The way most humans treat APs. I can make it worth your while. Truly I can. I never got my doxy certificate but I've had most of the training . . . and I *try*."

"Oh, my dear! Who hurt you so badly?"

"Me? I'm all right. I was just explaining that I know how the world wags. I'm not a kid still learning how to get along without the crutch of the crèche. An artificial person doesn't expect sentimental love from a human male; we both know that. You understand it far better than a layman can; you're in the profession. I respect you and sincerely like you. If you will permit me to go to bed with you, I'll do my best to entertain you."

"Friday!"

"Yes, sir?"

"You will not go to bed with me to entertain me."

I felt sudden tears in my eyes—a very seldom thing. "Sir, I'm sorry," I said miserably. "I didn't mean to offend you. I did not intend to presume."

"God damn it, STOP IT!"

"Sir?"

"Stop calling me 'sir.' Stop behaving like a slave! Call me Georges. If you feel like adding 'dear' or 'darling' as you have sometimes in the past, please do so. Or slang me. Just treat me as your friend. This 'human' and 'not-human' dichotomy is something thought up by ignorant laymen; everybody in the profession knows that it is nonsense. Your genes are *human* genes; they have been most carefully selected. Perhaps that makes you superhuman; it can't make you nonhuman. Are you fertile?"

"Uh, sterile reversible."

"In ten minutes with a local anesthetic I could change that. Then I could impregnate you. Would our baby be human? Or nonhuman? Or half human?"

"Uh . . . human."

"You can bet your life it would be! It takes a human mother to bear a human baby. Don't ever forget that."

"Uh, I won't forget." I felt a curious tingle, way down inside me. Sex, but not like anything I had ever felt before even though I'm rutty as a cat. "Georges? Do you want to do that? Impregnate me?"

He looked very startled. Then he moved to where I was standing, tilted my face up, put his arms around me, and kissed me. On the ten scale I would have to rate it at eight and a half, maybe nine—no way to do better vertically and with clothes on. Then he picked me up, moved to a chair, sat down with me in his lap, and started undressing me, casually and gently. Janet had insisted on dressing me in her clothes; I had more interesting things to take off than a jump suit. My Superskin job, freshly laundered by Janet, was in my jumpbag.

Georges said, as he unzipped and unbuttoned and undid, "That ten minutes would have to be in my lab and it would take another month, about, until your first breeding date, and that combination of circumstances saves you from a bulging belly . . . because that kind of remark acts on the human male like cantharides on a bull. So you are saved from your folly. Instead I'm going to take you to bed and try to entertain *you* . . . although I don't have my certificate, either. But we'll think of something, dear Friday." He lifted me up and pushed the last of my clothing to the floor. "You look good. You feel good. You smell good. Do you want first chance at the bathroom? I need a shower."

"Uh, I'd rather go second as I want to take quite a long time."

I did take quite a long time as I had not been fooling when I told him I was bloated. I'm an experienced traveler, careful never to invite either of the twin curses of travel. But no dinner, followed by an enormous "breakfast" at midnight had changed my timing a bit. If I was going to have weight on my chest—and my belly—it was time to get rid of the bloat.

It was after two before I came out of the bath—bathed, bloat taken care of, mouth fresh and breath sweet, and feeling as fit and cheerful as I have ever felt in my life. No perfume—not only do I not carry it but men prefer *fragrans feminae* to any other aphrodisiac even when they don't know it—they just don't like it stale.

Georges was in bed with a coverlet over him, sound asleep. The tent was not up, I noticed. So with extreme caution I crawled in and managed not to wake him. Truly, I was not disappointed as I am not that self-centered a slitch. I felt happily confident that he would wake me refreshed and it would thus be better for each of us—it had been a strenuous day for me, too.

XV

I was correct.

I don't want to take Georges away from Janet . . . but I look forward to happy visits and, if he ever does elect to reverse my sterility, doing it like a cat might be all right to make a baby for Georges—I cannot see why Janet has not done so.

I was awakened the third or fourth time by a lovely odor; Georges was unloading the dumb waiter. "You have twenty-one seconds to get in and out of the bath," he said, "as soup is on. You had a proper breakfast in the middle of the night, so you are going to have a most improper brunch."

I suppose it is improper to have fresh Dungeness crab for breakfast but I'm in favor of it. It was preceded by sliced banana with cream on cornflakes, which strikes me as breakfasty, and was accompanied by toasted rusks and a tossed green salad. I then tapered off with chicory coffee laced with a pony of Korbel champagne brandy. Georges is a loving lecher and a hearty gourmand and a gourmet chef and a gentle healer who can make an artificial person believe that she is human, or, if not, that it doesn't matter.

Query: Why are all three of that family so slender? I am certain that they do not diet and do not take masochistic exercise. A therapist once told me that all the exercise any person needs could be had in bed. Could that be it?

The above is the good news. The bad news—

The International Corridor was closed. It was possible to reach Deseret by changing at Portland, but there was no guarantee that the SLC-Omaha-Gary tube would be open. The only major international route running capsules regularly seemed to be San Diego—Dallas—Vicksburg—Atlanta. San Diego was no problem as the San Jose tube was open from Bellingham to La Jolla. But Vicksburg is not Chicago Imperium; it is simply a river port from which a person with cash and persistence might reach the Imperium.

I tried to call Boss. After forty minutes I felt about synthetic voices the way humans feel about my sort of people. Who thought up this idea of programming "politeness" into computers? To hear a machine voice say "Thank you for waiting" may be soothing the first time, but three times in a row reminds you that it is phony, and forty minutes of such stalls without even once hearing a living voice can try the patience of a guru.

I never did get that terminal to admit that it was not possible to phone into the Imperium. That confounded digital disaster was not programmed to say no; it was programmed to be polite. It would have been a relief if, after a certain number of futile tries, it had been programmed to say, "Buzz off, sister; you've had it."

I then tried to call the Bellingham post office to inquire about mail service into the Imperium—honest-to-goodness words on paper, paid for as a parcel, not a facsimile or mailgram or anything electronic.

I got a cheerful lecture on doing your Christmas mailing early. With Christmas half a year away this seemed less than urgent.

I tried again. I got scolded about zip codes.

I tried a third time and got Macy's customer service department and a voice: "All our friendly helpers are busy at the moment thankyouforwaiting."

I didn't wait.

I didn't want to phone or to send a letter anyhow; I wanted to report to Boss in person. For that I needed cash. That offensively polite terminal admitted that the local office of MasterCard was in the Bellingham main office of TransAmerica Corporation. So I punched the signal and got a sweet voice—recorded, not synthesized—saying: "Thank you for calling MasterCard. In the interests of efficiency and maximum savings to our millions of satisfied customers all of our California Confederacy district offices have been consolidated with the home office at San Jose. For speedy service please use the toll-free signal on the back of your MasterCard card." The sweet voice gave way to the opening bars of "Trees." I shut it off quickly.

My MasterCard card, issued in Saint Louis, did not have on it that San Jose toll-free signal, but only the signal of the Imperial Bank of Saint Louis. So I tried that number, not very hopefully.

I got Punch-a-Prayer.

While I was being taught humility by a computer, Georges was reading the Olympic edition of the *Los Angeles Times* and waiting for me to quit fiddling. I gave up and asked, "Georges, what's in the morning paper on the emergency?"

"What emergency?"

"Huh? I mean, Excuse me?"

"Friday my love, the only emergency mentioned in this newspaper is a warning by the Sierra Club concerning the threat to the endangered species *Rhus diversiloba*. A picketing demonstration against Dow Chemical is planned. Otherwise all is quiet on the western front."

I wrinkled my forehead to stimulate my memory. "Georges, I don't know much about California politics—"

"My dear, no one knows much about California politics, including California politicians."

"—but I do seem to recall reports on the news of maybe a dozen major assassinations in the Confederacy. Was that all a hoax?" Thinking back and figuring time zones—how long? Thirty-five hours?

"I find obituaries of several prominent ladies and gentlemen who were mentioned in the news night before last . . . but they are not listed as assassinated. One is an 'accidental gunshot wound.' Another died after a 'lingering illness.' Another was a victim in an 'unexplained crash' of a private APV and the Confederacy Attorney General has ordered an investigation. But I seem to recall that the Attorney General herself was assassinated."

"Georges, what is going on?"

"Friday, I do not know. But I suggest that it might be hazardous to inquire too closely."

"Uh, I'm not going to inquire; I'm not political and never have been. I'm going to move over into the Imperium as fast as possible. But to do that—since the border is closed no matter what the *L.A. Times* says—I need cash. I hate to bleed Janet through using her Visa card. Maybe I can use my own but I must go to San Jose to have any luck with it; they are being stuffy. Do you want to go to San Jose with me? Or back to Jan and Ian?"

"Sweet lady, all my worldly goods are at your feet. But show me the way to San Jose. Why do you balk at taking me into the Imperium? Is it not possible that your employer has use for my talents? I cannot now return to Manitoba for reasons we both know."

"Georges, it is not that I balk at taking you with me but the border is *closed* . . . which may force me to do a Dracula and flow through a crack. Or some unreasonable facsimile. I'm trained for that but I can do it only alone—you're in the profession; you can see that. Moreover, while we don't know what the conditions are inside the Imperium, the news shows that things are rough. Once inside, I may have to be very fast on my feet just to stay alive. And I'm trained for that, too."

"And you are enhanced and I am not. Yes, I can see."

"Georges! Dear, I do not mean to hurt your feelings. Look, once I have reported in, I will call you. Here, or at your home, or wherever you say. If it is safe for you to cross the border, I will know it then." (Georges ask Boss for a job? Impossible! Or was it? Boss might have use for an experienced genetic engineer. When it came right down to it, I had no idea of Boss's needs aside from that one small piece I worked in.) "Are you serious in wanting to see my boss about a job? Uh, what shall I tell him?"

Georges gave his gentle half-smile that he uses to cover his thoughts the way I use my passport-picture face. "How can I know? All I know about your employer is that you are reluctant to talk about him and that he can afford to use one such as yourself as a messenger. But, Friday, I may appreciate even more sharply than you do how much capital investment must have gone into your design, your nurture, and your training . . . and therefore what a price your employer must have paid for your indentures—"

"I'm not indentured. I'm a Free Person."

"Then it cost him even more. Which leads to conjectures. Never mind, dear; I'll stop guessing. Am I serious? A man can wonder mightily what lies beyond the range. I'll supply you with my *curriculum vitae*; if it contains anything of interest to your employer, no doubt he'll let me know. Now about money: You need not worry about 'bleeding' Janet; money doesn't mean anything to her. But *I* am most willing to supply you with whatever cash you need using my own credit—and I have already established that my credit cards are honored here despite any political troubles. I used Crédit Québec to pay for our midnight breakfast, I punched into this inn with American Express, then used Maple Leaf to pay for our brunch. So I have three valid cards and all match my ID." He grinned at me. "So bleed me, dear girl."

"But I don't want to bleed you any more than I want to bleed Janet. Look, we can try my card at San Jose; if that does not work, I'll happily borrow from you . . . and I can punch you the money as soon as I report in." (Or would Georges be willing to pull a swindle with Lieutenant Dickey's credit card for me?—damnably difficult for a woman to get cash with a man's card. Paying for something by sticking a card into a slot is one thing; using a card to draw cash money is a kettle of fish of another color.)

"Why do you speak of repayment? When I am forever in your debt?"

I chose to be obtuse. "Do you truly feel that you owe me something? Just for last night?"

"Yes. You were adequate."

I gasped. *"Oh!"*

He answered, unsmiling: "Would you rather I had said inadequate?"

I refrained from gasping. "Georges. Take off your clothes. I am going to take you back to bed, then kill you, slowly. At the end I am going to squeeze you and break your back in three places. 'Adequate.' 'Inadequate.' "

He grinned and started unzipping.

I said, "Oh, stop that and kiss me! Then we are going to San Jose. 'Inadequate.' *Which was I?*"

It takes almost as long to go from Bellingham to San Jose as it does to go from Winnipeg to Vancouver but this trip we had seats. We emerged above ground at fourteen-fifteen. I looked around with interest, never having visited the Confederacy capital before.

The thing I first noticed was the amazing number of APVs bouncing like fleas all over the place and most of them taxicabs. I know of no other modern city that permits its air space to be infested to this extent. The streets were loaded with hansom cabs, too, and there were slidewalks bordering every street; nevertheless these power-drive pests were everywhere, like bicycles in Canton.

The second thing I noticed was the *feel* of San Jose. It was not a city. I now understood that classic description: "A thousand villages in search of a city."

San Jose does not seem to have any justification save politics. But California gets more out of politics than any other country I know of—utter unashamed and uninhibited democracy. You run into democracy in many places—New Zealand uses it in an attenuated form. But only in California will you find the clear-quill, raw-gum, two-hundred-proof, undiluted democracy. The voting age starts when a citizen is tall enough to pull the lever without being steadied by her nurse, and registrars are reluctant to disenfranchise a citizen short of a sworn cremation certificate.

I did not fully appreciate that last until I saw, in an election news story, that the corpsicles at Prehoda Pines Patience Park constituted three precincts all voting through preregistered proxies. ("Death, be not proud!")

I will not try to pass judgment as I was a grown woman before I encountered democracy even in its milder, nonmalignant form. Democracy is probably all right used in sparing amounts. The British Canadians use a dilute form and they seem to do all right. But only in California is everyone drunk on it all the time. There does not seem to be a day when there is not an election somewhere in California, and, for any one precinct, there is (so I was told) an election of some sort about once a month.

I suppose they can afford it. They have a mellow climate from British Canada to the Mexican Kingdom and much of the richest farm land on Earth. Their second favorite sport (sex) costs almost nothing in its raw form; like marijuana it is freely available everywhere. This leaves time and energy for the true California sport: gathering and yabbering about politics.

They elect *everybody*, from precinct parasite to the Chief Confederate ("The Chief"). But they *un*elect them almost as fast. For example the Chief is supposed to serve one six-year term. But, of the last nine chiefs, only two served a full six years; the others were recalled except that one who was lynched. In many cases an official has not yet been sworn in when the first recall petition is being circulated.

But Californians do not limit themselves to electing, recalling, indicting, and (sometimes) lynching their swarms of officials; they also legislate directly. Every election has on the ballot more proposed laws than candidates. The provincial and national representatives show some restraint—I have been assured that the typical California legislator will withdraw a bill if you can prove to her that pi can't equal three no matter how many vote to make it so. But grassroots legislation ("the initiative") has no such limitation.

For example three years ago a grassroots economist noticed that college graduates earned, on the average, about 30 percent more than their fellow citizens who lacked bachelor's degrees. Such an undemocratic condition is anathema to the California Dream, so, with great speed, an initiative was qualified for the next election, the measure passed, and all California high-school graduates and/or California citizens attaining eighteen years were henceforth awarded bachelor's degrees. A grandfather clause backdated this benefit eight years.

This measure worked beautifully; the holder of a bachelor's degree no longer had any undemocratic advantage. At the next election the grandfather clause was expanded to cover the last twenty years and there is a strong movement to extend this boon to all citizens.

Vox populi, vox Dei. I can't see anything wrong with it. This benevolent measure costs nothing and makes everyone (but a few soreheads) happier.

About fifteen o'clock Georges and I were sliding along the south side of the National Plaza in front of the Chief's Palace, headed for the main offices of MasterCard. Georges was telling me that he saw nothing wrong with my having asked to stop at a Burger King for a snack in lieu of luncheon—that, in his opinion, the giant burger, properly prepared from top sirloin substitute and the chocolate malt made with a minimum of chalk, constitutes California's only contribution to international haute cuisine.

I was agreeing with him while burping gently. A group of women and men, a dozen to twenty, were moving down the grand steps in front of the Palace and Georges had started to swing off to avoid them when I noticed the eagle-feather headdress on a little man in the middle of the group, spotted the much-photographed face under it, and checked Georges with one hand.

And caught something out of the corner of my eye: a figure coming out from behind a pillar at the top of the steps.

It triggered me. I pushed the Chief down flat to the steps, knocking a couple of his staff aside to do it, then bounded up to that pillar.

I didn't kill the man who had lurked behind that pillar; I merely broke the arm he had his gun in, then kicked him sort of high when he tried to run. I hadn't been hurried the way I had been the day before. After reducing the target the Chief Confederate made (really, he should not wear that distinctive headdress), I had had time to realize that the assassin, if taken alive, might be a clue to the gang behind these senseless killings.

But I did not have time to realize what else I had done until two Capital police seized my arms. I then did realize it and felt glum indeed, thinking about the scorn there would be in Boss's voice when I had to admit that I had allowed myself to be publicly arrested. For a split moment I seriously considered disengaging and hiding behind the horizon—not impossible as one police officer clearly had high blood pressure and the other was an older man wearing frame spectacles.

Too late. If I ran now using full overdrive, I could almost certainly get away and, in a square or two, mingle with the crowd and be gone. But these bumblers would possibly burn half a dozen bystanders in trying to wing me. Not professional! Why hadn't this palace guard protected their chief instead of leaving it up to me? A lurker behind pillars fer Gossake!—nothing like that had happened since the assassination of Huey Long.

Why hadn't I minded my own business and let the killer burn down the Chief Confederate in his silly hat? Because I have been trained for defensive warfare only, that's why, and consequently I fight by reflex. I don't have any interest in fighting, don't like it—it just happens.

I did not then have time to consider the advisability of minding my own business because Georges was minding mine. Georges speaks unaccented (if somewhat stilted) BritCan English; now he was sputtering incoherently in French and trying to peel those two praetorians off me.

The one with the spectacles let go my left arm in an effort to deal with Georges so I jabbed him with my elbow just under his sternum. He *whooshed* and went down. The other was still holding on to my right arm, so I jabbed him in the same spot with the first three fingers of my left hand, whereupon he *whooshed* and laid himself across his mate, and both vomited.

All this happened much faster than it takes to tell it—i.e., the cows grabbed me, Georges intervened, I was free. Two seconds? Whatever it was, the assassin had disappeared, his gun with him.

I was about to disappear, too, with Georges even if I had to carry him, when I realized that Georges had made up my mind for me. He had me by my right elbow and had me firmly pointed toward the main entrance of the Palace just beyond that row of pillars. As we stepped into the rotunda he let go my elbow while saying softly, "Slow march, my darling—quietly, quietly. Take my arm."

I took his arm. The rotunda was fairly crowded but there was no excitement, nothing at all to suggest an attempt had just been made a few meters away to kill the nation's chief executive. Concession booths rimming the rotunda were busy, especially the off-track betting windows. Just to our left a young woman was selling lottery tickets—or available to sell them I should say, as she had no customers just then and was watching a detergent drama on her terminal.

Georges turned us and halted us at her booth. Without looking up she said, "Station break coming up. Be with you then. Shop around. Be my guest."

There were festoons of lottery tickets around the booth. Georges started examining them, so I pretended a deep interest, too. We stretched the time; presently the commercials started, the young woman punched down the sound and turned to us.

"Thanks for waiting," she said with a pleasant smile. "I never miss *One Woman's Woes*, especially right now when Mindy Lou is pregnant again and Uncle Ben is being so unreasonable about it. Do you follow the theater, dearie?"

I admitted that I rarely had time for it—my work interfered.

"That's too bad; it's very educational. Take Tim—that's my roommate—won't look at anything but sports. So he doesn't have a thought in his head for the finer things in life. Take this crisis in Mindy Lou's life. Uncle Ben is purely persecuting her because she won't tell him who did it. Do you think Tim cares? Not Tim! What neither Tim nor Uncle Ben realizes is that she *can't* tell because it happened at a precinct caucus. What sign were you born under?"

I should phrase a prepared answer for this question; human persons are always asking it. But when you weren't born, you tend to shy away from such things. I grabbed a date and threw it at her: "I was born on the twenty-third of April." That's Shakespeare's birthday; it popped into my mind.

"Oho! Have I got a lottery ticket for you!" She shuffled through one of the Maypole decorations, found a ticket, showed me a number. "See *that*? And you just walked in here and I had it! This is *your* day!" She detached the ticket. "That's twenty bruins."

I offered a BritCan dollar. She answered, "I don't have change for that."

"Keep the change for luck."

She handed me the ticket, took the dollar. "You're a real sport, dearie. When you collect, stop by and we'll have a drink together. Mister, have you found one you like?"

"Not yet. I was born on the ninth day of the ninth month of the ninth year of the ninth decade. Can you handle it?"

"Woo woo! What a terrific combo! I can try . . . and if I can't, I won't sell you anything." She dug through her piles and strings of paper, humming to herself. She ducked her head under the counter, stayed awhile.

She reappeared, red-faced and triumphant, clutching a lottery ticket. "Got it! Look at it, mister! Give a respectful gander."

We looked: 8109999

"I'm impressed," Georges said.

"Impressed? You're *rich*. There's your four nines. Now add the odd digits. Nine again. Divide that into the odd digits. Another nine. Add the last four—thirty-six. That's nine squared, for two more nines, making another four nines. Add all up at once and it's five nines. Take away the sum and you have four nines again. No matter what you do, you always keep getting your own birthday. What do you want, mister? Dancing girls?"

"How much do I owe you?"

"That's a pretty special number. You can have any other number on the rack for twenty bruins. But that one— Why don't you just keep piling money in front of me until I smile?"

"That seems fair. Then if you don't smile when I think you should, I'll pick up the money and walk away. No?"

"I may call you back."

"No. If you won't offer me a fixed price, I won't let you spar around about it after I've made a fair offer."

"You're a tough customer, sport. I—"

Speakers on all sides of us suddenly started blasting "Hail to the Chief," followed by "The Golden Bear Forever." The young woman shouted, *"Wait! Over soon!"* A crowd of people came in from outside, walked straight through the rotunda, and on down the main corridor. I spotted the eagle-feather headdress sticking up in the middle of the clump but this time the Chief Confederate was so tightly surrounded by his parasites that an assassin would have a hard time hitting him.

As it became possible to hear again the lottery saleswoman said, "That was a short one. Less than fifteen minutes ago he went through here heading out. If he was just going down to the corner for a pack of tokes, whyn't he send somebody instead of going himself? Bad for business, all that noise. Well, sport, have you figured out how much you'll pay to get rich?"

"But yes." Georges took out a three-dollar bill, laid it on the counter. He looked at the woman.

They locked gazes for about twenty seconds, then she said glumly, "I'm smiling. I guess I am." She picked up the money with one hand, handed Georges the lottery ticket with the other. "I bet I could have sweated you out of another dollar."

"We'll never know, will we?"

"Cut for double or nothing?"

"With *your* cards?" Georges asked gently.

"Sport, you'll make an old woman out of me. Be elsewhere before I change my mind."

"Rest room?"

"Down the corridor on my left." She added, "Don't miss the drawing."

As we walked toward the rest room Georges told me quietly in French that gendarmes had passed behind us while we were dickering, had gone into the rest room, come out, back into the rotunda, and down the main corridor.

I cut him off, speaking also in French—telling him that I knew but this place must be filled with Eyes, Ears—talk later.

I was not snubbing him. Two uniformed guards—not the two with stomach problems—had come in almost on our heels, hurried past us, checked the rest room first—reasonable; an amateur often tries to hide in a public rest room—had come out and hurried past us, then deep into the Palace. Georges had quietly shopped for lottery tickets while guards looking for us had brushed past him, twice. Admirable. Quite professional.

But I had to wait to tell him so. There was a person of indeterminate sex selling tickets to the rest room. I asked her(him) where the powder room was. She (I decided on "she" when closer observation showed that her T-shirt covered either falsies or small milk glands)—she answered scornfully, "You some kind of a nut? Trying to discriminate, huh? I ought to send for a cop." Then she looked at me more closely. "You're a foreigner."

I admitted it.

"Okay. Just don't talk that way; people don't like it. We're democratic here, see?—setters and pointers use the same fireplug. So buy a ticket or quit blocking the turnstile."

Georges bought us two tickets. We went in.

On our right was a row of open stalls. Above them floated a holo: THESE FACILITIES ARE PROVIDED *FREE* FOR YOUR HEALTH AND COMFORT BY THE CALIFORNIA CONFEDERACY—JOHN "WARWHOOP" TUMBRIL, CHIEF CONFEDERATE.

A life-size holo of the Chief floated above it.

Beyond the open stalls were pay stalls with doors; beyond these were doorways fully closed with drapes. On our left was a news-and-notions stand presided over by a person of very determined sex, bull dyke. Georges paused there and surprised me by buying several cosmetics and a flacon of cheap perfume. Then he asked for a ticket to one of the dressing rooms at the far end.

"*One* ticket?" She looked at him sharply. Georges nodded agreement. She pursed her lips. "Naughty, naughty. No hanky-panky, stud."

Georges did not answer. A BritCan dollar passed from his hand to hers, vanished. She said very softly, "Don't take too long. If I buzz the buzzer, get decent fast. Number seven, far right."

We went to number seven, the farthest dressing room, and entered. Georges closed the drapes, zipped them tight, flushed the water closet, then turned on the cold water and left it running. Speaking again in French, he told me that we were about to change our appearance without using disguises, so, please, my dear, get out of the clothes you are wearing and put on that suit you have in your jumpbag.

He explained in more detail, mixing French and English and continuing to flush the commode from time to time. I was to wear that scandalous Superskin job, more makeup than I usually do, and was to attempt to look like the famous Whore of Babylon or equivalent. "I know that's not your métier, dear girl, but try."

"I will attempt to be 'adequate.' "

"Ouch!"

"And you plan to wear Janet's clothes? I don't think they'll fit."

"No, no, I shan't drag. Just swish."

"Excuse me?"

"I won't dress in women's clothes; I will simply endeavour to appear effeminate."

"I don't believe it. All right, let's try."

We didn't do much to me—just that one-piece job with the wet look that had hooked Ian, plus more makeup than I am used to, applied by Georges (he seemed to feel that he knew more about it than I did—he felt that way because he did), plus—once we were outside—that here-it-is-come-and-get-it walk.

Georges used on himself rather more makeup than he had put on me, plus that vile perfume (which he did not ask me to wear), plus at his neck a shocking-orange scarf I had been using as a belt. He had me fluff his hair and spray it so that it stayed bouffant. That was all . . . plus a change in manner. He still looked like Georges—but he did *not* seem like the virile buck who had so wonderfully worn me out the night before.

I repacked my jumpbag and we left. The old moose at the news-stand widened her eyes and caught her breath when she saw me. But she said nothing as a man who had been leaning against the stand straightened up, pointed a finger at Georges, and said, "You. The Chief wants you." Then he added, almost to himself, "I don't believe it."

Georges stopped and gestured helplessly with both hands. "Oh, dear me! Surely there has been some mistake?"

The flunky bit a toothpick he had been sucking and answered, "I think so, too, citizen—but I ain't going to say so and neither are you. Come along. Not you, sister."

Georges said, "I positively am not going anywhere without my dear sister! So there!"

That cow said, "Morrie, she can wait here. Sweetie, come around behind here with me and sit down."

Georges gave me the barest negative shake of his head but I did not need it. If I stayed, either she would take me straight back to that dressing room or I would stuff her into her own trash can. I was betting on me. I will put up with that sort of nonsense in line of duty—she would not have been as unpleasant as Rocky Rockford—but not willingly. If and when I change my luck, it will be with someone I like and respect.

I moved closer to Georges, took his arm. "We have never been separated since Mama on her death bed told me to take care of him." I added, "So there!" while wondering what that phrase means, if anything. Both of us pouted and looked stubborn.

The man called Morrie looked at me, back at Georges, and sighed. "Hell with it. Tag along, sister. But keep your mouth shut and stay out of the way."

About six checkpoints later—at each of which an attempt was

made to peel me off—we were ushered into the Presence. My first impression of Chief Confederate John Tumbril was that he was taller than I had thought he was. Then I decided that not wearing his headdress might make the difference. My second impression was that he was even homelier than pictures, cartoons, and terminal images showed him to be—and that opinion stayed. Like many another politico before him, Tumbril had turned a distinctive, individual ugliness into a political asset.

(Is homeliness a necessity to a head of state? Looking back through history I cannot find a single handsome man who got very far in politics until we get clear back to Alexander the Great . . . and he had a head start; his father was a king.)

As may be, "Warwhoop" Tumbril looked like a frog trying to be a toad and just missing.

The Chief cleared his throat. "What's *she* doing here?"

Georges said quickly, "Sir, I have a most serious complaint to make! That man— *That man*"—he pointed at the toothpick chewer—"tried to separate me from my dear sister! He should be reprimanded!"

Tumbril looked at Morrie, looked at me, looked back at his parasite. "Did you do that?"

Morrie asserted that he had not but even if he did, he had done so because he had thought that Tumbril had ordered it but in any case he thought—

"You're not supposed to think," Tumbril ruled. "I'll talk to you later. And why are you leaving her standing? Get a chair! Do I have to do all the thinking around here?"

Once I was seated, the Chief turned his attention back to Georges. "That was a Brave Thing you did earlier today. Yes, sir, a Very Brave Thing. The Great Nation of California is Proud to have raised Sons of Your Caliber. What's your name?"

Georges gave his name.

" 'Payroll' is a Proud California Name, Mr. Payroll; one that shines down our Noble History, from the rancheros who threw off the Yoke of Spain to the Brave Patriots who threw off the Yoke of Wall Street. Do you mind if I call you George?"

"Not at all."

"And you can call me Warwhoop. That's the Crowning Glory of Our Great Nation, George; All of us are Equal."

I suddenly said, "Does that apply to artificial people, Chief Tumbril?"

"Eh?"

"I was asking about artificial people, like those they make at Berkeley and Davis. Are they equal, too?"

"Uh . . . little lady, you really shouldn't interrupt while your elders are speaking. But to answer your question: How can Human Democracy apply to creatures who are Not Human? Would you expect a cat to vote? Or a Ford APV? Speak up."

"No, but—"

"There you are. Everybody is Equal and Everybody has a vote. But you have to draw the line somewhere. Now, shut up, damn it, and don't interrupt while your betters are talking. George, what you did today—well, if that klutz had actually been making an attack on my life—he wasn't and don't you ever forget it—you could not have behaved in a manner more becoming to all the Heroic Traditions of Our Great California Confederacy. You Make Me Proud!"

Tumbril stood up and came out from behind his desk, hooked his hands behind him, and paced—and I saw why he had seemed taller here than he had outside.

He used some sort of a highchair or possibly a platform at his desk. When he stood with no fakery, he was about up to my shoulder. He seemed to be thinking aloud as he paced. "George, there is always a place in my official family for a man of your demonstrated courage. Who knows?—the day *might* come when you would save me from a criminal who seriously intended to harm me. Foreign agitators, I mean; I have nothing to fear from the Stalwart Patriots of California. They all love me for what I have done for them while occupying the Octagon Office. But other countries are jealous of us; they envy our Rich and Free and Democratic lifestyle and sometimes their smoldering hatred erupts in violence."

He stood with his head bowed for a moment, in reverent adoration of something. "One of the Prices of the Privilege of Serving," he said solemnly, "but one which, with All Humility, one must pay Gladly. George, tell me, if you were called upon to make the Last

Supreme Sacrifice that Your Country's Chief Executive might live, would you hesitate?"

"It all seems most unlikely," Georges answered.

"*Eh?* What?"

"Well, when I vote—not often—I usually vote *Réunioniste.* But the present Prime Minister is *Revanchiste.* I doubt that he would have me."

"What the devil are you talking about?"

"*Je suis Québecois,* M. *le chef d'état.* I'm from Montréal."

XVI

Five minutes later we were out on the street again. For some tense moments it seemed that we were going to be hanged or shot or at least locked up forever in their deepest dungeon for the crime of not being Californians. But cooler counsel prevailed when Warwhoop's leading legal eagle convinced him that it was better to let us go than it was to risk a trial, even one in chambers—the Québecois Consul General might cooperate but buying his whole staff could be horribly expensive.

That was not quite how he put it but he did not know that I was listening, as I had not mentioned enhanced hearing even to Georges. The Chief's chief counselor whispered something about the trouble we had with that little Mexicana doll after all those other greasers got aholt of the story. We can't afford another mess like that one. You wanta watch it, Chief; they gotcha by the short ones.

So at last we passed the Palace and went to MasterCard main California office, forty-five minutes late . . . and lost another ten minutes shucking off our false *personae* in a rest room of the California Commercial Credit Building. The rest room was nondiscriminatory and democratic but not aggressively so. There was no charge to get in and the stalls had doors on them and the women used one side and the men used the side that had those vertical bathtub things that men use as well as stalls, and the only place they mingled was in a middle room equipped with wash trays and mirrors and even there women tended to stay on their side and men on the other. I'm not upset by co-ed plumbing—after all, I was raised in a crèche—but I have noticed that men and women, given a chance to segregate, do segregate.

Georges looked a lot better without lip paint. He had used water on his hair, too, and slicked it down. I put that noisy scarf into my jumpbag. He said to me, "I guess I was silly, trying to camouflage us this way."

I glanced around. No one near and the high noise level of plumbing and air conditioning—"Not in my opinion, Georges. I think that in six weeks you could be turned into a real pro."

"What sort of a pro?"

"Uh, Pinkerton, maybe. Or a—" Someone came in. "Discuss it later. Anyhow, we got two lottery tickets out of it."

"So we did. When is the drawing on yours?"

I took mine out, looked at it. "Why, it's today! This very afternoon! Or have I lost track of the date?"

"No," Georges said, peering at my ticket, "it's today all right. About an hour from now we had better be near a terminal."

"No need," I told him. "I don't win at cards, I don't win at dice, I don't win lotteries. When I buy Cracker Jack, sometimes the box doesn't have a prize in it."

"So we'll watch the terminal anyhow, Cassandra."

"All right. When is your drawing?"

He took out his ticket; we looked at it. "Why, it's the same drawing!" I exclaimed. "Now we have much more reason to watch."

Georges was still looking at his ticket. "Friday. Look at this." He rubbed his thumb across the printing. The lettering stayed sharp; the serial number smeared heavily. "Well, well! How long did our friend have her head under the counter before she 'found' this ticket?"

"I don't know. Less than a minute."

"Long enough, that's clear."

"Are you going to take it back?"

"Me? Friday, why would I do that? Such virtuosity deserves applause. But she's wasting a major talent on a very minor scam. Let's get along upstairs; you want to finish with MasterCard before the lottery drawing."

I went back temporarily to being "Marjorie Baldwin" and we were allowed to talk to "our Mr. Chambers" in the main office of California MasterCard. Mr. Chambers was a most likable person—hospitable, sociable, sympathetic, friendly, and just the man, it appeared, that I needed to see, as the sign on his desk told us that he was Vice-President for Client Relations.

After several minutes I began to see that his authority was to say no and that his major talent lay in saying no in so many pleasant, friendly words that the client hardly realized that she was being turned down.

First, please understand, Miss Baldwin, that California Master-Card and Chicago Imperium MasterCard are separate corporations and that you do not have a contract with us. To our regret. True, as a matter of courtesy and reciprocity we ordinarily honor credit cards issued by them and they honor ours. But he was truly sorry to say that at the moment—he wanted to emphasize "at the moment"— the Imperium had cut off communication and, strange as it seems, there was not *today* even an established rate of exchange between bruins and crowns . . . so how can we possibly honor a credit card from the Imperium even though we want to and will gladly do so . . . later. But we do want to make your stay with us happy and what can we do for you toward that end?

I asked when he thought the emergency would be over.

Mr. Chambers looked blank. "Emergency? What emergency, Miss Baldwin? Perhaps there is one in the Imperium since they have seen fit to close their borders . . . but certainly not here! Look around you—did you ever see a country so glowing with peace and prosperity?"

I agreed with him and stood up, as there seemed no point in arguing. "Thank you, Mr. Chambers. You have been most gracious."

"My pleasure, Miss Baldwin. MasterCard service. And don't forget: Anything I can do for you, anything at all, I am at your service."

"Thank you, I'll remember. Uh, is there a public terminal somewhere in this building? I bought a lottery ticket earlier today and it turns out that the drawing is almost at once."

He grinned broadly. "My dear Miss Baldwin, I'm so happy that you asked! Right on this floor we have a large conference room and every Friday afternoon just before the drawing everything stops and our entire office staff—or at least those who hold tickets; attendance is not compulsory—all of us crowd in and watch the drawing. J.B.—that's our president and chief executive—old J.B. decided that it was better to do it that way than to have the punters sneaking away to washrooms and toke shops and pretending they weren't. Better for morale. When one of our people wins one—does happen—she or he gets a fancy cake with sparklers on it, just like a birthday, a gift from old J.B. himself. He comes out and has a piece with the lucky winner."

"Sounds like a happy ship."

"Oh, it is! This is one financial institution where computer crime is unheard of; they all love old J.B." He glanced at his finger. "Let's get on into the conference room."

Mr. Chambers saw to it that we were placed in VIP seats, fetched coffee to us himself, then decided to sit down and watch the drawing.

The terminal screen occupied most of the end wall of the room. We sat through an hour of minor prizes during which the master of ceremonies exchanged utterly sidesplitting jokes with his assistant, mostly about the physical charms of the girl who picked the slips out of the tumble bowl. She clearly had been picked for those physical charms, which were considerable—that and her willingness to wear a costume that not only displayed them but also assured the audience that she was not hiding anything. Each time she plunged in an arm and drew out a lucky number she was dressed principally in a blindfold. It looked like easy pleasant work if the studio was properly heated.

Halfway through there were loud squeals from up front; a Master-Card clerk had won a thousand bruins. Chambers grinned broadly. "Doesn't happen often but when it does, it cheers everyone up for days. Shall we go? No, you still have a ticket that might win, don't you? Unlikely as it is that lightning will strike here twice."

At last with a blare of trumpets we reached the week's grand prize—the "Giant, Supreme, All-California Super Prize!!!" The girl with the goose bumps drew two honorary prizes first, a year's supply of Ukiah Gold with hash pipe, and dinner with the great sensie star Bobby "The Brute" Pizarro.

Then she drew the last lucky ticket; the master of ceremonies read off the numbers and they appeared in blazing light above his head. "Mr. Zee!" he shouted. "Has the owner registered this number?"

"One moment— No, not registered."

"We have a Cinderella! We have an unknown winner! Somewhere in our great and wonderful Confederacy someone is two hundred thousand bruins richer! Is that child of fortune listening now? Will she—or he—call in and let us put her on the air before this program ends? Or will he wake up tomorrow morning to be told that she is rich? There is the number, folks! It will shine up there until the end of this program, then it will be repeated every news break until fortune's darling claims her prize. And now a message—"

"Friday," Georges whispered, "let me see your ticket."

"Not necessary, Georges," I whispered back. "That's it, all right."

Mr. Chambers stood up. "Show's over. Nice that one of our little family won something. Been a pleasure to have you with us, Miss Baldwin and Mr. Karo—and don't hesitate to call on me if we can help you."

"Mr. Chambers," I asked, "can MasterCard collect this for me? I don't want to do it in person."

Mr. Chambers is a nice man but a touch slow. He had to compare the numbers on my lottery ticket with the numbers still shining on the screen three times before he could believe it. Then Georges had to stop him when he was about to run in all directions, to order a photographer, call National Lottery headquarters, send for a holovision crew—and just as well that Georges stopped him because I might have been rough about it. I get annoyed by big males who won't listen to my objections.

"Mr. Chambers!" Georges said. "Didn't you hear her? She does *not* want to do it in person. No publicity."

"What? But the winners are always in the news; that's routine! This won't take a moment if that's what's worrying you because—you remember the girl who won earlier?—about now she is being photographed with J.B. and her cake. Let's go straight to his office and—"

"Georges," I said. "American Express."

Georges is *not* slow—and I wouldn't mind marrying him if Janet ever turned him loose. "Mr. Chambers," he said quickly, "what is the address of the San Jose main office of American Express?"

Chambers' four-winds flight stopped abruptly. "*What* did you say?"

"Can you tell us the address of American Express? Miss Baldwin will take her winning ticket there for collection. I will call ahead and make sure that they understand that banking privacy is a requisite."

"But you *can't* do that. She won it *here*."

"We can and we will. She did *not* win it here. She simply happened to be here when the drawing took place elsewhere. Please stand aside; we're leaving."

Then we had to do it all over again for J.B. He was a dignified old duck with a cigar in one side of his mouth and sticky white cake icing on his upper lip. He was neither slow nor stupid but he was in the habit of seeing his wishes carried out and Georges had to mention American Express quite loudly before he got it through his skull that I would not hold still for any publicity whatever (Boss would faint!) and that we were about to go to those Rialto money-changers rather than deal with his firm.

"But Miss Bulgrin is a MasterCard client."

"No," I disagreed. "I had thought that I was a MasterCard client but Mr. Chambers refused to honor my credit. So I'll start an account with American Express. Without photographers."

"Chambers." There was the knell of doom in his voice. "What Is This?"

Chambers explained that my credit card had been issued through the Imperial Bank of Saint Louis.

"A most reputable house," J.B. commented. "Chambers. Issue her another card. On us. At once. And collect her winning ticket for her." He looked at me and took his cigar out of his mouth. "No publicity. The affairs of MasterCard's clients are always confidential. Satisfactory, Miss Walgreen?"

"Quite, sir."

"Chambers. Do it."

"Yes, sir. What credit limit, sir?"

"What extent of credit do you require, Miss Belgium? Perhaps I should ask that in crowns—what is your amount with my colleagues in Saint Louis?"

"I am a gold client, sir. My account is always reckoned in bullion rather than crowns under their two-tier method for gold customers. Can we figure it that way? You see, I'm not used to *thinking* in bruins. I travel so much that it is easier for me to think in grams of gold." (It is almost unfair to mention gold to a banker in a soft-currency country; it clouds his thinking.)

"You wish to pay in gold?"

"If I may. By draft in grams, three nines, on Ceres and South Africa Acceptances, Luna City office. Would that be satisfactory? I usually pay quarterly—you see, I travel so much—but I can instruct C. and S. A. A. to pay you monthly if quarterly is not convenient."

"Quarterly is quite satisfactory." (Of course it was—the interest charges pile up.)

"Now the credit limit— Truthfully, sir, I don't like to place too much of my financial activity in any one bank or any one country. Shall we hold it down to thirty kilos?"

"If that is your wish, Miss Bedlam. If you ever wish to increase it, just let us know." He added, "Chambers. Do it."

So we went back to the same office in which I had been told that my credit was no good. Mr. Chambers offered me an application form. "Let me help you fill it out, miss."

I glanced at it. Parents' names. Grandparents' names. Place and date of birth. Addresses including street numbers for the past fifteen years. Present employer. Past employer immediately preceding. Reason for leaving past employment. Present rate of pay. Bank accounts. Three references from persons who have known you at least ten years. Have you ever applied for bankruptcy or had a petition of involuntary receivership filed against you or been a director or responsible officer of any business, partnership, or corporation that has applied for reorganization under paragraph thirteen of Public Law Ninety-Seven of the California Confederacy Civil Code? Have you ever been convicted of—

"Friday. No."

"So I was about to say." I stood up.

Georges said, "Good-bye, Mr. Chambers."

"Something wrong?"

"But yes. Your employer told you to issue to Miss Baldwin a gold credit card with a limit of thirty kilograms, fine gold; he did *not* tell you to subject her to an impertinent quiz."

"But this is a routine require—"

"Never mind. Just tell J.B. you flubbed again."

Our Mr. Chambers turned a light green. "Do please sit down."

Ten minutes later we left, me with a brand-new gold-colored credit card good anywhere (I hoped). In exchange I had listed my Saint Louis P.O. box number, my next-of-kin address (Janet), and my account number in Luna City with a written instruction to bill C and S.A.A., Ltd. quarterly for my debts. I also had a comfortable wad of bruins and another like it of crowns, and a receipt for my lottery ticket.

We left the building, crossed the corner into National Plaza, found a bench, and sat down. It was just eighteen, pleasantly cool but the sun was still high above the Santa Cruz Mountains.

Georges inquired, "Dear Friday, what are your wishes?"

"To sit here for a moment and collect my thoughts. Then I should buy you a drink. I won a lottery; that calls for buying a drink. At least."

"At least," he agreed. "You won two hundred thousand bruins for . . . twenty bruins?"

"A dollar," I agreed. "I tipped her the change."

"Near enough. You won about eight thousand dollars."

"Seventy-four hundred and seven dollars and some cents."

"Not a fortune but a respectable sum of money."

"Quite respectable," I agreed, "for a woman who started the day dependent on the charity of friends. Unless I'm credited something for my 'adequate' performance last night."

"My brother Ian would prescribe a fat lip for that remark. I wanted to add that, while seventy-four hundred is a respectable sum, I find myself more impressed by the fact that, with no assets other than that lottery ticket, you persuaded a most conservative credit banking firm to extend to you an open account in the amount of a million dollars, reckoned in gold. How did you do it, dear? You didn't even wiggle. Not even a sultry tone of voice."

"But, Georges, *you* caused them to issue me their card."

"I don't think so. Oh, I did try to back your play . . . but you initiated each move."

"Not the one about that horrid questionnaire! You got me out of *that*."

"Oh. That silly ass had no business quizzing you. His boss had already ordered him to issue the card."

"You saved me. I was about to lose my nerve. Georges—dear Georges!—I know that you have told me that I must *not* be uneasy about what I am—and I'm trying, I truly am!—but to be faced with a form that demands to know all about my parents and grandparents—it's dismaying!"

"Can't expect you to get well overnight. We'll keep working on it. You certainly did not lose your nerve over how much credit to ask."

"Oh. I once heard someone say"—it was Boss—"that it was much easier to borrow a million than it was to borrow ten. So when they asked me, that's what I named. Not quite a million BritCan dollars. Nine hundred and sixty-four thousand, about."

"I'm not going to quibble. When we passed nine hundred thousand I ran out of oxygen. Adequate one, do you know what a professor is paid?"

"Does it matter? From what I know of the profession one successful new design of a living artifact can pay in the millions. Even millions of grams, rather than dollars. Haven't you had any successful designs? Or is that a rude question?"

"Let's change the subject. Where are we sleeping tonight?"

"We could be in San Diego in forty minutes. Or in Las Vegas in thirty-five. Each has advantages and disadvantages for getting into the Imperium. Georges, now that I have enough money, I'm going to report in, no matter how many fanatics are assassinating officials. But I promise cross-my-heart to visit Winnipeg just as soon as I have a few days' leave."

"I may still be unable to return to Winnipeg."

"Or I'll come visit you in Montréal. Look, dear, we'll swap all the addresses we have; I'm not going to lose you. You not only assure me that I'm human, you tell me that I'm adequate—you're good for my morale. Now choose, for I'll take either one: San Diego and talk Spanglish, or Vegas and look at pretty naked ladies."

XVII

We did both and wound up in Vicksburg.

The Texas-Chicago border turned out to be closed from both sides all the way, so I decided to try the river route first. Of course Vicksburg is still Texas but, for my purpose, its situation as the major river port just outside the Imperium was the point that counted—especially that it was the leading smugglers' port, both directions.

Like ancient Gaul, Vicksburg is divided into three parts. There is the low town, the port, right on the water and sometimes flooded, and there is the high town sitting on a bluff a hundred meters high and itself divided into old town and new town. Old town is surrounded by battlefields of a war long forgotten (but not by Vicksburg!). These battlefields are sacred; nothing may be built on them. So the new town is outside this holy ground, and functions through being tied to old town and to itself by a system of tunnels and tubes. High town is joined to low town by escalators and funiculars to the city barricade.

To me, high town was just a place to sleep. We punched into the Vicksburg Hilton (twin to the Bellingham Hilton even to The Breakfast Bar in the basement) but my business was down on the river. It was a happy-sad time as Georges knew that I would not let him come any farther with me and we had quit discussing it. Indeed, I did not permit him to go with me to low town—and had warned him that any day I might not come back, might not even stop to punch a message to him to record in our hotel suite. When the moment came to jump, I would jump.

Vicksburg low town is a lusty, evil place, as swarmingly alive as a dunghill. In daylight city police travel in pairs; at night they leave the place alone. It is a city of grifters, whores, smugglers, pushers, drug wholesalers, spivs, pimps, hire hatchets, military mercenaries, recruiters, fences, fagins, beggars, clandestine surgeons, black-birders, glimjacks, outstanders, short con, long con, sting riggers, girlboys, you name it, they sell it in Vicksburg low town. It's a wonderful place and be sure to get a blood test afterward.

It is the only place I know of where a living artifact, marked by his design (four arms, no legs, eyes in the back of his skull, whatever) can step (or slither) up to a bar, buy a beer, and have absolutely no special attention paid to him or his oddity. As for my sort, being artificial meant nothing—not in a community where 95 percent of the residents did not dare step onto an escalator leading to the upper city.

I was tempted to stay there. There was something so warm and friendly about all these outcasts, no one of whom would ever point a finger of scorn. Had it not been for Boss on one hand and Georges and the memory of places that *smelled* better on the other hand, I might have stayed in (lower) Vicksburg and found a scam that suited my talents.

"But I have promises to keep, And miles to go before I sleep." Master Robert Frost knew why a person keeps on going when she would rather stop. Dressed as if I were a soldier out of work and shopping for the best recruiting deal, I frequented river town listening for a riverboat skipper willing to smuggle live cargo. I had been disappointed to learn how little traffic there was on the river. No news was coming out of the Imperium and no boats were coming down the river, so very few skippers were willing to risk going upriver.

So I sat in bars in river town, drinking small beer and letting the word filter around that I was prepared to pay a worthwhile price for a ticket up the river.

I considered advertising. I had been following the Opportunity

Ads, which were considerably more outspoken than those I had noticed in California—apparently *anything* was tolerated as long as it was limited to low town:

> Do You Hate Your Family?
> Are You Frustrated, Tied Down, Bored?
> Is Your Husband/Wife a Waste of Space?
> LET US MAKE A NEW (WO)MAN OF YOU!!!!!
> Plasticizing—Reorientation—Relocating
> Transsexualizing—Discreet Wet Work
> Consult Doc Frank Frankenstein
> Softly Sam's Bar Grill

This was the first time I'd ever seen murder for pay blatantly advertised. Or did I misunderstand it?

> Do You Have a PROBLEM?
> Nothing is illegal—it isn't what
> you do; it's the way that you do
> it. We have the most skilled
> shysters in the Lone Star State.
> LOOPHOLES, Inc.
> *(Special Rates to Bachelors)*
> Punch LEV 10101

With the above it helped to know that "LEV" call codes were assigned only to locations under the bluff.

Certainly all of the above services were available in any large city but they were *rarely* openly advertised. As for the warranty, I simply did not believe it.

I decided not to advertise my need because of doubt that anything so public could help in a matter essentially clandestine—I went on relying on chandlers and barkeeps and madams. But I continued to watch the ads on the chance of spotting something of use to me . . . and came across one probably not of use but decidedly of interest. I froze it and called it to Georges' attention:

W.K.—Make your will. You have
only ten days to live.

A.C.B.

"What about it, Georges?"

"The first one we saw gave W.K. only a week. More than a week has passed and he now has ten days. If this keeps up, W.K. will die of old age."

"You don't believe that."

"No, my love, I do not. It's a code."

"What sort of a code?"

"The simplest sort and thereby impossible to break. The first ad told the person or persons concerned to carry out number seven or expect number seven or it said something about something designated as seven. This one says the same with respect to code item number ten. But the meaning of the numbers cannot be deduced through statistical analysis because the code can be changed long before a useful statistical universe can be reached. It's an idiot code, Friday, and an idiot code can never be broken if the user has the good sense not to go too often to the well."

"Georges, you sound as if you had done military code and/or cipher work."

"I have but that's not where I learned it. The most difficult code analysis ever attempted—one that still goes on today and will never be complete—is the interpretation of living genes. An idiot code all of it . . . but repeated so many millions of times that we can eventually assign meaning to nonsense syllables. Forgive me for talking shop at meals."

"Piffle, I started it. No way to guess what A.C.B. means?"

"None."

That night the assassins struck the second time, right on schedule. I don't say that the two were related.

They struck ten days, almost to the hour, after their first attack. The timing did not tell us anything about which group was responsible as it matched the predictions of both the so-called Council for Survival and their rivals the Stimulators, whereas the Angels of the Lord had offered no prediction about a second strike.

There were differences between the first wave of terror and the second, differences that seemed to tell me something—or us something, as Georges and I discussed it as the reports came in:

a) No news at all from the Chicago Imperium. No change here, as *no* news had come out of the Imperium since the initial reports of the slaughter of Democrats . . . then nary a peep for over a week, which made me increasingly anxious.

b) No news from the California Confederacy concerning a second strike—routine news only. N.B.: a few hours after the initial news reports of a second wave of assassinations elsewhere a "routine" news item came out of the California Confederacy. Chief "Warwhoop" Tumbril, on the advice of his physicians, had named a three-person executive regency with plenipotentiary powers to govern the nation while he underwent long-postponed medical treatment. He had gone to his retreat, the Eagle's Nest, near Tahoe, for this purpose. Bulletins would be issued from San Jose, not from Tahoe.

c) Georges and I agreed on the most probable—almost certain—meaning of this. The medical treatment that pitiful poseur now needed was embalming and his "regency" would now give news handouts while they settled their power struggle.

d) This second time there were no reports from off-Earth.

e) Canton and Manchuria did not report attacks. Correction: No such reports reached Vicksburg, Texas.

f) So far as I could tell in ticking them off against a list, the terrorists did strike at all other nations. But my tally had holes in it. Of the four hundred–odd "nations" in the U.N. some produce news only during total solar eclipses. I don't know what happened in Wales or the Channel Isles or Swaziland or Nepal or Prince Edward Island and I can't see why anyone (who does not live in one of those nowhere places) should care. At least three hundred of those so-called sovereign nations that vote in the U.N. are ciphers, aboard only for quarters and rations—important to themselves, no doubt, but totally meaningless in Geopolitick. But in all major countries, except as noted above, the terrorists did strike and those strikes were reported *except where baldly censored.*

g) Most strikes failed. This was the glaring difference between the first wave and the second. Ten days earlier most assassins had killed their targets and most assassins had escaped. Now this was reversed: Most targets survived, most assassins died. A few had been captured, a very few had escaped.

This last aspect of the second-wave assassinations put to rest a nagging fret in my mind, i.e., Boss was *not* the mover behind these assassinations.

Why say I so? Because the second wave was a disaster for whoever was in charge.

Field operatives, even common soldiers, are expensive; management does not expend them casually. A trained assassin costs at least ten times as much as a common soldier: She is not expected to get herself killed—goodness me, *no*! She is expected to make the kill and get out, scot-free.

But whoever was running this show had gone bankrupt in one night.

Unprofessional.

Therefore it was not Boss.

But I still could not figure out who was behind the whole silly gymkhana because I could not see who benefitted. My earlier notion, that one of the corporate nations was paying for it, no longer looked as attractive because I could not conceive of one of the big ones (Interworld, for example) hiring any but the best professionals.

But it was even harder to picture one of the territorial nations planning such a grotesque attempt at world conquest.

As for a fanatic group, such as the Angels of the Lord or the Stimulators, the job was just too big. Nevertheless the whole thing seemed to have a fanatic flavor—not rational, not pragmatic.

It is not written in the stars that I will always understand what is going on—a truism that I often find damnably annoying.

The morning after that second strike Vicksburg low town buzzed with excitement. I had just stepped into a saloon to check with the head barkeep when a runner sidled up to me. "Good news," this youngster said in a prison whisper. "Rachel's Raiders is signing 'em on—Rachel said to tell *you* especially."

"Pig swill," I answered politely. "Rachel doesn't know me and I don't know Rachel."

"Scout's honor!"

"You were never a Scout and you can't spell honor."

"Look, Chief," he persisted, "I haven't had anything to eat today. Just walk in with me; you don't have to sign. It's only across the street."

He did look skinny but that probably reflected his having just reached the gangly stage, that sudden spurt in adolescence; low town is not a place where people go hungry. But the bartender chose that moment to snap, "Beat it, Shorty! Quit bothering the customers. You want to buy a broken thumb?"

"It's okay, Fred," I put in. "I'll check with you later." I dropped a bill on the bar, did not ask for change. "Come, Shorty."

Rachel's recruiting office turned out to be quite a lot of mud farther than across the street, and two more recruiter's runners tried to pluck me away from Shorty before we got there. They did not stand a chance as my only purpose was to see that this sorry youngster collected his cumshaw.

The recruiting sergeant reminded me of the old cow who had the concessions in the rest room of the Palace at San Jose. She looked at me and said, "No camp doxies, sugar tit. But stick around and I might buy you a drink."

"Pay your runner," I said.

"Pay him for what?" she answered. "Leonard, I told you. No idlers, I said. Now get back out there and hustle."

I reached across and grasped her left wrist. Quite smoothly her knife appeared in her right hand. So I rearranged things, taking the knife and sticking it into the desk in front of her, while changing my hold on her left paw to one much more annoying. "Can you pay him one-handed?" I asked. "Or do I break this finger?"

"Easy there," she answered, not fighting it. "Here, Leonard." She reached into a drawer, handed him a Texas two-spot. He grabbed it and vanished.

I eased the pressure on her finger. "Is that all you're paying? With every recruiter on the street fishing today?"

"He gets his real commission when you sign up," she answered. "Because I don't get paid until I deliver a warm body. And I get docked if it ain't to spec. Now would you mind letting go of my finger? I'll need it to make out your papers."

I surrendered her finger; quite suddenly the knife was again in her hand and moving toward me. This time I broke the blade before handing it back to her. "Please don't do that again," I said. "Please. And you should use a better steel. That's not a Solingen."

"I'm deducting the price of that blade from your bounty, dear," she answered, unperturbed. "There's been a beam on you since you walked in that door. Shall I trigger it? Or do we quit playing games?"

I did not believe her but her purpose suited me. "No more games, Sarge. What's the proposition? Your runner told me swabo."

"Coffee and cakes and guild scale. Guild bounty. Ninety days with company option to extend ninety days. Wooden overcoat payme fifty-fifty, you and the company."

"Recruiters around town are offering guild plus fifty." (This was a stab in the dark; the atmosphere felt that tense.)

She shrugged. "If they are, we'll match it. What weapons do you know? We aren't signing any raw recruits. Not this time."

"I can teach you any weapon you think you know. Where's the action? Who's on first?"

"Mmm, real salty. Are you trying to sign as a DI? I don't buy it."

I asked, "Where's the action? Are we going upriver?"

"You ain't even signed up and you're asking for classified information."

"For which I am prepared to pay." I took out fifty Lone-Star, in tens, laid them in front of her. "Where's the action, Sarge? I'll buy you a good knife to replace that carbon steel I had to expend."

"You're an AP."

"Let's not play the dozens. I simply want to know whether or not we'll be going upriver. Say about as far as Saint Louis."

"Are you expecting to sign on as sergeant instructor?"

"What? Heavens, no! As a staff officer." I should not have said that—or at least not so soon. While ranks tend to be vague in Boss's outfit, I was certainly a senior officer in that I reported to and took orders from Boss and Boss alone—and this was confirmed by the fact that I was *Miss* Friday to everyone but Boss—until and unless *I* asked for informal address. Even Dr. Krasny had not spoken to me *en tutoyant* until I asked him to. But I had never given much thought to my actual rank because, while I had no senior but Boss, I had no one working under me, either. On a formal T.O. (I had never seen one for Boss's company) I would have to be one of those little boxes leading out horizontally from the stem to the C.O.—

i.e., a senior staff specialist, if you like bureaucratese.

"Well, fiddledeedee! If you can back that up, you'll do it to Colonel Rachel, not to me. I expect her in around thirteen." Almost absentmindedly she reached out to pick up the cash.

I picked up the bills, tapped them even, put them down again in front of her but closer to me. "So let's chat a bit before she gets here. Every live outfit in town is signing them up today; there ought to be some good reason to sign with one rather than another. Is the expected action upstream, or not? And how far? Will we be against real pros? Or local yokels? Or possibly town clowns? Pitched battle? Or strike and run? Or both? Let's chat, Sarge."

She did not answer, she did not move. She did not take her eyes off the cash.

Shortly I took out another ten Lone-Star, placed it neatly on the fifty—waited.

Her nostrils dilated but she did not reach for the money. After several moments I added still another Texas ten-spot.

She said hoarsely, "Put that stuff out of sight or hand it to me; somebody might walk in."

I picked it up and handed it to her. She said, "Thanks, miss," and made it vanish. "I reckon we'll go upstream at least as far as Saint Louis."

"Whom do we fight?"

"Well . . . you repeat this and I'll not only deny it; I'll cut your heart out and feed it to the catfish. We may not fight. More likely we will but not in a set battle. We, all of us, are going to be bodyguard to the new Chairman. The newest Chairman, I should say; he's still-wet new."

(Jackpot!) "Interesting. Why are other outfits in town jockeying for recruits? Is the new Chairman hiring *everybody?* Just for his palace guard?"

"Miss, I wish I knew. I purely wish I knew."

"Maybe I had better try to find out. How much time do I have? When are we sailing?" I quickly amended this to: "Or are we sailing? Maybe Colonel Rachel has a handle on some APVs."

"Uh . . . damn it, how much classified do you expect for a lousy seventy stars?"

I thought about it. I didn't mind spending money but I needed to be certain of the merchandise. With troops moving upriver smugglers would not be moving, at least not this week. So I needed to move with the traffic available.

But not as an officer! I had talked too much. I took out two more ten-spots, fiddled with them. "Sarge, are you going upriver yourself?"

She eyed the bank notes; I dropped one of them in front of her. It disappeared. "I wouldn't miss it, dearie. Once I close down this office, I'm a platoon sergeant."

I dropped the other note; it joined its twin. I said, "Sarge, if I wait and talk to your colonel, if she signs me on, it will be as personnel adjutant, or logistics and supply, or something dreary like that. I don't need the money and don't want the worry; I want a holiday. Could you use a trained private? One you could brevet to corporal or even buck sergeant once you get to shaking down your recruits and see what vacancies you need to fill?"

She looked sour. "That's all I need, a millionaire in my platoon!"

I felt sympathy for her; no sergeant wants a cashiered officer in his/her ranks. "I'm not going to play the millionaire; I just want to be one of the troops. If you don't trust me, stick me in some other platoon."

She sighed. "I ought to have my head examined. No, I'll put you where I can keep an eye on you." She reached into a drawer, pulled out a form headed "Limited Indenture." "Read this. Sign it. Then I swear you. Any questions?"

I looked it over. Most of it was routine trivia about slop chest and toke money and medical benefits and guild pay rate and bounty— but interlined was a provision postponing payment of bounty to the tenth day after enlistment. Understandable. To me it was a guarantee that they really were going in harm's way and at once—i.e., upriver. The nightmare ruining every mercenary paymaster's sleep is the thought of bounty jumpers. Today, with all recruiters active, it would be possible for a veteran soldier to sign up five or six ways, collect a bounty from each, then head for the banana states—unless the indentures were worded to stop it.

The commitment was to Colonel Rachel Danvers personally or

to her lawful successor in case of her death or disability, and it required the signer to carry out her orders and those of officers and noncommissioned officers she placed over me. I agreed to fight faithfully and not to cry for quarter, according to international law and the usages of war.

It was so vaguely worded that it would require a squad of Philadelphia lawyers to define the gray areas . . . which did not matter at all because a difference in opinion when it counted would get the signer shot in the back.

The period was, as the sergeant had represented, ninety days with the Colonel's option to extend it ninety days on payment of another bounty. There was no provision for additional extension, which gave me pause. Just what sort of a political bodyguard contract could it be that would run for six months and then stop cold?

Either the recruiting sergeant was lying or someone had lied to her and she wasn't bright enough to spot the illogicality. Never mind, there was no point in quizzing her. I reached for a pen. "Do I see the medical officer now?"

"Are you kidding?"

"How else?" I signed, then said, " I do," when she read off rapidly an oath that more or less followed the indenture.

She peered at my signature. "Jones, what does F stand for?"

"Friday."

"That's a silly name. On duty, you're Jones. Off duty, you're Jonesie."

"Whatever you say, Sergeant. Am I on duty now, or off?"

"You'll be off duty in a moment. Here are your orders: Foot of Shrimp Alley is a godown. Sign says WOO FONG AND LEVY BROTHERS, INK. Be there by fourteen o'clock, ready to leave. Use the back door. You're free from now till then to wind up your private affairs. You are free to tell anyone of your enlistment but you are strongly admonished under penalty of disciplinary action not to make conjectures as to the nature of the duty on which you are embarking." She read off the last rapidly as if it were a recording. "Do you need lunch money? No, I'm sure you don't. That's all, Jonesie. Glad to have you aboard. We'll have a good tour." She motioned me toward her.

I went to her; she put an arm around my hips, smiled up at me. Inwardly I shrugged as I decided that this was no time to be getting my platoon sergeant sore at me. I smiled back, leaned down, and kissed her. Not bad at all. Her breath was sweet.

XVIII

The excursion boat *Skip to M'Lou* was a real Mark Twainer, much fancier transportation than I had expected—three passenger decks, four Shipstones, two for each of twin screws. But she was loaded to the gunwales and it seemed to me that a stiff breeze would swamp her. At that we were not the only troopship; the *Myrtle T. Hanshaw* was a few lengths ahead of us, carving the river at an estimated twenty knots. I thought about concealed snags and hoped that their radar/sonar was up to the task.

The Alamo Heroes were in the *Myrtle* as was Colonel Rachel, commanding both combat teams—and this was all I needed to nail down my suspicions. A bloated brigade is not a palace guard. Colonel Rachel was expecting field action—possibly we would disembark under fire.

We had not yet been issued weapons and recruits were still in mufti; this seemed to indicate that our colonel did not expect action at once and it fitted in with Sergeant Gumm's prediction that we were going upriver at least as far as Saint Louis—and of course the rest of what she said about our becoming bodyguard to the new Chairman indicated that we were going all the way up to the capital—

—if the new Chairman was in fact at the seat of government. —if Mary Gumm knew what she was talking about. —if someone didn't turn the river around while I was not looking. Too many "ifs," Friday, and too little hard data. All I really knew was that this vessel should be crossing into the Imperium about now—in fact I did not know which side of the border we were on or how to tell.

But I did not care greatly because sometime in the next several days, when we were close to Boss's headquarters, I planned to resign informally from Rachel's Raiders—before action, by strong preference. I had had time to size up this outfit and I believed strongly that it could not be combat-ready in less than six weeks of tough field training at the hands of tough and blooded sergeant instructors. Too many recruits, not enough cadre.

The recruits were all supposed to be veterans . . . but I was certain that some of them were farm girls run away from home and in some cases about fifteen years old. Big for their age, perhaps, and "when they're big enough, they're old enough," as the old saw goes—but it takes more than massing sixty kilos to make a soldier.

To take such troops into action would be suicide. But I did not worry about it. I had a belly full of beans and was settled on the fantail with my back against a spool of cordage, enjoying the sunset and digesting my first meal as a soldier (if that is the word) while contentedly contemplating the fact that, about now, the *Skip to M'Lou* was crossing into, or had crossed into, the Chicago Imperium.

A voice behind me said, "Hidin' out, trooper?"

I recognized the voice and turned my head. "Why, Sergeant, how could you say such a thing?"

"Easy. I just asked myself, 'Where would I go if I was goldbricking?'—and there you were. Forget it, Jonesie. Have you picked your billet?"

I had not done so because there were many choices, all bad. Most of the troops were quartered in staterooms, four to each double room, three to a single. But our platoon, along with one other, was to sleep in the dining salon. I could see no advantage to being at the Captain's table so I had not engaged in the scramble.

Sergeant Gumm nodded at my answer. "Okay. When you draw your blanket, don't use it to stake out a billet; somebody'll steal it. Portside aft, abreast the pantry, is the dining-room steward's stateroom—that's mine. It's a single but with a wide bunk. Drop your blanket there. You'll be a damn sight more comfortable than sleeping on the deck."

"That's mighty nice of you, Sergeant!" (How do I talk my way out of this? Or am I going to have to relax to the inevitable?)

"Call me Sarge. And when we're alone, my name is Mary. What did you say your first name was?"

"Friday."

"Friday. That's kind o' cute, when you stop to think about it. Okay, Friday, I'll see you around taps." We watched the last reddish slice of sun disappear into the bottomland astern of us, the *Skip* having swung east in one of the river's endless meanders. "Seems like it ought to sizzle and send up steam."

"Sarge, you have the soul of a poet."

"I've often thought I could. Write poetry, I mean. You got the word? About the blackout now?"

"No lights outside, no smoking outside. No lights inside except in spaces fully shuttered. Offenders will be shot at sunrise. Doesn't affect me much, Sarge; I don't smoke."

"Correction. Offenders will not be shot; they'll just wish to God they *had* been shot. You don't smoke at all, dear? Not even a friendly hit with a friend?"

(Give up, Friday!) "That's not really smoking; that's just friendly."

"That's the way I see it. I don't go around with my head stuffed full of rags, either. But an occasional hit with a friend when you're both in the mood, that's sweet. And so are you." She dropped to the deck by me, slipped an arm around me.

"Sarge! I mean Mary. Please don't. It's not really dark yet. Somebody'll see us."

"Who cares?"

"I do. It makes me self-conscious. Spoils the mood."

"In this outfit you'll get over that. You're a virgin, dear? With girls, I mean."

"Uh . . . please don't quiz me, Mary. And do let me go. I'm sorry but it does make me nervous. Here, I mean. Why, anybody could walk around the corner of that deckhouse."

She grabbed a feel, then started to stand up. "Kind o' cute, you bein' so shy. All right, I've got some mellow Omaha Black I've been saving for a special—"

The sky lit up with a dazzling light; on top of it came a tremendous *karoom*! and where the *Myrtle* had been the sky was filled with junk.

"Jesus *Christ!*"

"Mary, can you swim?"

"Huh? No."

"Jump in after me and I'll keep you afloat." I went over the port side in as long a dive as I could manage, took a dozen hard strokes to get well clear, turned over onto my back. Mary Gumm's head was silhouetted against the sky.

That was the last I saw of her as the *Skip to M'Lou* blew up.

In that stretch of the Mississippi there are bluffs on the east. The western limit of the river is simply higher land, not as clearly marked, ten or fifteen kilometers away. Between these two sides the location of the river can be a matter of opinion—often of legal opinion because the river shifts channels and chews up property rights.

The river runs in all directions and is almost as likely to run north as to run south. Well, half as likely. It had been flowing west at sundown; the *Skip*, headed upriver, had the sunset behind her. But while the sun was setting the boat had swung left as the channel turned north; I had noticed the red-and-orange display of sunset swinging to portside.

That's why I went over the side to port. When I hit the water, my immediate purpose was to get clear; my next purpose was to see if Mary followed me in. I did not really expect her to because (I've noticed!) most people, human people, don't make up their minds that fast.

I saw her, still aboard; she was staring at me. Then the second explosion took place and it was too late. I felt a brief burst of sorrow—in her own rutty, slightly dishonest way Mary was a good sort—then I wiped her out of my mind; I had other problems.

My first problem was not to be hit by debris; I surface-dived and stayed under. I can hold my breath *and* exercise almost ten minutes, although I don't like it at all. This time I stretched it almost to bursting before surfacing.

Long enough: It was dark but I seemed to be clear of floating debris.

Perhaps there were survivors in the water but I did not hear any and did not feel impelled to try to find any (other than Mary and no way to find her) as I was not well equipped to rescue anyone, even myself.

I looked around, spotted what was left of the loom of sunset, swam toward it. After a while I lost it, turned over on my back, searched the sky. Broken clouds and no moon. I spotted Arcturus, then both the Bears and Polaris, and I had north. I then corrected my course so that I was swimming west. I stayed on my back because, if you take it easy, you can swim forever and two years past, on your back. Never any problem to breathe and if you get a touch weary, you can just hold still and twiddle your fingers a trifle until you are rested. I wasn't in any hurry; I just wanted to reach the Imperium on the Arkansas side.

But of crash-priority importance I did *not* want to drift back down into Texas.

Problem: to navigate correctly at night with no map on a river a couple of kilometers wide, when your object is to reach a west bank you can't see . . . *without* giving any southing as you go.

Impossible?—the way the Mississippi winds around, like a snake with a broken back? But "impossible" is not a word one should use concerning the Mississippi River. There is one place where it is possible to make three short portages totaling less than ninety meters, float down the river in two bights totaling about thirty kilometers . . . *and end up more than one hundred kilometers up the river.*

No map, no sight of my destination—I knew only that I must go west and that I must not go south. So that is what I did. I stayed on my back and kept checking the stars to hold course west. I had no way of telling how much I might be losing to the south through the current, save for the certainty that, if and when the river turned south, my own progress west through the water would fetch me up on the bank on the Arkansas side.

And it did. An hour later—two hours later?—a lot of water later and Vega was high in the east but still far short of meridian, I realized that the bank was looming over me on my left side. I checked and corrected course west and kept on swimming. Shortly I bumped my head on a snag, reached behind me and grabbed it, pulled myself up, then pulled my way through endless snags to the bank.

Scrambling up on the bank was no problem as it was only half a meter high, about, at that point. The only hazard was that the mud was thick and loose underfoot. I managed it, stopped, and took stock.

Still inky-black all around with stars the only light. I could tell the smooth black of the water from the thick black of the brush behind me only by the faint glint of starlight on the water. Directions? Polaris was now blocked by cloud but the Big Dipper told me where it had to be and this was confirmed by Spica blazing in the south and Antares in the southeast.

This orientation by the stars told me that west sliced straight into that thick black brush.

My only alternative was to get back into the water, stick with the river . . . and wind up sometime tomorrow in Vicksburg.

No, thanks. I headed into the bush.

I'm going to skip rapidly over the next several hours. It may not have been the longest night of my life but it was surely the dullest. I am sure that there must be thicker and more dangerous jungles on Earth than the brush on the bottomland of the lower Mississippi. But I do not want to tackle them, especially without a machete (not even a Scout knife!).

I spent most of my time backing out, having decided, No, not through there—now how can I go around?—No, not on its *south* side!—how can I get around it to the north? My track was as contorted as the path of the river itself and my progress was possibly one kilometer per hour—or perhaps I exaggerate; it could have been less. Much of the time was spent reorienting, a necessity every few meters.

Flies, mosquitoes, gnats, crawly things I never saw, twice snakes underfoot that may have been water moccasins but I did not wait to find out, endless disturbed birds with a dozen different sorts of cries—birds that often flew up almost in my face to our mutual distress. My footing was usually mud and always included something to trip over, ankle-high, shin-high, or both.

Three times (four times?) I came to open water. Each time I held course west and when the water was deep enough I swam. Stagnant bayou mostly, but one stretch seemed to have a current and may have been a minor channel of the Mississippi. Once there was something large swimming by me. Giant catfish? Aren't they supposed to stay on the bottom? Alligator? But there aren't supposed to be *any* there at all. Perhaps it was the Loch Ness monster on tour; I never saw it, simply felt it—and levitated right out of the water through sheer fright.

About eight hundred years after the sinking of the *Skip* and the *Myrtle* came the dawn.

West of me about a kilometer was the high ground of the Arkansas side. I felt triumphant.

I also felt hungry, exhausted, dirty, insect-bitten, disreputable, and almost unbearably thirsty.

Five hours later I was the guest of Mr. Asa Hunter as a passenger in his Studebaker farm wagon hitched to a fine span of mules. We were approaching a small town named Eudora. I still had not had any sleep but I had had the next best and everything but—water, food, a wash-up. Mrs. Hunter had clucked over me, lent me a comb, and given me breakfast: basted fried eggs, home-cured bacon thick and fat, corn bread, butter, sorghum, milk, coffee made in a pot and settled with an eggshell—and to appreciate in fullness Mrs. Hunter's cooking I recommend swimming all night alternated with crawling through the thickets of Old Man River's bottomland mud. Ambrosia!

I ate wearing her wrapper as she insisted on rinsing out my bedraggled jump suit. It was dry by the time I was ready to leave, and I looked almost respectable.

I did not offer to pay the Hunters. There are human people who have very little but are rich in dignity and self-respect. Their hospitality is not for sale, nor is their charity. I am slowly learning to recognize this trait in human people who have it. In the Hunters it was unmistakable.

We crossed Macon Bayou and then the road dead-ended into a slightly wider road. Mr. Hunter stopped his mules, got down, came around to my side. "Miss, I'd thank you kindly to get down here."

I accepted his hand, let him hand me down. "Is something wrong, Mr. Hunter? Have I offended you?"

He answered slowly, "No, miss. Not at all." He hesitated. "You told us how your fishing boat was stove in by a snag."

"Yes?"

"Snags in the river are a pesky hazard." He paused. "Yesterday evening come sundown something bad happened on the river. Two explosions, about at Kentucky Bend. Big ones. Could see 'em and hear 'em from the house."

He paused again. I didn't say anything. My explanation of my presence and of my (deplorable) condition had been feeble at best. But the next best explanation was a flying saucer.

Mr. Hunter went on, "Wife and I have never had any words with the Imperial Police. We don't aim to. So, if you don't mind walking a short piece down this road to the left, you'll come to Eudora. And I'll turn my team around and go back to our place."

"I see. Mr. Hunter, I wish there were some way I could repay you and Mrs. Hunter."

"You can."

"Yes?" (Was he going to ask for money? No!)

"Someday you'll find somebody needs a hand. So give him a hand and think of us."

"Oh! I shall! I surely shall!"

"But don't bother to write to us about it. People who get mail get noticed. We don't crave to be noticed."

"I see. But I'll do it and think about you, not once but more than once."

"That's best. Bread cast upon the waters always comes back, miss. Mrs. Hunter told me to tell you that she plans to pray for you."

My eyes watered so quickly that I could not see. "Oh! And please tell her that I will remember her in my prayers. Both of you." (I had never prayed in my life. But I would, for the Hunters.)

"Thank y' kindly. I will tell her. Miss. May I offer you a word of advice and not have you take it amiss?"

"I need advice."

"You don't plan to stop in Eudora?"

"No. I must get north."

"So you said. Eudora's just a police station and a few shops. Lake Village is farther away but the Greyhound APV stops there. That's about twelve kilometers down the road to the right. If you can cover that distance between now and noon, you could catch the midday bus. But it's a dogtrottin' distance and a pretty hot day."

"I can do it. I will."

"Greyhound'll take you to Pine Bluff, even to Little Rock. Um. Bus costs money."

"Mr. Hunter, you've been more than kind. I have my credit card with me; I can pay for the bus." I had not come through the swim and the mud in very good shape but my credit cards, IDs, passport, and cash money had all been in that waterproof money belt Janet had given me so many light-years ago; all had come through untouched. Someday I would tell her.

"Good. Thought I'd better ask. One more thing. Folks around here mind their own business, mostly. If you just go straight aboard the Greyhound, the few nosy ones won't have any excuse to bother you. Better so, maybe. Well, good-bye and good luck."

I told him good-bye and got moving. I wanted to kiss him good-bye but strange women do not take liberties with such as Mr. Hunter.

I caught the noon APV and was in Little Rock at 12:52. An express capsule north was loading as I reached the tube station; I was in Saint Louis twenty-one minutes later. From a terminal booth in the tube station I called Boss's contact code to arrange for transportation to headquarters.

A voice answered, "The call code you have used is not in service. Remain in circuit and an operator—" I slapped the disconnect and got out fast.

I stayed in the underground city several minutes, walking at random and pretending to window-shop but putting distance between me and the tube station.

I found a public terminal in a shopping mall some distance away and tried the fallback call code. When the voice reached: "The call code you have used is not—" I slapped the disconnect but the voice failed to cut off. I ducked my head, dropped to my knees, got out of that booth, cutting to the right and being conspicuous, which I hate, but possibly avoiding being photographed through the terminal, which could be disaster.

I spent minutes mixing with the crowd. When I felt reasonably sure that no one was following me, I dropped down one level, entered the city's local tube system and went to East Saint Louis. I had one more top-emergency fallback call code, but I did not intend to use it without preparation.

Boss's new underground headquarters was just sixty minutes from anywhere but I did not know where it was. I mean to say that, when I left its infirmary to take a refresher course, the APV trip had taken exactly sixty minutes. When I returned it had taken sixty minutes. When I went on leave and asked to be placed to catch a capsule for Winnipeg, I had been dropped in Kansas City in exactly sixty minutes. And there was no way for a passenger to see out of an APV used for this.

By geometry, geography, and simplest knowledge of what an APV can do, Boss's new headquarters had to be someplace more or less around Des Moines—but in this case "more or less" meant a radius of at least a hundred kilometers. I did not conjecture. Nor did I conjecture as to which ones of us actually knew the location of HQ. It was a "need-to-know" and trying to guess how Boss decided such things was a waste of time.

In East Saint Louis I bought a light cloak with a hood, then a latex mask in a novelty shop, picking one that was not grotesque. Then I took careful pains to randomize my choice of terminal. I was of strong but not conclusive opinion that Boss had been hit again and this time smeared, and the only reason that I had not panicked was that I am trained not to panic until after the emergency.

Masked and hooded, I punched the last-resort call code. Same result and again the terminal could not be switched off. I turned my back on the pickup, pulled off that mask and dropped it on the floor, got out of there slow-march, around a corner, shed that cloak as I walked, folded it, shoved it into a trash can, went back to Saint Louis—

—where I, bold as brass, used my Imperial Bank of Saint Louis credit card to pay my tube fare to Kansas City. An hour earlier in Little Rock I had used it without hesitation but at that time I had had no suspicion that anything had happened to Boss—in fact I held a "religious" conviction that *nothing* could happen to Boss. ("Religious" = "absolute belief without proof.")

But now I was forced to operate on the assumption that something had indeed happened to Boss, which included the assumption that my Saint Louis MasterCard (based on Boss's credit, not my own) could drop dead on me at any moment. I might stick it into a slot to pay for something and have it burned out by a destruction bolt when the machine recognized the number.

So four hundred kilometers and fifteen minutes later I was in Kansas City. I never left the tube station. I made a free call at the information desk about service on the KC–Omaha–Sioux Falls–Fargo–Winnipeg tube and was told that there was full service to Pembina at the border, none beyond. Fifty-six minutes later I was at the British Canadian border directly south of Winnipeg. It was still early afternoon. Ten hours earlier I had been climbing up out of the bottomland of the Mississippi and wondering light-headedly whether I was in the Imperium or if I had floated back into Texas.

Now I was even more overpoweringly anxious to get out of the Imperium than I had been to get in. So far I had managed to stay one flea-hop ahead of the Imperial Police but there was no longer any doubt in my mind that they wanted to talk to me. I did not want to talk to them because I had heard tales about how they conducted an investigation. The laddies who had questioned me earlier this year had been moderately rough . . . but the Imperial Police were reputed to burn out a victim's brain.

XIX

Fourteen hours later I had moved only twenty-five kilometers east of where I had had to leave the tube system. An hour of that I had spent in shopping, most of an hour in eating, over two hours in close consultation with a specialist, a heavenly six hours in sleeping, and almost four in moving cautiously east parallel to the border fence without getting close to it—and now it was dawn and I did approach the fence, right up to it, and was walking it, a bored repairman.

Pembina is just a village; I had to go back to Fargo to find a specialist—a quick trip by local capsule. The specialist I wanted was the same sort as "Artists, Ltd." of Vicksburg save that such entrepreneurs do not advertise in the Imperium; it took time and some cautious grease to find him. His office was downtown near Main Avenue and University Drive but it was behind a more conventional business; it would not easily be noticed.

I was still wearing the faded blue neodenim jump suit I had been wearing when I dived off the *Skip to M'Lou*, not through any special affection for it but because a one-piece blue suit of coarse cloth is the nearest thing to an international unisex costume you can find. It will get by even at Ell-Five or in Luna City, where a monokini is more likely. Add a scarf and a smart housewife will wear it to shop; carry a briefcase and you are a respected businessman; squat with a hatful of pencils and it's a beggar's garb. Since it is hard to soil, easy to clean, won't wrinkle, and almost never wears out, it is ideal for a courier who wishes to fade into the scene and can't waste time or luggage on clothes.

To that jump suit had been added a greasy cap with "my" union badge pinned to it, a well-worn hip belt with old but serviceable tools, a bandolier of repair links over one shoulder and a torch kit to install them over the other.

Everything I had was well worn including my gloves. Zippered into my right hip pocket was an old leather wallet with IDs showing that I was "Hannah Jensen" of Moorhead. A worn newspaper clipping showed that I had been a high-school cheerleader; a spotted Red Cross card gave my blood type as O Rh pos sub 2 (which in fact it is) and credited me with having won my gallon pin—but the dates showed that I had neglected to donate for over six months.

Other mundane trivia gave Hannah a background in depth; she even carried a Visa card issued by Moorhead Savings and Loan Company—but on this item I had saved Boss more than a thousand crowns: Since I did not expect to use it, it lacked the invisible magnetic signature without which a credit card is merely a piece of plastic.

It was just full light and I had, I figured, a maximum of three hours to get through that fence—only that long because the real fence maintenance men started working then and I was most unanxious to meet one. Before that time Hannah Jensen should disappear . . . possibly to resurface in the late afternoon for a final effort. Today was go-for-broke; my cash crowns were used up. True, I still had my Imperium credit card—but I am extremely leery of electronic sleuths. Had my three attempts yesterday to call Boss, all with the same card, tripped some subprogram under which I could be identified? I seemed to have gotten away with using the card for tube fare immediately thereafter . . . but had I really escaped all electronic traps? I did not know and did not want to find out—I simply wanted to get through that fence.

I sauntered along, resisting a powerful urge to fall out of character by hurrying. I wanted a place where I could cut the fence without being watched, despite the fact that the ground was scorched for about fifty meters on each side of the fence. I had to accept that; what I wanted was a stretch shielded along the scorched band by trees and bush about like Normandy hedgerows.

Minnesota does not have Normandy hedgerows.

Northern Minnesota almost does not have trees—or at least not in the stretch of the border I was covering. I was eyeing a piece of fence, trying to tell myself that a wide reach of open space with no one in sight was just as good as being shielded, when a police APV came into sight cruising slowly west along the fence. I gave them a friendly wave and kept on trudging east.

They circled, came back, and squatted, about fifty meters from me. I turned and went toward them, reaching the car as the best boy got out, followed by his driver, and I saw by their uniforms (hell, damn, and spit) that they were not Minnesota Provincial Police but Imperials.

Best boy says to me, "What are you doing here this early?"

His tone was aggressive; I answered it to match: "I was *working*, until you interrupted me."

"The hell you say. You don't go on until eight hundred hours."

I answered, "Get the news, big man. That was *last* week. Two shifts now. First shift comes on at 'can.' Shifts change at noon; second shift goes off at 'can't.' "

"Nobody notified *us*."

"You want the Superintendent to write you a personal letter? Give me your badge number and I'll tell him you said so."

"None of your lip, slitch. I'd as lief run you in as look at you."

"Go ahead. A day's rest for me . . . while you explain why this stretch was not maintained."

"Stow it." They started climbing back in.

"Either of you turkeys got a toke?" I asked.

The driver said, "We don't hit on duty and neither should you."

"Brown nose," I answered politely.

The driver started to reply, but best boy slammed the lid, and they took off—right over my head, forcing me to duck. I don't think they liked me.

I went back to the fence while concluding that Hannah Jensen was not a lady. She had no excuse to be rude to the Greenies merely because they are unspeakably vile. Even black widows, body lice, and hyenas have to make a living although I could never see why.

I decided that my plans were not well thought out; Boss would not approve. Cutting that fence in broad daylight was too conspicuous. Better to pick a spot, then hide until dark, and return to it. Or spend the night on plan number two: Check the possibility of going under the fence at Roseau River.

I wasn't too crazy about plan number two. The lower reach of the Mississippi had been warm enough but these northern streams would chill a corpse. I had checked the Pembina late the day before yesterday. *Brrr!* A last resort.

So pick a piece of fence, decide exactly how you are going to cut it, then try to find some trees, wrap yourself in some nice warm leaves, and wait for dark. Rehearse every move, so that you go through that fence like pee through snow.

At this point I topped a slight rise and came face to face with another maintenance man, male type.

When in doubt, attack. "What the hell are *you* doing, buster?"

"I'm walking the fence. *My* stretch of the fence. What are *you* doing, sister?"

"Oh, fer Gossake! I'm not your sister. And you are either on the wrong stretch or the wrong shift." I noticed with unease that the well-dressed fence-walker carries a walkie-talkie. Well, I had not been one very long; I was still learning the job.

"Like hell," he answered. "Under the new schedule I come on at dawn; I'm relieved at noon. Maybe by you, huh? Yeah, that's probably it; you read the roster wrong. I had better call in."

"You do that," I said, moving toward him.

He hesitated. "On the other hand, maybe—" I did *not* hesitate.

I do not kill everyone with whom I have a difference of opinion and I would not want anyone reading this memoir to think that I do. I didn't even hurt him other than temporarily and not much; I merely put him to sleep rather suddenly.

From a roll on my belt I taped his hands behind him and fastened his ankles together. If I had had some wide surgical tape, I would have gagged him but all I had was two-centimeter mechanics friction tape, and I was far more anxious to cut fence than I was to keep him from yelling for help to the coyotes and jackrabbits. I got busy.

A torch good enough to repair fence will cut fence—but my torch was a bit better than that; I had bought it out the back door of Fargo's leading fence (the other sort of fence). It was a steel-cutting laser rather than the oxyacetylene job it appeared to be. In moments I had a hole big enough, barely, for Friday. I stooped to leave.

"Hey, take me with you!"

I hesitated. He was saying insistently that he was just as anxious to get away from the goddam Greenies as I was—untie me!

What I did next is matched in folly only by Lot's wife. I grabbed the knife at my belt, cut the tape at his wrists, at his ankles—dived through my scuttle hole and started to run. I didn't wait to see whether or not he came through, too.

There was one of the rare stands of trees about half a kilometer north of me; I headed that way at a new record speed. That heavy tool belt impeded me; I shucked it without slowing. A moment later I brushed that cap off and "Hannah Jensen" went back to Never-Never Land, as torch, gloves, and repair links were still in the Imperium. All that was left of her was a wallet I would jettison when I was not so busy.

I got well inside the trees, then circled back and found a place to observe my back track, as I was uncomfortably aware that I was wearing a tail.

My late prisoner was about halfway from fence to trees . . . and *two* APVs were homing in on him. The one closer to him carried the big Maple Leaf of British Canada. I could not see the insigne on the other as it was headed right toward me, coming *across* the international boundary.

The BritCan police car grounded; my quondam guest appeared to surrender without argument—reasonable, as the APV from the Imperium grounded immediately thereafter, at least two hundred meters inside British Canada—and, yes, Imperial Police—possibly the car that had stopped me.

I'm not an international lawyer but I'm sure wars have started over less. I held my breath, extended my hearing to the limit, and listened.

There were no international lawyers among those two sorts of police, either; the argument was noisy but not coherent. The Imperials were demanding surrender of the refugee under the doctrine of hot pursuit and a Mountie corporal was maintaining (correctly, it seemed to me) that hot pursuit applied only to criminals caught in the act, but the only "crime" here was entering British Canada not at a port of entry, a matter not lying in the jurisdiction of the Imperial Police. "Now get that crock off BritCan soil!"

The Greenie gave a monosyllabic nonresponse that annoyed the Mountie. He slammed the lid and spoke through his loudspeaker: "I arrest you for violation of British Canadian air and ground space. Get out and surrender. Do not attempt to take off."

Whereupon the Greenies' car took off at once and retreated across the international border—then went elsewhere. Which may have been exactly what the Mountie intended to accomplish. I held very still, as now they would have time to give their attention to me.

I assume conclusively that my companion escapee now paid me for his ticket through the fence: No search was made for me. Certainly he saw me run into the woods. But it is unlikely that the RCMP saw me. No doubt cutting the fence sounded alarms in police stations on both sides of the border; this would be a routine installation for electronics people—even to pinpointing the break— and so I had assumed in planning to do it *fast*.

But counting the number of warm bodies that passed through a gap would be a separate electronics problem—not impossible but an added expense that might not be considered worthwhile. As may be, my nameless companion did not snitch on me; no one came looking for me. After a time a BritCan car fetched a repair crew; I saw them pick up the tool belt I had discarded near the fence. After they left another repair crew showed up on the Imperium side; they inspected the repair and went away.

I wondered a bit about tool belts. On thinking back I could not recall seeing such a belt on my erstwhile prisoner when he surrendered. I concluded that he had had to shed his belt to go through the fence; that hole was just barely big enough for Friday; for him it must have been a jam fit.

Reconstruction: The BritCans saw one belt, on their side; the Greenies saw one belt, on their side. Neither side had any reason to assume that more than one wetback had passed through the hole . . . as long as my late prisoner kept mum.

Pretty decent of him, I think. Some men would have held a grudge over that little tap I had to give him.

I stayed in those woods until dark, thirteen tedious hours. I did not want to be seen by anyone until I reached Janet (and, with luck, Ian); an illegal immigrant does not seek publicity. It was a long day but in middle training my mind-control guru had taught me to cope with hunger, thirst, and boredom when it is necessary to remain quiet, awake, and alert. When it was full dark I started out. I knew the terrain as well as one can from maps, as I had studied all of it most carefully in Janet's house less than two weeks earlier. The problem ahead of me was neither complex nor difficult: move approximately one hundred and ten kilometers on foot before dawn while avoiding notice.

The route was simple. I must move east a trifle to pick up the road from Lancaster in the Imperium to La Rochelle in British Canada, at the port of entry—easy to spot. Go north to the outskirts of Winnipeg, swing to the left around the city and pick up the north-south road to the port. Stonewall was just a loud shout from there, with the Tormey estate nearby. All of the last and more difficult part I knew not just from maps but from having recently been over it in a surrey with nothing to distract me but a little friendly groping.

It was just dawn when I spotted the Tormey outer gates. I was tired but not in too bad shape. I can maintain the walk-jog-run-walk-jog-run routine for twenty-four hours if necessary and have done so in training; keeping it up all night is acceptable. Mostly my feet hurt and I was very thirsty. I punched the announcing button in happy relief.

And at once heard: "Captain Ian Tormey speaking. This is a recording. This house is protected by the Winnipeg Werewolves Security Guards, Incorporated. I have retained this firm because I do not consider their reputation for being trigger-happy to be justified; they are simply zealous in protecting their clients. Calls coded to this house will not be relayed but mail sent here will be forwarded. Thank you for listening."

And thank *you*, Ian! Oh, damn, damn, damn! I knew that I had no reason to expect them to remain at home . . . but my mind had never entertained the thought that they might *not* be at home. I had "transferred," as the shrinks call it; with my Ennzedd family lost,

Boss missing and perhaps dead, the Tormey estate was "home" and Janet the mother I had never had.

I wished that I were back on the Hunters' farm, bathed in the warm protectiveness of Mrs. Hunter. I wished that I were in Vicksburg, sharing mutual loneliness with Georges.

In the meantime the Sun was rising and soon the roads would begin to fill and I was an illegal alien with almost no BritCan dollars and a deep need not to be noticed, not to be picked up and questioned, and light-headed from fatigue and lack of sleep and hunger and thirst.

But I did not have to make difficult decisions as one was forced on me, Hobson's choice. I must again hole up like an animal, and quickly, before traffic filled the roads.

Woods are not common anywhere near Winnipeg but I recalled some hectares left wild, back and around to the left, off the main road, and more or less behind the Tormey place—uneven land, below the low hill on which Janet had built. So I went in that direction, encountering one delivery wagon (milk) but no other traffic.

Once abreast the scrub I left the road. The footing became very uneven, a series of gullies, and I was going "across the furrows." But quickly I encountered something even more welcome than trees: a tiny stream, so narrow I could step across it.

Which I did, but not until I had drunk from it. Clean? Probably contaminated but I gave it not a thought; my curious "birthright" protects me against most infection. The water tasted clean and I drank quite a lot and felt much better physically—but not the sick weight in my heart.

I went deeper into the scrub, looking for a place where I could not only hide but could dare risk sleeping. Six hours of sleep two nights ago seemed awfully far away but the trouble with hiding in the wild this close to a big city is that a troop of Boy Scouts is awfully likely to come tromping through and step on your face. So I hunted for a spot not only bushy but inaccessible.

I found it. Quite a steep stretch up one side of a gully and made still more inaccessible by thornbushes, which I located by Braille.

Thornbushes?

It took me about ten minutes to find it as it looked like an exposed face of a boulder left over from the time when the great ice flow had planed all this country down. But, when I looked closely, it did not look quite like rock. It took still longer to get fingers into any purchase and lift it, then it swung up easily, partly counterbalanced. I ducked inside quickly and let it fall back into place—

—and found myself in darkness save for fiery letters: PRIVATE PROPERTY—KEEP OUT

I stood very still and thought. Janet had told me that the switch that disarmed the deadly booby traps was "concealed a short distance inside."

How long is a "short distance"?

And how concealed?

It was concealed well enough simply because the place was dark as ink except for those ominous glowing letters. They might as well have spelled "All hope abandon, ye who enter here."

So whip out your pocket torch, Friday, powered with its own tiny lifetime Shipstone, and search. But don't go too far!

There was indeed a torch in a jumpbag I had left behind me in the *Skip to M'Lou*. It might even be shining, entertaining fish on the bottom of the Mississippi. And I knew that there were other torches stockpiled straight down this black tunnel.

I didn't even have a match.

If I had a Boy Scout, I could make a fire by rubbing his hind legs together. Oh, shut up, Friday!

I sank down to the floor and let myself cry a little. Then I stretched out on that (hard, cold) (welcome and soft) concrete floor and went to sleep.

XX

I woke up a long time later and the floor was indeed hard and cold. But I felt so enormously rested that I did not mind. I stood up and rubbed the kinks out and realized that I no longer felt hopeless—just hungry.

The tunnel was now well lighted.

That glowing sign still warned me not to go any farther but the tunnel was no longer black; the illumination seemed about equal to a well-lighted living room. I looked around for the source of the light.

Then my brain came back into gear. The only illumination came from the glowing sign; my eyes had adjusted while I slept. I understand that human people also experience this phenomenon, but possibly to a lesser degree.

I started to hunt for the switch.

I stopped and started using my brain instead. That's harder work than using muscles but it's quieter and burns fewer calories. It's the only thing that separates us from the apes, although just barely. If I were a concealed switch, where would I be?

The significant parameters of this switch had to be that it must be well enough hidden to frustrate intruders but it nevertheless must save Janet's life and that of her husbands. What did that tell me?

It would not be too high for Janet to reach; therefore I could reach it, we are much the same size. So that switch was in my reach without using a stool.

Those floating, glowing letters were about three meters inside the door. The switch could not be much past that point because Janet had told me that the second warning, the one that promised death, was triggered not far inside—"a few meters" she had said. "A few" is rarely over ten.

Janet would not hide the switch so thoroughly that one of her husbands, dodging for his life, would have to remember *exactly* where it was. The simple knowledge that there was such a switch must be sufficient clue to let him find it. But any intruder who did not know that there was such a switch must not notice it.

I moved down the tunnel until I stood right under that glowing sign, looked up. The light from that warning sign made it easy to see anywhere but that small part of the tunnel arch just above the letters. Even with my dark-adjusted and enhanced vision I could not see the ceiling directly over the sign.

I reached up and felt the ceiling where I could not see it. My fingers encountered something that felt like a button, possibly the end of a solenoid. I pushed it.

The warning sign blinked out; ceiling lights came on, shining far down the tunnel.

Frozen food and the means to cook it and big towels and hot and cold running water and a terminal in the Hole on which I could get the current news and summaries of past news . . . books and music and cash money stored in the Hole against emergency and weapons and Shipstones and ammunition and clothes of all sorts that fit me because they fitted Janet and a clock-calendar in the terminal that told me that I had slept thirteen hours before the hardness of the concrete "bed" woke me and a comfy soft bed that invited me to finish the night by sleeping again after I had bathed and eaten and satisfied my hunger for news . . . a feeling of total security that let me calm down until I no longer had to use mind control to suppress my real feelings in order to function. . . .

The news told me that British Canada had scaled the emergency down to "limited emergency." The border with the Imperium remained closed. The Québec border was still closely controlled but permits were granted for any legitimate business. The remaining dispute between the two nations lay in how much reparation Québec should pay for what was now admitted to be a military attack made through error and/or stupidity. The internment order was still in effect but over 90 percent of Québecois internees had been released on their own paroles . . . and about 20 percent of internees from the Imperium. So I had done well to dodge because, no question about it, I was a suspicious character.

But it looked as if Georges could come home whenever he wished. Or were there angles I did not understand?

The Council for Survival promised a third round of "educational" killings ten days plus or minus two days from the last round. The Stimulators followed this a day later with a matching statement, one which again condemned the so-called Council for Survival. The Angels of the Lord did not this time make any announcement, or at least none that issued through the BritCan Data Net.

Again I had tentative conclusions, shaky ones: The Stimulators were a dummy organization, all propaganda, no field operatives. The Angels of the Lord were dead and/or on the run. The Council for Survival had extremely wealthy backing willing to pay for more unprofessional stooges to be sacrificed in mostly futile attempts—but that was merely a guess, to be dropped in a hurry if the third round of attacks turned out to be efficient and professional—which I did not expect, but I have a long record for being wrong.

I still couldn't decide who was back of this silly reign of terror. It could not be (I felt certain) a territorial nation; it might be a multinational, or a consortium, although I could see no sense in it. It could even be one or more extremely wealthy individuals—if they had holes in their heads.

Under "retrieval" I also punched "Imperium" and "Mississippi River" and "Vicksburg" as singles, each pair, and the triple. Negative. I added in the names of the two vessels and tried all the combinations. Still negative. Apparently what had happened to me and several hundred others had been suppressed. Or was it considered trivial?

Before I left I wrote Janet a note telling her what clothes I had taken, how many BritCan dollars I had taken and added that amount to what she had given me earlier, and I detailed what I had charged to her Visa card: one capsule fare Winnipeg to Vancouver, one shuttle fare Vancouver to Bellingham, nothing since. (Or had I paid my fare to San Jose with her card, or was that when Georges started being masterful? My expense accounts were in the bottom of the Mississippi.)

Having taken enough of Janet's cash to get me out of British Canada (I hoped!) I was strongly tempted to leave her Visa card with my note to her. But a credit card is an insidious thing—just a cheap little piece of plastic . . . that can equate to great stacks of gold bullion. It was up to me to protect that card personally and at any cost, until I could place it in Janet's hand. Nothing less was honest.

A credit card is a leash around your neck. In the world of credit cards a person has *no* privacy . . . or at best protects her privacy only with great effort and much chicanery. Besides that, do you *ever* know what the computer network is doing when you poke your card into a slot? I don't. I feel much safer with cash. I've never heard of anyone who had much luck arguing with a computer.

It seems to me that credit cards are a curse. But I'm not human and probably lack the human viewpoint (in this as in so many, many other things).

I set out the next morning, dressed in a beautiful three-piece pantsuit in powder-blue glass (I felt sure that Janet was beautiful in it and it made me feel beautiful despite the evidence of mirrors), and intending to hire a rig in nearby Stonewall, only to find that I had a choice of a horsedrawn omnibus or a Canadian Railways APV, both going to the tube station, Perimeter and McPhillips, where Georges and I had left on our informal honeymoon. Much as I prefer horses I picked the faster method.

Going into town would not let me pick up my luggage, still in bond at the port. But was it possible to pick it up from transit bond without being pinpointed as an alien from the Imperium? I decided to order it forwarded from *outside* British Canada. Besides, those bags were packed in New Zealand. If I could live without them this long, I could live without them indefinitely. How many people have died because they would not abandon their baggage?

I have this moderately efficient guardian angel who sits on my shoulder. Only days ago Georges and I had walked right up to the proper turnstile, stuck Janet's and Ian's credit cards into the slot without batting an eye, and zipped merrily to Vancouver.

This time, although a capsule was then loading, I discovered that I was headed on past the turnstiles toward the British Canadian Tourist Bureau travel office. The place was busy, so there was no danger of an attendant rubbernecking what I was doing—but I waited until I could get a console in a corner. One became available; I sat down and punched for capsule to Vancouver, then stuck Janet's card into the slot.

My guardian angel was awake that day; I snatched the card out, got it out of sight fast, and hoped that no one had caught the stink of scorched plastic. And I left, quick-march and nose in the air.

At the turnstiles, when I asked for a ticket to Vancouver, the attendant was busy studying the sports page of the *Winnipeg Free Press*. He lowered his paper slightly, peered at me over it. "Why don't you use your card like everyone else?"

"Do you have tickets to sell? Is this money legal tender?"

"That's not the point."

"It is to me. Please sell me a ticket. And give me your name and clock number in accordance with that notice posted back of your head." I handed him the exact amount.

"Here's your ticket." He ignored my demand for his identification; I ignored his failure to comply with the regulations. I did not want a hooraw with his supervisor; I simply wanted to create a diversion from my own conspicuous eccentricity in using money rather than a credit card.

The capsule was crowded but I did not have to stand; a Galahad left over from the last century stood up and offered me his seat. He was young and not bad-looking and clearly was being gallant because he classed me as having the apposite female qualities.

I accepted with a smile and he stood over me and I did what I could to repay him by leaning forward a bit and letting him look down my neckline. Young Lochinvar seemed to feel repaid—he stared the whole way—and it cost me nothing and was no trouble. I appreciated his interest and what it got me in comfort—sixty minutes is a long time to stand up to the heavy surges of an express capsule.

As we got out at Vancouver he asked me if I had any plans for lunch. Because, if I didn't, he knew of a really great place, the Bayshore Inn. Or if I liked Japanese or Chinese food—

I said that I was sorry but I had to be in Bellingham by noon.

Instead of accepting the brush-off, his face lit up. "That's a happy coincidence! I'm going to Bellingham, too, but I thought I would wait until after lunch. We can have lunch together in Bellingham. Is it a deal?"

(Isn't there something in international law about crossing international boundaries for immoral purposes? But can the simple, straightforward rut of this youngster correctly be classed as "immoral"? An artificial person *never* understands human people's sexual codes; all we can do is memorize them and try to stay out of trouble. But this isn't easy; human sexual codes are as contorted as a plate of spaghetti.)

My attempt at polite brush-off having failed, I was forced to decide quickly whether to be rude or to go along with his clear purpose. I scolded myself: Friday, you are a big girl now; you know better. If you intended to give him no hope whatever of getting you into bed, the time to back out was when he offered you his seat at Winnipeg.

I made one more attempt: "It's a deal," I answered, "if I am allowed to pay the check, with no argument." This was a dirty trick on my part, as we both knew that, if he let me pay for lunch, that canceled his investment in me of one hour of standing up and hanging on and fighting the surge of the capsule. But barnyard protocol did not allow him to claim the investment; his act of gallantry was supposed to be disinterested, knightly, no reward expected.

The dirty, sneaking, underhanded, rutty scoundrel proceeded to chuck protocol.

"All right," he answered.

I swallowed my astonishment. "No argument later? It's *my* check?"

"No argument," he agreed. "Obviously you don't want to be under the nominal obligation of the price of a lunch even though I issued the invitation and therefore should have a host's privilege. I don't know what I have done to annoy you but I will not force on you even a trivial obligation. There is a McDonald's at surface level as we arrive in Bellingham; I'll have a Big Mac and a Coke. You pay for it. Then we can part friends."

I answered, "I'm Marjorie Baldwin; what is your name?"

"I'm Trevor Andrews, Marjorie."

"Trevor. That's a nice name. Trevor, you are dirty, sneaky, underhanded, and despicable. So take me to the best restaurant in Bellingham, ply me with fine liquor and gourmet food, and *you* pay the check. I'll give you a fair chance to sell your fell designs. But I don't think that you will get me into bed; I'm not feeling receptive."

That last was a lie; I was feeling receptive and very rutty—had he possessed my enhanced sense of smell he would have been certain of it. Just as I was certain of his rut toward me. A human male cannot possibly dissemble with an AP female who has enhanced senses. I learned this at menarche. But of course I am never offended by male rut. At most I sometimes imitate a human woman's behavior by pretending to be offended. I don't do this often and tend to avoid it; I'm not that convincing an actress.

From Vicksburg to Winnipeg I had felt no sexual urge. But, with a double night's sleep, a hot, hot bath with lots of soap, plenty of food, my body now was restored to its normal behavior. So why was I lying about it to this harmless stranger? "Harmless?" In any rational sense, yes. Short of corrective surgery I am sterile. I am not inclined to catch even a sniffle and I am specifically immunized against the four commonest venereal diseases. I was taught in crèche to class coition with eating, drinking, breathing, sleeping, playing, talking, cuddling—the pleasant necessities that make life a happiness instead of a burden.

I lied to him because human rules call for a lie at that point in the dance—and I was passing as human and didn't dare be honestly myself.

He blinked down at me. "You feel that I would be wasting my investment?"

"I'm afraid so. I'm sorry."

"You're mistaken. I never try to get a woman into bed; if she wants me in her bed, she will find some way to let me know. If she does *not* want me there, then I would not enjoy being there. But you seem to be unaware of the fact that it is worth the price of a good lunch just to sit and look at you, while ignoring any silly babble that comes out of your mouth."

"Babble! That had better be a *very* good restaurant. Let's catch the shuttle."

I had thought that I might have to argue my way through the barrier on arrival.

But the CHI officer looked most carefully at Trevor's IDs before validating his tourist card, then barely glanced at my San Jose MasterCard and waved me on through. I waited for Trevor just past the CHI barrier and looked at the sign THE BREAKFAST BAR while feeling double *déjà vu*.

Trevor joined me. "If I had seen," he said mournfully, "that gold card you were flashing just now, I would not have offered to pay for the lunch. You're a wealthy heiress."

"Now look, buster," I answered, "a deal's a deal. You told me it was worth the price just to sit and drool over me. In spite of my 'babble.' I'm willing to cooperate to the extent of easing the neckline a little. One button, maybe two. But I won't let you back out. Even a rich heiress likes to show a profit now and then."

"Oh, the shame and the pity of it all!"

"Quit complaining. Where's this gourmet restaurant?"

"Well, now— Marjorie, I'm forced to admit that I don't know the restaurants in this glittering metropolis. Will you name the one you prefer?"

"Trevor, your seduction technique is terrible."

"So my wife says."

"I thought you had that harness-broken look. Get out her picture. Back in a moment; I'm going to find out where we eat."

I caught the CHI officer between shuttles, asked him for the name of the best restaurant. He looked thoughtful. "This isn't Paris, you know."

"I noticed."

"Or even New Orleans. If I were you, I would go to the Hilton dining room."

I thanked him, went back to Trevor. "We're eating in the dining room, two floors up. Unless you want to send out your spies. Now let's see her picture."

He showed me a wallet picture. I looked at it carefully, then gave a respectful whistle. Blondes intimidate me. When I was little, I thought I could get to be that color if I scrubbed hard enough. "Trevor, with that at home why are you picking up loose women on the streets?"

"Are you loose?"

"Quit trying to change the subject."

"Marjorie, you wouldn't believe me and you would babble. Let's go up to the dining room before all the martinis dry up."

Lunch was okay but Trevor did not have Georges' imagination, knowledge of cooking, and skill at intimidating a maître d'hôtel. Without Georges' flair the food was good, standard, North American cuisine, the same in Bellingham as in Vicksburg.

I was preoccupied; discovering that Janet's credit card had been invalidated had upset me almost more than the horrid disappointment of not finding Ian and Janet at home. Was Janet in trouble? *Was she dead?*

And Trevor had lost some of the cheerful enthusiasm a stud should display when the game is afoot. Instead of staring lecherously at me, he too seemed preoccupied. Why the change in manner? My demand to see a picture of his wife? Had I made him self-conscious thereby? It seems to me that a man should not engage in the hunt unless he is on such terms with his wife or wives that he can recount the lurid details at home to be giggled over. Like Ian. I don't expect a man to "protect my reputation" because, to the best of my knowledge and belief, they never do. If I want a man to refrain from discussing my sweaty clumsiness in bed, the only solution is to stay out of bed with him.

Besides, Trevor had mentioned his wife first, hadn't he? I reviewed it—yes, he had.

After lunch he perked up some. I was telling him to come back here after his business appointment because I was punching in as a guest in order to have comfort as well as privacy in making satellite calls (true) and that I might stay overnight (also true), so come back and call me and I would meet him in the lounge (conditionally true—I was so lonely and troubled I suspected that I would tell him to come straight up).

He answered, "I'll call first so that you can get that man out but I'll come straight up. No need to make the trip twice. But I'll send the bubbly up; I won't carry it."

"Hold it," I said. "You have not yet sold me your nefarious purpose. All I promised was the opportunity to present your sales talk. In the lounge. Not in my bedroom."

"Marjorie, you're a hard woman."

"No, you're a hard man. I know what I'm doing." A sudden satori told me that I did know. "How do you feel about artificial persons? Would you want your sister to marry one?"

"Do you know one who might be willing to? Sis is getting to be a bit long in the tooth; she can't afford to be particular."

"Don't try to evade me. Would *you* marry one?"

"What would the neighbors think? Marjorie, how do you know I haven't? You saw my wife's picture. Artifacts are supposed to make the very best wives, horizontally or vertically."

"Concubines, you mean. It isn't necessary to marry them. Trevor, you not only are not married to one; you don't know anything about them but the popular myths . . . or you wouldn't say 'artifact' when the subject is 'artificial persons.' "

"I'm sneaky, underhanded, and despicable. I misused the term so that you would not suspect that I am one."

"Oh, babble! You aren't one, or I would know it. And while you probably would go to bed with one, you wouldn't dream of marrying one. This is a futile discussion; let's adjourn it. I need about two hours; don't be surprised if my room terminal is busy. Tape a message and curl up with a good drink; I'll be down as soon as possible."

I punched in at the desk and went up, not to the bridal suite—in the absence of Georges that lovely extravagance would have made me *triste*—but to a very nice room with a good, big, wide bed, a luxury I had ordered from a deep suspicion that Trevor's low-key (almost reverse) salesmanship was going to cause him to wind up in it. The difficult louse.

I put the thought aside and got to work.

I called the Vicksburg Hilton. No, Mr. and Mrs. Perreault had punched out. No, no forwarding address. Sorree!

So was I, and that synthetic computer voice was no comfort. I called McGill University in Montréal and wasted twenty minutes "learning" that, Yes, Dr. Perreault was a senior member of this university but was now at the University of Manitoba. The only new fact was that this Montréal computer synthesized English or French with equal ease and always answered in the language in which it was addressed. Very clever, these electron pushers—too clever, in my opinion.

I tried Janet's (Ian's) call code in Winnipeg, learned that their terminal was out of service at the subscribers' request. I wondered why I had been able to receive news on the terminal in the Hole earlier this day. Did "out of service" mean only "no incoming calls"? Was such arcanum a close-held secret of S.T. and T.?

ANZAC Winnipeg bounced me around through parts of its computer meant for the traveling public before I got a human voice to admit that Captain Tormey was on leave because of the Emergency and the interruption of flights to New Zealand.

Ian's Auckland code answered only with music and an invitation to record a message, which was no surprise as Ian would not be there until semiballistic service resumed. But I had thought that I might catch Betty and/or Freddie.

How could one go to New Zealand with the SBs out of service? You can't ride a seahorse; they're too small. Did those big waterborne, Shipstone-driven freighters ever carry passengers? I didn't think they had accommodations. Hadn't I heard somewhere that some of them didn't even have crews?

I believed that I had a detailed knowledge of ways to travel superior to the professional knowledge of travel agents because, as a courier, I often moved around by means that tourists can't use and ordinary commercial travelers don't know about. It vexed me to realize that I had never given thought to how to outwit the fates when all SBs are grounded. But there is a way, there is *always* a way. I ticked it off in my mind as a problem to solve—later.

I called the University of Sydney, spoke with a computer, but at last got a human voice that admitted knowing Professor Farnese but he was on sabbatical leave. No, private call codes and addresses were never given out—sorry. Perhaps customer service might help me.

The Sydney information service computer seemed lonely, as it was willing to chat with me endlessly—anything but admit that either Federico or Elizabeth Farnese was in its net. I listened to a sales pitch for the World's Biggest Bridge (it isn't) and the World's Grandest Opera House (it is), so come Down Under and— I switched off reluctantly; a friendly computer with a Strine accent is better company than most people, human or my sort.

I then tackled the one I had hoped to be able to skip: Christchurch. There was a probability that Boss's HQ had sent word to me care of my former family when the move was made—if it was a move and not a total disaster. There was a very remote possibility that Ian, unable to send a message to me in the Imperium, would send one to my former home in hopes that it would be forwarded. I recalled that I had given him my Christchurch call code when he gave me the code for his Auckland flat. So I called my erstwhile home—

—and got the shock that one gets in stepping on a step that isn't there. "Service is discontinued at the terminal you have signaled. Calls are not being relayed. In emergency please signal Christchurch—" A code followed that I recognized as Brian's office.

I found myself doing the time-zone correction backward to get a wrong answer that would let me put off calling—then I snapped out of it. It was afternoon here, just past fifteen, so it was tomorrow morning in New Zealand, just past ten, a most likely time of day for Brian to be in. I punched his call, got a satellite hold of only a few seconds, then found myself staring into his astonished face. "Marjorie!"

"Yes," I agreed. "Marjorie. How are you?"

"Why are you calling me?"

I said, "Brian, please! We were married seven years; can't we at least speak politely with each other?"

"Sorry. What can I do for you?"

"I am sorry to disturb you at work but I called the house and found the terminal out of service. Brian, as you no doubt know from the news, communications with the Chicago Imperium have been interrupted by the Emergency. The assassinations. What the newscasters have been calling Red Thursday. As a result of this I am in California; I never did reach my Imperium address. Can you tell me anything about mail or messages that may have come for me? You see, nothing has reached me."

"I really could not say. Sorry."

"Can't you even tell me whether anything had to be forwarded? Just to know that a message had been forwarded would help me in tracing it."

"Let me think. There would have been all that money you drew out—no, you took the draft for that with you."

"What money?"

"The money you demanded we return to you—or be faced with an open scandal. A bit more than seventy thousand dollars. Marjorie, I am surprised that you have the gall to show your face . . . when your misbehavior, your lies, and your cold cupidity destroyed our family."

"Brian, what in the world are you talking about? I have not lied to anyone, I don't think I have misbehaved, and I have not taken one penny out of the family. 'Destroyed the family' *how?* I was kicked out of the family, out of a clear blue sky—kicked out and sent packing, all in a matter of minutes. I certainly did not 'destroy the family.' Explain yourself."

Brian did, in cold and dreary detail. My misbehavior was all of a piece with my lies, of course, that ridiculous allegation that I was a living artifact, not human, and thereby I had forced the family to ask for an annulment. I tried to remind him that I had proved to him that I was enhanced; he brushed it aside. What I recalled, what he recalled, did not match. As for the money, I was lying again; he had seen the receipt with my signature.

I interrupted to tell him that any signature that appeared to be mine on any such receipt had to be a forgery as I had not received a single dollar.

"You are accusing Anita of forgery. Your boldest lie yet."

"I'm not accusing Anita of anything. But I received no money from the family."

I *was* accusing Anita and we both knew it. And possibly accusing Brian as well. I recalled once that Vickie had said that Anita's nipples erected only over fat credit balances . . . and I had shushed her and told her not to be catty. But there were hints from others that

Anita was frigid in bed—a condition that an AP can't understand. In retrospect it did seem possible that her total passion was for the family, its financial success, its public prestige, its power in the community.

If so, she must hate me. I did not destroy the family, but kicking me out appeared to be the first domino in its collapse. Almost immediately after I left, Vickie went to Nuku'alofa . . . and instructed a solicitor to sue for divorce and financial settlement. Then Douglas and Lispeth left Christchurch, married each other separately, then entered the same sort of suit.

One tiny crumb of comfort. I learned from Brian that the vote against me had not been six to nothing but seven to nothing. An improvement? Yes. Anita had ruled that voting must be by shares; the major stockholders, Brian, Bertie, and Anita, had voted first, casting seven votes against me, a clear majority to expel me— whereupon Doug, Vickie, and Lispeth had abstained from voting.

A very small crumb of comfort, however. They had not bucked Anita, not tried to stop her, they had not even warned me of what was afoot. They abstained . . . then stood aside and let the sentence be executed.

I asked Brian about the children—and was told bluntly that they were none of my business. He then said that he was quite busy and must switch off, but I held him for one more question: What was done with the cats?

He looked about to explode. "Marjorie, are you utterly heartless? When your acts have caused so much pain, so much real tragedy, you want to know about something as trivial as cats?"

I restrained my anger. "I do want to know, Brian."

"I think they were sent to the SPCA. Or it might have been to the medical school. Good-bye! Please do not call me again."

"The medical school—" Mister Underfoot tied to a surgical table while a medical student took him apart with a knife? I am not a vegetarian and I am not going to argue against the use of animals in science and in teaching. But if it must be done, dear God if there is One anywhere, don't let it be done to animals who have been brought up to think they are people!

SPCA or medical school, Mister Underfoot and the younger

cats were almost certainly dead. Nevertheless, if SBs had been running, I would have risked going back to British Canada to catch the next trajectory for New Zealand in the forlorn hope of saving my old friend. But without modern transportation Auckland was farther away than Luna City. Not even a forlorn hope—

I dug deep into mind-control training and put matters I could not help out of my mind—

—and found that Mister Underfoot was still brushing against my leg.

On the terminal a red light was blinking. I glanced at the time, noted that it had been just about the two hours I had estimated; that light was almost certainly Trevor.

So make up your mind, Friday. Put cold water on your eyes and go down and let him try to persuade you? Or tell him to come on up, take him straight to bed, and cry on him? At first, that is. You certainly don't feel lecherous this minute . . . but tuck your face into a nice, warm male shoulder and let your feelings sag and pretty soon you will feel eager. You know that. Female tears are reputed to be a powerful aphrodisiac to most men and your own experience bears that out. (Crypto-sadism? Machismo? Who cares? It works.)

Invite him up. Have some liquor sent up. Maybe even put on some lip paint, try to look sexy. No, the hell with lip paint; it would not last long anyway. Invite him up; take him to bed. Cheer yourself up by doing your damnedest to cheer him up. Give it everything you've got!

I fitted a smile onto my face and answered the terminal.

And found myself speaking to the hotel's robot voice: "We are holding a box of flowers for you. May we send them up?"

"Certainly." (No matter who or what, a box of flowers is better than a slap in the belly with a wet fish.)

Shortly the dumbwaiter buzzed; I went to it and took out a floral package as big as a baby's coffin, put it on the floor to open it.

Long-stemmed, dusky red roses! I decided to give Trevor a better time than Cleopatra ever managed on her best days.

After admiring them I opened the envelope that came with them, expecting just a card with perhaps a line asking me to call the lounge, or such.

No, a note, almost a letter:

Dear Marjorie,

    I hope that these roses will be at least as welcome as I would have been.

["—would have been"? What the devil?]

    I must confess that I have run away. Something came up that made me realize that I must desist from my attempts to force my company on you.

    I am not married. I don't know who that pretty lady is; the picture is just a prop. As you pointed out, my sort is not considered suitable for marriage. I'm an artificial person, dear lady. "My mother was a test tube; my father was a knife." So I should not be making passes at human women. I pass for human, yes, but I would rather tell you the truth than to continue to try to pass with you—then have you learn the truth later. As you would, eventually, as I am the dirt-proud sort who would sooner or later tell you.

    So I would rather tell you now than hurt you later.

    My family name is not Andrews, of course, as my sort do not have families.

    But I can't help wishing that you were an AP yourself. You really are sweet (as well as extremely sexy) and your tendency to babble about matters, such as APs, that you don't understand, is probably not your fault. You remind me of a little fox terrier bitch I once had. She was cute and very affectionate, but quite willing to fight the whole world by herself if that was the program for the day. I confess to liking dogs and cats better than most people; they never hold it against me that I'm not human.

Do enjoy the roses,
Trevor

I wiped my eyes and blew my nose and went down fast and rushed through the lounge and then through the bar and then down one floor to the shuttle terminal and stood by the turnstiles leading to the departing shuttles . . . and stood there, and waited, and waited, and waited some more, and a policeman began eyeing me and finally he came over and asked me what I wanted and did I need help?

I told him the truth, or some of it, and he let me be. I waited and waited and he watched me the whole time. Finally he came over again and said, "Look here, if you insist on treating this as your beat, I'm going to have to ask to see your license and your medical certificate, and take you in if either one is not in order. I don't want to do that; I've got a daughter at home about your age and I'd like to think that a cop would give her a break. Anyhow you ought not to be in the business; anybody can see from your face that you're not tough enough for it."

I thought of showing him that gold credit card—I doubt that there is a streetwalker anywhere who carries a gold credit card. But the old dear really did think that he was taking care of me and I had humiliated enough people for one day. I thanked him and went up to my room.

Human people are so cocksure that they can always spot an AP— *blah!* We can't even spot each other. Trevor was the only man I had ever met whom I could have married with an utterly clear conscience—and I had chased him away.

But he was too sensitive!

Who is too sensitive? *You* are, Friday.

But, damn it, most humans do discriminate against our sort. Kick a dog often enough and he becomes awfully jumpy. Look at my sweet Ennzedd family, the finks. Anita probably felt self-righteous about cheating me—I'm not human.

Score for the day: Humans 9—Friday 0.

Where is Janet?

XXI

After a short nap that I spent standing on an auction block, waiting to be sold, I woke up—woke up because prospective buyers were insisting on inspecting my teeth and I finally bit one and the auctioneer started giving me a taste of the whip and woke me. The Bellingham Hilton looked awfully good.

Then I made the call I should have made first. But the other calls had to be made anyhow and this call cost too much and would have been unnecessary if my last call had paid off. Besides, I don't like to phone the Moon; the time lag upsets me.

So I called Ceres and South Africa Acceptances, Boss's banker— or one of them. The one who took care of my credit and paid my bills.

After the usual hassle with synthetic voices that seemed more deliberately frustrating than ever through the speed-of-light lag, I finally reached a human being, a beautiful female creature who clearly (it seemed to me) had been hired to be a decorative receptionist—one-sixth gee is far more effective than a bra. I asked her to let me speak to one of the bank's officers.

"You are speaking to one of the vice-presidents," she answered. "You managed to convince our computer that you needed help from a responsible officer. That's quite a trick; that computer is stubborn. How may I help you?"

I told a portion of my unlikely story. "So it took a couple of weeks to get inside the Imperium and when I did, all my contact codes were sour. Does the bank have another call code or address for me?"

"We'll see. What is the name of the company for which you work?"

"It has several names. One is System Enterprises."

"What is your employer's name?"

"He doesn't have a name. He is elderly, heavyset, one-eyed, rather crippled, and walks slowly with two canes. Does that win a prize?"

"We'll see. You told me that we backed your MasterCard credit issued through the Imperial Bank of Saint Louis. Read the card's number, slowly."

I did so. "Want to photograph it?"

"No. Give me a date."

"Ten sixty-six."

"Fourteen ninety-two," she answered.

"Four thousand four B.C.," I agreed.

"Seventeen seventy-six," she riposted.

"Two thousand twelve," I answered.

"You have a grisly sense of humor, Miss Baldwin. All right, you're tentatively you. But if you're not, I'll make a small bet with you that you won't live past the next checkpoint. Mr. Two-Canes is reputed to be unamused by gatecrashers. Take down this call code. Then read it back to me."

I did so.

One hour later I was walking past the Palace of the Confederacy in San Jose, again headed for the California Commercial Credit Building and firmly resolved not to get into any fights in front of the Palace no matter what assassinations were being attempted. I thought about the fact that I was on the exact spot I had been on, uh, two weeks ago?—and if this relay point sent me to Vicksburg I would go quietly mad.

My appointment at the CCC Building was not with MasterCard but with a law firm on another floor, one I had called from Bellingham after obtaining the firm's terminal code from the Moon. I had just reached the corner of the building when a voice almost in my ear said, "Miss Friday."

I looked quickly around. A woman in a Yellow Cab uniform. I looked again. "Goldie!"

"You ordered a cab, miss? Across the Plaza and down the street. They won't let us squat here."

We crossed the Plaza together. I started to babble, bursting with euphoria. Goldie shushed me. "Do please try to act like a cab fare, Miss Friday. The Master wants us to be inconspicuous."

"Since when do you call me miss?"

"Better so. Discipline is very tight now. My picking you up is a special permission, one that would never have been granted if I had not been able to point out that I could make positive identification without buzz words."

"Well. All right. Just don't call me miss when you don't have to. Golly gosh, Goldie darling, I'm so happy to see you I could cry."

"Me, too. Especially since you were reported dead just this Monday. And I did cry. And several others."

"Dead? *Me?* I haven't even been close to being dead, not at all, not anywhere. I haven't been in the slightest danger. Just lost. And now I'm found."

"I'm glad."

Ten minutes later I was ushered into Boss's office. "Friday reporting, sir," I said.

"You're late."

"I came the scenic route, sir. Up the Mississippi by excursion boat."

"So I heard. You seem to be the only survivor. I meant that you are late today. You crossed the border into California at twelve-oh-five. It is now seventeen-twenty-two."

"Damn it, Boss; I've had problems."

"Couriers are supposed to be able to outwit problems and move fast anyhow."

"Damn it, Boss, I wasn't on duty, I wasn't being a courier, I was still on leave; you've no business chewing me out. If you hadn't moved without notifying me, I wouldn't have had the slightest trouble. I *was* here, two weeks ago, in San Jose, just a loud shout from right here."

"Thirteen days ago."

"Boss, you're nitpicking to avoid admitting that it was your fault, not mine."

"Very well, I will accept the blame if any in order that we may cease quibbling and stop wasting time. I made extreme effort to notify you, much more than the routine alert MSG that was sent to other field operatives not at headquarters. I regret that this special effort failed. Friday, what must I do to convince you that you are unique and invaluable to this organization? In anticipation of the events tagged Red Thursday—"

"Boss! Were *we* in *that?*" I was shocked.

"What causes you to entertain such an obscene idea? No. Our intelligence staff projected it—in part from data you delivered from Ell-Five—and we started making precautionary arrangements in good time, so it seemed. But the first attacks took place in advance of our most pessimistic projection. At the onset of Red Thursday we were still moving impedimenta; it was necessary to crash our way across the border. With bribes, not with force. The notices of change of address and of call code had gone out earlier but it was not until we were here and our comm center reestablished that I was notified that you had not made routine acknowledgment."

"For the bloody good reason that I did not receive routine notice!"

"Please. On learning that you had not acknowledged, I attempted to call you at your New Zealand home. Possibly you are aware that there was an interruption in satellite service—"

"I heard."

"Precisely. The call got through some thirty-two hours later. I spoke to Mrs. Davidson, a woman about forty, rather sharp features. Senior wife in your S-group?"

"Yes. Anita. Both Lord High Executioner and Lord High Everything Else."

"That was the impression I received. I received also an impression that you had become *persona non grata.*"

"I'm sure that it was more than an impression. Go ahead, Boss; what did the old bat have to say about me?"

"Almost nothing. You had left the family quite suddenly. No, you had left no forwarding address or call code. No, she would not accept a message for you or forward any that arrived. I'm very busy; Marjorie has left us in a dreadful mess. Good-bye."

"Boss, she had your Imperium address. She also had the address in Luna City of Ceres and South Africa because I made my monthly payments to her through them."

"I could see the situation. My New Zealand representative"—the first I had ever heard of one!—"obtained for me the business address of your S-group's senior husband, Brian Davidson. He was more polite and somewhat more helpful. From him we learned what shuttle you had taken from Christchurch and that led us to the passenger list of the semiballistic you took from Auckland to Winnipeg. There we lost you briefly, until my agent there established that you had left the port in the company of the skipper of the semiballistic. When we reached him—Captain Tormey—he was helpful, but you had left. I am pleased to be able to tell you that we were able to return the favor to Captain Tormey. An inside source enabled us to let him know that he and his wife were about to be picked up by the local police."

"Fer Gossake! What for?"

"The nominal charge is harboring an enemy alien and harboring an unregistered Imperium subject during a declared emergency. In fact the Winnipeg office of the provincial police are not interested in you or in Dr. Perreault; that is an excuse to pull in the Tormeys. They are wanted on a much more serious charge that has not been filed. A Lieutenant Melvin Dickey is missing. The last trace of him is an oral statement made by him as he left police HQ that he was going to Captain Tormey's home to pick up Dr. Perreault. Foul play is suspected."

"But that's not evidence against Jan and Ian! The Tormeys."

"No, it is not. That is why the provincial police intend to hold them on a lesser charge. There is more. Lieutenant Dickey's APV crashed near Fargo in the Imperium. It was unoccupied. The police are very anxious to check that wreck for fingerprints. Possibly they are doing so at this very moment as, about one hour ago, a news bulletin reported that the common border between the Chicago Imperium and British Canada had been reopened."

"Oh, my God!"

"Compose yourself. On the controls of that APV there were indeed fingerprints that were not Lieutenant Dickey's. They matched Captain Tormey's prints on file with ANZAC Skyways. Note the tense I used; there *were* such prints; there no longer are. Friday, although I found it prudent to move our seat of operations out of the Imperium, after many years I am not without contacts there. And agents. And past favors I can collect. No prints matching those of Captain Tormey are now in that wreckage but there are prints on it from many sources living and dead."

"Boss, may I kiss your feet?"

"Hold your tongue. I did not do this to frustrate the British Canadian police. My field agent in Winnipeg is a clinical psychologist as well as having our usual training. It is his professional opinion that either Captain Tormey or his wife could kill in self-defense but that it would take extreme conditions indeed to cause either of them to kill a policeman. Dr. Perreault is described as being even less disposed toward violent solutions."

"I killed him."

"So I assumed. No other explanation fitted the data. Do you wish to discuss it? Is it any of my business?"

"Uh, perhaps not. Except that you made it your business when you got rid of those damning fingerprints. I killed him because he was threatening Janet, Janet Tormey, with a gun. I could have simply disabled him; I had time to pull my punch. But I meant to kill him and I did."

"I would be—and will be—much disappointed in you if you *ever* simply injure a policeman. A wounded policeman is more dangerous than a wounded lion. I had reconstructed it much as you described save that I had assumed that you were protecting Dr. Perreault . . . since you seemed to find him an acceptable surrogate husband."

"He's that, all right. But it was that crazy fool threatening Janet's life that made me go *spung!* Boss, until this happened I didn't know that I loved Janet. Didn't know I *could* love a woman that intensely. You know more than I do about how I was designed, or so you have hinted. Are my glands mixed up?"

"I know quite a lot about your design but I shan't discuss it with you; you have no need to know. Your glands are no more mixed up than those of any healthy human—specifically, you do *not* have a redundant Y chromosome. All normal human beings have *soi-disant* mixed-up glands. The race is divided into two parts: those who know this and those who do not. Stop the stupid talk; it ill befits a genius."

"Oh, so I'm a genius now. Hully gee, Boss."

"Don't be pert. You are a supergenius but you are a long way from realizing your potential. Geniuses and supergeniuses always make their own rules on sex as on everything else; they do not accept the monkey customs of their lessers. Let us return to our muttons. Is it possible that this body will be found?"

"I would bet long odds against it."

"Any point in discussing it with me?"

"Uh, I don't think so."

"Then I have no need to know and will assume that the Tormeys can safely return home as soon as the police conclude that they cannot establish *corpus delicti*. While *corpus delicti* does not require a corpse, it is enormously more difficult to make a charge of murder stand up without one. If arrested, a good lawyer would have the Tormeys out in five minutes—and they would have a *very* good lawyer, I assure you. You may be pleased to know that you helped them to escape from the country."

"I *did?*"

"You and Dr. Perreault. By leaving British Canada as Captain and Mrs. Tormey, and by using their credit cards and by filling out tourist-card applications in their names. You two left a trail that 'proved' that the Tormeys fled the country immediately after Lieutenant Dickey disappeared. This worked so well that the police wasted several days trying to trace down the suspects in the California Confederacy—and blaming inefficiency of their colleagues in the Confederacy for their lack of success. But I'm somewhat surprised that the Tormeys were not arrested in their own home as my agent had no great difficulty interviewing them there."

(I'm not. If a cop shows up—zip! down the Hole. If it's not a cop and he satisfies Ian that he is okay—) "Boss, did your Winnipeg agent mention my name? My 'Marjorie Baldwin' name, I mean."

"Yes. Without that name and a picture of you, Mrs. Tormey

would never have let him in. Without the Tormeys I would have lacked necessary data for picking up your rather elusive trail. We benefitted each other. They helped you to escape; we helped them to escape, after I told them—after my agent told them—that they were being actively sought. A pleasant ending."

"How did you get them out?"

"Friday, do you wish to know?"

"Um, no." (When will I learn? Had Boss wished to disclose the method, he would have told me. "Careless slips sink ships." Not around Boss.)

Boss came out from behind his desk . . . and shocked me. Ordinarily he does not move around much and in his old office his ubiquitous tea service was within his reach at his desk. Now he *rolled* out. No canes. A powered wheelchair. He guided it to a side table, started fiddling with tea things.

I stood up. "May I pour?"

"Thank you, Friday. Yes." He left the service table, rolled back to his place behind his desk. I took over, which let me stand with my back to him—that was what I needed right then.

There is no reason to feel shock when a cripple decides to substitute a powered wheelchair for canes—it is simply efficiency. Except that this was *Boss*. If the Egyptians at Giza woke up some morning and found the Pyramids switched around and the Sphinx with a new nose, they would not be more shocked than was I. Some things—and some people—are not supposed to change.

After I had served his tea—warm milk, two lumps—and had poured mine, I sat back down, my composure restored. Boss uses the very latest technology and quite old-fashioned customs; I have never known him to ask a woman to wait on him but if a woman is present and offers to pour tea, it is a certainty that he will accept graciously and turn the incident into a minor ceremony.

He chatted of other matters until we each had finished one cup. I refilled his cup, did not myself take another; he resumed business. "Friday, you changed names and credit cards so many times that we were always one jump behind you. We might not have traced you to Vicksburg had not your progress suggested something about your plan. Although it is not my practice to interfere with an agent no matter how closely he is being watched, I might have decided to head you off from going up the river—knowing that that expedition was doomed—"

"Boss, what was that expedition? I never believed the song and dance."

"A coup d'état. A clumsy one. The Imperium has had three Chairmen in two weeks . . . and the current one is no better and no more likely to survive. Friday, a well-run tyranny is a better base for my work than is any form of free government. But a well-run tyranny is almost as scarce as an efficient democracy. To resume—you got away from us in Vicksburg because you moved without hesitation. You were aboard that comic-opera troopship and gone before our Vicksburg agent knew that you had signed up. I was vexed with him. So much so that I have not yet disciplined him. I must wait."

"No reason to discipline him, Boss. I moved fast. Unless he breathed down my neck—which I notice and always take steps—he could not have kept up with me."

"Yes, yes, I know your techniques. But I think that you will agree that I was understandably annoyed when it was reported to me that our man in Vicksburg actually had you physically in sight . . . and twenty-four hours later he reports you dead."

"Maybe, maybe not. A man got too close on my heels coming into Nairobi earlier this year—breathed down my neck and it was his last breath. If you have me shadowed again, better warn your agents."

"I do not ordinarily use a shadow on you, Friday. With you, point checks work better. Fortunately for all of us you did not stay dead. While the terminals of my contact agents in Saint Louis have all been tapped by the government, I still get some use from them. When you attempted to report in, three times and never got caught, I heard of it at once and deduced that it had to be you, then knew it with certainty when you reached Fargo."

"Who in Fargo? The paper artist?"

Boss pretended not to hear. "Friday, I must get back to work. Complete your report. Make it brief."

"Yes, sir. I left that excursion boat when we entered the Imperium, proceeded to Saint Louis, found your contact call codes trapped, left, visited Fargo as you noted, crossed into British Canada twenty-six klicks east of Pembina, crossed to Vancouver and down to Bellingham today, then reported to you here."

"Any trouble?"

"No, sir."

"Any novel aspects of professional interest?"

"No, sir."

"At your convenience tape a detailed report for staff analysis. Feel free to suppress facts not yours to disclose. I will send for you some time in the next two or three weeks. You start school tomorrow morning. Oh-nine hundred."

"*Huh?*"

"Don't grunt; it is not pleasing in a young woman. Friday, your work has been satisfactory but it is time you entered on your true profession. Your true profession at this stage, perhaps I should say. You are woefully ignorant. We will change that. Nine o'clock tomorrow."

"Yes, sir." (Ignorant, huh? Arrogant old bastard. Gosh, I was glad to see him. But that wheelchair fretted me.)

XXII

Pajaro Sands used to be a resort seaside hotel. It's a nowhere place on Monterey Bay outside a nowhere city, Watsonville. Watsonville is one of the great oil export ports of the world and has all the charm of cold pancakes with no syrup. The nearest excitement is in the casinos and bawdy houses of Carmel, fifty kilometers away. But I don't gamble and am not interested in sex for hire, even the exotic sorts to be had in California. Not many from Boss's headquarters patronized Carmel as it was too far away to go by horse other than for a weekend, there was no direct capsule, and, while California is liberal in authorizing power vehicles, Boss did not release his APVs for anything but business.

The big excitements for us at Pajaro Sands were the natural attractions that caused it to be built, surf and sand and sunshine.

I enjoyed surfboarding until I became skilled at it. Then it bored me. I usually sunned a bit each day and swam a little and stared out at the big tankers suckling at the oil moles and noted with amusement that the watchstander aboard each ship often was staring back, with binoculars.

There was no reason for any of us to be bored as we had full individual terminal service. People are so used to the computer net today that it is easy to forget what a window to the world it can be—and I include myself. One can grow so canalized in using a terminal only in certain ways—paying bills, making telephonic calls, listening to news bulletins—that one can neglect its richer uses. If a subscriber is willing to pay for the service, almost anything can be done at a terminal that can be done out of bed.

Live music? I could punch in a concert going on live in Berkeley this evening, but a concert given ten years ago in London, its conductor long dead, is just as "live," just as immediate, as any listed on today's program. Electrons don't care. Once data *of any sort* go into the net, time is frozen. All that is necessary is to remember that all the endless riches of the past are available any time you punch for them.

Boss sent me to school at a computer terminal and I had far richer opportunities than any enjoyed by a student at Oxford or the Sorbonne or Heidelberg in any earlier year.

At first it did not seem to me that I was going to school. At breakfast the first day I was told to report to the head librarian. He was a fatherly old dear, Professor Perry, whom I had met first during basic training. He seemed harried—understandably, as Boss's library was probably the bulkiest and most complex thing shipped from the Imperium to Pajaro Sands. Professor Perry undoubtedly had weeks of work ahead before everything would be straightened out—and in the meantime all Boss would expect would be utter perfection. The work was not made easier by Boss's eccentric insistence on paper books for much of his library rather than cassettes or microfiche or disks.

When I reported to him, Perry looked bothered, then pointed to a console over in one corner. "Miss Friday, why don't you sit down over there?"

"What am I to do?"

"Eh? That's hard to say. No doubt we'll be told. Um, I'm awfully busy now and terribly understaffed. Why don't you just get acquainted with the equipment by studying anything you wish?"

There wasn't anything special about the equipment except that there were extra keys giving direct access to several major libraries such as Harvard's and the Washington Library of the Atlantic Union and the British Museum without going through a human or network linkup—plus the unique resource of direct access to Boss's library, the one right beside me. I could even read his bound paper books if I wanted to, on my terminal's screen, turning the pages from the keyboard and never taking the volume out of its nitrogen environment.

That morning I was speed-searching the index of the Tulane University library (one of the best in the Lone Star Republic), looking for history of Old Vicksburg, when I stumbled onto a cross-reference to spectral types of stars and found myself hooked. I don't recall why there was such a cross-referral but these do occur for the most unlikely reasons.

I was still reading about the evolution of stars when Professor Perry suggested that we go to lunch.

We did but I made some notes first about types of mathematics I wanted to study. Astrophysics is fascinating—but you have to talk the language.

That afternoon I got back to Old Vicksburg and was footnoted to *Show Boat*, a musical play concerning that era—and then spent the rest of the day looking at and listening to Broadway musical plays from the happy days before the North American Federation fell to pieces. Why can't they write music like that today? Those people must have had fun! I certainly did—I played *Show Boat*, *The Student Prince*, and *My Fair Lady* one after the other and noted a dozen more to play later. (*This* is going to school?)

Next day I resolved to stick to serious study of professional subjects in which I was weak, because I felt sure that once my tutors (whoever they were) assigned my curriculum, I would have no time at all for my own choices—earlier training in Boss's outfit had taught me the need for a twenty-six-hour day. But at breakfast my friend Anna asked me, "Friday, what can you tell me about the influence of Louis Onze on French lyric poetry?"

I blinked at her. "Is there a prize? Louis Onze sounds like a cheese to me. The only French verse I can recall is 'Mademoiselle from Armentières.' If that qualifies."

"Professor Perry said that you are the person to ask."

"He's pulling your leg." When I reached the library Papa Perry looked up from his console. I said, "Good morning. Anna said that you had told her to ask me about the effect of Louis the Eleventh on French verse."

"Yes, yes, of course. Would you mind not bothering me now? This bit of programming is very tricky." He looked back down and closed me out of his world.

Frustrated and irritated I punched up Louis XI. Two hours later I came up for air. I had not learned anything about poetry—so far as I could tell the Spider King had never even rhymed *ton con* with *c'est bon* or ever been a patron of the art. But I learned a lot about politics in the fifteenth century. Violent. Made the little scrapes I had been in seem like kiddie quarrels in the crèche.

I spent the rest of the day punching up French lyric verse since 1450. Good in spots. French is suited to lyric poetry, more so than is English—it takes an Edgar Allan Poe to wring beauty consistently out of the dissonances of English. German is unsuited to lyricism, so much so that translations fall sweeter on the ear than do the German originals. This is no fault of Goethe or Heine; it is a defect of an ugly language. Spanish is so musical that a soap-powder commercial in Spanish is more pleasing to the ear than the best free verse in English—the Spanish language is so beautiful that much of its poetry sounds best if the listener does not understand the meaning.

I never did find out what effect, if any, Louis XI had on verse.

One morning I found "my" console occupied. I looked inquiringly at the head librarian. Again he looked harried. "Yes, yes, we're quite crowded today. Um, Miss Friday, why not use the terminal in your room? It has the same additional controls and, if you need to consult me, you can do so even more quickly than you can here. Just punch local seven and your signature code and I'll instruct the computer to give you priority. Satisfactory?"

"Just fine," I agreed. I enjoyed the warm camaraderie of the library study room but in my own room I could take off my clothes without feeling that I was annoying Papa Perry. "What should I study today?"

"Goodness. Isn't there some subject you are interested in that merits further listening? I dislike disturbing Number One."

I went to my room and went on with French history since Louis Onze and that led me to the new colonies across the Atlantic and that led me into economics and that took me to Adam Smith and from there to political science. I concluded that Aristotle had had his good days but that Plato was a pretentious fraud and that led to my being called three times by the dining room with the last call including a recorded message that any later arrival would mean nothing but cold night-rations and a live message from Goldie threatening to drag me down by my hair.

So I rushed down, barefooted and still zipping into a jump suit. Anna asked what I had been doing that was so urgent I would forget to eat. "Most unFridayish." She and Goldie and I usually ate together, with or without male company—residents at HQ were a club, a fraternity, a noisy family, and some two dozen of them were "kissing friends" of mine.

"Improving my brain," I said. "You are looking at the World's Greatest Authority."

"Authority on what?" Goldie asked.

"Anything. Just ask me. The easy ones I answer at once; the hardest ones I'll answer tomorrow."

"Prove it," said Anna. "How many angels can sit on the point of a needle?"

"That's an easy one. Measure the angels' arses. Measure the point of the needle. Divide A into B. The numerical answer is left as an exercise for the student."

"Smart-aleck. What is the sound of one hand clapping?"

"Even easier. Switch on a recorder, using any nearby terminal. Clap with one hand. Play back the result."

"You try her, Goldie. She's been eating meat."

"What is the population of San Jose?"

"Ah, that's a hard one! I'll report tomorrow."

This fiddling went on for over a month before it filtered through my skull that someone (Boss, of course) was in fact trying to force me to become "the World's Greatest Authority."

At one time there really was a man known as "the World's Greatest Authority." I ran across him in trying to nail down one of the many silly questions that kept coming at me from odd sources. Like this: Set your terminal to "research." Punch parameters in succession "North American culture," "English-speaking," "mid–twentieth century," "comedians," "the World's Greatest Authority." The answer you can expect is "Professor Irwin Corey." You'll find his routines timeless humor.

Meanwhile I was being force-fed, like a Strasbourg goose.

Nevertheless it was a very happy time. Often, as often as not, one of my true friends would invite me to share a bed. I don't recall ever refusing. Rendezvous would usually be arranged during afternoon sunbathing and the prospect added a tingle to the sensuous pleasure of lying in the sun. Because *everyone* at HQ was so civilized—sweet through and through—it was possible to answer, "Sorry, Terence asked me first. Tomorrow maybe? No? Okay, sometime soon"— and have no hurt feelings. One of the shortcomings of the S-group I used to belong to was that such arrangements were negotiated among the males under some protocol that was never explained to me but was not free from tension.

The silly questions speeded up. I found myself just getting acquainted with the details of Ming ceramics when a message showed up in my terminal saying that someone in staff wanted to know the relationships between men's beards, women's skirts, and the price of gold. I had ceased to wonder at silly questions; around Boss anything can happen. But this one seemed supersilly. Why should there be *any* relationship? Men's beards did not interest me; they tickle and often are dirty. As for women's skirts, I knew even less. I have almost never worn skirts. Skirted costumes can be pretty but they aren't practical for travel and could have gotten me killed three or four times—and when you're home, what's wrong with skin? Or as near as local custom permits.

But I had learned not to ignore questions merely because they were obvious nonsense; I tackled this one by calling up all the data I could, including punching out some most unlikely association chains. I then told the machine to tabulate all retrieved data by categories.

Durned if I didn't begin to find connections!

As more data accumulated I found that the only way I could see all of it was to tell the computer to plot and display a three-dimensional graph—and that looked so promising that I told it to convert to holographic in color. Beautiful! I did not know why these three variables fitted together but they did. I spent the rest of that day changing scales, X versus Y versus Z in various combinations—magnifying, shrinking, rotating, looking for minor cycloid relations under the obvious gross ones . . . and noticed a shallow double sinusoidal hump that kept showing up as I rotated the holo—and suddenly, for no reason I can assign, I decided to subtract the double sunspot curve.

Eureka! As precise and necessary as a Ming vase! Before dinnertime I had the equation, just one line that encompassed all the silly data I had spent five days dragging out of the terminal. I punched the chief of staff's call and recorded that one-line equation, plus definitions of variables. I added no comment, no discussion; I wanted to force the faceless joker to ask for my opinions.

I got the same answer back—i.e., none.

I fiddled for most of a day, waiting, and proving to myself that I could retrieve a group picture from any year and, through looking only at male faces and female legs, make close guesses concerning the price of gold (falling or rising), the time of that picture relative to the double sunspot cycle, and—shortly and most surprising—whether the political structure was falling apart or consolidating.

My terminal chimed. No face. No pat on the back. Just a displayed message: "Operations requests soonest depth analysis of possibility that plague epidemics of sixth, fourteenth, and seventeenth centuries resulted from political conspiracy."

Fooey! I had wandered into a funny farm and was locked up with the inmates.

Oh, well! The question was so complex that I might be left alone a long time while I studied it. That suited me; I had grown addicted to the possibilities of a terminal of a major computer hooked into a world research net—I felt like Little Jack Horner.

I started by listing as many subjects as possible by free association: plague, epidemiology, fleas, rats, Daniel Defoe, Isaac Newton, conspiracies, Guy Fawkes, Freemasonry, Illuminati, OTO, Rosicrucians, Kennedy, Oswald, John Wilkes Booth, Pearl Harbor, Green Bowlers, Spanish influenza, pest control, etc.

In three days my list of possibly related subjects was ten times as long.

In a week I knew that one lifetime was not nearly long enough to study in depth all of my list. But I had been told to tackle the subject so I started in—but I placed my own meaning on "soonest"—i.e., I would study conscientiously at least fifty hours per week but when and how I wished and with no cramming or rawhiding . . . unless somebody came along and explained to me why I should work harder or differently.

This went on for weeks.

I was wakened in the middle of the night by my terminal—override alarm; I had shut it off as usual when I went to bed (alone, I don't recall why). I answered sleepily, "All right, all right! Speak up, and it had better be good."

No picture. Boss's voice said, "Friday, when will the next major Black Death epidemic occur?"

I answered, "Three years from now. April. Starting in Bombay and spreading worldwide at once. Spreading off planet at first transport."

"Thank you. Good night."

I dropped my head to the pillow and went right back to sleep.

I woke up at seven hundred as usual, held still for several moments and thought, while I grew colder and colder—decided that I really had heard from Boss in the night and really had given him that preposterous answer.

So bite the bullet, Friday, and climb the Thirteen Steps. I punched "local one." "Friday here, Boss. About what I told you in the night. I plead temporary insanity."

"Nonsense. See me at ten-fifteen."

I was tempted to spend the next three hours in lotus, chanting my beads. But I have a deep conviction that one should not attend even the End of the World without a good breakfast . . . and my decision was justified as the special that morning was fresh figs with cream, corned-beef hash with poached eggs, and English muffins with Knott's Berry Farm orange marmalade. Fresh milk. Colombian high-altitude coffee. That so improved things that I spent an hour trying to find a mathematical relationship between the past history of plague and the date that had popped into my sleep-drenched mind. I did not find one but was beginning to see some shape to the curve when the terminal gave me a three-minute warning I had punched in.

I had refrained from having my hair cut and my neck shaved but otherwise I was ready. I walked in on the tick. "Friday reporting, sir."

"Sit down. Why Bombay? I would think that Calcutta would be a more likely center."

"It might have something to do with long-range weather forecasts and the monsoons. Fleas can't stand hot, dry weather. Eighty percent of a flea's body mass is water and, if the percentage drops below sixty, the flea dies. So hot, dry weather will stop or prevent an epidemic. But, Boss, the whole thing is nonsense. You woke me up in the middle of the night and asked me a silly question and I gave you a silly answer without really waking up. I probably pulled it out of a dream. I've been having nightmares about the Black Death and there really was a bad epidemic that started in Bombay. Eighteen ninety-six and following."

"Not as bad as the Hong Kong phase of it three years later. Friday, the analytical section of Operations says that the next Black Death epidemic won't start until a year later than your prediction. And not Bombay. Djakarta and Ho Chi Minh City."

"That's preposterous!" I stopped abruptly. "Sorry, sir, I guess I was back in that nightmare. Boss, can't I study something pleasanter than fleas and rats and Black Death? It's ruining my sleep."

"You may. You are through studying plague—"

"Hooray!"

"—other than to whatever extent your intellectual curiosity causes you to tidy up any loose ends. The matter now goes to Operations for action. But action will be based on your prediction, not on that of the mathematical analysts."

"I have to say it again. My prediction is nonsense."

"Friday, your greatest weakness is lack of awareness of your true strength. Wouldn't we look silly if we depended on the professional analysts but the outbreak was one year earlier, as you predicted? Catastrophe. But to be a year early in taking prophylactic measures does no harm."

"Are we going to try to stop it?" (People have been fighting rats and fleas throughout history. So far, the rats and fleas are ahead.)

"Heavens, no! In the second place, the contract would be too big for this organization. But in the first place I do not accept contracts that I cannot fulfill; this is one such. In the third place, from the strictest humanitarian viewpoint, any attempt to stop the processes by which overcrowded cities purge themselves is not a kindness. Plague is a nasty death but a quick one. Starvation also is a nasty death . . . but a very slow one."

Boss grimaced, then continued. "This organization will limit itself to the problem of keeping *Pasteurella pestis* from leaving this planet. How will we do this? Answer at once."

(Ridiculous! Any government public health department, faced with such a question, would set up a blue-ribbon study group, insist on ample research funds, and schedule a reasonable time—five years or more—for orderly scientific investigation.) I answered at once, "Explode them."

"The space colonies? That seems a drastic solution."

"No, the fleas. Back during the global wars of the twentieth century somebody discovered that you could kill off fleas and lice by taking them up to high altitude. They explode. About five kilometers as I recall but it can be looked up and checked by experiment. I thought of it because I noticed that Beanstalk Station on Mount Kenya was above the critical altitude—and almost all space traffic these days goes up the Beanstalk. Then there is the simple method of heat and dryness—works but not as fast. But the key to it, Boss, is *absolutely no exceptions*. Just one case of diplomatic immunity or one VIP allowed to skip the routines and you've had it. One lapdog. One gerbil. One shipment of laboratory mice. If it took the pneumonic form, Ell-Five would be a ghost town in a week. Or Luna City."

"If I did not have other work for you, I would put you in charge. How about rats?"

"I don't want the job; I'm sick of the subject. Boss, killing a rat is no problem. Stuff it into a sack. Beat the sack with an ax. Then shoot it. Then drown it. Burn the sack with the dead rat in it. Meanwhile its mate has raised another litter of pups and you now have a dozen rats to replace it. Boss, all we've ever been able to do with rats is fight them to a draw. We never win. If we let up for a moment the rats pull ahead." I added sourly, "I think they're the second team." This plague assignment had depressed me.

"Elucidate."

"If *Homo sapiens* doesn't make it—he keeps trying to kill himself off—there are the rats, ready to take over."

"Piffle. Soft-headed nonsense. Friday, you overstress the human will to die. We have had the means to commit racial suicide for generations now and those means are and have been in many hands. We have not done so. In the second place, to replace us, rats would have to grow enormously larger skulls, develop bodies to support them, learn to walk on two feet, develop their front paws into delicate manipulative organs—and grow more cortex to control all this. To *replace* man another breed must *become* man. Bah. Forget it. Before we leave the subject of plague, what conclusions did you reach concerning the conspiracy theory?"

"The notion is silly. You specified sixth, fourteenth, and seventeenth centuries . . . and that means sailing ships or caravans and no knowledge of bacteriology. So here we have the sinister Dr. Fu Manchu in his hideaway raising a million rats and the rats are infested with fleas—easy. Rats and fleas are infected with the bacillus—possible even without theory. But how does he hit his target city? By ship? In a few days all the million rats will be dead and so would be the crew. Even harder to do it overland. To make such a conspiracy work in those centuries would require modern science and a largish time machine. Boss, who thought up that silly question?"

"I did."

"I thought it had your skid to it. Why?"

"It caused you to study the subject with a much wider approach than you otherwise would have given it, did it not?"

"Uh . . ." I had spent much more time studying relevant political history than I had spent studying the disease itself. "I suppose so."

"You know so."

"Well, yes. Boss, there ain't no such animal as a well-documented conspiracy. Or sometimes too well documented but the documents contradict each other. If a conspiracy happened quite some time ago, a generation or longer, it becomes impossible to establish the truth. Have you ever heard of a man named John F. Kennedy?"

"Yes. Chief of state in the middle twentieth century of the Federation then occupying the land between Canada—British Canada and Québec—and the Kingdom of Mexico. He was assassinated."

"That's the man. Killed in front of hundreds of witnesses and every aspect, before, during, and after, heavily documented. All that mountain of evidence adds up to is this: Nobody knows who shot him, how many shot him, how many times he was shot, who did it, why it was done, and who was involved in the conspiracy if there was a conspiracy. It isn't even possible to say whether the murder plot was foreign or domestic. Boss, if it is impossible to untangle one that recent and that thoroughly investigated, what chance is there of figuring out the details of the conspiracy that did in Gaius Iulius Caesar? Or Guy Fawkes and the Gunpowder Plot? All that can truthfully be said is that the people who come out on top write the official versions found in the history books, history that is no more honest than is autobiography."

"Friday, autobiography is usually honest."

"*Huh!* Boss, what have you been smoking?"

"That will do. Autobiography is usually honest but it is never truthful."

"I missed a turn."

"Think about it. Friday, I can't spend more time on you today; you chatter too much and change the subject. Hold your tongue while I say some things. You are now permanently on staff work. You are getting older; no doubt your reflexes are a touch slower. I will not again risk you in field work—"

"I'm not complaining!"

"Pipe down. —But you must not get swivel-chair spread. Spend less time at the console, more time in exercise; the day will come when your enhanced reflexes will again save your life. And possibly the lives of others. In the meantime give thought to the day when you will have to shape your life unassisted. You should leave this planet; for you there is nothing here. The Balkanization of North America ended the last chance of reversing the decay of the Renaissance Civilization. So you should think about off-planet possibilities not only in the solar system but elsewhere—planets ranging from extremely primitive to well developed. Investigate for each the cost and the advantages of migrating there. You will need money; do you want my agents to collect the money of which you were cheated in New Zealand?"

"How did you know I was cheated?"

"Come, come! We are not children."

"Uh, may I think about it?"

"Yes. Concerning your ex-migration: I recommend that you not move to the planet Olympia. Otherwise I have no specific advice other than to migrate. When I was younger, I thought I could change this world. Now I no longer think so but for emotional reasons I must keep on fighting a holding action. But you are young and, because of your unique heritage, your emotional ties to this planet and to this portion of humanity are not great. I could not mention this until you shuffled off your sentimental connection in New Zealand—"

"I didn't 'shuffle' it off; I was kicked out on my arse!"

"So. While you are deciding, look up Benjamin Franklin's parable of the whistle, then tell me—no, ask yourself—whether or not you paid too much for your whistle. Enough of that— Two assignments for you: Study the Shipstone corporate complex, including its interlocks outside the complex. Second, the next time I see you I want you to tell me precisely how to spot a sick culture. That's all."

Boss turned his attention to his console, so I stood up. But I was not ready to accept so abrupt a dismissal as I had had no opportunity to ask important questions. "Boss. Don't I have any duties? Just random study that goes nowhere?"

"It goes somewhere. Yes, you have duties. First, to study. Second, to be awakened in the middle of the night—or stopped in the hallway— to answer silly questions."

"Just that?"

"What do you want? Angels and trumpets?"

"Well . . . a job title, maybe. I used to be a courier. What am I now? Court jester?"

"Friday, you are developing a bureaucratic mind. 'Job title' indeed! Very well. You are staff intuitive analyst, reporting to me only. But the title carries an injunction: You are forbidden to discuss anything more serious than a card game with any member of the analytical section of the general staff. Sleep with them if you wish—I know that you do, in two cases—but limit your conversation to the veriest trivia."

"Boss, I could wish that you spent less time under my bed!"

"Only enough to protect the organization. Friday, you are well aware that the absence of Eyes and Ears today simply means that they are concealed. Be assured that I am shameless about protecting the organization."

"You are shameless, unlimited. Boss, answer me one more question. Who is behind Red Thursday? The third wave sort of fizzled; will there be a fourth? What's it all about?"

"Study it yourself. If I told you, you would not know; you simply would have been told. Study it thoroughly and some night—when you are sleeping alone—I will ask you. You will answer and then you will know."

"Fer Gossake. Do you *always* know when I'm sleeping alone?"

"Always." He added, "Dismissed," and turned away.

XXIII

As I left the sanctum sanctorum I ran into Goldie coming in. I was feeling grouchy and simply nodded. Not sore at Goldie. Boss! Damn him. Supercilious, arrogant voyeur! I went to my room and got to work, so that I could stop fuming.

First I punched for the names and addresses of all the Shipstone corporations. While these were printing I called for histories of the complex. The computer named two, an official company history combined with a biography of Daniel Shipstone, and an unofficial history footnoted "muckrake." Then the machine suggested several other sources.

I told the terminal to print out both books and I asked it for printouts of other sources if four thousand words or less, summarized if not. Then I looked over the corporations list:

Daniel Shipstone Estate, Inc.	Shipstone Never-Never
Muriel Shipstone Memorial Research Laboratories	Shipstone Ell-Four
	Shipstone Ell-Five
Shipstone Tempe	Shipstone Stationary
Shipstone Gobi	Shipstone Tycho
Shipstone Aden	Shipstone Ares
Shipstone Sahara	Shipstone Deep Water
Shipstone Arica	Shipstone Unlimited, Ltd.
Shipstone Death Valley	Sears-Montgomery, Inc.
Shipstone Karroo	Prometheus Foundation

Coca-Cola Holding Company	Billy Shipstone School for
Interworld Transport Corporation	Handicapped Children
Jack and the Beanstalk, Pty.	Wolf Creek Pass Nature Preserve
Morgan Associates	Año Nuevo Wild Life Refuge
Out-Systems Colonial	Shipstone Visual Arts Museum
Corporation	and School

I looked at this list with easily controlled enthusiasm. I had known that the Shipstone trust had to be big—who does not have half a dozen Shipstones within easy reach, not counting the big one in your basement or foundation? But now it seemed to me that studying this monster would be a lifetime career. I was not that much interested in Shipstones.

I was nibbling around the edges when Goldie stopped by and told me that it was time to put on the nosebag. "And I have instructions to see to it that you do not spend more than eight hours a day at your terminal and you are to take a full weekend every week."

"Ah so. Tyrannical old bastard."

We started for the refectory. "Friday . . ."

"Yes, Goldie?"

"You are finding the Master grumpy and sometimes difficult."

"Correction. He is always difficult."

"Mmm, yes. But what you may not know is that he is in constant pain." She added, "He can no longer take drugs to control it."

We walked in silence while I chewed and swallowed that one. "Goldie? What is wrong with him?"

"Nothing, really. I would say that he is in good health . . . for his age."

"How old is he?"

"I don't know. From things I have heard I know that he is over a hundred. How much over I can't guess."

"Oh, no! Goldie, when I went to work for him, he could not have been more than seventy. Oh, he used canes but he was very spry. He moved as fast then as anyone."

"Well . . . it's not important. But you might remember that he hurts. If he is rude to you, it is pain talking. He thinks highly of you."

"What makes you think so?"

"Ah . . . I've talked too much about my patient. Let's eat."

In studying the Shipstone corporate complex I did not attempt to study Shipstones. The way—the only way—to study Shipstones would be to go back to school, get a Ph.D. in physics, add on some intense postdoctoral study in both solid state and plasma, get a job with one of the Shipstone companies and so impress them with your loyalty and your brilliance that you are at long last part of the inner circle controlling fabrication and quality.

Since that involves about twenty years that I should have started back in my teens, I assumed that Boss did not intend me to take that route.

So let me quote from the official or propaganda history:

Prometheus, a Brief Biography and Short Account of the Unparalleled Discoveries of Daniel Thomas Shipstone, B.S., M.A., Ph.D., LL.D., L.H.D., and of the Benevolent System He Founded.

—thus young Daniel Shipstone saw at once that the problem was not a shortage of energy but lay in the transporting of energy. Energy is everywhere—in sunlight, in wind, in mountain streams, in temperature gradients of all sorts wherever found, in coal, in fossil oil, in radioactive ores, in green growing things. Especially in ocean depths and in outer space energy is free for the taking in amounts lavish beyond all human comprehension.

Those who spoke of "energy scarcity" and of "conserving energy" simply did not understand the situation. The sky was "raining soup"; what was needed was a bucket in which to carry it.

With the encouragement of his devoted wife Muriel (née Greentree), who went back to work to keep food on the table, young Shipstone resigned from General Atomics and became the most American of myth-heroes, the basement inventor. Seven frustrating and weary years later he had fabricated the first Shipstone by hand. He had found—

What he had found was a way to pack more kilowatt-hours into a smaller space and a smaller mass than any other engineer had ever dreamed of. To call it an "improved storage battery" (as some early accounts did) is like calling an H-bomb an "improved firecracker." What he had achieved was the utter destruction of the biggest industry (aside from organized religion) of the western world.

For what happened next I must draw from the muckraking history and from other independent sources as I just don't believe the sweetness and light of the company version. Fictionalized speech attributed to Muriel Shipstone:

> "Danny Boy, you are not going to patent the gadget. What would it get you? Seventeen years at the most . . . and no years at all in three-fourths of the world. If you did patent or try to, Edison, and P. G. and E., and Standard would tie you up with injunctions and law suits and claimed infringements and I don't know what all. But you said yourself that you could put one of your gadgets in a room with the best research team G.A. has to offer and the best they could do would be to melt it down and the worst would be that they would blow themselves up. You said that. Did you mean it?"
>
> "Certainly. If they don't know how I insert the—"
>
> "*Hush!* I don't want to know. And walls have ears. We don't make any fancy announcements; we simply start manufacturing. Wherever power is cheapest today. Where is that?"

The muckraking author fairly frothed at the "cruel, heartless monopoly" held by the Shipstone complex over the prime necessities of "all the little people everywhere." I could not see it that way. What Shipstone and his companies did was to make plentiful and cheap what used to be scarce and dear—this is "cruel" and "heartless"?

The Shipstone companies do not have a monopoly over energy. They don't own coal or oil or uranium or water power. They do lease many, many hectares of desert land . . . but there is far more desert not being cropped for sunshine than the Shipstone trust is using. As for space, it is impossible to intercept even one percent of all the sunshine going to waste inside the orbit of Luna, impossible by a factor of many millions. Do the arithmetic yourself; otherwise you'll never believe the answer.

So what is their crime?

Twofold:

a) The Shipstone companies are guilty of supplying energy to the human race at prices below those of their competitors;

b) They meanly and undemocratically decline to share their industrial secret of the final assembly stage of a Shipstone.

This latter is, in the eyes of many people, a capital offense. My terminal dug out many editorials on "the people's right to know," others on "the insolence of giant monopolies," and other displays of righteous indignation.

The Shipstone complex is mammoth, all right, because they supply cheap power to billions of people who want cheap power and want more of it every year. But it is not a monopoly because they don't own any power; they just package it and ship it around to wherever people want it. Those billions of customers could bankrupt the Shipstone complex almost overnight by going back to their old ways—burn coal, burn wood, burn oil, "burn" uranium, distribute power through continent-wide stretches of copper and aluminum wires and/or long trains of coal cars and tank cars.

But no one, so far as my terminal could dig out, wants to go back to the bad old days when the landscape was disfigured in endless ways and the very air was loaded with stinks and carcinogens and soot, and the ignorant were scared silly by nuclear power, and *all* power was scarce and expensive. No, nobody wants the bad old ways—even the most radical of the complainers want cheap and convenient power . . . they just want the Shipstone companies to go away and get lost.

"The people's right to know"—the people's right to know *what?* Daniel Shipstone, having first armed himself with great knowledge of higher mathematics and physics, went down into his basement and patiently suffered seven lean and weary years and thereby learned an applied aspect of natural law that let him construct a Shipstone.

Any and all of "the people" are free to do as he did—he did not even take out a patent. Natural laws are freely available to everyone equally, including flea-bitten Neanderthals crouching against the cold.

In this case, the trouble with "the people's right to know" is that it strongly resembles the "right" of someone to be a concert pianist— but who does not want to practice.

But I am prejudiced, not being human and never having had any rights.

Whether you prefer the saccharine company version or the vitriolic muckraker's version, the basic facts about Daniel Shipstone and the

Shipstone complex are well known and beyond argument. What surprised me (shocked me, in fact) was what I learned when I started digging into ownership, management, and direction.

My first hint came from that basic printout when I saw what companies were listed as Shipstone complex companies but did not have "Shipstone" in their names. When one pauses for a Coke . . . the deal is with Shipstone!

Ian had told me that Interworld had ordered the destruction of Acapulco—does this mean that the trustees of Daniel Shipstone's estate ordered the killing of a quarter of a million innocent people? Can these be the same people who run the best hospital/school for handicapped children in the world? And Sears-Montgomery—hell's bells, I own some Sears-Montgomery stock myself. Do I share by concatenation some part of the guilt for the murder of Acapulco?

I programmed the machine to display how the directorates interlocked inside the Shipstone complex, and then what directorships in other companies were held by directors of Shipstone companies—and the results were so startling that I asked the computer to list stock ownership of one percent or more of the voting stock in all Shipstone companies.

I spent the next three days fiddling with and rearranging and looking for better ways to display the great mass of data that came back in answer to those two questions.

At the end of that time I wrote out my conclusions:

a) The Shipstone complex is all one company. It just looks like twenty-eight separate organizations.

b) The directors and/or stockholders of the Shipstone complex own or control everything of major importance in all the major territorial nations in the solar system.

c) Shipstone is potentially a planetwide (systemwide?) government. I could not tell from the data whether it acted as such or not as control (if indeed it were exerted) would be through corporations not overtly part of the Shipstone empire.

d) It scared me.

Something I had noticed in connection with one Shipstone company (Morgan Associates) caused me to run a search on credit companies and banks. I was unsurprised but depressed to learn that the very company now extending me credit (MasterCard of California) was in effect the same company as the one guaranteeing payment (Ceres and South Africa Acceptances) and that was duplicated right down the line, whether it was Maple Leaf, Visa, Crédit Québec, or what. That is not news; fiscal theorists have been asserting that as long as I can remember. But it struck home when I saw it spelled out in terms of directorates interlocking and ownership shared.

On impulse I suddenly asked the computer: "Who owns you?"

I got back: "Null Program."

I rephrased it, conforming most carefully to its language. The computer represented by this terminal was a most forgiving machine and very smart; ordinarily it did not mind somewhat informal programming. But there are limits to what one may expect in machine understanding of verbal language; a reflexive question such as this might call for semantic exactness.

Again: "Null Program."

I decided to sneak up on the idea. I asked it the following question, doing it step by step exactly in accordance with this computer's language, computer grammar, computer protocol: "What is the ownership of the information-processing network that has terminals throughout British Canada?"

The answer was displayed and flashed several times before wiping—and it wiped without my order: "Requested data are not in my membanks."

That scared me. I knocked off for the day and went swimming and sought out a friend to share a bed with me that night, not waiting to be asked. I wasn't superhorny, I was superlonely and dern well wanted a warm living body close to mine to "protect" me from an intelligent machine that refused to tell me who (what) it really was.

During breakfast next morning Boss sent word to me to see him at ten hundred. I reported, somewhat mystified because in my opinion there had not been nearly enough time for me to complete my two assignments: Shipstone, and the marks of a sick culture.

But when I came in, he handed me a letter, of the old-fashioned sort, sealed into an envelope and physically forwarded, just like junk mail.

I recognized it, for I had sent it—to Janet and Ian. But I was surprised to see it in Boss's hands, as the return address on it was phony. I looked and saw that it had been readdressed to a law firm in San Jose, the one that had been my contact to find Boss. "Pixies."

"You can hand it back to me and I will send it to Captain Tormey . . . when I know where he is."

"Uh, when you know where the Tormeys are, I will write a very different letter. This one is sort of blind."

"Commendably so."

"You've read it?" (Damn it, Boss!)

"I read everything that is to be forwarded to Captain and Mrs. Tormey—and Dr. Perreault. By their request."

"I see." (Nobody tells me a damn thing!) "I wrote the way I did, phony name and all, because the Winnipeg police might open it."

"They undoubtedly did. I think you covered adequately. I regret that I did not inform you that all mail sent to their home would be forwarded to me. If indeed the police are forwarding all of it. Friday, I do not know where the Tormeys are . . . but I have a contact method that I can use—once. The plan is to use it when the police drop all charges against them. I expected that weeks ago. It has not taken place. From this I conclude that the police in Winnipeg are very much in earnest in their intention of hanging the disappearance of Lieutenant Dickey on the Tormeys as a murder charge. Let me ask you again: Can that body be found?"

I thought hard, trying to put "worst case" on it. If the police ever moved in on that house, what would they find? "Boss, have the police been inside that house?"

"Certainly. They searched it the day after the owners departed."

"In that case the police had not found the body the morning of the day I reported here. If they found it, or were to find it, since that date, would you know?"

"I think it probable. My lines of communication into that police headquarters are less than perfect but I pay highest for freshest information."

"Do you know what was done with the livestock? Four horses, a cat and five kittens, a pig, maybe other animals?"

"Friday, where is your intuition leading you?"

"Boss, I don't know exactly how that body is hidden. But Janet, Mrs. Tormey, is an architect who specialized in two-tier active defense of buildings. What she did about her animals would tell me whether or not she thought there was the slightest possibility of that body ever being found."

Boss made a notation. "We'll discuss it later. What are the marks of a sick culture?"

"Boss, fer Gossake! I'm still learning the full shape of the Shipstone complex."

"You will never learn its full shape. I gave you two assignments at once so that you could rest your mind with a change of pace. Don't tell me that you've given no thought to the second assignment."

"Thought is about all I've given to it. I've been reading Gibbon and studying the French Revolution. Also Smith's *From the Yalu to the Precipice*."

"A very doctrinaire treatment. Read also Penn's *The Last Days of the Sweet Land of Liberty*."

"Yes, sir. I did start making tallies. It is a bad sign when the people of a country stop identifying themselves with the country and start identifying with a group. A racial group. Or a religion. Or a language. Anything, as long as it isn't the whole population."

"A very bad sign. Particularism. It was once considered a Spanish vice but any country can fall sick with it."

"I don't really know Spain. Dominance of males over females seems to be one of the symptoms. I suppose the reverse would be true but I haven't run across it in any of the history I've listened. Why not, Boss?"

"You tell me. Continue."

"So far as I have listened, before a revolution can take place, the population must lose faith in both the police and the courts."

"Elementary. Go on."

"Well . . . high taxation is important and so is inflation of the currency and the ratio of the productive to those on the public payroll. But that's old hat; everybody knows that a country is on the skids when its income and outgo get out of balance and stay that way—even though there are always endless attempts to wish it away by legislation. But I started looking for little signs, what some call silly-season symptoms. For example, did you know that it is against the law here to be naked outside your own home? Even *in* your own home if anybody can see in?"

"Rather difficult to enforce, I suspect. What significance do you see in it?"

"Oh, it isn't enforced. But it can't be repealed, either. The Confederacy is loaded with such laws. It seems to me that any law that is not enforced and can't be enforced weakens all other laws. Boss, did you know that the California Confederacy subsidizes whores?"

"I had not noticed it. To what end? For their armed forces? For their prison population? Or as a public utility? I confess to some surprise."

"Oh, not that way at all! The government pays them to keep their legs crossed. Take it off the market entirely. They are trained, licensed, examined—and stockpiled. Only it doesn't work. The designated 'surplus artists' draw their subsidy checks . . . then go right ahead peddling tail. When they aren't supposed to do it even for fun because that hurts the market for the unsubsidized whores. So the hookers' union, who sponsored the original legislation to support the union scale, is now trying to work out a voucher system to plug up the holes in the subsidy law. And that won't work either."

"Why won't it work, Friday?"

"Boss, laws to sweep back the tide never do work; that's what King Canute was saying. Surely you know that?"

"I wanted to be sure that you knew it."

"I think I've been insulted. I ran across a goody. In the California Confederacy it is against the law to refuse credit to a person merely because that person has taken bankruptcy. Credit is a civil right."

"I assume that it does not work but what form does noncompliance take?"

"I have not yet investigated, Boss. But I think a deadbeat would be at a disadvantage in trying to bribe a judge. I want to mention one of the obvious symptoms: Violence. Muggings. Sniping. Arson. Bombing. Terrorism of any sort. Riots of course—but I suspect that little incidents of violence, pecking away at people day after day, damage a culture even more than riots that flare up and then die down. I guess that's all for now. Oh, conscription and slavery and arbitrary compulsion of all sorts and imprisonment without bail and without speedy trial—but those things are obvious; all the histories list them."

"Friday, I think you have missed the most alarming symptom of all."

"I have? Are you going to tell me? Or am I going to have to grope around in the dark for it?"

"Mmm. This once I shall tell you. But go back and search for it. Examine it. Sick cultures show a complex of symptoms such as you have named . . . but a *dying* culture invariably exhibits personal rudeness. Bad manners. Lack of consideration for others in minor matters. A loss of politeness, of gentle manners, is more significant than is a riot."

"Really?"

"Pfui. I should have forced you to dig it out for yourself; then you would know it. This symptom is especially serious in that an individual displaying it never thinks of it as a sign of ill health but as proof of his/her strength. Look for it. Study it. Friday, it is too late to save this culture—this worldwide culture, not just the freak show here in California. Therefore we must now prepare the monasteries for the coming Dark Age. Electronic records are too fragile; we must again have books, of stable inks and resistant paper. But that may not be enough. The reservoir for the next renaissance may have to come from beyond the sky." Boss stopped and breathed heavily. "Friday . . ."

"Yes, sir?"

"Memorize this name and address." His hands moved at his console; the answer appeared on his high screen. I memorized it.

"Do you have it?"

"Yes, sir."

"Shall I repeat it for check?"

"No, sir."

"You are sure?"

"Repeat it if you wish, sir."

"Mmm. Friday, would you be so kind as to pour a cup of tea for me before you leave? I find that my hands are unsteady today."

"My pleasure, sir."

XXIV

Neither Goldie nor Anna showed up next day at breakfast. I ate by myself and consequently fairly quickly; I dawdle over food only when shared with company. This was just as well for I was just standing up, finished, when Anna's voice came over the speaking system:

"Attention, please. I have the unhappy duty to announce that during the night our Chairman died. By his wish there will be no memorial service. The body has been cremated. At nine hundred hours, in the large conference room, there will be a meeting to wind up the affairs of the company. Everyone is urged to attend and to be on time."

I spent the time until nine o'clock crying. Why? Feeling sorry for myself, I suppose. I'm certain that's what Boss would think. He didn't feel sorry for himself, he didn't feel sorry for me, and he scolded me more than once for self-pity. Self-pity, he said, is the most demoralizing of all vices.

Just the same, I was feeling sorry for myself. I had always spatted with him, even way back when he broke my indentures and made me a Free Person after I had run away from him. I found myself regretting every time I had answered him back, been impudent, called him names.

Then I reminded myself that Boss would not have liked me at all if I had been a worm, subservient, no opinions of my own. He had to be what he was and I had to be what I was and we had lived for years in close association that had never, not once, involved even touching hands. For Friday, that is a record. One I am not interested in surpassing.

I wonder if he knew, years ago when I first went to work for him, how quickly I would have swarmed into his lap had he invited it. He probably did know. As may be, even though I had never touched his hand, he was the only father I ever had.

The big conference room was very crowded. I had never seen even half that number at meals and some of the faces were strange to me. I concluded that some had been called in and had been able to arrive quickly. At a table at the front of the room Anna sat with a total stranger. Anna had folders of paper, a formidable terminal relay, and secretarial gear. The stranger was a woman about Anna's age but with a stern schoolmarmish look instead of Anna's warmth.

At two seconds past nine the stranger rapped loudly on the table. "Quiet, please! I am Rhoda Wainwright, Executive Vice-Chairman of this company and chief counsel to the late Dr. Baldwin. As such I am now Chairman *pro tem* and paymaster for the purpose of winding up our affairs. You each know that each of you was bound to this company by contract to Dr. Baldwin personally—"

Had I ever signed such a contract? I was bemused by "the late Dr. Baldwin." Was that really Boss's name? How did it happen that his name matched my commonest *nom de guerre*? Had he picked it? That was so very long ago.

"—since you are all now free agents. We are an elite outfit and Dr. Baldwin anticipated that every free company in North America would wish to recruit from our ranks once his death released you. There are hiring agents in each of the small conference rooms and in the lounge. As your names are called please come forward to receive and sign for your packet. Then examine it at once but do not, repeat do *not*, stand at this table and attempt to discuss it. For discussion you must wait until all the others have received their termination packets. Please remember that I have been up all night—"

Hire out with some other free company at once? Did I have to? Was I broke? Probably, except for what was left of that two hundred thousand bruins I had won in that silly lottery—and most of that I probably owed to Janet on her Visa card. Let me see, I had won 230.4 grams of fine gold, deposited with MasterCard as Br.200,000 but credited as gold at that day's fix. I had drawn thirty-six grams of that as cash and— But I must reckon my other account, too, the one through Imperial Bank of Saint Louis. And the cash and the Visa credit I owed Janet. And Georges ought to let me pay half of—

Someone was calling my name.

It was Rhoda Wainwright, looking vexed. "Please be alert, Miss Friday. Here is your packet and sign here to receipt for it. Then move aside to check it."

I glanced at the receipt. "I'll sign after I've checked it."

"Miss Friday! You're holding up the proceedings."

"I'll step aside. But I won't sign until I confirm that the packet matches the receipt list."

Anna said soothingly, "It's all right, Friday. I checked it."

I answered, "Thanks. But I'll handle it just the way you handle classified documents—sight and touch."

The Wainwright biddy was ready to boil me in oil but I simply moved aside a couple of meters and started checking—a fair-size packet: three passports in three names, an assortment of IDs, very sincere papers matching one or another identity, and a draft to "Marjorie Friday Baldwin" drawn on Ceres and South Africa Acceptances, Luna City, in the amount of Au-0.999 grams 297.3— which startled me but not nearly as much as the next item did: adoption papers by Hartley M. Baldwin and Emma Baldwin for female child Friday Jones, renamed Marjorie Friday Baldwin, executed at Baltimore, Maryland, Atlantic Union. Nothing about Landsteiner Crèche or Johns Hopkins, but the date was the day I left Landsteiner Crèche.

And two birth certificates: one was a delayed birth certificate for Marjorie Baldwin, born in Seattle, and one was for Friday Baldwin, borne by Emma Baldwin, Boston, Atlantic Union.

Two things were certain about each of these documents: Each was phony and each could be relied on utterly; Boss never did things by halves. I said, "It checks, Anna." I signed.

Anna accepted the receipt from me, adding quietly: "See me after."

"Suits. Where?"

"See Goldie."

"Miss Friday! Your credit card, please!" Wainwright again.

"Oh." Well, yes, with Boss gone and the company dissolved, I could not use my Saint Louis credit card again. "Here it is."

She reached for it; I held on. "The punch, please. Or the shears. Whatever you're using."

"Oh, come now! I'll incinerate yours along with many others, after I check the numbers."

"Ms. Wainwright, if I am to surrender a credit card charged against me—and I am; no argument about that—it will be destroyed or mutilated, rendered useless, right in front of me."

"You are very tiresome! Don't you trust anyone?"

"No."

"Then you'll have to wait, right here, until everyone else is through."

"Oh, I don't think so." I think MasterCard of California uses a phenolic-glass laminate; in any case their cards are tough, as credit cards must be. I had been careful not to show any enhancements around HQ, not because it would matter there but because it isn't polite. But this was a special circumstance. I tore the card two ways, handed her the bits. "I think you can still make out the serial number."

"Very well!" She sounded as annoyed as I felt. I turned away. She snapped, "Miss Friday! Your other card, please!"

"What card?" I was wondering who among my dear friends was suddenly being deprived of that utter necessity of modern life, a valid credit card, and being left with only a draft and some small change. Clumsy. Inconvenient. I felt certain that Boss had not planned it that way.

"MasterCard . . . of . . . California, Miss Friday, issued in San Jose. Hand it over."

"The company has nothing to do with that card. I arranged that credit on my own."

"I find that hard to believe. Your credit on it is guaranteed by Ceres and South Africa—that is to say, by the company. The affairs of which are being liquidated. So hand over that card."

"You're mixed up, counselor. While payment is made through

Ceres and South Africa, the credit involved is my own. It's none of your business."

"You'll soon find out whose business it is! Your account will be canceled."

"At your own risk, counselor. If you want a law suit that will leave you barefooted. Better check the facts." I turned away, anxious not to say another word. She had me so angry that, for the moment, I was not feeling grief over Boss.

I looked around and found that Goldie had already been processed. She was sitting, waiting. I caught her eye and she patted an empty chair by her; I joined her. "Anna said for me to see you."

"Good. I made a reservation at Cabaña Hyatt in San Jose for Anna and me for tonight, and told them that there might be a third. Do you want to come with us?"

"So soon? Are you already packed?" What did I have to pack? Not much, as my New Zealand luggage was still sitting in bond in Winnipeg port because I suspected that the Winnipeg police had placed a tag on it—so there it would sit until Janet and Ian were in the clear. "I had expected to stay here tonight but I really hadn't thought about it."

"Anyone can sleep here tonight but it's not being encouraged. The management—the new management—wants to get everything done today. Lunch will be the last meal served. If anyone is still here tonight at dinnertime, it's cold sandwiches. Breakfast, nit."

"Fer Gossake! That doesn't sound like anything Boss would have planned."

"It isn't. This woman— The Master's arrangements were with the senior partner, who died six weeks ago. But it doesn't matter; we'll just leave. Coming with us?"

"I suppose so. Yes. But I had better see these recruiters first; I'm going to need a job."

"Don't."

"Why not, Goldie?"

"I'm looking for a job, too. But Anna warned me. The recruiters here today all have arrangements with La Wainwright. If any of them are any good, we can get in touch with them at Las Vegas Labor Mart . . . without handing this snapping turtle a commission. I know what I want—head nurse in a field hospital of a crack mercenary outfit. All the best ones are represented in Las Vegas."

"I guess that's the place for me to look, too. Goldie, I've never had to hunt for a job before. I'm confused."

"You'll do all right."

Three hours later, after a hasty lunch, we were in San Jose. Two APVs were shuttling between Pajaro Sands and the National Plaza; Wainwright was getting rid of us as fast as possible—I saw two flat-bed trucks, big ones, each drawn by six horses, being loaded as we left, and Papa Perry looking harried. I wondered what was being done with Boss's library—and felt a little separate, selfish sadness that I might never again have such an unlimited chance to feed the Elephant's Child. I'll never be a big brain but I'm curious about everything and a terminal hooked directly to all the world's best libraries is a luxury beyond price.

When I saw what they were loading I suddenly recalled something with near panic. "Anna, who was Boss's secretary?"

"He didn't have one. I sometimes helped him if he needed an extra hand. Seldom."

"He had a contact address for my friends Ian and Janet Tormey. What would have become of it?"

"Unless it's in this"—she took an envelope from her bag and handed it to me—"it's gone . . . because I have had standing orders for a long time to go to his personal terminal as soon as he was pronounced dead and to punch in a certain program. It was a wipe order, I know, although he did not say so. Everything personal he had in the memory banks was erased. Would this item be personal?"

"Very personal."

"Then it's gone. Unless you have it there."

I looked at what she had handed me: a sealed envelope with nothing but "Friday" on the outside. Anna added, "That should have been in your packet but I grabbed it and held it out. That nosy slitch was reading everything she could get her hands on. I knew that this was private from Mr. Two-Canes—Dr. Baldwin, I should say now—to you. I was not going to let her have it." Anna sighed. "I worked with her all night. I didn't kill her. I don't know why I didn't."

Goldie said, "We had to have her to sign those drafts."

Riding with us was one of the staff officers, Burton McNye—a quiet man who rarely expressed opinions. But now he spoke. "I'm sorry you restrained yourself. Look at me; I have no cash, I always used my credit card for everything. That snotty shyster wouldn't give me my closing check until I handed over my credit card. What happens with a draft on Lunar bank? Can you cash it, or do they simply accept it for collection? I may be sleeping in the Plaza tonight."

"Mr. McNye—"

"Yes, Miss Friday?"

"I'm no longer 'Miss' Friday. Just Friday."

"Then I'm Burt."

"Okay, Burt. I've got some cash bruins and a credit card that Wainwright could not touch, although she tried. How much do you need?"

He smiled and reached over and patted my knee. "All the nice things I've heard about you are true. Thanks, dear, but I'll handle it. First I'll take this to the Bank of America. If they won't cash it offhand, perhaps they will advance me some pending collection. If not, I shall go to her office in the CCC Building and stretch out on her desk and tell her that it is up to her to find me a bed. Damn it; the Chief would have seen to it that each of us got a few hundred in cash; she did it on purpose. Maybe to force us to sign up with her buddies; I wouldn't put it past her. If she makes any fuss, I'm feeling just ornery enough to find out whether or not I remember any of the things they taught me in basic."

I answered, "Burt, don't ever tackle a lawyer with your hands. The way to fight a lawyer is with another lawyer, a smarter one. Look, we'll be in the Cabaña. If you can't cash that draft, better accept my offer. It won't inconvenience me."

"Thanks, Friday. But I'm going to choke her until she gives in."

The room Goldie had reserved turned out to be a small suite, a room with a big waterbed and a living room with a couch that opened into a double bed. I sat down on the couch to read Boss's letter while Anna and Goldie used the bath—then got up to use it myself when they came out. When I came out, they were on the big bed, sound asleep—not surprising; both of them had been up all night in nervously exhausting work. I kept very quiet and sat back down, resumed reading the letter:

Dear Friday,

Since this is my last opportunity to communicate with you, I must tell you things I have not been able to say while alive and still your employer.

Your adoption: You do not remember it because it did not happen that way. You will find that all records are legally correct. You are indeed my foster daughter. Emma Baldwin has the same sort of reality as your Seattle parents, i.e., real for all practical and legal purposes. You need be careful of only one thing: Don't let your several identities trip each other. But you have walked that tight-wire many times, professionally.

Be sure to be present or represented at the reading of my will. Since I am a Lunar citizen

(Huh?)

this will be at Luna City immediately after my death, Luna Republic not having all the lawyer-serving delays one finds in most Earthside countries. Call Fong, Tomosawa, Rothschild, Fong, and Finnegan, Luna City. Do not anticipate too much; my will does not relieve you of the necessity of earning a living.

Your origin: You have always been curious about this, understandably so. Since your genetic endowment was assembled from many sources and since all records have been destroyed, I can tell you little. Let me mention two sources of your genetic pattern in whom you may take pride, two known to history as Mr. and Mrs. Joseph Green. There is a memorial to them in a crater near Luna City, but it is hardly worth the trip as there is nothing much to see. If you will query the Luna City Chamber of Commerce concerning this memorial, you can obtain a cassette with a reasonably accurate account of what they did. When you hear it, you will know why I told you to suspend judgment on assassins. Assassination is usually a dirty business . . . but honorable hatchet men can be heroes. Play the cassette and judge for yourself.

The Greens were colleagues of mine many years ago. Since their work was very dangerous, I had caused each of them to deposit genetic material, four of her ova, a supply of his sperm. When they were killed, I caused gene analysis to be made with an eye to posthumous children—only to learn that they were incompatible; simple fertilization would have caused reinforcement of some bad alleles.

Instead, when creation of artificial persons became possible, their genes were used selectively. Yours was the only successful design; other attempts at including them were either not viable or had to be destroyed. A good genetic designer works the way a good photographer does: A perfect result derives from a willingness to discard drastically any attempt less than perfect. There will be no more attempts using the Greens; Gail's ova are gone and Joe's sperm is probably no longer useful.

It is not possible to define your relationship to them but it is equivalent to something between granddaughter and great-granddaughter, the rest of you being from many sources but you can take pride in the fact that *all* of you was most carefully selected to maximize the best traits of *H. sapiens*. This is your potential; whether or not you achieve your potential is up to you.

Before your records were destroyed, I once scratched my curiosity by listing the sources that went into creating you. As near as I can recall they are:

Finnish, Polynesian, Amerindian, Innuit, Danish, red Irish, Swazi, Korean, German, Hindu, English—and bits and pieces from elsewhere since none of the above is pure. You can never afford to be racist; you would bite your own tail!

All that the above really means is that the best materials were picked to design you, regardless of source. It is sheer luck that you wound up beautiful as well.

["Beautiful"! Boss, I do own a mirror. Was it possible that he had really thought so? Surely, I'm built okay; that just reflects the fact that I'm a crack athlete—which in turn reflects the fact that I was planned, not born. Well, it's nice that he thought so if he did . . . because it's the only game in town; I'm me, whatever.]

On one point I owe you an explanation if not an apology. It was intended that you should be reared by selected parents as their natural child. But when you still weighed less than five kilos, I was sent to prison. Although I was able, eventually, to escape, I could not return to Earth until after the Second Atlantic Rebellion. The scars of this mix-up are still with you, I know. I hope that you someday will purge yourself of your fear and mistrust of "human" persons; it gains you nothing and handicaps you mightily. Someday, somehow, you must realize emotionally what you know intellectually, that they are as tied to the Wheel as you are.

As for the rest, what can I say in a last message? That unfortunate coincidence, my conviction at just the wrong time, left you too easily bruised, much too sentimental. My dear, you must cure yourself utterly of all fear, guilt, and shame. I think you have rooted out self-pity

[The hell I have!]

but, if not, you must work on it. I think that you are immune to the temptations of religion. If you are not, I cannot help you, any more than I could keep you from acquiring a drug habit. A religion is sometimes a source of happiness and I would not deprive anyone of happiness. But it is a comfort appropriate for the weak, not for the strong—and you are strong. The great trouble with religion—*any* religion—is that a religionist, having accepted certain propositions by faith, cannot thereafter judge those propositions by evidence. One may bask at the warm fire of faith or choose to live in the bleak uncertainty of reason—but one cannot have both.

I have one last thing to tell you—for my own satisfaction, for my own pride. I am one of your "ancestors"—not a major one but some of my genetic pattern lives on in you. You are not only my foster daughter but also in part my natural daughter as well. To my *great* pride.

So let me close this with a word I could not say while I was alive—
Love,
Hartley M. Baldwin

I put the letter back into its envelope and curled up and indulged in that worst of vices, self-pity, doing it thoroughly, with plenty of tears. I don't see anything wrong with crying; it lubricates the psyche.

Having gotten it out of my system I got up and washed my face and decided that I was all through grieving over Boss. I was pleased and flattered that he had adopted me and it warmed me all through to know that a bit of him was used in designing me—but he was still Boss. I thought that he would allow me one cathartic session of grief but if I kept it up, he would be annoyed with me.

My chums were still sawing wood, exhausted, so I closed the door that shut them off, was pleased to note that it was a sound-silencer door, and I sat down at the terminal, stuck my card into the slot, and coded Fong, Tomosawa, and so forth, having routed through exchange service to get the code, then coding directly; it's cheaper that way.

I recognized the woman who answered. Low gee certainly is better than a bra; if I lived in Luna City, I would wear only a monikini, too. Oh, stilts, maybe. An emerald in my bellybutton. "Excuse me," I said. "Somehow I've managed to code Ceres and South Africa when I intended to punch for Fong, Tomosawa, Rothschild, Fong, and Finnegan. My subconscious is playing tricks. Sorry to have bothered you and thanks for the help you gave me a few months ago."

"Wups!" she answered. "You didn't punch wrong. I'm Gloria Tomosawa, senior partner in Fong, Tomosawa, et al., now that Grandpa Fong has retired. But that doesn't interfere with my being a vice-president of Ceres and South Africa Acceptances; we are also the legal department of the bank. And I'm the chief trust officer, too, which means that I'm going to have business with you. Everybody here is sorry as can be at the news of Dr. Baldwin's death and I hope that it did not distress you too much—Miss Baldwin."

"Hey, back up and start over!"

"Sorry. Usually when people call the Moon they want to make it as brief as possible because of the cost. Do you want me to repeat all that, a sentence at a time?"

"No. I think I've assimilated it. Dr. Baldwin left a note telling me to be at the reading of his will or to be represented. I can't be there. When will it be read and can you advise me as to how I can get someone in Luna City to represent me?"

"It will be read as soon as we get official notification of death from the California Confederacy, which should be any time now as our

San Jose representative has already paid the squeeze. Someone to represent you—will I do? Perhaps I should say that Grandpa Fong was your father's Luna City attorney for many years . . . so I inherited him and now that your father has died, I inherit you. Unless you tell me otherwise."

"Oh, would you?—Miss—Mrs. Tomosawa—is it Miss or Mrs.?"

"I could and I would and it's Mrs. It had better be; I have a son as old as you are."

"Impossible!" (This beauty-contest winner twice my age?)

"Most possible. Here in Luna City we are all old-fashioned cubes, not like California. We get married and we have babies and always in that order. I wouldn't dare be a Miss with a son your age; nobody would retain me."

"I mean the idea that you have a son my age. You can't have a baby at the age of five. Four."

She chuckled. "You say the nicest things. Why don't you come here and marry my son? He's always wanted an heiress."

"Am I an heiress?"

She sobered. "Um. I can't break the seal on that will until your father is officially dead, which he is not, in Luna City, not yet. But he will be shortly and there is no sense in making you call back. I drafted that will. I checked it for changes when I got it back. Then I sealed it and put it into my safe. So I know what's in it. What I'm about to tell you, you don't know until later today. You're an heiress but fortune-hunters won't be chasing you. You are not getting a gram in cash. Instead the bank is instructed—that's me—to subsidize you in migrating off Earth. If you pick Luna, we pay your fare. If you picked a bounty planet, we would give you a Scout knife and pray for you. If you pick a high-priced place like Kaui or Halcyon, the trust pays your fare and your contribution and assists you with starting capital. If you never do migrate off Terra, on your death funds earmarked to assist you revert to the other purposes of the trust. But your migration needs have first call. Exception: If you migrate to Olympia, you pay for it yourself. Nothing from the trust."

"Dr. Baldwin said something about that. What's so poisonous about Olympia? I don't recall a colony world named that."

"You don't? No, I guess you're too young. That's where those

263

self-styled supermen went. No real point in warning you against it, however; the corporation doesn't run ships there. Dear, you are running up a fancy comm bill."

"I guess so. But it would cost me more if I had to call back. All I mind is having to pay for the speed-of-light dead time. Can you switch hats and be Ceres and South Africa for a moment? Or maybe not; I may need legal advice."

"I'm wearing both hats, so fire away. Ask anything; today there's no fee. My advertising loss leader."

"No, I pay for what I get."

"You sound like your late father. I think he invented tanstaafl."

"He's not really my father, you know, and I never thought of him as such."

"I know the score, dear; I drew up some of the papers about you. He thought of you as his daughter. He was inordinately proud of you. I was most interested when you first called me—having to keep quiet about things I knew but looking you over. What is on your mind?"

I explained the trouble I had had with Wainwright over credit cards. "Certainly MasterCard of California has given me a credit ceiling far beyond my needs or assets. But is that any of her business? I haven't even used up my predeposit and I'm about to back it up with my closing pay. Two hundred and ninety-seven and three-tenths grams, fine."

"Rhoda Wainwright never was worth a hoot as a lawyer; when Mr. Esposito died, your father should have changed representation. Of course it's none of her business what credit MasterCard extends to you, and she has no authority over this bank. Miss Baldwin—"

"Call me Friday."

"Friday, your late father was a director of this bank and is, or was, a major stockholder. Although you do not receive any of his wealth directly, you would have to run up an enormous unsecured debt and neglect to reduce it for quite some time and refuse to answer queries about it before your account would be red-flagged. So forget it. But, now that Pajaro Sands is closing down, I do need another address for you."

"Uh, right now, *you* are the only address I have."

"I see. Well, get me one as soon as you have one. There are others with that same problem, a problem unnecessarily made worse by Rhoda Wainwright. There are others who should be represented at the reading of the will. She should have notified them, did not, and now they have left Pajaro Sands. Do you know where I can find Anna Johansen? Or Sylvia Havenisle?"

"I know a woman named Anna who was at the Sands. She was the classified documents clerk. The other name I don't recognize."

"She must be the right Anna; I have her listed as 'confidential clerk.' Havenisle is a trained nurse."

"Oh! Both of them are just beyond a door I'm looking at. Sleeping. Up all night. Dr. Baldwin's death."

"My lucky day. Please tell them—when they wake up—that they should be represented at the reading of the will. But don't wake them; I can fix it afterwards. We aren't all that fussy here."

"Could you represent them?"

"On your say-so, yes. But have them call me. I'll need new mailing addresses for them, too. Where are you now?"

I told her, we said good-bye and switched off. Then I held very still and let my head catch up with events. But Gloria Tomosawa had made it easy. I suspect that there are just two sorts of lawyers: those who spend their efforts making life easy for other people—and parasites.

A little jingle and a red light caused me to go to the terminal again. It was Burton McNye. I told him to come on up but be mouse-quiet. I kissed him without stopping to think about it, then remembered that he was not a kissing friend. Or was he? I did not know whether he had helped rescue me from "the Major" or not— must ask.

"No trouble," he told me. "Bank of America accepted it for deposit subject to collection but advanced me a few hundred bruins for overnight money. They tell me that a gold draft can be cleared through Luna City in about twenty-four hours. That, combined with our late employer's sound financial reputation, got me out of the bind. So you don't have to let me sleep here tonight."

"I'm supposed to cheer? Burt, now that you are solvent again, you can take me out to dinner. Out. Because my roommates are zombies. Dead, maybe. The poor dears were up all night."

"It's too early for dinner."

It wasn't too early for what we did next. I hadn't planned on it but Burt claimed that he had, in the APV; and I didn't believe him. I asked him about that night on the farm and, sure enough, he was part of the combat team. He claimed that he had been held in reserve and thus was merely along for the ride, but nobody yet has admitted doing anything dangerous that night—but I recall Boss telling me that anybody at all was taken because bodies were so scarce—even Terence, who doesn't really have to shave yet.

He didn't protest when I started taking his clothes off.

Burt was just what I needed. Too much had happened and I felt emotionally battered. Sex is a better tranquilizer than any of those drugs and much better for your metabolism. I don't see why human people make such a heavy trip out of sex. It isn't anything complex; it is simply the best thing in life, even better than food.

The bath in that suite could be reached without going through the bedroom, laid out that way, probably, because the living room could double as a second bedroom. So we each tidied up a bit and I put on that Superskin jump suit with the wet look that had been the bait with which I had hooked Ian last spring—and learned that I had put it on through thinking sentimentally about Ian but that I was no longer worried about Ian and Jan—and Georges. I would find them, I was now serenely sure. Even if they never went home, I would at worst track them down through Betty and Freddie.

Burt made appropriate animal noises over how I looked in the Superskin job, and I let him look and wiggled some and told him that was exactly why I had bought it, because I was a slitch who wasn't even mildly ashamed of being female, and I wanted to thank him for what he had done for me; my nerves had been twanging like a harp and now they were so relaxed they dragged on the ground and I had decided to pay for dinner to show my appreciation.

He offered to wrestle me for it. I didn't tell him that I had to be very careful in moments of passion not to break male bones; I just giggled. I guess giggling looks silly on a woman my age but there it is—when I'm happy, I giggle.

I was careful to leave a note for my chums.

When we got back, latish, they were gone, so Burt and I went to bed, this time stopping to open out that folding double bed. I woke up when Anna and Goldie tiptoed through, returning from supper. But I pretended not to wake, figuring that morning was soon enough.

Sometime the next morning I became aware that Anna was standing over us and not looking happy—and, truthfully, that was the very first time that it occurred to me that Anna might be displeased at finding me in bed with a man. Certainly I had realized which way she leaned a long time ago; certainly I knew that she leaned in my direction. But she herself had cooled it and I had stopped thinking of her as unfinished business I would have to cope with someday; she and Goldie were simply my chums, hair-down friends who trusted each other.

Burt said plaintively, "Don't scowl at me, lady; I just came in to get out of the rain."

"I wasn't scowling," she answered too soberly. "I was simply trying to figure out how to get around the end of the bed to the terminal without waking you two. I want to order breakfast."

"Order for all of us?" I asked.

"Certainly. What do you want?"

"Some of everything and fried potatoes on the side. Anna hon, you know me—if it's not dead, I'll kill it and eat it raw, bones and all."

"And the same for me," agreed Burt.

"Noisy neighbors." Goldie was standing in the doorway, yawning. "Chatterboxes. Go back to bed." I looked at her and realized two things: I had never really looked at her before, even at the beach. And, second, if Anna was annoyed with me for sleeping with Burt, she didn't have any excuse for such feelings; Goldie looked almost indecently satiated.

"It means 'harbor island,' " Goldie was saying, "and it really ought to have a hyphen in it because nobody can ever spell it or pronounce it. So I just go as Goldie—easy to do in the Master's outfit where last names were always discouraged. But it's not as hard a name as Mrs. Tomosawa's—after I mispronounced hers about the fourth time, she asked me to call her Gloria."

We were finishing off a big breakfast and both of my chums had talked to Gloria and the will had been read and both of them (and Burt, too, to my surprise and his) were now a bit richer and we were all getting ready to leave for Las Vegas, three of us to shop for jobs, Anna simply to stay with us and visit until we shipped out, or whatever.

Anna was then going to Alabama. "Maybe I'll get tired of loafing. But I promised my daughter that I would retire and this is the right time. I'll get reacquainted with my grandchildren before they get too big."

Anna a grandmother? Does anyone ever know anyone else?

XXV

Las Vegas is a three-ring circus with a hangover.

I enjoy the place for a while. But after I've seen all the shows I reach a point where the lights and the music and the noise and the frenetic activity are too much. Four days is a-plenty.

We reached Vegas about ten, after a late start because each of us had business to do—everybody but me with arrangements to make for the collection of moneys from Boss's will and me to deposit my closing draft with MasterCard. That is, I started to. I stopped abruptly when Mr. Chambers said, "Do you want to execute an order to us to pay your income tax on this?"

Income tax? What a filthy suggestion! I could not believe my ears. "What was that, Mr. Chambers?"

"Your Confederacy income tax. If you ask us to handle it—here's the form—our experts prepare it and we pay it and deduct it from your account and you aren't bothered. We charge only a nominal fee. Otherwise you have to calculate it yourself and make out all the forms and then stand in line to pay it."

"You didn't say anything about any such tax when I made the deposit the day I opened this account."

"But that was a national lottery prize! That's *yours*, utterly free— that's the Democratic Way! Besides, the government gets its cut off the top in running the lottery."

"I see. How much cut does the government take?"

"Really, Miss Baldwin, that question should be addressed to the government, not to me. If you'll just sign at the bottom, I'll fill in the rest."

"In a moment. How much is this 'nominal fee'? And how much is the tax?"

I left without depositing my draft and again poor Mr. Chambers was vexed with me. Even though bruins are so inflated that you have to line up quite a few of them to buy a Big Mac, I do not consider a thousand bruins "nominal"—it's more than a gram of gold, $37 BritCan. With their 8 percent surcharge on top, MasterCard would be getting a fat fee for acting as stooge for the Confederacy's Eternal Revenue Service.

I wasn't sure that I owed income tax even under California's weird laws—most of that money had not been earned in California and I couldn't see what claim California had on my salary anyway. I wanted to consult a good shyster.

I went back to Cabaña Hyatt. Goldie and Anna were still out but Burt was there. I told him about it, knowing that he had been in logistics and accounting.

"It's a moot point," he said. "Personal-service contracts with the Chairman were all written 'free of tax' and in the Imperium the bribe was negotiated each year. Here an umbrella bribe should have been paid through Mr. Esposito—that is to say, through Ms. Wainwright. You can ask her."

"In a pig's eye!"

"Precisely. She should have notified Eternal Revenue and paid any taxes due—after negotiation, if you understand me. But she may be skimming; I don't know. However— You do have a spare passport, do you not?"

"Oh, certainly! Always."

"Then use it. That's what I'll be doing. Then I'll transfer my money after I know where I'll be. Meanwhile I'll leave it safe on the Moon."

"Uh, Burt, I'm pretty sure Wainwright has every spare passport listed. You seem to be saying that they'll be checking us at exit?"

"What if Wainwright has listed them? She won't turn over the list to the Confederates without arranging her cut, and I doubt that she's had time to dicker it. So pay only the regular squeeze and stick your nose in the air and walk on through the barrier."

This I understood. I had been so indignant at that filthy notion that for a moment I had ceased to think like a courier.

We crossed the border into Vegas Free State at Dry Lake; the capsule stopped just long enough for Confederacy exit stamps. Each of us used an alternate passport with the standard squeeze folded inside—no trouble. And no entrance stamp as the Free State doesn't bother with CHI; they welcome any solvent visitor.

Ten minutes later we checked into the Dunes, with much the same accommodations we had had in San Jose save that this was described as an "orgy suite." I could not see why. A mirror on the ceiling and aspirin and Alka-Seltzer in the bath are not enough to justify that designation; my doxyology instructor would have laughed in scorn. However I suppose that most of the marks would not have had the advantages of advanced instruction—I've been told that most people don't have *any* formal training. I've often wondered who teaches them. Their parents? Is that rigid incest taboo among human persons actually a taboo against talking about it but not against doing it?

Someday I hope to find out such things but I've never known anybody I could ask. Maybe Janet will tell me. Someday . . .

We arranged to meet for dinner, then Burt and Anna went to the lounge and/or casino while Goldie and I went out to the Industrial Park. Burt intended to job-hunt but expressed an intention of raising a little hell before settling down. Anna said nothing but I think she wanted to savor the fleshpots before taking up the life of a grandmother-in-residence. Only Goldie was dead-serious about job-hunting that day. I intended to find a job, yes—but I had some thinking to do first.

I was probably—almost certainly—going to out-migrate. Boss thought I should and that was reason enough. But besides that, the study he had started me on concerning the symptoms of decay in cultures had focused my mind on things I had long known but never analyzed. I've never been critical of the cultures I've lived in or traveled through—please understand that an artificial person is a permanent stranger wherever she is, no matter how long she stays. No country could ever be mine so why think about it?

But when I did study it, I saw that this old planet is in sorry shape. New Zealand is a pretty good place and so is British Canada, but even those two countries showed major signs of decay. Yet those two are the best of the lot.

But let's not rush things. Changing planets is something a person doesn't do twice—unless she is fabulously wealthy, and I was not. I was subsidized for *one* out-migration . . . so I had better by a durn sight pick the right planet because no mistakes were going to be corrected after I left the window.

Besides— Well, *where* was Janet?

Boss had had a contact address or a call code. Not me!

Boss had had an ear in the Winnipeg police HQ. Not me!

Boss had had his own Pinkerton net over the whole planet. Not me!

I could try to phone them from time to time. I would. I could check with ANZAC and the University of Manitoba. I would. I could check that Auckland code and also the biodep of the University of Sydney. I would.

If none of those worked, what more could I do? I could go to Sydney and try to sweet-talk somebody out of Professor Farnese's home address or sabbatical address or whatever. But that would not be cheap and I had suddenly been forced to realize that travel I had taken for granted in the past would now be difficult and perhaps impossible. A trip to New South Wales before semiballistics started to run again would be *very* expensive. It could be done—by tube and by float and by going three-fourths the way around the world . . . but it would be neither easy nor cheap.

Perhaps I could sign on as a ship's doxy out of San Francisco for Down Under. That would be cheap and easy . . . but time-consuming even if I shipped in a Shipstone-powered tanker out of Watsonville. A sail-powered freighter? Well, no.

Maybe I had better hire a Pinkerton in Sydney. What did they charge? Could I afford it?

It took less than thirty-six hours from Boss's death for me to bump my nose into the fact that I had never learned the true value of a gram.

Consider this: Up to then my life had had just three modes of economy:

a) On a mission I had spent whatever it took.

b) At Christchurch I spent some but not much—mainly presents for the family.

c) At the farm, at the next HQ, then still later at Pajaro Sands, I didn't spend *any* money, hardly. Room and board were in my contract. I did not drink or gamble. If Anita had not been bleeding me, I would have accumulated a tidy sum.

I had led a sheltered life and had never really learned about money.

But I can do simple arithmetic without using a terminal. I had paid in cash my share at Cabaña Hyatt. I used my credit card for my fare to the Free State but jotted down the cost. I noted the daily rate at the Dunes and kept track of other costs, whether card or cash or on the hotel bill.

I could see at once that room and board in first-class hotels would very shortly use up every gram I owned even if I spent zero, nit, swabo, nothing, on travel, clothes, luxuries, friends, emergencies. Q.E.D. I must either get a job or ship out on a one-way colonizing trip.

I acquired a horrid suspicion that Boss had been paying me a lot more than I was worth. Oh, I'm a good courier, none better—but what's the going rate on couriers?

I could sign up as a private, then (I was fairly sure) make sergeant in a hurry. That did not really appeal to me but it might be where I would wind up. Vanity isn't one of my faults; for most civilian jobs I am unskilled labor—I know it.

Something else was pulling me, something else was pushing me. I didn't *want* to go alone to a strange planet. It scared me. I had lost my Ennzedd family (if indeed I ever had them), Boss had died, and I felt like Chicken Little when the sky was falling, my true friends among my colleagues had gone to the four winds—except these three and they were leaving quickly—and I had managed to lose Georges and Janet and Ian.

Even with Las Vegas giddy around me I felt as alone as Robinson Crusoe.

I wanted Janet and Ian and Georges to out-migrate with me. Then I would not be afraid. Then I could smile all the way.

Besides— The Black Death. Plague was coming.

Yes, yes, I had told Boss that my midnight prediction was nonsense. But he had told me that his analytical section had predicted the same thing, in four years instead of three. (Small comfort!)

I was forced to take my own prediction seriously. I must warn Ian and Janet and Georges.

I did not expect to frighten them with it—I don't think you can scare those three. But I did want to say, "If you won't migrate, at least take my warning seriously to the extent of staying out of big cities. If inoculation becomes available, get it. But heed this warning."

The Industrial Park is on the road to Hoover Dam; the Labor Mart is there. Vegas does not permit APVs inside the city but there are slidewalks everywhere and one runs out to Industrial Park. To go beyond there, to the dam or to Boulder City, there is an APV commuter line. I planned to use it as Shipstone Death Valley leases a stretch of desert between East Las Vegas and Boulder City for a charging station and I wanted to see it to supplement my study.

Could the Shipstone complex be the corporation state behind Red Thursday? I could see no reason for it. But it had to be a power rich enough to blanket the globe and reach all the way out to Ceres in a single night. There were not many such. Could it be a superrich man or group of men? Again, not many possibilities. With Boss dead I probably never would know. I used to slang him—but he was the one I turned to when I didn't understand something. I had not known how much I leaned on him until his support was taken away.

The Labor Mart is a large covered mall, with everything from fancy offices of the *Wall Street Journal* to scouts who have their offices in their hats and never sit down and seldom stop talking. There are signs everywhere and people everywhere and it reminds me of Vicksburg river town but it smells better.

The military and quasi-military free companies cluster together at the east end. Goldie went from one to the other and I went with her. She left her name and a copy of her brag sheet with each one. We had stopped in town to get her brag sheet printed and she had arranged a mail drop with a public secretary, and she had induced me to pay for a mail and telephonic accommodation address, too. "Friday, if we are here more than a day or two, I'm moving out of the Dunes. You noticed the room tariff, did you not? It's a nice place but they sell you the bed all over again each day. I can't afford it. Maybe you can but—"

"I can't."

So I established an address of sorts, and sent my brain a memo to tell Gloria Tomosawa. I paid a year's fee in advance—and discovered that it gave me an odd feeling of security. It was not even a little grass shack . . . but it was a base, an address, that would not wash away.

Goldie did not sign up that afternoon but did not seem disappointed. She said to me, "No war going on now, that's all. But peace never lasts more than a month or two. Then they'll start hiring again and my name will be on file. Meanwhile I'll list with the city registry and work substitute jobs. One thing about the bedpan business, Friday; a nurse *never* starves. The current emergency shortage of nurses has been going on for more than a century and won't let up soon."

The second recruiter she called on—representative of Royer's Rectifiers, Caesar's Column, and the Grim Reapers, all crack outfits, worldwide reputations—turned to me after Goldie had made her statement. "How about you? Are you an RN, too?"

"No," I said, "I'm a combat courier."

"Not much call for that. Today most outfits use express mail if a terminal won't serve."

I found myself somewhat piqued—Boss has warned me against that. "I'm elite," I replied. "I go anywhere . . . and what I carry gets there when the mail is shut down. Such as the late Emergency."

"That's true," said Goldie. "She's not exaggerating."

"There still isn't much call for your talents. Can you do anything else?"

(I should not boast!) "What's your best weapon? I'll duel you with it, either contest rules, or blood. Phone your widow and we'll do it."

"My, you're a sparky little slitch! You remind me of a fox terrier I once had. Look, dear, I can't play games with you; I have to keep this office open. Now tell me the truth and I'll put your name on file."

"Sorry, chief. I shouldn't have sounded off. All right, I'm an elite courier. If I carry it, it gets there and my fees are high. Or my salary if I'm hired as a specialist staff officer. As for the rest, of course I have to be the best, bare-handed or with weapons, because what I carry *must* go through. You can list me as a DI if you wish—bare-handed or any weapon. But I'm not interested in combat unless the pay is high. I prefer courier duty."

He made notes. "All right. Don't get your hopes up. The hairy characters I work for aren't likely to use couriers other than battle-field couriers—"

"I'm that, too. What I carry gets through."

"Or you get killed." He grinned. "They're more likely to use a superdog. Look, sweetheart, a corporate has more need for your sort of messenger than does a military. Why don't you leave your name with each of the multinationals? All the big ones are represented here. And they've got more money. Lots more money."

I thanked him and we left. At Goldie's urging I stopped in at the local branch post office and made printouts of my own brag sheet. I was going to ease off on the required salary, being sure that Boss had favored me—but Goldie wouldn't let me. "Raise it! This is your best chance. Outfits that need you will either pay without a quiver . . . or will at least call you and try to dicker. But cut your price? Look, dear, nobody buys at a fire sale if they can afford the best."

I dropped one at each multinational. I didn't really expect any nibbles but if anyone wanted the world's best courier, they could study my qualifications.

When the offices started to close, we slid back to the hotel to keep our dinner date, and found both Anna and Burt just a leetle tipsy. Not drunk, just happy and a touch too deliberate in their movements.

Burt struck a pose and declaimed, "Ladies! Look at me and admire! I am a great man—"

"You're swacked."

"That, too, Friday, m'love. But you see before you wup! the man who banked the broke at Monte Carlo. I'm a genius, a blinkin', true-blue, authentic, f'nanchal genius. You may touch me."

I had been planning to touch him, later that night. Now I wondered. "Anna, did Burt break the bank?"

"No, but he certainly bent it." She stopped to belch carefully, covering up. "'Scuse me. We dropped a little here, then went over to the Flamingo to change our luck. Got there just before post time for the third at Santa Anita and Burt put a superbuck on the nose of a little mare with his mother's name—a long shot and she romped home. So here is a wheel right outside the track room and Burt put his winnings on double zero—"

"He was drunk," Goldie stated.

"I am genius!"

"Both. Double zero hit, and Burt put this enormous stack on black and hit, and left it there and hit, and moved it to red and hit—and the croupier sent for the pit boss. Burt wanted to go for broke but the pit boss limited him to five kilobucks."

"Peasants. Gestapo. Hired menials. Not a gentleman sportsman in their entire casino. I took my patronage elsewhere."

"And lost it all," said Goldie.

"Goldie m'old frien', you do not show proper respec'."

"He might have lost it all," agreed Annie, "but I saw to it that he followed the pit boss's advice. With six of the casino's sheriffs around us we went straight to their casino's office of the Lucky Strike State Bank and deposited it. Otherwise I would not have let him leave. Imagine carrying a half a megabuck from the Flamingo to the Dunes *in cash*. He wouldn't have lived to cross the street."

"Preposterous! Vegas has less violent crime 'nany other city North Amer'ca. Anna, m'true love, you are a bossy, notional woman. A henpecker. I shall not marry you even when you fall on your knees at Fremont 'n' Main 'n' beg me to. Instead I shall take your shoes away from you and beat you and feed you on crusts."

"Yes, dear. You can put your own shoes on now because you are going to feed all three of us. On crusts of caviar and truffles."

"And champagne. But not because you are henpeckering me. Ladies. Friday, Goldie, my true loves—will you help me celebrate my f'nanchal genius? With libations and pheasant under glass and gorgeous show girls in fancy hats?"

"Yes," I answered.

"Yes before you change your mind. Anna, did you say 'half a megabuck'?"

"Burt. Show them."

Burt produced a new bankbook, let us look at it while he buffed his nails on his stomach and looked smug. Bk504,000. Over half a million in the only hard currency in North America. Uh, slightly over thirty-one kilos of fine gold. No, I wouldn't want to carry that much across the street, either—not in bullion. Not without a wheelbarrow. It would mass almost half as much as I do. A bankbook is more convenient.

Yes, I would drink Burt's champagne.

Which we did, in the theater at the Stardust. Burt knew how much cumshaw to give the captain of waiters to get us ringsides (or paid too much, I don't know which) and we sopped up champagne and had a lovely dinner centered around Cornish game hen but billed as squab and the show girls were young and pretty and cheerful and healthy and smelled freshly bathed. And they had show boys with stuffed codpieces for us women to look at, only I didn't, not much, because they didn't smell right and I got the feeling that they were more interested in each other than they were in women. Their business, of course, but on the whole I preferred the show girls.

And they had a swell magician who plucked live pigeons out of the air the way most magicians pluck coins. I love magicians and never understand how they do it and I watch them with my mouth hanging open.

This one did something that had to involve a pact with the Devil. At one point he had one of the show girls replace his pretty assistant. His assistant was not overdressed but the show girl was wearing shoes at one end and a hat at the other and just a smile in between.

The magician started taking pigeons from her.

I don't believe what I saw. There isn't that much room and it would tickle. So it didn't happen.

But I'm planning on going back to watch it from a different angle. It simply *can't* be true.

When we got back to the Dunes, Goldie wanted to catch the lounge show but Anna wanted to go to bed. So I agreed to sit with Goldie. Burt said to save him a seat as he would be right back after he took Anna up.

Only he didn't. When we went up I was unsurprised to find the door to the other room closed; before dinner my nose had warned me that it was unlikely that Burt would soothe my nerves two nights in a row. Their business and I had no kick coming. Burt had done nobly by me when I really needed it.

I thought perhaps Goldie would have her nose out of joint but she didn't seem to. We simply went to bed, giggled over the impossibility of where he got those pigeons, and went to sleep. Goldie was snoring gently as I dropped off.

Again I was awakened by Anna but this morning she was not looking sober; she was radiant. "Good morning, darlings! Pee and brush your teeth; breakfast will be up in two jounces. Burt is just getting out of the bath, so don't dally."

Along toward the second cup of coffee Burt said, "Well, dear?"

Anna said, "Shall I?"

"Go ahead, hon."

"All right. Goldie, Friday— We hope you can spare us some time this morning because we both love you both and want you to be with us. We're getting married this morning."

Goldie and I put on fine exhibitions of utter astonishment and great pleasure, along with jumping up and kissing each of them. In my case the pleasure was sincere; the surprise was faked. With Goldie I thought that it might have been reversed. I kept my suspicions to myself.

Goldie and I went out to buy flowers with arrangements to meet at the Gretna Green Wedding Chapel later—and I was relieved and pleased to find that Goldie seemed to be just as happy about it out of their presence as in it. She said to me, "They're going to be very good for each other. I never did think well of Anna's plans to become a professional grandmother; that's a form of suicide." She added, "I hope you didn't get your nose out of joint."

I answered, "Huh? *Me?* Why in the world would I?"

"He slept with you night before last; he slept with her last night. Today he's marrying her. Some women would be quite upset."

"Fer Gossake, *why?* I'm not in love with Burt. Oh, I do love him because he was one of you who saved my life one busy night. So night before last I tried to thank him—and he was awfully sweet to me, too. When I needed it. But that's no reason for me to expect Burt to devote himself to me every night or even a second night."

"You're right, Friday, but not many women your age can think that straight."

"Oh, I don't know; I think it's obvious. You didn't get your feelings hurt. Same deal."

"Eh? What do you mean?"

"Exactly the same deal. Night before last she slept with you; last night she slept with him. Doesn't seem to fret you."

"Why should it?"

"It should not. But the cases are parallel." (Goldie, please don't take me for a fool, dear. I not only saw your face but I smelled you.) "Matter of fact, you surprised me a little. I didn't know you leaned that way. Of course I knew that Anna did—she surprised me a bit in taking Burt to bed. I wasn't aware that she did. Men, I mean. Hadn't known that she had ever been married."

"Oh. Yes, I suppose it could look that way. But it's much what you said about Burt: Anna and I love each other, have for years— and sometimes we express it in bed. But we're not 'in love.' Each of us leans heavily toward men . . . no matter what impression you gained the other night. When Anna practically stole Burt out of your arms, I cheered—despite fretting a bit about you. But not fretting too much because you always have a pack of men sniffing around after you whereas with Anna it had become a seldom thing. So I cheered. Hadn't expected it to lead to marriage but it's grand that it has. Here's the Golden Orchid—what shall we buy?"

"Wait a moment." I stopped her outside the florist shop. "Goldie . . . at great risk to her life somebody went charging up to the bedroom of the farmhouse, carrying a basket stretcher. For me."

Goldie looked annoyed. "Somebody talks too much."

"I should have talked sooner. I love you. More than I love Burt for I've loved you longer. Don't need to marry him, can't marry you. Just love you. All right?"

XXVI

Maybe I did marry Goldie, sort of. Once we had Anna and Burt formally married, we all went back to the hotel; Burt moved them into the "bridal suite" (no mirror on the ceiling, interior decorations white and pink instead of black and red, otherwise much the same—but much more expensive), and Goldie and I moved out of the hotel and sublet a little crackerbox near where Charleston slants into Fremont. This placed us in walking distance of the slidewalk connecting the Labor Mart with town and that gave Goldie transportation to any of the hospitals and made it easy for me to shop— otherwise we would have had to buy or rent a horse and buggy, or bicycles.

Location was that house's sole virtue, maybe, but to me it was a fairy-tale honeymoon cottage with roses over the door. It had no roses and was ugly and the only thing modern in it was a limited-service terminal. But for the first time in my life I had a home of my own and was a "housewife." My home in Christchurch had never truly been mine; I certainly was never mistress of that household, and I had been steadily reminded in various ways that I was a guest rather than a permanent fixture.

Do you know what fun it is to buy a saucepan for your very own kitchen?

I was a housewife at once as Goldie was called on that very day and went on watch at twenty-three hundred to work all night to oh-seven hundred. The following day I cooked my first dinner while

Goldie slept . . . and burned the potatoes beyond salvage and cried, which is, I understand, a bride's privilege. If so, I've used mine up against the day when I'm really a bride if ever—and not a phony bride as in Christchurch.

I was a proper housewife; I even bought sweet-pea seeds and planted them in lieu of that missing climbing rose over the door— and discovered that gardening has more to it than sticking seeds in the ground; those seeds did not germinate. So I consulted the Las Vegas library and bought a book, a real book with looseleaf pages and pictures of what the compleat gardener should do. I studied it. I memorized it.

One thing I did not do. Although enormously tempted I did not get a kitten. Goldie might ship out any day; she warned me that, if I was out of the house, she might be gone without saying good-bye (as I had warned Georges—and did do).

Were I to get a kitten I would be honor-bound to keep it. A courier can't carry a kitten everywhere in a travel case; that's no way to bring up a baby. Someday I would ship out. So I did not adopt a kitten.

Aside from that I enjoyed all the warm delights of being a house-wife . . . including ants in the sugar and a waste pipe line that broke in the night, two delights that I don't care to repeat. It was a very happy time. Goldie slowly got my cooking straightened out—I had thought I knew how to cook; now I *do* know how. And I learned to stir a martini exactly the way she preferred it: Beefeater gin three-point-six to one of Noilly Prat dry vermouth, a twist, no bitters— while I took Bristol Cream on rocks. Martinis are too rugged for me but I can see why a nurse with tired feet would want one the minute she is home.

Swelp me, had Goldie been male, I would have had my sterility reversed and happily have raised children and sweet peas and cats.

Burt and Anna left for Alabama early in this period and we all made careful arrangements not to lose track of each other. They did not intend to live there but Anna felt that she owed her daughter a visit (and owed herself, I think, a chance to show off her new hus-band). Thereafter they intended to sign up with a military or quasi-military, one that would take both of them and contract to keep them together. In combat. Yes. Both were tired of desk work; both were willing to take a bust in grade to leave staff and join a combat team. "Better one crowded hour of life than a cycle of Cathay." Maybe so. It was their life.

I kept in touch at the Labor Mart because the day was coming when I not only would want to ship out but would have to ship out. Goldie was working quite steadily and she tried to insist on paying all the household expenses. I laid my ears back and insisted on paying half right down the middle. Since I was keeping track of every buck, I knew exactly what it cost to live in Las Vegas. Too much, even in a crackerbox. When Goldie left, I could live there a few months, then I would be broke.

But I would not do so. A honeymoon cottage is a no-good place to live alone.

I continued to try to reach Georges and Ian and Janet, and Betty and Freddie, but I limited myself to twice a month; the terminal charges were considerable.

Twice a week I spent half a day at the Labor Mart, checking everything. I no longer expected to find a courier job even half as good as the one I had had with Boss but I still checked the multinationals—who did indeed use experienced couriers. And I checked all other job opportunities, looking for something, anything, to match my decidedly odd talents. Boss had hinted that I was some sort of a superman—if so, I can testify that there is very little demand for supermen.

I considered going to school to become a croupier or dealer— then moved that possibility to the bottom of the pile. A skilled dealer or stick man or wheel man can work for many years at good wages . . . but to me it would be a treadmill. A way to stay alive but not a life. Better to join up as a private and buck for field rank.

But there were other possibilities I had never thought about. Consider these:

Host Mother—Unlimited License, Bonded by TransAmerica and/or Lloyd's—no extra charge for multiple births up to quadruplets. Fee by arrangement. Standard interview fee with physical examination by your-choice physiometricist.
BABIES UNLIMITED, Inc.
LV 7962M 4/3

I could try to sign with Babies Unlimited or I could freelance. My conditional sterility would be a selling point, as the thing customers of host mothers are most leery of is the host mother who slips one over on the client—gets pregnant on her own just before submitting herself for hosting. Sterility is no handicap as bringing down an ovum is not the purpose; the technologist simply manipulates to change the body chemistry to make the field ripe for implantation. Ovulation is simply a nuisance.

Having babies for other people could be only a stopgap—but a possible one; it paid well.

WANTED: 90-day wife for off-planet vacation.
All expenses, luxury 9+, guild bonus scale. Phys. range S/W, temperament sanguine 8, amativeness scale 7 or above. Client holds procreation license Chicago Imperium, will surrender it to holiday wife if she becomes pregnant or both will undergo 120-day sterilization, her choice.
See Amelia Trent, Licensed Sex Broker,
#18/20 New Cortez Mezzanine.

Not a bad deal for someone who wanted a three-months' vacation and enjoyed Russian roulette. To me, pregnancy was no danger and my horny scale rating is higher than seven—much! But the doxy bonus scale in the Free State is not high enough to make the accumulated pay enough to justify losing chances at more permanent work—and that faceless client was almost certainly a crashing bore or he wouldn't consider hiring a stranger for his holiday bed.

URGENTLY NEEDED—Two Time-Space Engineers, any sex, experienced in n-dimensional design. Must be willing to risk nonreversible temporal dislocation.
Participation—Amenities—Assurance
Terms to be negotiated
Babcock and Wilcox, Ltd.
Care *Wall Street Journal*, LV Lbr Mrt

The above is exactly the sort of job I wanted. The only hitch was that I was in no slightest degree qualified.

The First Plasmite Church ("In the Beginning was Plasma, without form and void") off the Mall had a sign advertising times of services. A smaller notice with movable letters included in it caught my eye: "The Next Virgin Will Be Sacrificed at 0251 Oct 22"

That looked like a permanent position but again not one for which I was qualified. It fascinated me. While I was gawking, a man came out and changed the sign and I realized that I had missed last night's sacrament and the next altar sacrifice was two weeks away, which left me undismayed. But my curiosity got me, as usual. I asked him: "Do you actually sacrifice virgins?"

He answered, "Not me. I'm just an acolyte. But— Well, no, they don't actually have to *be* virgins. But they do have to *look* like virgins." He looked me up and down. "I think you could make it. Want to come in and talk to the priest?"

"Uh, no. Do you mean that he actually sacrifices them?"

He looked at me again. "You're a stranger here, aren't you?"

I admitted it. "Well, it's like this," he went on. "If you were to advertise that you were casting for a snuff film, you could cast every part by noon and not one of 'em would ask if they were actually going to be snuffed. It's that kind of a town."

Maybe so. More likely I'm a yokel come to town. Or both.

There were lots of ads for off-planet jobs or concerning off-planet matters. I did not expect to hire out for an off-planet job because I did expect to go off planet as a colonist so lavishly subsidized that I would have free choice of any colony, from Proxima, almost in our laps, to The Realm, so far away that both cargo and people went by *n*-ship—except that the late word on The Realm was that The First Citizen had closed it to migrants at any price, except certain artists and scientists by individual negotiation. Not that I wanted to go to The Realm, rich as it is reputed to be. Too far! But the Proximates are our close neighbors; from South Island their sun is right overhead, a big bright star. Friendly.

But I read all the ads:

Transuranics Golden Division on Golden around Procyon-B wanted experienced mining engineers to supervise kobolds, five-year renewable, bonuses, perks. The ad did not mention that on Golden an unmodified human person seldom lives five years.

HyperSpace Lines was hiring for the run to The Realm via Proxima, Outpost, Fiddler's Green, Forest, Botany Bay, Halcyon, and Midway. Four months round trip from Stationary Station, one month paid leave Earthside or Luna, and repeat. I skipped over the requirements and pay for ultra-astrogator and warp engineer and supercargo and communicator and medical officer but looked at the other ratings:

Waiter, room steward, maintenance carpenter, electrician, plumber, electronicist, electronicist (computer), plumber, cook, baker, sous chef, pantryman, chef, specialty cook, bartender, croupier/dealer, social director, holographer/photographer, dental assistant, singer, dance instructor, games supervisor, companion-secretary-maid/valet, cruise director's assistant, art instructor, cards instructor, cruise hostess, swimming instructor, hospital nurse, children's nurse, master-at-arms (armed), master-at-arms (unarmed), director/bandmaster, theatrical director, musician (twenty-three instruments named but doubling on two or more required), cosmetician, barber, masseur, stores clerk, retail sales clerk, sales manager, excursion escort—

—and that's just a sample. In general, if they do it on the ground, they do it or something like it in the sky. Some of the jobs concerned uniquely with spaceship matters I can't even translate—what in the world (or out of it) is an "over kippsman 2/c"?

One profession not listed is "doxy" despite the fact that Hyper-Space Lines is an Equal Opportunity Employer. By word of mouth I learned how very equal this is. If you want to be hired for any of the not so very technical jobs, it helps enormously to be young, handsome/pretty, healthy, horny, bisexual, money-hungry, and open to any reasonable proposition.

The Port Captain himself has two left feet and was purser of the old *Newton*, up from room steward. In his sky-voyaging days he made certain that his first-class passengers got *anything* they wanted—and that they paid well for it. As Port Captain this is still his purpose. He is said to favor married couples or equivalent over any single if they can work as a team both in and out of bed. I heard a story around the Mall of one gigolo/doxy team who made themselves rich in only four trips—dance instructors in the morning, swimming instructors in the afternoon, dancing host and hostess before and after dinner, a singing and comedy act, then private entertainment singly or as a team at night—four voyages and ready to retire . . . and had to retire because they were fired, as they were no longer very attractive, no longer brimming with vitality; they had maintained this impossible pace on uppers and downers.

I don't think money can tempt me that much. I'll stay awake all night most anytime I'm asked but I do want to catch up on sleep the next day.

I wondered how it was that HyperSpace Lines, with only four passenger liners, was apparently hiring all their many ratings all the time. The line's assistant hiring agent said to me, "You really don't know?"

I told her I did not.

"At each of three of the stops it takes lots and lots of what makes the world go round to buy your way in. Three more are not cheap although some skills are accepted in lieu of contribution. Only one is a bounty planet. So desertion is a major problem. Fiddler's Green is so desirable a place that the first officer of the *Dirac* jumped ship there a few years back. The company does not have too much trouble with crew recruited here . . . but suppose your home was Rangoon or Bangkok or Canton and you were working cargo on Halcyon and the pusher took his eyes off you just long enough. What would you do?"

She shrugged and went on, "I'm telling you no secrets. Anybody who thinks about it knows that the only possible way for most people to get off Earth—even to Luna—is to sign on as crew of a spaceship, then jump ship. I'd do it myself if I could."

"Why don't you?" I asked.

"Because I have a six-year-old son."

(I should learn to mind my own business!)

Some of the ads stirred my imagination; this was one:

> New Planet Just Opening—Type T-8
> Guaranteed Maximum Danger
> Couples or Groups Only
> Augmented Survival Plan
> Churchill and Son, Realtors
> Las Vegas Labor Mart 96/98

I remembered something Georges had said, that anything above Terran scale eight called for a big bonus or bounty. But I knew more about that scale now; eight was Earth's own basic rating. Most of this planet wasn't too easy to tame. Most of it had to be worked over, rebuilt. This very land I stood on had been fit only for gila monsters and desert crawlies until it had been treated with tons of money and many, many tons of water.

I wondered about that "maximum danger." Was it something that called for the talents of a woman who was fast on her feet when triggered? I really didn't yearn to be a platoon leader of Amazons because some of my girls would get killed and I wouldn't like that. But I wouldn't mind tackling a saber-toothed tiger or equivalent because I felt certain that I could move in, clobber him, and back off while he was still finding out that something was up.

Maybe a raw T-8 would be a better place for Friday than a manicured place like Fiddler's Green.

On the other hand that "maximum danger" might derive from too many volcanoes or too much radioactivity. Who wants to glow in the dark? Find out first, Friday; you won't get two chances.

I stayed quite late at the Mall that day because Goldie was again on the night shift. I had served her dinner when she got home that morning, put her to bed about ten, and hoped that she would sleep till at least eighteen. So I dallied until the Mall offices started closing.

When I got home our house was dark, which pleased me as it tended to indicate that Goldie had slept straight through. With luck I could get her breakfast before she woke up. So I let myself in most quietly . . . and realized that the house was empty. I won't try to define this but an empty house doesn't feel, smell, sound, or taste like one with a person sleeping in it. I went straight to the bedroom. Empty bed. Empty bath. I switched on lights and presently I found it, a long printout for me in the terminal:

Dearest Friday,
It looks now as if you won't be home before I leave—and that is probably just as well because we would just cry on each other and that's no help.

My job came through but not as expected. Keeping in touch with my former boss paid off; Dr. Krasny called me shortly after I went to bed. He is C.O. of a brand-new MASH being set up to serve the Sam Houston Scouts. An expanded Scouts of course; each battalion is cadre for a triangular combat team, a pony brigade. I am not supposed to tell you where we are mounting or where we will go but (burn this printout after you read it!) if you were to go west from Plainview, you might run across us in Los Llanos Estacados, before you reach Portales.

Where are we going? That's *really* classified! But if we don't hit Ascension, some wives will draw a pension. I called Anna and Burt; they are meeting me in El Paso at ten past eighteen

["1810"? Then Goldie is *already* in Texas. Oh, dear!]

because Dr. Krasny assured me that they would have jobs, either as combat troops or as auxiliary medical if any hitch develops. There is a job for you, too, my dear one—combat if that's what you want. Or I'll rate you medtech-3 and use you myself and upgrade you to master sergeant (medadmin) in nothing flat, as I know your quality and so does Colonel Krasny. It would be good to have all four of us—five, I mean—back together again.

But I'm not trying to twist your arm. I know you have things troubling you about your Canadian friends who disappeared. If you feel that you must stay loose to look for them—bless you and good luck. But if you want to get in a little action with bonus pay, come straight to El Paso. The address is Panhandle Investments, El Paso Division, Field Operations Office, Environmental Factors, Attention John

Krasny, Chief Engineer—and don't laugh; just memorize it and destroy it.

Once this operation is in the news you can reach any of us openly through the Houston office of the Scouts. But in the meantime I am "personnel chief clerk" in "Environmental Factors."

May a gracious God watch over you and keep you safe from harm.

All my love,
Goldie

XXVII

I burned it at once. Then I went to bed. I didn't feel like eating dinner.

Next morning I went to the Labor Mart, looked up Mr. Fawcett, agent for HyperSpace Lines, and told him that I wanted to sign on as a master-at-arms, unarmed.

The supercilious slob laughed at me. I glanced at his assistant for moral support but she kept her eyes averted. I restrained my temper and said gently, "Would you mind explaining the joke?"

He stopped his raucous cawing and said, "Look, chicken, 'master' as in 'master-at-arms' designates a *male*. Although we might be able to hire you as 'mistress' in some other department."

"Your sign says Equal Opportunity Employer. The fine print under it states that 'waiter' includes 'waitress,' 'steward' includes 'stewardess,' and so forth. Is that true?"

Fawcett stopped grinning. "Quite true. But it also says: 'physically able to carry out the normal duties of the position.' Master-at-arms is a police officer aboard ship. Master-at-arms, unarmed, is a cop who can keep order without having to resort to weapons. He can wade into a fight and arrest the center of the disturbance, barehanded. Obviously you can't. So don't give me any quack about taking it to the union."

"I shan't. But you didn't read my brag sheet."

"Can't see that it matters. However—" He glanced casually down the page. "Says here you're a combat courier, whatever that is."

"That means that when I have a job to do, nobody stops me. If somebody tries too hard, he's dog meat. A courier goes unarmed. I sometimes carry a laser knife or one-shot tear gas. But I depend on my hands. Note my training."

He looked it over. "Okay, so you've been to a martial-arts school. That still doesn't mean that you can cope with some big bruiser over a hundred kilos heavier and a head taller than you are. Don't waste my time, girlie; you couldn't even arrest *me*."

I went over his desk, then turkey-walked him to the door and turned him loose before anyone outside could see. Even his assistant did not see it—she most carefully did not see it.

"There," I said, "that's how I do it without hurting anyone. But I want to be tested against your biggest male master-at-arms. I'll break his arm. Unless you tell me to break his neck."

"You grabbed me when I wasn't looking!"

"Of course I did. That's how to handle a nasty drunk. But you're looking now, so let's run through it again. Are you ready? This time I might have to hurt you a little but not much. I won't break any bones."

"Stay where you are! This is ridiculous. We don't hire masters-at-arms merely because they've been trained in some Oriental tricks; we hire *big* men, men so big they carry authority just by their size. They don't have to fight."

"Okay," I said. "Hire me as a plainclothes cop. Put me into an evening dress; call me a dance hostess. When somebody about my size and hopped up on sleet pokes your big cop in his solar plexus and he goes down, I stop pretending to be a lady and go in and rescue him."

"Our masters-at-arms don't need to be protected."

"Maybe. A really big man is usually slow and clumsy. He hardly ever knows much about fighting because he's never really had to fight. He's okay to keep order at a card party. Or to handle one drunk. But suppose the Captain *really* needs help. A riot. A mutiny. Then you need someone who can fight. Me."

"Leave your application with my assistant. Don't call us; we'll call you."

I went home and thought about where else I could look—or should I go to Texas? I had made the same silly, unpardonable mistake with Mr. Fawcett that I had made with Brian . . . and Boss would have been ashamed of me. Instead of picking up his challenge I should have insisted on a fair test—but I should *never* have laid a finger on the man I was asking to hire me. Stupid, Friday, *stupid!*

It was not losing that job that bothered me; it was losing *any* chance of getting a spaceside job with HyperSpace Lines. I was going to have to have a job pretty soon to accomplish the sacred duty of seeing to it that Friday eats (let's face it; I eat like a pig) but it didn't have to be *this* job. I had decided to ship out with Hyper-Space because one voyage with them would let me size up more than half of the colonized planets in explored space.

While I had made up my mind to migrate as Boss had advised, the idea of picking a planet solely from brochures written by advertising copywriters—with no return-and-exchange privilege—bothered me. I wanted to shop first.

For example: Eden has received more favorable publicity than any other colony in the sky. Hearken to its virtues: A climate much like Southern California over most of its land mass, no dangerous predators, no noxious insects, surface gravity 9 percent less than Earth, oxygen content of air 11 percent higher, metabolic environment compatible with Terran life and soil so rich that two or three bumper crops a year are routine. Scenery delightful no matter where you look. Population today just under ten million.

So what's the catch? I found out one evening in Luna City through letting a ship's officer pick me up and take me to dinner. The company placed a high price on Eden from the time it was discovered and touted it as the perfect retirement home. And it is. After the pioneer party had prepared it, nine-tenths of the people who moved there were elderly and wealthy.

The government is a democratic republic but not one like the California Confederacy. To be eligible to vote a person must be seventy Terran years old and a taxpayer (i.e., landowner). Residents from ages twenty to thirty perform public service, and if you think that means waiting on the elderly hand and foot you are utterly right, but it includes also anything else unpleasant that needs to be done and therefore would command high wages if it were not done by conscript labor.

Is any of this in any of the company brochures? Hollow laugh!

I needed to know the unadvertised facts about each colonial planet before buying a one-way ticket to one of them. But I spoiled my best chance by "proving" to Mr. Fawcett that an unarmed female can place a come-along on a male bigger than she is—that merely got me on his blacklist.

I do hope I grow up before Cheyne-Stokes breathing sets in.

Boss scorned crying over spilt milk quite as much as he despised self-pity. Having killed my chances of being hired by HyperSpace it was time to leave Las Vegas while I was still solvent. If I couldn't make the Grand Tour myself, there was still a way to get the ungarnished word about colonial planets the way I had acquired the truth about Eden: cultivate ships' crew members.

The way to do that was by going to the one place where I was sure to find them: Stationary Station, up the Beanstalk. Freighters were not likely to come farther down Earth's gravity well than to Ell-Four or -Five—that is, to Lunar orbit without the disadvantage of entering Luna's own gravity well. But passenger ships usually touched at Stationary Station. All of HyperSpace Lines' giant liners, *Dirac*, *Newton*, *Forward*, and *Maxwell*, left from there, returned there, received maintenance and chandlery there. Shipstone complex had a branch there (Shipstone Stationary) primarily to sell power to ships and especially these big ships.

Officers and ratings going on leave arrived and left from there; those not on leave might sleep in their ships but they were likely to drink and eat and party a bit in the Station.

I dislike the Beanstalk and I don't care much for the twenty-four-hour Station. Aside from its spectacular and always changing view of Earth it has nothing to offer but high prices and cramped quarters. Its artificial gravity surges uncomfortably and always seems to go out just in time to put soup in your face.

But there are jobs to be had there if you are not fussy. I should be able to support myself there long enough to be sure that I received frank opinions concerning each of the colonized planets from one or more jaundiced spacemen.

It was even possible that I might bypass Fawcett and ship out from there with HyperSpace. Ships are reputed always to sign on a few at the last minute to fill unexpected vacancies. If such a chance opened up, I would not compound my folly—I would not ask for a master-at-arms billet. Waitress, scullery, chambermaid, bath attendant—if the job would swing me around the Grand Tour, I would grab it.

Having thus picked my new home, I looked forward to boarding the same ship, by choice, as a luxury-class passenger, passage paid under the odd terms of my foster father's will.

I gave notice to the leaseholder of the mousetrap I lived in, then took care of some chores before leaving for Africa. Africa— Would I have to cross via Ascension? Or would SBs be running again? Africa made me think of Goldie, and Anna and Burt, and sweet Doc Krasny. I might reach Africa before they did. Irrelevant as there was only one probable war there now (that I knew of) and I intended to shun that area like the plague.

Plague! I must at once prepare a report on plague for Gloria Tomosawa and for my friends at Ell-Five, Mr. and Mrs. Mortenson. It seemed preposterously unlikely that anything I could say would persuade them or anyone else that a Black Death epidemic was coming in only two and a half years—I hadn't believed it myself. But, if I could make responsible people uneasy enough so that antirat measures were tightened and health checks at CHI barriers be made more than a meaningless ritual, it might—it just might—save space colonies and Luna.

Unlikely— But I had to try.

The only other thing I had to do was make one more check on my missing friends . . . then let the matter rest until I came down from Stationary Station or (one may hope!) returned from the Grand Tour. Surely one can call Sydney or Winnipeg or anywhere from Stationary Station . . . but at much higher cost. I had learned lately that wanting something and being able to pay for it were not the same.

I punched the Tormeys' Winnipeg call code, resigned to hearing:

"The code you have signaled is temporarily out of service at the subscriber's request."

What I got was: "Pirates Pizza Palace!"

I muttered, "Sorry, I punched wrong," and cleared the board. Then I punched again, most carefully—

—and got: "Pirates Pizza Palace!"

This time I said, "I'm sorry to bother you. I'm in Las Vegas Free State and have been trying to reach a friend in Winnipeg—but twice I've reached you. I don't know what I'm doing wrong."

"What code did you punch?"

I told the friendly voice. "That's us," she agreed. "Best giant pizzas in British Canada. But we opened just ten days ago. Maybe your friend used to have this call code?"

I agreed with that, thanked the pleasant voice, and cleared—sat back and thought. Then I punched ANZAC Winnipeg while wishing mightily that this minimum-service terminal could bring in a picture from farther away than Las Vegas itself; in trying to play Pinkerton it helps to watch faces. Once ANZAC's computer answered, I asked for the operations duty officer, I having become somewhat more sophisticated in how to handle that computer. I told the woman who answered, "I'm Friday Jones, a New Zealand friend of Captain and Mrs. Tormey. I tried to call their home and could not reach them. I wonder if you can help me?"

"I'm afraid not."

"Really? Not even a suggestion?"

"I'm sorry. Captain Tormey resigned. He even cashed in his pension rights. I understand that he's sold his house, so I assume that he is gone for good. I do know that the only address we have for him is his brother-in-law's address at the University of Sydney. But we can't give out addresses."

I said, "I think you mean Professor Federico Farnese, Biology Department, at the University."

"That's right. I see you know it."

"Yes, Freddie and Betty are old friends; I knew them when they lived in Auckland. Well, I'll wait till I'm home to call Freddie and that will get me Ian. Thanks for being so helpful."

"My pleasure. When you talk to Captain Tormey, please tell him that Junior Piloting Officer Pamela Heresford sends her best."

"I will remember."

"If you are going home soon, I have good news for you. The semi schedule for Auckland is now fully restored. We've run ten days of cargo-only and we are now certain that there is no longer any way our ships can be sabotaged. We are offering a forty percent discount on all fares now, too; we want to get our old friends back."

I thanked her again but told her that, since I was in Vegas, I expected to leave from Vandenberg, then switched off before I had to improvise more lies.

Again I sat and thought. Now that the SBs were running should I go to Sydney first? There was—or used to be—a weekly trajectory from Cairo to Melbourne, and vice versa. If it was not running it was possible to go by tube and float craft via Singapore, Rangoon, Delhi, Teheran, Cairo, then down to Nairobi—but it would be expensive, long, and uncertain, with squeeze at every move and always the chance of being grounded by some local disturbance. I might wind up in Kenya without money enough to go up the Beanstalk.

A last resort. A desperate one.

I called Auckland, was unsurprised to be told by the computer that Ian's call code was not operative. I checked to see what time it was in Sydney, then called the university, not doing it the routine way through its admin office but punching straight through to its biology department, a call code I had obtained a month back.

I recognized a familiar Strine accent. "Marjorie Baldwin here, Irene. Still trying to find my lost sheep."

"My word! Luv, I tried, I did try, to deliver your message. But Professor Freddie never did come back to his office. He's left us. Gone."

"Gone? Gone where?"

"You wouldn't believe how many people would like to know! I'm not even supposed to be telling you this. Somebody cleaned out his desk, there's no hide nor hair in his flat—gone! I can't tell you more than that, because nobody knows."

After that dismaying call I sat still and thought, then called the Winnipeg Werewolves Security Guards. I went as high as I could, to a man who described himself as Assistant Commandant, and told him truthfully who I was (Marjorie Baldwin), where I was (Las Vegas), and what I wanted, a lead to my friends. "Your company was guarding their home before it was sold. Can you tell me who bought it, or who the agent was who sold it, or both?"

Then I certainly wished for vision as well as sound! He answered, "Look, sister, I can smell a cop even through a terminal. Go back and tell your chief that he got nothing off us last time and he gets nothing off us this time."

I held my temper and answered quietly, "I am not a cop although I can see why you might think so. I really am in Las Vegas, which you can confirm by calling me back, collect."

"Not interested."

"Very well. Captain Tormey owned a matched pair of black Morgans. Can you tell me who bought them?"

"Copper, get lost."

Ian had shown excellent judgment: The Werewolves really were loyal to their clients.

If I had plenty of time and money, I might dig up something by going to Winnipeg and/or Sydney and rooting at it myself. If wishes were horses— Forget it, Friday; you are at last totally alone; you've lost them.

Do you want to see Goldie badly enough to get involved in a war in East Africa?

But Goldie did not want to stay with you badly enough to stay out of that war—doesn't that tell you something?

Yes, it tells me something I know but always hate to admit: I always need people more than they need me. It's your old basic insecurity, Friday, and you know where it comes from and you know what Boss thought about it.

All right, we go to Nairobi tomorrow. Today we write up the Black Death report for Gloria and for the Mortensons. Then get a full night's sleep and leave. Uh, eleven hours time difference; try to get an early start. Then don't worry about Janet and Co. until you get back from the Beanstalk with your mind made up about where to colonize. Then you can afford to spend your last gram in a flat-out attempt to find them . . . because Gloria Tomosawa will handle things once you tell her what planet you have picked.

I actually did get a long night's sleep.

The next morning I had packed—same old jumpbag, nothing

much in it—and was puttering around the kitchen, dumping some items and saving others with a note to my landlord, the leaseholder, when the terminal buzzed.

It was the nice gal with the six-year-old boy at HyperSpace. "Glad I caught you," she said. "My boss has a job for you."

(*Timeo Danaos et dona ferentes.*) I waited.

Fawcett's silly face showed. "You claim to be a courier."

"I'm the best."

"In this case, you had better be. This is an off-planet job. Okay?"

"Certainly."

"Take this down. Franklin Mosby, Finders, Inc., suite six hundred, Shipstone Building, Beverly Hills. Now hurry; he wants to interview you before noon."

I didn't write down the address. "Mr. Fawcett, that costs you one kilobuck, plus round-trip tube fare. In advance."

"Huh? Ridiculous!"

"Mr. Fawcett, I suspect that you may hold a grudge. It might strike you as funny to send me on a wild-goose chase and cause me to waste a day and the price of a round-trip fare to Los Angeles."

"Funny girl. Look, you can pick up your fare here at the office—after the interview; you've got to leave now. As for that kilobuck . . . shall I tell you what to do with it?"

"Don't bother. For master-at-arms I would expect only master-at-arms wages. But as courier . . . I am the best and if this man really does want the best, he will pay my interview fee without a second thought." I added, "You're not serious, Mr. Fawcett. Good-bye." I cleared.

He called back seven minutes later. He talked as if it hurt him. "Your round trip and the kilobuck will be at the station. But that kilobuck is against your salary and you pay it back if you don't get the job. Either way, I get my commission."

"It will not be paid back under any circumstances, and you get no commission from me because I have not appointed you my agent. Perhaps you can collect something from Mosby but, if so, it does not come out of my salary or my interview fee. And I'm not going down to the station to wait around like a boy playing snipe hunt. If you mean business, you'll send the money here."

"You're impossible!" His face left the screen but he did not clear it. His assistant came on. "Look," she said, "this job really does have heat behind it. Will you meet me at the station under the New Cortez? I'll get there as fast as I can make it and I'll have your fare and your fee."

"Certainly, dear. A pleasure."

I called my landlord, told him I was leaving the key in the refrigerator and be sure to salvage the food.

What Fawcett did not know was that *nothing* could have induced me *not* to keep this appointment. The name and address was that which Boss had caused me to memorize just before he died. I had never done anything about it because he had not told me *why* he wanted me to memorize it. Now I would see.

XXVIII

All the sign on the door said was FINDERS, INC. and SPECIALISTS IN OFF-PLANET PROBLEMS. I went in and a live receptionist said to me, "They filled the job, dearie; I got it."

"I wonder how long you will keep it. I'm here by appointment to see Mr. Mosby."

She looked me over carefully, in no hurry. "Call girl?"

"Thank you. Where do you get your hair dyed? Look, I'm sent here by HyperSpace Lines, Las Vegas office. Every second is costing your boss bruins. I'm Friday Jones. Announce me."

"You're kidding." She touched her console, spoke into a hushphone. I stretched my ears. "Frankie, there's a floozie out here says she has an appointment with you. Claims to be from Hypo in Vegas."

"God damn it, I've told you not to call me that at work. Send her in."

"I don't think she's from Fawcett. Are you two-timing me?"

"Shut up and send her in."

She pushed aside the hushphone. "Sit down over there. Mr. Mosby is in conference. I'll let you know as soon as he is free."

"That isn't what he told you."

"Huh? Since when do you know so much?"

"He told you not to call him Frankie at work, and to send me in. You gave him some backtalk and he told you to shut up and to send me in. So I'm going in. Better announce me."

Mosby appeared to be about fifty trying to look thirty-five. He had an expensive tan, expensive clothes, a big, toothy smile, and cold eyes. He motioned me toward a visitor's chair. "What took you so long? I told Fawcett I wanted to see you before noon."

I glanced at my finger, then at his desk clock. Twelve-oh-four. "I've come four hundred and fifty kilometers plus a crosstown shuttle since eleven o'clock. Shall I go back to Vegas and see if I can beat that time? Or shall we get down to business?"

"I told Fawcett to see to it that you caught the ten o'clock. Oh, well. I understand you need a job."

"I'm not hungry. I was told that you needed a courier for an off-planet job." I took out a copy of my brag sheet, handed it to him. "Here are my qualifications. Look it over and, if I am what you want, tell me about the job. I'll listen and tell you whether or not I'm interested."

He glanced at the sheet. "The reports I have tell me that you *are* hungry."

"Only in that it is getting on toward lunchtime. My fee schedule is on that sheet. It is subject to negotiation—upwards."

"You're pretty sure of yourself." He looked again at my brag sheet. "How's Kettle Belly these days?"

"Who?"

"It says here that you worked for System Enterprises. I asked you, 'How is Kettle Belly?' Kettle Belly Baldwin."

(Was this a test? Had everything since breakfast been carefully calculated to cause me to lose my temper? If so, the proper response would be not to lose my temper no matter what.) "The Chairman of System Enterprises was Dr. Hartley Baldwin. I've never heard him called Kettle Belly."

"I believe he does have some sort of a doctor's degree. But everybody in the trade calls him Kettle Belly. I asked you how he is."

(Watch it, Friday!) "He's dead."

"Yeah, I know. I wondered if you knew. In this business you get a lot of ringers. All right, let's see this marsupial pouch of yours."

"Excuse me?"

"Look, I'm in a hurry. Show me your bellybutton."

(Just where did the leak occur? Uh— No, we killed that gang. All of them—or so Boss thought. Doesn't mean it couldn't have leaked from there before we killed them. No matter—it *did* leak . . . as Boss said it would.) "Frankie boy, if you want to play bellybuttons with me, I must warn you that the bleached blonde in your outer office is listening and almost certainly recording."

"Oh, she doesn't listen. She has her instructions about that."

"Instructions she carries out the way she carries out your injunction not to call you Frankie during working hours. Look, Mr. Mosby, you started discussing classified matters under not-secure conditions. If you want her to be part of this conference, bring her in. If not, get her out of the circuit. But let's have no more breaches of security."

He drummed on his desk, then got up very suddenly, went into his outer office. The door was not totally soundproof; I heard angry voices, muffled. He came back in, looking annoyed. "She's gone to lunch. Now don't give me any more guff. If you are who you say you are, Friday Jones, also known as Marjorie Baldwin, formerly a courier for Kettle—for Dr. Baldwin, managing director of System Enterprises, you have a pouch created by surgery back of your navel. Show it to me. Prove your identity."

I thought about it. A requirement that I prove my identity was not unreasonable. Fingerprint identification is a joke, at least inside the profession. Clearly the existence of my courier's pouch was now a broached secret. It would never be useful again—except that right now it could be used to prove that I was me. I was I? It sounds silly either way. "Mr. Mosby, you paid a kilobuck to interview me."

"I certainly did! So far I've had nothing from you but static."

"I'm sorry. I've never been asked to show my trick bellybutton before, because up to recently it has been a closely held secret. Or so I thought. Evidently it is no longer a secret, since you know of it. That tells me that I can no longer use it for classified work. If the job you have for me requires the use of it, perhaps you had better reconsider. A secret just a little bit broached is like a girl just a little bit pregnant."

"Well . . . yes and no. Show me."

I showed him. I keep a smooth nylon sphere one centimeter in diameter in my pouch so that the pouch won't shrink between jobs.

I popped out the sphere, letting him watch, and then replaced it—then let him see that it was not possible to tell my navel from a normal navel. He studied it carefully. "It doesn't hold very much."

"Maybe you would rather hire a kangaroo."

"It's big enough for the purpose—barely. You'll be carrying the most valuable cargo in the galaxy, but it won't occupy much space. Zip up and adjust your clothing; we're going to lunch and we mustn't—*must not*—be late."

"What is all this?"

"Tell you on the way. Hurry up."

A carriage was already waiting for us. Back of Beverly Hills, in the hills that name that town, is a very old hotel that is also very swank. It has the stink of money, an odor I don't despise. Between fires and the Big Quake it has been rebuilt several times, always to look just as it did but (so I hear) the last time it was rebuilt to be totally fire- and earthquakeproof.

It took about twenty minutes to drive, at a spanking trot, from the Shipstone Building to the hotel; Mosby used it to fill me in. "During this ride is about the only time that both of us can be sure that we don't have an Ear planted on us—"

(I wondered if he believed that. I could think of three obvious places for an Ear: my jumpbag, his pockets, and the cushions of the carriage. And there were always endless unobvious places. But it was his problem. I had no secrets. None, now that my bellybutton was a window to the world.)

"—so let me talk fast. I'm meeting your price. Furthermore there will be a bonus on completed performance. The trip is from Earth to The Realm. That's what you're paid for; the trip back is deadhead but, since the round trip is four months, you'll be paid for four months. You collect your bonus at the far end at the imperial capital. Salary—one month in advance, the rest as you go. Okay?"

"Okay." I had to avoid sounding too enthusiastic. A round trip to The Realm? My dear man, only yesterday I was anxious to make this trip at petty officer's wages. "What about my expenses?"

"You won't have much in the way of expenses. Those luxury liners are all-expense deals."

"Gratuities, squeeze, groundside excursions, walking-around money, Bingo and such aboard ship—at a minimum such expenses are never less than twenty-five percent of the price of the ticket. If I'm going to pretend to be a rich tourist, I must behave like one. Is that my cover?"

"Uh . . . Well, yes. All right, all right—nobody's going to fuss if you spend a few thousand pretending to be Miss Rich Bitch. Keep track and bill us at the end."

"No. Advance the money, twenty-five percent of the ticket cost. I won't keep records as it would not be in character; Miss Rich Bitch would not keep track of such trivia."

"All right already! Shut up and let me talk; we'll soon be there. You're a living artifact."

I had not felt that cold chill in quite a while. Then I braced up and resolved to make him pay heavily for that one crude, rude remark. "Are you being intentionally offensive?"

"No, I'm not. Don't get in a flutter. You and I know that an artificial person can't be told, offhand, from a natural person. You'll be carrying, in stasis, a modified human ovum. You will carry it in your navel pouch, where the constant temperature and the cushioning will protect the stasis. When you reach The Realm, you will catch a flu bug or some such and go to hospital. While you are in this hospital, what you are carrying will be transferred to where it will do the most good. You'll be paid the bonus and will leave the hospital . . . with the happy knowledge that you have enabled a young couple to have a perfect baby when they were dead-certain, almost, to have a defective one. Christmas disease."

I decided that the story was mostly true. "The Dauphiness."

"What? Don't be silly!"

"And it is considerably more than Christmas disease, which, by itself, might be ignored in a royal person. The First Citizen himself is concerned with this since this time succession is passing through his daughter rather than through a son. This job is much more important and much more hazardous than you told me . . . so the price goes up."

That pair of beautiful bays went clopping on up Rodeo Drive another hundred meters before Mosby answered. "All right. God help you if you talk. You wouldn't live long. We'll increase the bonus. And—"

"You'll damn well double the bonus and deposit it to my account before we warp. This is the kind of a job where people grow forgetful after it's over."

"Well—I'll do what I can. We are about to have lunch with Mr. Sikmaa—and you are expected not to spot the fact that he is personal representative of The First Citizen with an interworld rank of Ambassador Extraordinary and Minister Plenipotentiary. Now straighten up and mind your table manners."

Four days later I was again minding my table manners at the right of the Captain of H. S. *Forward*. My name was now Miss Marjorie Friday and I was so offensively rich that I had been fetched up from groundside to Stationary Station in Mr. Sikmaa's own antigrav yacht and whisked through into the *Forward* without having to bother with anything so plebeian as passport control, health, and so forth. My luggage had come aboard at the same time—box after box of expensive, stylish clothing, appropriate jewelry—but others took care of it; I did not have to bother with anything.

Three of those days I had spent in Florida in what felt like a hospital but was (I knew!) a superbly equipped genetic engineering laboratory. I could infer which one it was but I kept my guesses to myself as speculation about *anything* was not encouraged. While I was there I was given the most thorough physical examination I have ever heard of. I did not know why they were checking my health in a style ordinarily reserved for heads of state and chairmen of multinationals but I presumed that they were jumpy about entrusting to anyone not in perfect health the protecting and delivering of an ovum that would become, in the course of years, First Citizen of the fabulously wealthy Realm. It was a good time to keep my mouth shut.

Mr. Sikmaa used none of the sharpshooting that both Fawcett and Mosby had tried. Once he decided that I would do, he sent Mosby home and catered to me so lavishly that I had no need to dicker. Twenty-five percent for casual money?—not enough; make that fifty percent. Here it is; take it—in gold and in Luna City gold certificates—and, if you need more, just tell the purser and sign for it, a draft on me. No, we won't use a written contract; this is not that sort of a mission—just tell me what you want and you shall have it. And here is a little booklet that tells you who you are and where you went to school and all the rest. You will have plenty of time in the next three days to memorize it and if you forget to burn it, don't fret; the fibers are impregnated so that it self-destroys in the next three days—don't be surprised if the pages are yellow and somewhat brittle on the fourth day.

Mr. Sikmaa had thought of everything. Before we left Beverly Hills, he brought a photographer in; she shot me from several angles, me dressed in a smile, in high heels, in low heels, in bare feet. When my luggage showed up in the *Forward*, every item fitted me perfectly, all the styles and colors suited me, and the clothes carried a spread of famous designer's names from Italy, from Paris, from Bei-Jing, et al.

I'm not used to haute couture and don't know how to handle it, but Mr. Sikmaa had that covered, too. I was met at the airlock by a pretty little Oriental creature named Shizuko who told me that she was my personal maid. Since I had been bathing and dressing myself since I was five, I felt no need for a maid, but again it was time to roll with the blow.

Shizuko conducted me to cabin BB (not quite big enough for a volley-ball court). Once there, it appeared that (in Shizuko's opinion) there was just barely time enough to get me ready for dinner.

With dinner three hours away this struck me as excessive. But she was firm and I was going along with whatever was suggested—I did not need a diagram to tell me that Mr. Sikmaa had planted her there.

She bathed me. While this was going on, there was a sudden surge in the grav control as the ship warped away. Shizuko steadied me and kept it from being a wet disaster and did it so skillfully that she convinced me that she was used to warp ships. She didn't look old enough.

She spent a full hour on my hair and my face. In the past I had washed my face when it seemed to need it and styled my hair mostly by whacking it off enough to keep it out of way. I learned what a bumpkin I·was. While Shizuko was reincarnating me as the Goddess of Love and Beauty the cabin's little terminal chimed. Letters appeared on the screen while the same message extruded from the printout, an impudent tongue:

> The Master of HyperSpaceShip *Forward*
> Requests the Pleasure of the Company
> of Miss Marjorie Friday
> for Sherry and Bonhomie
> in the Captain's Lounge
> at nineteen hundred hours
> regrets only

I was surprised. Shizuko was not. She had already hung out and touched up a cocktail dress. It covered me completely and I have never been so indecently dressed.

Shizuko refused to let me be on time. She led me to the Captain's Lounge timed so that I went through the receiving line at seven minutes after the hour. The cruise hostess already knew my (current) name and the Captain bowed over my hand. It is my considered opinion that being a VIP in a spaceship is a better deal than being a spaceship master-at-arms.

"Sherry" includes highballs, cocktails, Icelandic Black Death, Spring Rain from The Realm (deadly—don't touch it), Danish beer, some pink stuff from Fiddler's Green, and, I have no doubt, Panther Sweat if you ask for it. It also includes thirty-one different sorts (I counted) of tasty tidbits you eat with your fingers. I was a credit to Mr. Sikmaa; I really did take sherry and only one small glass, and I greatly restrained myself when offered, again and again and again and again, those thirty-one tasty temptations.

And it is well that I resisted. This ship puts on the nosebag eight times a day (again I counted): early morning coffee (*café complet*—that is, with pastry), breakfast, midmorning refreshment, tiffin, afternoon tea with sandwiches and more pastry, cocktail-hour hors d'oeuvres (those thirty-one sinful traps), dinner (seven courses if you can stay the route), midnight buffet supper. But if you feel peckish at any hour, you can always order sandwiches and snacks from the pantry.

The ship has two swimming pools, a gymnasium, a Turkish bath, a Swedish sauna, and a "Girth Control" clinic. Two and a third times around the main promenade is a kilometer. I don't think this is enough; some of our shipmates are eating their way across the galaxy. My own major problem will be to arrive at the imperial capital still able to find my bellybutton.

Dr. Jerry Madsen, Junior Medical Officer, who doesn't look old enough to be a sawbones, cut me out of the mob at the Captain's sherry, then was waiting for me after dinner. (He does not eat at the Captain's table or even in the dining room; he eats with the other younger officers in the wardroom.) He took me to the Galactic Lounge, where we danced, then there was a cabaret show—singing, specialty dancing, and a juggler who did magic tricks on the side (which made me think of those pigeons, and of Goldie, and I felt suddenly wistful but suppressed it).

Then there was more dancing and two other young officers, Tom Udell and Jaime Lopez, rotated with Jerry, and finally the lounge shut down and all three took me to a little cabaret called The Black Hole, and I firmly declined to get drunk but danced whenever I was asked. Dr. Jerry managed to outsit the others and took me back to cabin BB at an hour quite late by ship's time but not especially late by the Florida time by which I had gotten up that morning.

Shizuko was waiting, dressed in a beautiful formal kimono, silk slippers, and high makeup of another sort. She bowed to us, indicated that we should sit down at the lounge end—the bedroom end is shut off by a screen—and served us tea and little cakes.

After a short time Jerry stood up, wished me a good night, and left. Then Shizuko undressed me and put me to bed.

I did not have any firm plans about Jerry though no doubt he could have persuaded me had he worked on it—my heels are quite short, I know. But both of us were sharply aware that Shizuko was sitting there, hands folded, watching, waiting. Jerry did not even kiss me good-night.

After putting me to bed, Shizuko went to bed on the other side of the screen—some deal with bedclothes she took out of a cupboard.

I was never before quite so closely chaperoned, even in Christchurch. Could this be part of my unwritten contract?

XXIX

A spaceship—a hyperspaceship—is a terribly interesting place. Of course it takes very, very advanced knowledge of wave mechanics and multidimensional geometry to understand what pushes the ship, education that I don't have and probably never will (although I would like to back up and study for it, even now). Rockets—no problem; Newton told us how. Antigrav—a mystery until Dr. Forward came along and explained it; now it's everywhere. But how does a ship massing about a hundred thousand tonnes (so the Captain told me) manage to speed up to almost eighteen hundred times the speed of light?—without spilling the soup or waking anyone.

I don't know. This ship has the biggest Shipstones I've ever seen . . . but Tim Flaherty (he's second assistant engineer) tells me that they are charged down only at the middle of each jump, then they finish the voyage having used only "parasitic" power (ship's heat, cooking, ship's auxiliary services, etc.).

That sounds to me like a violation of the Law of Conservation of Energy. I was brought up to bathe regularly and to believe that There Ain't No Such Thing as a Free Lunch; I told him so. He grew just a touch impatient and assured me that it was indeed the Law of Conservation of Energy that caused it to work out that way—it worked just like a funicular; you got back what you put in.

I don't know. There aren't any cables out there; it can't be a funicular. But it *does* work.

The navigation of this ship is even more confusing. Only they don't call it navigation; they don't even call it astrogation; they call it "cosmonautics." Now somebody is pulling Friday's leg because the engineer officers told me that the officers on the bridge (it's not a bridge) who practice cosmonautics are cosmetic officers because they are there just for appearances; the computer does all the work—and Mr. Lopez the second officer says that the ship has to have engineering officers because the union requires it but the computer does it all.

Not knowing the math for either one is like going to a lecture and not knowing the language.

I have learned one thing: Back in Las Vegas I thought that every Grand Tour was Earth, Proxima, Outpost, Fiddler's Green, Forest, Botany Bay, Halcyon, Midway, The Realm, and back to Earth because that's how the recruiting posters read. Wrong. Each voyage is tailored. Usually all nine planets are touched but the only fixed feature in the sequence is that Earth is at one end and The Realm, almost a hundred light-years away (98.7 +), is at the other. The seven way stations can be picked up either going out or coming back. However, there is a rule that controls how they are fitted in: Going out the distance from Earth must be greater at each stop, coming back the distance must decrease. This is not nearly as complex as it sounds; it simply means the ship does not double back—just the way you would plan a shopping trip of many stops.

But this leaves lots of flexibility. The nine stars, the suns of these planets, are lined up fairly close to a straight line. See the sketch with the Centaur and the Wolf. Looking from Earth, all those stars, as you can see, are either at the front end of the Centaur or close by in the Wolf. (I know the Wolf doesn't look too well but the Centaur has been clobbering him for thousands of years. Besides, I've never seen a wolf—a four-legged wolf, that is—and it's the best I can do. Come to think of it, I've never seen a Centaur, either.)

That's the way those stars cluster in Earth's night sky. You have to be about as far south as Florida or Hong Kong to see them at all, and even then, with bare eyes you will see only Alpha Centauri.

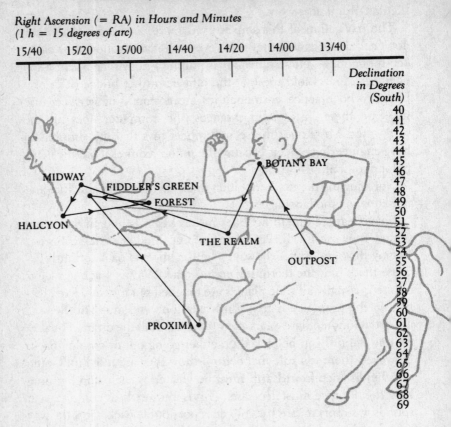

Right Ascension (= RA) in Hours and Minutes
(1 h = 15 degrees of arc)

15/40   15/20   15/00   14/40   14/20   14/00   13/40

Declination in Degrees (South)

MIDWAY
FIDDLER'S GREEN
FOREST
HALCYON
THE REALM
BOTANY BAY
OUTPOST
PROXIMA

But Alpha Centauri (Rigil Kentaurus) really shines out, third brightest star in Earth's sky. Three stars it is, actually, a brilliant one that is the twin brother of Sol, one not as bright that it is paired with, and a distant, dim, small companion that swings around both of them about a fifteenth of a light-year away. Years ago Alpha Centauri was known as Proxima. Then somebody bothered to measure the distance to this inconsequential third cousin and found that it was a hair closer, so the title of Proxima or "Nearest" was moved to this useless chunk of real estate. Then, when we set up a colony on the third planet of Alpha Centauri A (the twin of Sol), the colonists called their planet Proxima.

Eventually the astronomers who tried to shift the title to the dim companion were all dead and the colonists got their way. Just as well, because that dim star, while a hair closer today, will soon be farther away—just hold your breath a few millennia. Being "ballistically linked" it averages the same distance from Earth as the other two in the triplet.

Look at the second sketch, the one with "right ascension" across the top and "light-years" down the side.

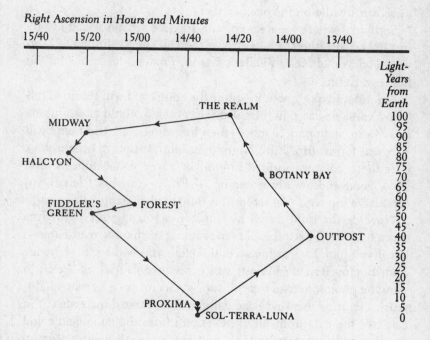

Right Ascension in Hours and Minutes

I must be the only person out of the hundreds in this ship who did not know that our first stop on this voyage would *not* be Proxima. Mr. Lopez (who was showing me the bridge) looked at me as if I were a retarded child who had just made another unfortunate slip. (But that did not matter because he is not interested in my brain.) I didn't dare explain to him that I had been snatched aboard at the last moment; it would have blown my cover. However, Miss Rich Bitch is not required to be bright.

The ship usually stops at Proxima both going and coming. Mr. Lopez explained that this time they had little cargo and only a few passengers for Proxima, not enough to pay for the stop. So that cargo and those passengers were put off until the *Maxwell* warps next month; this trip the *Forward* will call at Proxima on the way home, with cargo and, possibly, passengers from the other seven ports. Mr. Lopez explained (and I did not understand) that traveling many light-years in space costs almost nothing—mostly rations for passengers—but stopping at a planet is terribly expensive, so any stop has to be worthwhile on the balance sheet.

So here is where we are going this trip (see second sketch again): first to Outpost, then to Botany Bay, then to The Realm, on to Midway, Halcyon, Forest, Fiddler's Green, Proxima (at last!), and on home to Earth.

I'm not unhappy about it—quite the contrary! I will get rid of this "most valuable cargo in the galaxy" less than a month after warping away from Stationary Station—then the whole long trip home will be a real tourist trip. Fun! No responsibilities. Lots of time to look over these colonies squired around by eager young officers who smell good and are always polite. If Friday (or Miss Rich Bitch) can't have fun with that setup, it is time to cremate me; I'm dead.

Now see the third sketch, declination across the top, light-years down the side. This one makes the routing seem quite reasonable—but if you look back at the second sketch, you will see that the leg from Botany Bay to Outpost, which seems on the third sketch to skim the photosphere of Forest's sun, in fact misses it by many light-years. Picturing this voyage actually calls for three dimensions. You can take the data from the sketches and from the table below and punch it into your terminal and pull out a three-dimensional hologram; it all makes sense seen that way. There is one on the bridge, frozen so that you can examine it in detail. Mr. Lopez, who made these sketches (all but Joe Centaur and the sad wolf) warned me that a flat plot simply could not portray three-dimensional cosmonautics. But it helps to think of these three sketches as plan view, side view, and front elevation, as in visualizing a house from its plans; that is exactly analogous.

When Mr. Lopez gave me a printout of this table, he warned me

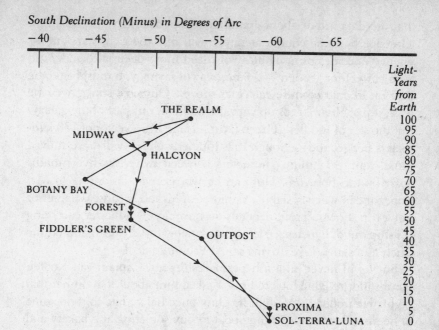

Data Concerning Eight Colonial Planets and Their Stars

Lt-yrs away	Name	Ctlg Number	Spctrl Type	Surf Temp K	Abslt Mgntd	RA Decl	Notes
40.7	Outpost	DM-54 5466	G8	5300	5.5	13h53m -54/27	cold, bleak
67.9	Botany Bay	DM-44 9181	G4	5900	4.7	14h12m -44/46	Earthlike
98.7	The Realm	DM-51 8206	G5	5700	5.4	14h24m -53/43	rich empire
4.38	Proxima	Alpha Cen.A	G2	5600	4.35	14h36m -60/38	oldest colony
57.15	Forest	DM-48 9494	G5	5500	5.1	14h55m -48/39	new, primitive
50.1	Fiddler's Green	Nu(2) Lupi	G2	5800	4.7	15h18m -48/08	restricted
90.5	Midway	DM-47 9926	G5	5600	6.1	15h20m -47/44	theocracy
81.45	Halcyon	DM-49 9653	G5	5300	5.7	15h26m -49/47	restricted
—	Sol	—	G2	5800	4.85	—	(for comparison)

that the data are of about grammar-school accuracy. If you aim a telescope by these coordinates, you will find the right star, but for science and for cosmonautics you need more decimal places, and then correct for "epoch"—a fancy way of saying you must bring the data up to date because each star moves. Outpost's sun moves the least; it just about keeps up with the traffic in our part of the galaxy. But the star of Fiddler's Green (Nu[2] Lupi) has a vector of 138 kilometers per second—enough that Fiddler's Green will have moved more than 1.5 billion kilometers between two visits five months apart by the *Forward*. This can be worrisome—according to Mr. Lopez it can worry a skipper right out of his job because whether or not a trip shows a profit depends on how closely a master can bring his ship out of hyperspace to a port planet without hitting something (such as a star!). Like driving an APV blindfolded!

But I will never pilot a hyperspaceship and Captain van Kooten has a solid, reliable look to him. I asked him about it at dinner that night. He nodded. "Ve find it. Only once haf ve had to send some of de boys down in a landing boat to buy someting at a bakery and read de signs."

I didn't know whether he expected me to laugh or to pretend to believe him, so I asked what they bought at the bakery. He turned to the lady on his left and pretended not to hear me. (The bakeshop in the ship makes the best pastry I have ever tasted and should be padlocked.)

Captain van Kooten is a gentle, fatherly man—yet I have no trouble visualizing him with a pistol in one hand and a cutlass in the other, holding off a mob of mutinous cutthroats. He makes the ship feel safe.

Shizuko is not the only guard placed on me. I think I have identified four more and I am wondering if I have them all. Almost certainly not, as I have sometimes looked around and not spotted any of them—yet the drill seems to be to have someone near me at all times.

Paranoid? It sounds like it but I'm not. I am a professional who has stayed alive through always noticing anything offbeat. This ship has six hundred and thirty-two first-class passengers, some sixty-odd uniformed officers, crew also in uniforms, and the cruise director's staff of hosts and hostesses and dancing partners and entertainers and such. The latter dress like passengers but they are young and they smile and they make it their business to see to it that the passengers are happy.

The passengers: In this ship a first-class passenger under age seventy is a rarity—me, for example. We have two teen-age girls, one teen-age boy, two young women, and a wealthy couple on their honeymoon. All others in first class are candidates for a geriatrics home. They are very old, very rich, and extremely self-centered—save for a bare handful who have managed to grow old without turning sour.

Of course none of these old dodderers are my guards, and neither are the youngsters. The cruise staff I got sorted out in the first forty-eight hours, whether they were musicians or whatever. I might have suspected that some of the younger officers had been assigned to watch me were it not that all of them stand duty watches, usually eight hours out of twenty-four, and therefore can't take on another full-time job. But my nose does not play me false; I *know* why they follow me around. I don't get this much attention dirtside but there is an acute shortage of beddable young females in this ship—thirty young male officers versus four young, single females in first class, other than Friday. With those odds a nubile female would have to have very bad breath indeed not to carry a train like a comet.

But, with all these categories accounted for, I found some men not accounted for. First class? Yes, they eat in the Ambrosia Room. Business travelers? Maybe—but according to the first assistant purser, business travelers go second class, not as swank but just as comfortable, at half the cost.

Item: When Jerry Madsen takes me to The Black Hole with his friends, here is this solitary bloke nursing a drink over in the corner. Next morning Jimmy Lopez takes me swimming; this same bloke is in the pool. In the card room I'm playing one-thumb with Tom—my shadow is playing solitaire over on the far side.

Once or twice can be coincidence . . . but at the end of three days I am certain that, anytime I am outside of suite BB, some one of four men is somewhere in sight. He usually stays as far from me as the geometry of the space permits—but he's there.

Mr. Sikmaa did impress on me that I was to carry "the most valuable package any courier ever carried." But I did not expect him to find it necessary to place guards around inside this ship. Did he think that someone could sneak up and steal it out of my bellybutton?

Or are the shadows not from Mr. Sikmaa? Was the secret broached before I left Earth? Mr. Sikmaa seemed professionally careful . . . but how about Mosby and his jealous secretary? I just don't know—and I don't know enough about politics in The Realm to make any guesses.

Later: Both of the young women are part of the watchful eye over me but they close in only when and where the men cannot—the beauty parlor, the dress shop, the women's sauna, etc. They never bother me but I'm tired of it already. I'll be glad to deliver the package so that I can fully enjoy this wonderful trip. Luckily the best part is after we leave The Realm. Outpost is such a frost (literally!) that no groundside excursions are planned there. Botany Bay is said to be very pleasant and I must see it because it is a place to which I may migrate later.

The Realm is described as rich and beautiful and I do want to see it as a tourist—but I won't be moving there. While it is reputed to be quite well governed, it is as absolute a dictatorship as is the Chicago Imperium—I've had enough of that. But for a stronger reason I would not consider asking for an immigrant's visa: I know too much. Officially I don't know anything as Mr. Sikmaa never admitted it and I didn't ask—but I won't stretch my luck by asking to live there.

Midway is another place I want to see but don't want to live. Two suns in its sky are enough to make it special . . . but it is the Pope-in-Exile that makes it very special—to visit, not to stay. It really is true that they celebrate Mass there *in public!* Captain van Kooten says so and Jerry tells me that he has seen it with his own eyes and that I can see it, too—no charge, but a contribution for charity on the part of a gentile is good manners.

I'm tempted to do it. It's not *really* dangerous and I'll probably never have a chance like this again in my whole life.

Of course I'll check out Halcyon and Fiddler's Green. Each must be extra-special or they would not command such high prices . . . but I'll be looking for the joker in the deck every minute—such as that at Eden. I would hate to ask Gloria to pay a high fee to get me in . . . then discover that I hated the place.

Forest is supposed to be nothing much for a tourist—no amenities—but I want to give it a very careful look. It is the newest colony, of course, still in the log-cabin stage and totally dependent on Earth and/or The Realm for tools and instruments.

But isn't that just the time to join a colony in order to feel great gusty joy in every minute?

Jerry just looks sour. He tells me to go look at it . . . and learn for myself that life in the forest primeval is greatly overrated.

I don't know. Maybe I could make a deal for stopover privilege: pick up this ship or one of her sisters some months from now. Must ask the Captain.

Yesterday there was a holo at the Stardust Theater that I wanted to see, a musical comedy, *The Connecticut Yankee and Queen Guinevere*. It was supposed to be quite funny, with romantic-revival music, and loaded with beautiful horses and beautiful pageantry. I avoided my swains and went alone. Or almost alone; I could not avoid my guards.

This man—"number three" in my mind, although the passenger list said that he was "Howard J. Bullfinch, San Diego"—followed me in and settled down right behind me . . . unusual, since they normally stayed as far away from me as the size of a room permitted. Perhaps he thought he might lose track of me after they lowered the lights; I don't know. His presence behind me distracted me. When the Queen sank her fangs into the Yankee and dragged him into her boudoir, instead of thinking about the fun going on in the holotank, I was trying to sort out and analyze all the odors that reached me— not easy in a crowded theater.

When the play was over and the lights came up, I reached the side aisle just as my shadow did; he gave way. I smiled and thanked him, then made exit by the forward door; he followed. That exit leads to a short staircase, four steps. I stumbled, fell backward, and he caught me.

"Thank you!" I said. "For that I am taking you to the Centaur Bar to buy you a drink."

"Oh, not at all!"

"Oh, most emphatically. You are going to explain to me why you have been following me and who hired you and several other things."

He hesitated. "You have made some mistake."

"Not me, Mac. Would you rather come quietly . . . or would you rather explain it to the Captain?"

He gave a little quizzical smile. (Or was it cynical?) "Your words are most persuasive even though you are mistaken. But I insist on paying for the drinks."

"All right. You owe me that. And then some."

I picked a table in the corner where we could not be overheard by other customers . . . thereby ensuring that we *could* be overheard by an Ear. But, aboard ship, how can one avoid an Ear? You can't.

We were served, then I said to him almost silently, "Can you read lips?"

"Not very well," he admitted at the same low level.

"Very well, let's keep it as low as possible and hope that random noise will confuse the Ear. Mac, tell me one thing: Have you raped any other helpless females lately?"

He flinched. I don't think anyone can be hit that hard and not flinch. But he paid me the courtesy of respecting my brain and showed that he was a brain, too, by answering, "Miss Friday, how did you recognize me?"

"Odor," I answered. "Odor at first; you sat too close to me. Then, as we left the theater, I forced on you a voice check. And I stumbled on the stairs and forced you to put your arms around me. That did it. Is there an Ear on us here?"

"Probably. But it may not be recording and it is possible that no one is monitoring it now."

"Too much." I worried it. Walk side by side on the promenade? An Ear would have trouble with that setup without continuous tracking, but tracking could be automatic if Mac had a beacon on him. Or I myself might be booby-trapped. Aquarius Pool? Acoustics in a swimming pool are always bad, which was good. But, damn it, I needed more privacy. "Leave your drink and come with me."

I took him to cabin BB. Shizuko let us in. So far as I could tell she stood a twenty-four-hour watch except that she slept when I did. Or I thought she did. I asked her, "What do we have later, Shizuko?"

"Purser's party, Missy. Nineteen o'clock."

"I see. Go take a walk or something. Come back in one hour."

"Too late. Thirty minutes."

"One hour!"

She answered humbly, "Yes, Missy"—but not before I caught her glance at him and his scant five-millimeter nod.

With Shizuko gone and the door bolted I said quietly, "Are you her boss or is she yours?"

"Some argument," he admitted. "Maybe 'cooperating independent agents' describes it."

"I see. She's quite professional. Mac, do you know where the Ears are in here or will we have to work out some way to defeat them? Are you willing to have your sordid past discussed and recorded on tape somewhere? I can't think of anything that would embarrass me—after all, I was the innocent victim—but I want *you* to speak freely."

Instead of answering he pointed: over my couch on the lounge side, over the head of my bed, into my bathroom—then he touched his eye and pointed to a spot where the bulkhead met the overhead opposite the couch.

I nodded. Then I dragged two chairs off into the corner farthest from the couch and out of line of sight for the Eye location he had indicated. I switched on the terminal, punched it for music, selected a tape featuring the Salt Lake City Choir. Perhaps an Ear could reach through and sort out our voices but I did not think so.

We sat down and I continued, "Mac, can you think of any good reason why I should not kill you right now?"

"Just like that? Without even a hearing?"

"Why do we need a hearing? You raped me. You know it, I know it. But I *am* giving you this much of a hearing. Can you think of any reason why you should not be summarily executed for your crime?"

"Well, since you put it that way— No, I can't."

Men will be the death of me. "Mac, you are a most exasperating man. Can't you see that I don't want to kill you and am looking for a reasonable excuse not to do so? But I can't manage it without your help. How did you get mixed up in so dirty a business as a gang rape of a blindfolded, helpless woman?"

I sat and let him stew and that's just what he did. At last he said, "I could claim that I was so deep into it by then that, if I balked at raping you, I would have been killed myself, right then."

"Is that true?" I asked, feeling contempt for him.

"True enough, but not relevant. Miss Friday, I did it because I *wanted* to. Because you are so sexy you could corrupt a Stylite. Or cause Venus to switch to Lesbos. I tried to tell myself that I couldn't avoid it. But I knew better. All right, do you want my help in making it look like suicide?"

"Not necessary." (So sexy I could corrupt a Stylite. What in the world is a Stylite?—must find out. He seemed to mean it as a superlative.)

He persisted. "Aboard ship you can't run away. A dead body can be embarrassing."

"Oh, I think not. You were hired to watch over me; do you think anything would be done to *me?* But you already know that I intend to let you get away with it. However, I want explanations before I let you go. How did you escape the fire? When I smelled you, I was astonished; I had assumed that you were dead."

"I wasn't at the fire; I ran for it before that."

"Really? Why?"

"Two reasons. I planned to leave as soon as I learned what I had come for. But mostly on your account."

"Mac, don't expect me to believe too many unlikely things. What was this you had come there to learn?"

"I never found out. I was after the same thing they were after: Why you had gone to Ell-Five. I heard them interrogate you and I could see that you did not know. So I left. Fast."

"That's true. I was a carrier pigeon . . . and when does a carrier pigeon know what a war is about? They wasted their time, torturing me."

Swelp me, he looked shocked. "They *tortured* you?"

I said sharply, "Are you trying to play innocent?"

"Eh? No, no, I'm guilty as sin and I know it. Of rape. But I didn't have any notion that they had *tortured* you. That's stupid, that's centuries out of date. What I heard was straight interrogation, then they shot you with babble juice—and you told the same story. So I knew you were telling the truth and I got out of there. Fast."

"The more you tell me, the more questions you raise. Who were you working for, why were you doing it, why did you leave, why did they let you leave, who was that voice that gave you orders—the one called the Major—why was everybody so anxious to know what I was carrying—so anxious that they would mount a military attack and waste a lot of lives and wind up torturing me and sawing off my right tit? *Why?*"

"They did *that* to you?" (Swelp me, Mac's face was utterly impassive until I mentioned damage done to my starboard milk gland. Will somebody explain males to me? With diagrams and short words?)

"Oh. Complete regeneration, functional as well as cosmetic. I'll show you—later. If you answer my questions fully. You can check it against how it used to look. Now back to business. Talk."

Mac claimed to have been a double agent. He said that, at the time, he was an intelligence officer in a quasi-military hired out to Muriel Shipstone Laboratories. As such, and working alone, he had penetrated the Major's organization—

"Wait a minute!" I demanded. "Did he die in the fire? The one called the Major?"

"I'm fairly sure he did. Although Mosby may be the only one who knows."

"Mosby? Franklin Mosby? Finders, Incorporated?"

"I hope he doesn't have brothers; one is too many. Yes. But Finders, Inc. is just a front; he's a stooge for Shipstone Unlimited."

"But you said you were working for Shipstone, too—the laboratories."

Mac looked surprised. "But the whole Red Thursday ruckus was an intramural fight amongst the top boys; everybody knows that."

I sighed. "I seem to have led a protected life. All right, you were working for Shipstone, one piece of it, and as a double agent you were working for Shipstone, another piece of it. But why was *I* the bone being fought over?"

"Miss Friday, I don't know; that is what I was supposed to find out. But you were believed to be an agent of Kettle Belly Bal—"

"Stop right there. If you are going to talk about the late Dr. Baldwin, please do not use that dreadful nickname."

"Sorry. You were thought to be an agent of System Enterprises, that is to say, of Dr. Baldwin, and you confirmed it by going to his headquarters—"

"Stop again. Were you part of the gang that jumped me there?"

"I am happy to say that I was not. You killed two and one died later and none of them was unhurt. Miss Friday, you're a wildcat."

"Go on."

"Ket— Dr. Baldwin was a mugwump, a maverick, not part of the system. With Red Thursday being mounted—"

"What's Red Thursday got to do with this?"

"Why, everything. Whatever it was that you carried was bound to affect the timing, at least. I think the Council for Survival—that's the side Mosby's goons were working for—got the wind up and moved before they were ready. Perhaps that's why nothing much ever came of it. They compromised their differences in the board-rooms. But I've never seen an analysis."

(Nor had I, and now I probably never would. I longed for a few hours at the unlimited-service terminal I had had at Pajaro Sands. What *directors* if any had been killed on Red Thursday and its *sequelae*? What had the stock market done? I suspect that all really important answers never get into the history books. Boss had been requiring me to learn the sort of things that would eventually have led me to the answers—but he had died and my education stopped abruptly. For now. But I would *still* feed the Elephant's Child! Someday.)

"Mac, did Mosby hire you for this job? Guarding me in this ship."

"Eh? No, I've only had that one contact with Mosby and that under a phony. I was hired for this through a recruiter working for a cultural attaché of the Ambassador for The Realm in Geneva. This job isn't one to be ashamed of, truly. We are taking care of you. The best care."

"Must be dull with no rape."

"Ouch."

"What are your instructions about me? And how many of you are there? You're in charge, are you not?"

He hesitated. "Miss Friday, you are asking me to tell my employer's secrets. In the profession we don't do that . . . as I think you know."

"Fiddlesticks. You knew when you walked in that door that your life depended on answering my questions. Think back to that gang that jumped me on Dr. Baldwin's farm—think what happened to them. Then speak up."

"I've thought about it, many times. Yes, I'm in charge . . . except, possibly, for Tilly—"

"Which one is Tilly?"

"Sorry. Shizuko. That's a professional name. At UCLA she was Matilda Jackson. We all had been waiting in the Sky High Hotel almost two months—"

" 'We,' plural. Name them. Ship's roster names. And don't try to stall me with guff about the mercenary's code; Shizuko will be back in a few minutes."

He named them—no surprises; I had spotted them all. Clumsy. Boss would never have tolerated it. "Go on."

"We waited and the *Dirac* warped without us and only twenty-four hours before warping time for the *Forward* we were suddenly alerted to leave in the *Forward*. Then I was supplied with color holos of you for us to study—and, Miss Friday, when I saw your picture, I almost fainted."

"Pictures were that bad? Oh, come, now."

"Huh? No, they were quite good. But consider where I saw you last. I thought that you had died in that fire. I, uh, well, you might say I had grieved over you. Some at least."

"Thank you. I think. Okay, seven, with you in charge. This trip isn't cheap, Mac; why do I need seven chaperons?"

"I had thought that *you* might tell *me*. Not that it is any of my business why you are making this trip. All I can tell you are my instructions. You are to be delivered to The Realm in perfect condition. Not a hangnail, not a bruise, not a sniffle. When we arrive, an officer of the palace guard comes aboard and then you're his problem. But we don't get paid our delivery bonus until you've had a physical examination. Then we are paid, and we deadhead home."

I thought about it. It was consistent with Mr. Sikmaa's worry over the "most valuable package a courier ever carried"—but there was something phony about it. The old belt-and-suspenders redundant-backups principle was understandable—but *seven* people, full-time, just to see that I did not fall downstairs and break my neck? It did not taste right.

"Mac, I can't think of anything else to ask you now, and Shizuko—I mean 'Tilly'—is due back. We'll talk later."

"Very well. Miss Friday, why do you call me Mac?"

"That's the only name I've ever heard you called. Socially, I mean. At a gang rape we both attended. I'm reasonably sure that you are not 'Howard J. Bullfinch.' What do you prefer to be called?"

"Oh. Yes, I was Mac on that mission. But I'm usually called Pete."

"Your name is Peter?"

"Uh, well, not exactly. It's—Percival. But I'm not called that."

I refrained from laughing. "I don't see why not, Pete. Brave and honorable men have been named Percival. I think that's Tilly at the door, anxious to bathe me and to dress me. One last word: Do you know why you are still breathing? Not dead?"

"No."

"Because you let me pee. Thank you for letting me pee before you handcuffed me to that bed."

He suddenly looked wry. "I got chewed out for that."

"You did? Why?"

"The Major intended to force you to wet the bed. He figured that it would help to make you crack."

"So? The bloody amateur. Pete, that was the point at which I decided that you were not totally beyond hope."

XXX

Outpost isn't much. Its sun is a G8 star, which puts it pretty far down the list of Sol-like stars since Sol is a G2. This is markedly cooler than our solar system star. But the star is not that important as long as it is a sol-type (G-type) star. (It may be possible to colonize around other types of stars someday but it seems reasonable to stick to stars with spectral distributions that match the human eye and don't pass out too much lethal radiation—I'm quoting Jerry. Anyhow there are over four hundred G-type stars no farther from Earth than is The Realm—so says Jaime Lopez—which could keep us busy for a few years.)

But assume a G-type star. Then you need a planet the right distance from it for it to be warm but not too warm. Then its surface gravity should be strong enough to hold its atmosphere firmly in place. That atmosphere must have had time to cook, in connection with evolving life, long enough to offer air suitable for life-as-we-know-it. (Life-as-we-*don't*-know-it is a fascinating subject but has nothing to do with colonization by Earth people. Not this week. Nor are we discussing colonies of living artifacts or cyborgs. This is about colonists from Dallas or Tashkent.)

Outpost just barely qualifies. It's a poor relation. Its sea-level oxygen is so scanty that one needs to walk slowly, as on top of a high mountain. It sits back so far from its star that it has just two sorts of weather, cool and freezing. Its axis stands almost straight up; it gets its seasons from an eccentric orbit—so you don't go south for the winter because the winter comes to you wherever you are. There is a growing season of sorts about twenty degrees each side of the equator but the winter is much longer than the summer—of course. That "of course" refers to Kepler's Laws, the one about radius vectors and equal areas. (I cribbed most of this out of the *Daily Forward*.) When the prizes were handed out, Outpost was ahint the door.

But I was frantically eager to see it.

Why? Because I had never been farther away from home than Luna—and Luna almost is home. Outpost is over forty light-years from Earth. Do you know how many kilometers that is? (Neither did I.) Here's what it is:

$$300,000 \times 40.7 \times 31,557,600 = 385,318,296,000,000 \text{ kilometers.}$$

Round it off. Four hundred million *million* kilometers.

Ship's schedule called for us to achieve stationary orbit (22.1 hours' orbital period, that being the length of the day at Outpost) at oh-two-four-seven and for the starboard landing boat to drop away very early in the morning (ship's time "morning")—oh-three hundred sharp. Not many signed up for the ride—that's all it would be since no passenger would set foot on the ground—as the midwatch isn't too popular an hour with most of our passengers.

But I would as lief miss Armageddon. I left a good party and went to bed at twenty-two hundred in order to soak up several hours of sleep before rise and shine. I got up at two o'clock and ducked into my bathroom, latching the door behind me—if I don't latch it, Shizuko comes straight in behind me; I learned that my first day in the ship. She was up and dressed when I woke up.

Latched the door behind me and promptly threw up.

This surprised me. I am not immune to motion sickness but I had not been bothered this trip. Riding the Beanstalk plays hob with my stomach and it goes on for endless hours. But in the *Forward* I had noticed one surge when we warped into hyperspace, then just before dinner last night when we broke into normal space I had felt a similar tremor, but the bridge had warned us to expect it.

Did the (artificial) gravity feel steady now? I couldn't be sure. I was quite dizzy but that might be an aftereffect of vomiting—for I had certainly thrown up as thoroughly as if I had been riding that goddam Beanstalk.

I rinsed my mouth, brushed my teeth without dentifrice, rinsed my mouth again, and said to myself, "Friday, that's your breakfast; you are not going to let an unexpected case of Beanstalk tummy keep you from seeing Outpost. Besides, you've gained two kilos and it is time to cut down on the calories."

Having given my stomach that fight talk and then turned it over to mind-control discipline, I went out, let Tilly-Shizuko help me into a heavy jump suit, then headed for the starboard landing-boat airlock, with Shizuko paddling along behind, carrying heavy coats for each of us. At first I had been inclined to be chummy with Shizuko, but after deducing, then confirming, her true role, I tended to resent her. Petty of me, no doubt. But a spy is not entitled to the friendly consideration that a servant always rates. I was not rude to her; I simply ignored her much of the time. This morning I did not feel sociable at best.

Mr. Woo, purser's assistant in charge of ground excursions, was at the airlock with a clipboard. "Miss Friday, your name isn't on my list."

"I certainly signed up. Either add it to your list or call the Captain."

"I can't do that."

"So? Then I am going on a sit-down strike right in the middle of your airlock. I don't like this, Mr. Woo. If you are trying to suggest that I should not be here because of some clerical error in your office, I shall like it still less."

"Mmm, I suppose it is a clerical error. There's not much time, so why don't you go in, let them show you to a seat, and I'll straighten it out after I get these other people checked off."

He did not object to Shizuko's following me. We went forward along a long passageway—even the landing boats of the *Forward* are enormous—following arrows that said "This Way to Bridge" and arrived in a fairly large room, something like the interior of an omnibus APV: dual controls up front, seats for passengers behind, a big windshield—and for the first time since we left Earth I was seeing "sunlight."

The light of Outpost's sun, it was, lighting a white, very white, curve of planet ahead, with black sky beyond. The sun-star was itself not in sight. Shizuko and I found seats and fastened seatbelts, the five-way sort used in SBs. Knowing that we were going by antigrav I was going to let it go simply with fastening the lap belt. But my little shadow twittered over me and fastened everything.

After a while Mr. Woo came looking, finally spotted me. He leaned across the man between me and the aisle and said, "Miss Friday, I'm sorry but you still aren't on the list."

"Indeed? What did the Captain say?"

"I couldn't reach him."

"That's your answer then. I stay."

"I'm sorry. No."

"Really? Which end are you going to carry? And who is going to help you carry me? For you will have to drag me kicking and screaming and, I assure you, I do kick and scream."

"Miss Friday, we can't have this."

The passenger next to me said, "Young man, aren't you making a fool of yourself? This young lady is a first-class passenger; I've noticed her in the dining room—at the Captain's table. Now get that silly clipboard out of my face and find something better to do."

Looking worried—junior pursers always look worried—Mr. Woo went away. After a bit the red light came on, the siren sounded, and a loud voice said, "Leaving orbit! Prepare for surges in weight."

I had a miserable day.

Three hours to get down to the surface, two hours on the ground, three hours to get back up to stationary orbit—the trip down had music varied by an amazingly dull lecture on Outpost; the trip back had nothing but music, which was better. The two hours on the ground might have been okay had we been able to leave the landing craft. But we had to stay inboard. We were allowed to unbelt and go aft to what was called the lounge but was really just a space with a coffee-and-sandwiches bar on the port side and transparent ports on the after end. Through these you could see the migrants getting out on the deck below and cargo being unloaded.

Low rolling hills covered with snow . . . some sort of stunted growth in the middle distance . . . near the ship low buildings connected by snow sheds. The immigrants were all bundled up but they wasted no time in hurrying toward the buildings. The cargo was going onto a string of flatbed trucks pulled by a machine of some sort that puffed out clouds of black smoke . . . exactly the sort of thing you see pictured in children's history books! But this was not a picture.

I heard one woman say to her companion, "Why would anyone decide to settle here?"

Her companion made some pious answer about "the Lord's will" and I moved away. How can anyone get to be seventy years old (she was at least that) without knowing that no one "decided" to settle on Outpost . . . except in the limited sense that one "decides" to accept transportation as the only alternative to death or life imprisonment?

My stomach still felt queasy so I did not risk the sandwiches, but I thought a cup of coffee might help—until I whiffed it. Then I went straight to the rest rooms forward of the lounge, and won the title of "Ironjaw Friday." I won it fair and square but nobody knows about it but me—I found the stalls all occupied and had to wait . . . and wait I did, jaw muscles rigid. After a century or two a stall was vacated and I grabbed it and threw up again. Dry heaves, mostly—I should not have smelled the coffee.

The trip back up was endless.

Once in the *Forward* I called my friend Jerry Madsen, the junior ship's surgeon, and asked to see him professionally. By ship's rules the medical department holds clinic at oh-nine hundred each day, then handles only emergencies at other times. But I knew that Jerry would be willing to see me, whatever the excuse. I told him that it was nothing serious; I just wanted to get from him some of those pills he prescribed for old ladies with jumpy tummies—the motion-sickness pills. He asked me to meet him at his office.

Instead of having the pills waiting for me he ushered me into an examination room and closed the door. "Miss Friday, shall I send for a nurse? Or would you rather be seen by a female doctor? I can call Dr. Garcia but I hate to wake her; she was up most of the night."

I said, "Jerry, what is this? When did I stop being Marj to you? And why the prissy protocol? I just want a handful of those seasick pills. The little pink ones."

"Sit down, please. Miss Friday—okay, Marj—we don't prescribe that drug or its derivatives for young females—to be precise, females of childbearing age—without making certain that they are not pregnant. It can cause birth defects."

"Oh. Set your mind at rest, lover boy; I am not knocked up."

"That's what we are here to find out, Marj. If you are—or if you become so—we have other drugs that will make you comfortable."

Ah so! The dear thing was just trying to take care of me. "Boss man, suppose I tell you, Cub Scout honor, that I ain't done nothin' a-tall for my last two periods? Although several have tried. You among them."

"Why, I would say, 'Take this cup and get me a urine sample' and then I'll take a blood sample, and a saliva sample. I've dealt before with women who hadn't done nothin'."

"You're a cynic, Jerry."

"I'm trying to take care of you, dear."

"I know you are, you sweet thing. All right, I'll go along with the nonsense. If the mouse squeals—"

"It's a gerbil."

"If the gerbil says yes, you can notify the Pope-in-Exile that it's happened at last, and I'll buy you a bottle of champagne. This has been the longest dry spell of my life."

Jerry took his samples and did nineteen other things, and gave me a blue pill to take before dinner and a yellow pill to make me sleep and another blue pill to take before breakfast. "These don't have quite the authority of the stuff you asked for but they will do and they don't cause a baby to be born with his feet on backwards or some such. I'll call you tomorrow morning as soon as I'm through with office hours."

"I thought that pregnancy tests today were service-while-you-wait?"

"Get along with you. Your great-grandmother used to find out through her waistband becoming too tight. You're spoiled. Just hope I don't have to run the test over."

So I thanked him and kissed him, which he pretended to try to avoid but not very hard. Jerry is a lamb.

The blue pills did let me eat dinner and breakfast.

I stayed in my cabin after breakfast. Jerry called about on time. "Brace yourself, Marj. You owe me a bottle of champagne."

"*What?*" Then I quieted down for Tilly's benefit. "Jerry, you are certifiably insane. Out of your skull."

"Certainly," he agreed. "But that's no handicap in this business. Stop in and we'll discuss a regime for you. Say at fourteen?"

"Say at right now. I want to talk to that gerbil."

Jerry convinced me. He went over the details, showing just how each test was conducted. Miracles do happen and I was demonstrably pregnant . . . so *that's* why my breasts had been feeling sort of tender lately. He had a little pamphlet for me, telling me what to do, what to eat, how to bathe, what to avoid, what to expect, and dreary so forth. I thanked him and took it and left. Neither of us mentioned the possibility of abortion and he made no wisecracks about women "who hadn't done nothin'."

Only I *hadn't*. Burt was the last time and that was two periods back and anyhow I had been rendered surgically sterile at menarche and had never used contraception of any sort in all my very busy social life. All those hundreds and hundreds of times and *now* he tells me I'm pregnant!

I am not totally stupid. Having accepted the fact, the old Sherlock Holmes rule told me when and where and how it had happened. Once back in cabin BB I went into the bathroom, latched the door, took off my clothes, and lay down on the floor—spread both hands around my navel, tensed my muscles, and pushed.

A little nylon sphere popped out and I grabbed it.

I examined it carefully. No doubt about it; this was the same little marble I had worn in there since the trick surgery was done to me, always worn except when I was carrying a message there. Not a container for an ovum in stasis, not a container for anything—just a small, featureless, translucent sphere. I looked at it again and popped it back in.

So they had lied to me. I had wondered at the time about "stasis" at body temperature because the only stasis for living tissues I had ever heard of involved cryogenic temperatures, liquid nitrogen or lower.

But that was Mr. Sikmaa's problem and I don't claim to be a biophysicist—if he had confidence in his scientists, it was not my place to argue. I was a courier; my sole responsibility was to deliver the package.

What package? Friday, you know durn well what package. Not one in your navel. One about ten centimeters farther inside. One that was planted in you one night in Florida when you were induced to sleep sounder than you knew. One that takes nine months to unload. That postpones your plans to complete the Grand Tour, does it not? If this fetus is what it *has* to be, they won't let you leave The Realm until after you unload.

If they wanted a host mother, why the blinkin' hell didn't they say so? I would have been reasonable about it.

Wait a moment! The *Dauphiness* has to give birth to this baby. That is what the whole hanky-panky is about: an heir to the throne, free of any congenital defects, from the Dauphiness—unarguably from the Dauphiness, born in the presence of about four court physicians and three nurses and a dozen members of the court. Not you, you mongrel AP with the phony birth certificate!

Which took me back to the original scenario with just the slightest variation: Miss Marjorie Friday, wealthy tourist, goes groundside on The Realm to enjoy the glories of the imperial capital . . . and catches a bad cold and has to go to hospital. And the Dauphiness is brought to the same hospital and—no, hold it! Would the Dauphiness do anything so plebeian as to be a patient in a hospital open to tourists?

Okay, try this: You enter hospital with a bad cold, as instructed. About three in the morning you go out the back door on a meat wagon with a sheet draped over you. You wind up in the Palace. How soon? How long will it take the Palace physicians to fiddle her royal body chemistry into receptiveness for the fetus? Oh, forget it, Friday; you don't know and don't have to know. When she is ready, they place both of you on operating tables and spread your legs and take it out of you and plant it in her, while it's small and no problem.

Then you get paid a fancy price and you leave. Does The First Citizen thank you? Probably not in person. But possibly incognito if— Stop it, Friday! Don't daydream; you know better. At a lecture clear back in basic—one of Boss's orientation lectures, it was—

"The trouble with this sort of mission is that, after an agent has successfully completed it, something permanent happens to that agent, something that keeps him from talking, then or later. So, no matter how lavish the fee, it is well to avoid this class of mission."

XXXI

During the leg to Botany Bay I mulled that thought over and over, trying to find some flaw in it. I recalled the classic case of J. F. Kennedy. His putative assassin had been killed (assassinated) too quickly for even a preliminary hearing. Then there was that dentist who had gunned down Huey Long—gunned down himself a few seconds later. And any number of agents during the long Cold War who had lived just long enough to carry out their missions and "just happened" to walk in front of speeding vehicles.

But the picture that kept coming back to my mind was so old that it is almost mythology: A lonely beach and a pirate chief supervising the burying of treasure. The hole is dug, the chests of loot placed therein—and the men who dug the hole are shot; their bodies help to fill the hole.

Yes, I'm being melodramatic. But it is *my* womb we are talking about, not yours. Everybody in the Known Universe knows that the father of the present First Citizen climbed to the throne over uncounted dead bodies and his son stays on that throne by being even more ruthless than his father.

Is he going to thank me for having improved his line? Or is he going to bury my bones in his deepest dungeon?

Don't kid yourself, Friday; knowing too much is a capital offense. In politics it always has been. If they ever had any intention of treating you fairly, you would not be pregnant. Therefore you are forced to assume that they will not treat you fairly *after* they take this royal fetus out of you.

What I had to do was obvious.

What was not obvious was how I could do it.

It no longer seemed a clerical error that my name had not been on the list to go down to the surface at Outpost.

At the cocktail hour the next evening I saw Jerry and asked him to dance with me. It was a classic waltz, which brought my face close enough to his to talk privately. "How's the tummy?" he asked.

"The blue pills do the trick," I assured him. "Jerry, who knows about this besides you and me?"

"Now there's an odd thing. I've been so busy that I haven't had time to enter anything in your medical folder. The notes are in my safe."

"So? How about the lab technician?"

"He's been so overworked that I ran those tests myself."

"Well, well. Do you think that there is a possibility that those notes might be lost? Burned, maybe?"

"We never burn anything in the ship; it annoys the air-conditioning engineer. Instead we shred and recycle. Fear not, little girl; your shameful secret is safe with me."

"Jerry, you're my pal. Dear, if it hadn't been for my maid, I think I could have blamed this baby on you. My first night in the ship— remember?"

"I'm not likely to forget. I had an attack of acute frustration."

"Having a maid along is not my idea; my family planted her on me, and she sticks to me like a leech. One would think my family does not trust me merely because they know they can't—as you know all too well. Can you think of a way to avoid her chaperonage? I'm feeling very pliable. With you. A man I can trust with secrets."

"Um. I must give it some thought. My stateroom is no good; you have to pass two dozen other officers' rooms and go through the wardroom to reach it. Watch it; here comes Jimmy."

Yes, of course I was trying to bribe him into silence. But besides that I was grateful and felt that I owed him something. If congress with my unvirgin carcass was what he wanted (and it was), I was willing—and willing on my own account, too; I had been quite underprivileged lately and Jerry is an attractive man. I was not embarrassed over being pregnant (although the idea was decidedly novel to me) but I did want to keep my condition secret (if possible—if there were not already a platoon of people in the ship who knew of it!)—keep it secret, if it was, while I sorted out what to do.

The extent of my predicament may not be clear; maybe I had better draw a diagram. If I went on to The Realm, I expected to be killed in a surgical operating room, all quiet and legal and proper. If you don't believe that such things can happen, we aren't living in the same world and there is no point in your reading any more of this memoir. Throughout history the conventional way of dealing with an awkward witness has been to arrange for him to stop breathing.

This might not happen to me. But all the signs suggested that it would—*if* I went to The Realm.

Just stay aboard? I thought of that . . . but Pete-Mac's words echoed in my ears: "When we arrive, an officer of the palace guard comes aboard and then you're his problem." Apparently they weren't even going to wait for me to go groundside and pretend to fall ill.

Ergo, I must leave the ship *before* we reached The Realm—i.e., Botany Bay, no other choice.

Simple. Just walk off the ship.

Oh, sure! Walk down the gangway and wave good-bye from the ground.

This is not an ocean ship. The closest the *Forward* ever gets to a planet is its stationary orbit—for Botany Bay that is about thirty-five thousand kilometers. That's a long way to go in some very thin vacuum. The only possible way I could get down to the surface of Botany Bay would be in one of the ship's landing boats, just as I had at Outpost.

Friday, they are not going to let you walk aboard that landing boat. At Outpost you bulled your way aboard. That has alerted them; you won't manage it a second time. What will happen? Mr. Woo or somebody will be at the airlock with a list—and again your name is not on it. But this time he has an armed master-at-arms with him. What do you do?

Why, I disarm him, bang their heads together, step over their unconscious bodies, and take a seat. You can do it, Friday; you've been trained for it and genetically designed for just that sort of rough stuff.

Then what happens? The landing boat does not leave on time. It waits in its cradle while a squad of eight comes in and by brute force and a tranquilizer dart takes you out of the boat and locks you into cabin BB—where you stay until that officer of the palace guard takes custody of your carcass.

This is not a problem rough stuff can solve.

That leaves sweet talk, sex appeal, and bribery.

Wait! What about *honesty?*

Huh?

Certainly. Go straight to the Captain. Tell him what Mr. Sikmaa promised you, tell him how you were swindled, get Jerry to show him the pregnancy report, tell him that you are frightened and have decided to wait on Botany Bay until some ship calls that is headed back to Earth, not to The Realm. He's a sweet, fatherly old dear; you've seen pictures of his daughters—he'll take care of you!

What would Boss's opinion be of that?

He would note that you sit on the Captain's right—*why?*

You were given one of the ship's most posh cabins at the last minute—*why?*

Space was found for seven others, people who spend all their time watching you—*do you think the Captain does not know this?*

Somebody took your name off the ground-trip list for Outpost—*who?*

Who owns HyperSpace Lines? Thirty percent is owned by Interworld, which in turn is owned or controlled by various segments of the Shipstone group. And you noticed that 11 percent was owned by three banks on The Realm—you noticed this because other chunks of Shipstone companies were owned from The Realm.

So don't expect too much from sweet old Captain van Kooten. You can hear him now: "Oh, I don't zink so. Mr. Sikmaa is a goot friend of mine; I haf known him for years. Yes, I did promise him zat no chances would be taken wiz your safety; zat's vy I can't let you go down to vild, uncivilized planets. But ven ve go back, I show you real, goot time on Halcyon, I promise. Now you yust be a goot girl and not make me any more troubles—henh?"

He might even believe it.

He almost certainly knows that you are not "Miss Rich Bitch" and probably has been told that you contracted as a host mother (probably not told that it was for the Royal Family—although he may guess it) and he would simply think that you are trying to welch on a legal and equitable contract. Friday, you have *not one word in writing* that would even tend to indicate that you were swindled.

Don't expect help from the Captain. Friday, you're on your own.

It was only three days before our scheduled arrival at Botany Bay that any change took place. I did a lot of pondering but most of it was maundering—futile and time-wasting imaginings about what I would do if I could *not* manage to jump ship in Botany Bay. Like this: "You heard me, Captain! I'm locking myself in my cabin until we leave The Realm. If you have the door broken down so that you can turn me over to that palace guard officer, I can't stop you—but a dead body is all you'll find!"

(Ridiculous. Sleepy gas through the air pipes is all it would take to outflank me.)

Or— "Captain, have you ever seen a knitting-needle abortion? You are invited to come watch; I understand that one can be quite bloody."

(Even more ridiculous. I can talk about abortion; I can't do it. Even though this wart inside me is no kin to me, it is nevertheless my innocent guest.)

I tried not to waste time on such useless thoughts but to concentrate my mind on subversion while continuing to behave normally. When the purser's office announced that it was time to sign up for excursions on Botany Bay, I was one of the first to show up, going over all the possibilities, asking questions, taking brochures to my cabin, and signing up for and paying cash for all the best and most expensive trips.

That night at dinner I chattered to the Captain about the trips I had picked, asked his opinions on each, and complained again about my name having been left off the list at Outpost and asked him to check on it for me this time—as if the Captain of a giant liner had nothing better to do than to run errands for Miss Rich Bitch. So far as I could see, he did not flinch under any of this—he certainly did not tell me that I could not go groundside. But he may be as steeped in sin as I am; I learned to lie with a straight face long before I left the crèche.

That evening (ship's schedule time) I found myself in The Black Hole with my first three swains: Dr. Jerry Madsen, Jaime "Jimmy" Lopez, and Tom Udell. Tom is first assistant supercargo and I had never known quite what that is. All that I really knew was that he wore one more stripe than the other two. That first night aboard Jimmy had told me solemnly that Tom was the head janitor.

Tom had not denied it. He answered, "You forgot 'furniture mover.' "

This night, less than seventy-two hours out from Botany Bay, I found out part of what Tom did. The starboard landing boat was being loaded with cargo for Botany Bay. "The port boat we loaded at Beanstalk," he told me. "But we had to load the starboard boat for Outpost. We need both of them to handle Botany Bay, so we have to shift cargo this leg." He grinned. "Lots of sweaty work."

"It's good for you, Tommy; you're getting fat."

"Speak for yourself, Jaime."

I asked how they loaded the boat. "That airlock looks pretty small to me."

"We don't move cargo through that. Would you like to see how we handle it?"

So I made a date with him for the next morning. And learned things.

The holds in the *Forward* are so enormous that they breed agoraphobia rather than claustrophobia. But even the holds in the landing boats are huge. Some of the items shipped are enormous, too, especially machinery. Botany Bay was receiving a Westinghouse turbogenerator—big as a house. I asked Tom how in the world they would move *that?*

He grinned. "Black magic." Four of his cargomen placed a metallic net around it and fastened a suitcase-size metal box to it. Tom inspected it, then said, "Okay, fire it up."

The leader—the "snapper"—did so . . . and this metal behemoth quivered and lifted a touch: a portable antigrav unit, not unlike that for an APV, but out in the open instead of built into a shell.

With extreme care, by hand, using lines and poles, they moved this thing through an enormous door and into the hold of the starboard boat. Tom pointed out that, while this huge monster was floating, free of the ship's artificial gravity, it was as ponderously massive as ever and could crush a man as easily as a man can crush an insect. "They depend on each other and have to trust each other. I'm responsible—but it's no use to a dead man for me to take the blame; they must take care of each other."

What he was really responsible for, he told me, was being certain that each item was placed by plan and was tied down solidly against surges, and also being absolutely certain that the big cargo doors, both sides, were actually vacuum-tight each time they were closed after being opened.

Tom showed me through the landing boat's migrant-passenger spaces. "We've got more new colonists for Botany Bay than for anywhere else. When we leave there, third class will be almost deserted."

"Are they all Aussies?" I asked.

"Oh, no. Lots of them are but about a third of them are not. But one thing they all do have in common; they are all fluent in English. It's the only colony with a language requirement. They are trying to ensure that their whole planet will have a single language."

"I heard something about that. Why?"

"Some notion that they are less likely to have wars. Maybe so . . . but the bloodiest wars in history have been fratricidal wars. No language problem."

I didn't have an opinion so I didn't comment. We left the boat through the passenger airlock and Tom closed it behind us. Then I recalled that I had left a scarf behind. "Tom, did you see it? I know I had it in the migrants' hold."

"No, but we'll find it." He turned back and unlocked the airlock door.

The scarf was where I had dropped it between two benches in the migrants' space. I flipped it around Tom's neck and pulled his face down to mine and thanked him, and let my appreciation progress as far as he cared to push it—which was pretty far but not that far as he was still on duty.

He deserved my best thanks. That door has a combination lock. Now I could open it.

When I returned from inspecting the cargo holds and the landing boat, it was almost lunchtime. Shizuko, as usual, was doing some sort of busywork (it can't take all of one woman's time to see that another woman is well groomed).

I said to her, "I don't want to go to the dining room. I want to take a quick shower, grab a robe, and eat here."

"What will Missy have? I will order."

"Order for both of us."

"For *me?*"

"For you. I don't want to eat alone, I just don't want to have to dress up and go to the dining room. Don't argue; just punch for the menu." I headed for the bath.

I heard her start to order but by the time I switched off the shower she was ready with a big fluffy towel, with a smaller one wrapped around her, the perfect bath girl. When I was dry and she had helped me into a robe, the dumbwaiter was chiming. While she opened the delivery drawer, I pulled a small table over into the corner where I had talked with Pete-Mac. Shizuko raised her eyebrows but did not argue; she started laying out lunch on it. I set the terminal for music and again punched up a tape with some loud singing, classic rock.

Shizuko had set only one place at the table. I said, facing her so that my words would reach her through the music, "Tilly, put your plate there, too."

"What, Missy?"

"Knock it off, Matilda. The farce is over. I've set this up so that we can talk."

She barely hesitated. "Okay, Miss Friday."

"Better call me Marj so that I won't have to call you Miss Jackson. Or call me Friday, my real name. You and I have got to take our hair down. By the way, your lady's-maid act is perfect, but there is no longer any need to bother with it when we're in private. I can dry myself after a bath."

She almost smiled. "I rather enjoy taking care of you, Miss Friday. Marj. Friday."

"Why, thank you! Let's eat." I spooned sukiyaki over onto her plate.

After some chomping—conversation goes better with food—I said, "What do you get out of it?"

"Out of what, Marj?"

"Out of riding herd on me. Turning me over to the palace guard on The Realm."

"Contract rates. Paid to my boss. There is supposed to be a bonus in it for me but I believe in bonuses only when I spend them."

"I see. Matilda, I'm cutting out at Botany Bay. You're going to help me."

"Call me Tilly. I am?"

"You are. Because I'm going to pay you a large chunk more than you would get otherwise."

"Do you really think you can switch me that easily?"

"Yes. Because you have just two choices." Between us was a large stainless-steel serving spoon. I picked it up, squeezed the bowl, crushed it. "You can help me. Or you can be dead. Rather quickly. Which is it?"

She picked up the mutilated spoon. "Marj, you don't have to be so dramatic. We'll work something out." With her thumbs she ironed out the crumpled steel. "What's the problem?"

I stared at the spoon. " 'Your mother was a test tube—' "

" '—and my father was a knife.' So was yours. That's why I was recruited. Let's talk. Why are you jumping ship? I'll catch hell if you do."

"I'll be dead if I don't." Without trying to hold back, I told her about the deal I had made, how I had turned up pregnant, why I thought my chances of living through a visit to The Realm were slim. "So what does it take to persuade you to look the other way? I think I can meet your price."

"I'm not the only one watching you."

"Pete? I'll handle Pete. The other three men and the other two women I think we can ignore. If I have your active help. You—you and Pete—are the only professionals. Who recruited these others? Clumsy."

"I don't know. I don't know who hired me, for that matter; it was done through my boss. Perhaps we can forget the others—depends on your plan."

"Let's talk money."

"Let's talk plans first."

"Uh . . . do you think you can imitate my voice?"

Tilly answered, " 'Uh . . . do you think you can imitate my voice?' "

"Do that again!"

" 'Do that again!' "

I sighed. "Okay, Tilly, you can do it. The *Daily Forward* says that breakout near Botany Bay is sometime tomorrow and, if the figures are as sharp as they were for Outpost, we'll hit stationary orbit and put boats down about midday the day after tomorrow—less than forty-eight hours from right now. So tomorrow I fall ill. Very sad. Because I had had my heart set on going down to the surface for all those wonderful excursions. The exact timing on my plan depends on when those landing boats are scheduled, which must wait—if I understand the matter—until we break out into normal space and they can predict exactly when we will hit stationary orbit. Whenever that is, the night before the boats go down, around oh-one hundred when the corridors are empty, I leave. From there on you're both of us. You don't let anyone in; I'm too ill.

"If anyone calls for me by terminal, be careful not to switch on the video pickup—I never do. You're both of us on anything you can handle, or, if you can't, I'm asleep. If you start to impersonate me and it gets too sticky, why, you're just so fogged up with fever and medicine that you're not coherent.

"You'll order breakfast for both of us—your usual breakfast for you, and tea and milk toast and juice for the invalid."

"Friday, I can see that you're planning on stowing away in a landing boat. But the doors to the landing boats are always locked when not in use. I know."

"So they are. Not your worry, Til."

"All right. Not my worry. Okay, I can cover for you after you leave. What do I tell the Captain after you've gone?"

"So the Captain *is* in on it. I thought so."

"He knows about it. But we get our orders from the purser."

"Makes sense. Suppose I arrange for you to be tied up and gagged . . . and your story is that I jumped you and did it to you. I can't, of course, because you have to be both of us from very early morning to whatever time the boats leave. But I can arrange to have you tied and gagged. I think."

"That would certainly improve my alibi! But who is the philanthropist?"

"You remember our first night in the ship? I came in late, with a date. You served us tea and almond cakes."

"Doctor Madsen. You're counting on *him?*"

"I think so. With your help. That night he was kind of eager."

She snorted. "His tongue was dragging on the rug."

"Yes. It still is. Tomorrow I become ill; he comes to see me, professionally. You are here, as usual. We have the lights turned off in the bedroom end. If Dr. Jerry has the steady nerves I think he has, he'll take what I'll offer. Then he'll cooperate." I looked at her. "Okay? He comes to see me the next morning—and ties you up. Simple."

Tilly sat and looked thoughtful for long moments. "No."

"No?"

"Let's keep it *really* simple. Don't let anyone else in on it. Not *anybody.* I don't need to be tied up; that would just cause suspicion. Here's my story: Sometime not very long before the boats go down you decide that you are well; you get up, get dressed, and leave the cabin. You don't tell me your plans; I'm just the poor dumb maid— you never tell me such things. Or maybe you've changed your mind and are going on the ground excursion anyhow. It doesn't matter either way. I am not charged with keeping you in the ship. My sole responsibility is to keep an eye on you here in the cabin. I don't think it's Pete's responsibility to keep you in the ship, either. If you manage to jump ship, probably the only one who gets burned is the Captain. And I'm not crying over him."

"Tilly, I think you are right, on all points. I had assumed that you would want an alibi. But you're better off without one."

She looked at me and smiled. "Don't let that keep you from taking Dr. Madsen to bed. Enjoy yourself. One of my jobs was to keep men out of your bed—as I think you know—"

"I figured it out," I agreed dryly.

"But I am switching sides, so that is no longer the case." Suddenly she dimpled. "Maybe I should offer Dr. Madsen a bonus. When he calls on his patient the next morning and I tell him that you're well and have gone to the sauna or something."

"Don't offer him that sort of bonus unless you mean business. As I know that *he* means business." I shivered. "I'm *certain*."

"If I advertise, I deliver. Are we all straight?" She stood up, I followed.

"All but what I owe you."

"I've been thinking about that. Marj, you know your circumstances better than I do. I'll leave it up to you."

"But you didn't quite tell me what you are being paid."

"I don't know. My master hasn't told me."

"Are you *owned*?" I felt sudden distress. Any AP would.

"No longer. Or not quite. I was sold on a twenty-year indenture. Thirteen years to go. Then I'm free."

"But— Oh, God, Tilly, let's get *you* off the ship, too!"

She put a hand on my arm. "Take it easy. You've got me thinking about it. That's the main reason I don't want to be tied up. Marj, I'm not on the ship's rolls as indentured. Consequently I can take a groundside excursion if I can pay for it—and I can. Maybe I'll see you down there."

"Yes!" I kissed her.

She pulled me to her strongly, and the kiss gained speed. She was moaning against my tongue and I felt her hand inside my robe.

Presently I broke the kiss and looked into her eyes. "Is that how it is, Tilly?"

"Hell, yes! From the first time I bathed you."

That evening the migrants leaving the ship at Botany Bay staged a lounge show for the first-class passengers. The Captain told me that such shows were traditional and that the first-class passengers customarily contributed to a purse for the colonists—but that it was not compulsory. He himself went to the lounge that night—also traditional—and I found myself sitting with him. I used the opportunity to mention that I was not feeling well. I added that I might have to cancel my reservations for dirtside excursions. I groused about it a bit.

He told me that, if I did not feel perfectly fit, I certainly should not risk exposing myself on the surface of a strange planet—but not to worry about missing Botany Bay, which wasn't much at best. The rest of the trip was the wonderful part. So be a goot girl or should I lock you in your room?

I told him that, if my tummy didn't stop acting up, it wouldn't be necessary to lock me up. The trip down to Outpost had been horrid—spacesick all the way—and I wouldn't risk anything like that again. I had laid groundwork for this by pecking at my food at dinner.

The show was amateurish but jolly—some skits but mostly group singing: "Tie Me Kangaroo Down," "Waltzing Matilda," "Botany Bay," and, for an encore, "The Walloping Window Blind." I enjoyed it but would have thought nothing of it were it not for a man in the second row of the group singers, a man who looked familiar.

I looked at him and thought: Friday, have you become the sort of careless, sloppy slitch who can't remember whether she's slept with a man or not?

He reminded me of Professor Federico Farnese. But this man was wearing a full beard, whereas Freddie had been smooth-shaven—which proves nothing as there had been time enough to grow a beard and almost all men get overtaken by the beard mania one time or another. But it did make it impossible for me to be certain by looking at him. This man never sang a solo, so voice did not help.

Body odor—at a range of thirty meters no way to sort it out from dozens of others.

I was greatly tempted not to be a lady—stand up, walk straight across the dance floor, confront him: "Are you Freddie? Didn't you take me to bed in Auckland last May?"

What if he says no?

I'm a coward. What I did do was tell the Captain that I thought I had spotted an old acquaintance from Sydney among the migrants and how could I check? That resulted in my writing "Federico Farnese" on a program and the Captain passed it to the purser, who passed it to one of his assistants, who went away and came back soon with a report that there were several Eyetalian names among the migrants but no name, Eyetalian or otherwise, even vaguely like "Farnese."

I thanked him and thanked the purser and thanked the Captain— and thought about asking for a check on "Tormey" and "Perreault," but decided that it was damfoolishness; I certainly had not seen Betty or Janet—and they didn't grow beards. I had seen a face behind a full beaver—meaning I hadn't seen it. Put a full beard on a man and all you see is the shredded wheat.

I decided that all the old wives' tales about pregnant women were probably true.

XXXII

It was two hours past midnight, ship's time. Breakout into normal space had taken place on time, about eleven in the morning, and the figures had been so good that the *Forward* was expected to achieve stationary orbit around Botany Bay at oh-seven-forty-two, several hours better than had been estimated before breakout. I was not pleased because an early morning landing-boat departure increased the hazard (I judged) that people might be prowling around the corridors in the still hours of the night.

No choice. It was rushing at me, no second chance. I finished last-minute adjustments, kissed Tilly good-bye, cautioned her with a finger to make no noise, and let myself out the door of cabin BB.

I had to go far aft and down three decks. Twice I slowed down to avoid night watchmen making their rounds. Once I ducked through a transverse passage to avoid a passenger, continued aft to the next passageway across the ship, then went back to starboard. Eventually I reached the short, dead-end corridor that led to the passenger airlock door for the starboard landing boat.

I found Mac-Pete-Percival waiting there.

I moved quickly to him, smiling, put a finger to my lips for silence, and clipped him under the ear.

I eased him to the deck, pulled him out of my way, and got to work on that combination lock—

—and discovered that it was almost impossible to read the marks on the dial, even with my enhanced night-sight. There was nothing but night-lights in the corridors and this short dead end had none of its own. Twice I muffed the combination.

I stopped and thought about it. Go back to cabin BB for a torch-light? I had none there, but perhaps Tilly had one. If she did not, should I wait until morning lights were turned on? That would be cutting it too fine; people would be stirring. But did I have a choice?

I checked Pete—still out but his heart was strong . . . and lucky for you, Pete; had I been fully triggered, you would be dead. I searched him.

I found, with no surprise, a pencil light on him—his job (tailing me) could need a torchlight, whereas Miss Rich Bitch does not bother with such things.

A few seconds later I had the door open.

I dragged Pete through, closed and locked the door, spinning the wheel both clockwise and counterclockwise. I turned back, noted that Pete's eyelids moved a touch—clipped him again.

There followed a bloody awkward chore. Pete masses about eighty-five kilos, not gross for a man. But it's twenty-five kilos more than I do and he's much bigger. I knew from Tom that the engineers were holding the artificial gravity at 0.97 gee to match Botany Bay. At that moment I could have wished for free fall or antigrav gear as I could not leave Pete behind, dead or alive.

I managed to get him up into that cross-shoulder carry that some call fireman's carry, then discovered that the best way for me to see ahead and still have a hand free for dogs on airtight doors and such was to hold Pete's pencil light in my mouth like a cigar. I really needed that light—but, given a choice, I would have felt my way through in the dark, sans unconscious body.

With only one false turn I arrived at last in that biggest cargo hold . . . which seemed even bigger with only a pencil beam to cut through the total darkness. I had not anticipated total darkness; I had visualized the landing boat as faintly illuminated with night-lights as was the ship proper from midnight to oh-six hundred.

At last I reached the hidey-hole I had picked out the day before: that giant Westinghouse turbogenerator.

I guessed that this big mass was intended to run on gas of some sort, or possibly steam—it certainly was not meant for Shipstones. There is a lot of obsolete engineering that is still useful in the colonies but is no longer used anywhere that Shipstones are readily available. None of it is familiar to me but I was not concerned with how this thing worked; my interest lay in the fact that half of it was somewhat like a frustrum of a giant cone laid on its side—and this formed a space in the middle under the narrow end of the frustrum, a space over a meter high. Big enough for a body. Mine. Even for two, luckily, since I had this unwelcome guest whom I could neither kill nor leave behind.

That space was made downright cozy by the fact that the cargo men had placed a fitted glass tarpaulin over this monster before tying it down. I had to wiggle in, between tiedowns, then I had to strain like the very devil to drag Pete in after me. I made it. Minus some skin.

I checked him again, then peeled him. With any luck I would get a little sleep—impossible had I left one of my guards loose behind me.

Pete was wearing trousers, belt, shirt, shorts, socks, sneakers, and a sweater. I took everything off, then tied his wrists behind him with his shirt, tied his ankles with his trouser legs, fastened his ankles to his wrists with his belt behind his back—this is one hell of an awkward position, taught to me in basic as a way to discourage attempts to escape.

Then I started to gag him, using his shorts and sweater. He said quietly, "No need to do that, Miss Friday. I've been awake quite a while. Let's talk."

I paused. "I thought you were awake. But I was willing to go along with the pretense as long as you were. I assumed that you would realize that, if you gave me any trouble, I would tear off your gonads and stuff them down your throat."

"I figured something of the sort. But I didn't expect you to be quite that drastic."

"Why not? I've run into your gonads before. Not favorably. They are mine to tear off if I wish. Any argument?"

"Miss Friday, will you let me talk?"

"Sure, why not? But one peep out of you louder than a whisper and these toys come off." I made sure he knew what I meant.

"Uh! Easy there—please! The purser put us on double watch to-night. I—"

"Double watch? How?"

"Ordinarily Tilly—Shizuko—is the only one on duty from the time you go to your cabin until you get up. When you do get up, she punches a button and that tells me to set the watch. But the purser—or maybe the Captain—is itchy about you. Worries that you might try to jump ship at Botany Bay—"

I made my eyes round. "Goodness gracious! How can anyone have such wicked thoughts about little ole me?"

"I can't imagine," he answered solemnly. "But why are we here in this landing boat?"

"I'm getting ready to go sight-seeing. How about you?"

"Me, too. I hope. Miss Friday, I realized that, if you were going to try to jump ship at Botany Bay, the most likely time would be tonight during the midwatch. I didn't know how you expected to get into the landing boat but I had confidence in you—and I see that my confidence is justified."

"Thank you. Some, anyhow. Who's watching the portside boat? Or is there someone?"

"Graham. Little sandy bloke. Perhaps you've noticed him?"

"Too often."

"I picked this side because you toured this boat with Mr. Udell yesterday. Day before yesterday, depending on how you figure it."

"I don't care how you figure it. Pete, what happens when you are missed?"

"I may not be missed. Joe Stupid—sorry, Joseph Steuben—the other is just my private name for him—I have instructed to relieve me after he eats breakfast. If I know Joe, he'll make no fuss at not finding me at the door; he will just sit down on the deck with his back to the door and sleep until someone comes along and unlocks it. Then he'll stay there until this boat drops away . . . whereupon he will go to his room and sack in until I look for him. Joe is steady but not bright. Which I figured on."

"Pete, it sounds as if you had planned this."

"I didn't plan to get a sore neck and a headache out of it. If you had waited long enough to let me speak, you wouldn't have had to carry me."

"Pete, if you're trying to sweet-talk me into untying you, you are barking down the wrong well."

"Don't you mean 'up the wrong tree'?"

"The wrong one, in any case, and you aren't improving your chances by criticizing my figures of speech. You're in deep trouble, Pete. Give me one good reason why I shouldn't kill you and leave you here. For the Captain is right; I'm jumping ship. I can't be bothered with you."

"Well . . . one reason is that they'll find my body later this morning, while they are unloading. Then they'll be looking for you."

"I'll be many kilometers the other side of the horizon. But why would they look for me? I'm not going to leave my fingerprints on you. Just some purple bruises around your neck."

"Motive and opportunity. Botany Bay is a pretty law-abiding community, Miss Friday. You can probably talk your way out of trouble in jumping ship there—others have. But if you are wanted for a murder aboard ship, the local people will cooperate."

"I'll plead self-defense. A known rapist. Fer Gossake, Pete, what am I going to do with you? You're an embarrassment. You know I won't kill you; I can't kill in cold blood. It has to be forced on me. But if I keep you tied up— Let me see—five and three is eight, then add at least two hours before they work back to here in unloading— that's ten hours at least—and I'll have to gag you—and it's getting cold—"

"You bet it's getting cold! Could you sort of drape my sweater around me?"

"All right, but I'll have to use it later when I gag you."

"And besides being cold, my hands and feet are going to sleep. Miss Friday, if you leave me tied up this way for ten hours, I'll have gangrene in both hands and both feet—and lose them. No regeneration out here. By the time I'm back where they can do it, I'll be a permanent basket case. Kinder to kill me."

"Damn it, you're trying to work on my sympathy!"

"I'm not sure you have any."

"Look," I told him, "if I untie you and let you put your clothes back on so that you won't freeze, will you let me tie you up and gag you later without fussing about it? Or must I clip you a good deal harder than I did and knock you out cold? Run a risk of breaking your neck? I can, you know. You've seen me fight—"

"I didn't see it; I just saw the results. Heard about it."

"Same thing. Then you know. And you must know why I can do such things. 'My mother was a test tube—' "

" '—and my father was a knife,' " he interrupted. "Miss Friday, I didn't have to let you clip me. You're fast . . . but I'm just as fast and my arms are longer. I knew that you were enhanced but you did not know that I am. So I would have had the edge."

I was sitting in lotus, facing him, when he made this astounding statement. I felt dizzy and wondered if I was going to throw up again. "Pete," I said, almost pleadingly, "you wouldn't lie to me?"

"I've had to lie all my life," he answered, "and so have you. However—" He paused and twisted his wrists; his bonds broke. Do you know the breaking strength of a twisted sleeve of a good shirt? It is more than that of a manila line of equal thickness—try it.

"I don't mind ruining the shirt," he said conversationally. "The sweater will cover. But I would rather not ruin my trousers; I expect to have to appear in public in them before I can get more. You can reach the knots more easily than I can; will you untie them, Miss Friday?"

"Stop calling me Miss Friday, Pete; we're APs together." I started working on the knots. "Why didn't you tell me a long time ago?"

"I should have. Other things got in the way."

"There! Oh, your feet are cold! Let me rub them. Get the circulation back."

We got some sleep, or I did. Pete was shaking my shoulder and saying quietly, "Better wake up. We must be about to ground. Some lights have come on."

A dim twilight trickled in, under, around, and through the tarpaulin covering the dinosaur we had slept under. I yawned at it. "I'm cold."

"Complaints. You had the inside of the snuggle. That's warmer than the outside. I'm frozen."

"Just what you deserve. Rapist. You're too skinny; you don't make much of a blanket. Pete, we've got to put some fat on you.

Which reminds me that we didn't have breakfast. And the thought of food— I think I'm about to throw up."

"Uh— Slide past me and sort o' heave it back into that corner. Not here where we would have to lie in it. And keep as quiet as you can; there may be someone in here by now."

"Brute. Unfeeling brute. Just for that I won't throw up."

On the whole I felt fairly good. I had taken one of the little blue pills just before leaving cabin BB, and it seemed to be holding. I had a butterfly or two in my tummy but they weren't very muscular butterflies—not the sort that shout "Lemme outa here!" I had with me the rest of the supply Dr. Jerry had given me. "Pete, what are the plans?"

"You're asking me? You planned this jailbreak, not me."

"Yes, but you are a big, strong, masculine man who snores. I assumed that you would take charge and have it all planned out while I napped. Am I mistaken?"

"Well— Friday, what are *your* plans? The plans you made when you didn't expect to have me along."

"It wasn't much of a plan. After we ground they are going to have to open a door, either a people door or a big cargo door; I don't care which, 'cause when they do, I go out of here like a frightened cat, running roughshod over anything or anybody in my way . . . and I don't stop until I'm a long way from the ship. I don't want to hurt anybody but I hope nobody tries too hard to stop me . . . for I won't be stopped."

"That's a good plan."

"You think so? It's not really a plan at all. Just a determination. A door opens, I crush out."

"It's a good plan because it doesn't have any fancies to go wrong. And you have one big advantage. They don't dare hurt you."

"I wish I could be sure of that."

"If you are hurt, it will be by accident, and the man who does it will be strung up by his thumbs. At least. After hearing the rest of your story I now know why the instructions to me were so emphatic. Friday, they don't want you dead-or-alive; they want you in perfect health. They'll let you escape before they will hurt you."

"Then it's going to be easy."

"Don't be too sure of it. Wildcat that you are, it has already been proved that enough men can grab you and hold you; we both know that. If they know you are gone—and I think they do; this boat was over an hour late in leaving orbit—"

"Oh!" I glanced at my finger. "Yes, we should have grounded by now. Pete, they are searching for me!"

"I think so. But there was no point in waking you until the lights came on. By now they have had about four hours to make certain that you are not on the deck above with the first-class excursionists. They will have mustered the migrants as well. So, if you are here—and not simply hiding out in the ship proper—you have to be in this cargo hold. That's an oversimplification as there are all sorts of ways to play hide-and-seek in a space as big as this boat. But they'll watch the two bottlenecks, the cargo door on this level and the passenger door on the level above. Friday, if they use enough people—and they will—and if those jimmylegs are equipped with nets and sticky ropes and tanglefoot—and they will be—they will catch you without hurting you as you come out of this boat."

"Oh." I thought about it. "Pete . . . if it comes to that, there will be some dead and wounded first. I may wind up dead myself—but they'll pay a high price for my carcass. Thanks for alerting me."

"They may not do it quite that way. They may make it very obvious that the doors are being watched in order to cause you to hang back. So they get the migrants out—I suppose you know that they go out the cargo door?"

"I didn't."

"They do. Get them out and checked off—then close the big door and shoot this place full of sleepy gas. Or tear gas and force you to come out wiping your eyes and tossing your cookies."

"Brrr! Pete, are they really equipped in the ship with those gases? I wondered."

"Those and worse. Look, the skipper of this ship operates many light-years from law and order and he has only a handful of people he can depend on in a crunch. In fourth class this ship carries, almost every trip, a gang of desperate criminals. Of *course* he is equipped to gas every compartment, selectively. But, Friday, you won't be here when they use the gas."

"Huh? Keep talking."

"The migrants walk down the center aisle of this hold. Almost three hundred of them this trip; they'll be packed into their compartment tighter than is safe. So many of them this trip that I am assuming that they can't possibly all know each other in the short time they've had to get acquainted. We'll use that. Plus a very, very old method, Friday; the one Ulysses used on Polyphemus . . ."

Pete and I were hanging back in an almost dark corner formed by the high end of the generator and a something in a big crate. The light changed, and we heard a murmur of many voices. "They're coming," Pete whispered. "Remember, your best bet is someone who has too much to carry. There'll be plenty of those. Our clothes are okay—we don't *look* first class. But we must have something to carry. Migrants are always loaded down; I got the straight word on that."

"I'm going to try to carry some woman's baby," I told him.

"Perfect, if you can swing it. Hush, here they come."

They were indeed loaded down—because of what seems to me a rather chinchy company policy: A migrant can take on his ticket anything he can stuff into those broom closets they call staterooms in third class—as long as he can carry it off the ship unassisted; that's the company's definition of "hand luggage." But anything he has to have placed in the hold he pays freight charges on. I know that the company has to show a profit—but I don't have to like this policy. However, today we were going to try to turn it to our advantage.

As they passed us most of them never glanced our way and the rest seemed uninterested. They looked tired and preoccupied and I suppose they were, both. There were lots of babies and most of them were crying. The first couple of dozen in the column were strung out with those in front hurrying. Then the line moved more slowly—more babies, more luggage—and clumped together. It was coming time to pretend to be a "sheep."

Then suddenly, in that medley of human odors, of sweat and dirt and worry and fear and musk and soiled diapers, one odor cut through as crystal clear as the theme of the Golden Cockerel in Rimsky-Korsakov's *Hymn to the Sun* or a Wagnerian leitmotif in the Ring Cycle—and I yelped:

"Janet!"

A heavyset woman on the other side of the queue turned and looked at me, and dropped two suitcases and grabbed me. *"Marjie!"* And a man in a beard was saying, "I *told* you she was in the ship! I told you!" And Ian said accusingly, "You're dead!" and I pulled my mouth away from Janet's long enough to say, "No, I'm not. Junior Piloting Officer Pamela Heresford sends you her warmest regards."

Janet said, *"That* slitch!" Ian said, "Now, Jan" and Betty looked at me carefully and said, "It *is* she. Hello, luv! Good on you! My word!" and Georges was being incoherent in French around the edges while trying gently to take me away from Janet.

Of course we had fouled up the progress of the queue. Other people, burdened down and some of them complaining, pushed past us, through us, around us. I said, "Let's get moving again. We can talk later." I glanced back at the spot where Pete and I had lurked; he was gone. So I quit worrying about him; Pete is smart.

Janet wasn't really heavyset, not corpulent—she was simply several months gone. I tried to take one of her suitcases; she wouldn't let me. "Better with two; they balance."

So I wound up carrying a cat's travel cage—Mama Cat. And a large brown-paper parcel Ian had carried under one arm. "Janet, what did you do with the kittens?"

"They," Freddie answered for her, "have, through my influence, gained excellent positions with fine prospects for advancement as rodent-control engineers on a large sheep station in Queensland. And now, Helen, pray tell me how it chances that you, who, only yesterday it seems, were seen on the right hand of the lord and master of a great superliner, today find yourself consorting with the peasantry in the bowels of this bucket?"

"Later, Freddie. After we're through here."

He glanced toward the door. "Ah, yes! Later, with a friendly libation and many a tale. Meanwhile we have yet to pass Cerberus."

Two watchdogs, both armed, were at the door, one on each side. I started saying mantras in my mind while chattering double-talk inanities with Freddie. Both masters-at-arms looked at me, both seemed to find my appearance unexceptionable. Possibly a dirty face and scraggly hair acquired in the night helped, for, up to then, I had never once been seen outside cabin BB unless Shizuko had labored mightily to prepare me to fetch top prices on the auction block.

We got outside the door, down a short ramp, and were queued up at a table set just outside. At it sat two clerks with papers. One called out, "Frances, Frederick J.! Come forward!"

"*Here!*" answered Federico and stepped around me to go to the table. A voice behind me called out, "There she is!"—and I sat Mama Cat down quite abruptly and headed for the skyline.

I was vaguely aware of much excitement behind me but paid no attention to it. I simply wanted to get out of range of any stun gun or sticky-rope launcher or tear-gas mortar as fast as possible. I could not outrace a radar gun or even a slug rifle—but those were no worry if Pete was right. I just kept placing one in front of the other. There was a village off to my right and some trees dead ahead. For the time being the trees seemed a better bet; I kept going.

A glance back showed that most of the pack had been left behind—not surprising; I can do a thousand meters in two minutes flat. But two seemed to be keeping up and possibly closing the gap. So I checked my rush, intending to bang their heads together or whatever was needed.

"Keep going!" Pete rasped. "We're supposed to be trying to catch you."

I kept going. The other runner was Shizuko. My friend Tilly.

Once I was well inside the trees and out of sight of the landing boat I stopped to throw up. They caught up with me; Tilly held my head and then wiped my mouth—tried to kiss me. I turned my face away. "Don't, I must taste dreadful. Did you come out of the ship like *that?*" She was dressed in a leotard that made her look taller, more slender, more western, and much more female than I was used to in my quondam "maid."

"No. A formal kimono with obi. They're back there somewhere. Can't run in them."

Pete said irritably, "Stop the chatter. We got to get out of here." He grabbed my hair, kissed me. "Who cares what you taste like? Get moving!"

So we did, staying in the woods and getting farther from the landing boat. But it quickly became clear that Tilly had a sprained ankle and was becoming more crippled each step. Pete grumbled again.

"When you broke for it, Tilly was only halfway down the gangway from the first-class deck. So she jumped and made a bad landing. Til, you're clumsy."

"It's these damn Nip shoes; they give no support. Pete, take the kid and get moving; the busies won't do anything to me."

"Like hell," Pete said bitterly. "We three are in it together all the way. Right, Miss— Right, Friday?"

"Hell, yes! 'One for all, all for one!' Take her right side, Pete; I'll take this side."

We did pretty well as a five-legged race, not making fast time but nevertheless putting more bush between us and pursuit. Somewhat later Pete wanted to take her piggyback. I stopped us. "Let's listen."

No sound of pursuit. Nothing but the strange sounds of a strange forest. Birdcalls? I wasn't sure. The place was a curious mix of friendly and outré—grass that wasn't quite grass, trees that seemed to be left over from another geological epoch, chlorophyll that was heavily streaked with red—or was this autumn? How cold would it be tonight? It didn't seem smart to go looking for people for the next three days, in view of the ship's schedule. We could last that long without food or water—but suppose it froze?

"All right," I said. "Piggyback. But we take turns."

"Friday! You can't carry me."

"I carried Pete last night. Tell her, Pete. You think I can't handle a little Japanese doll like you?"

"Japanese doll, my sore feet. I'm as American as you are."

"More so, probably. Because I'm not very. Tell you later. Climb aboard."

I carried her about fifty meters, then Pete carried her about two hundred, and so on, that being Pete's notion of fifty-fifty. After an hour of this we came to a road—just a track through the bush, but you could see marks of wheels and horses' hooves. To the left the road went away from the landing boat and the town, so we went left, with Shizuko walking again but leaning quite a lot on Pete.

We came to a farmhouse. Perhaps we should have ducked around it but by then I wanted a drink of water more than I yearned to be totally safe, and I wanted to strap Tilly's ankle before it got bigger than her head.

There was an older woman, gray-haired, very neat and prim, sitting in a rocking chair on the front veranda, knitting. She looked up as we got closer, motioned to us to come up to the house. "I'm Mrs. Dundas," she said. "You're from the ship?"

"Yes," I agreed. "I'm Friday Jones and this is Matilda Jackson and this is our friend Pete."

"Pete Roberts, ma'am."

"Come sit down, all of you. You'll forgive me if I don't get up; my back is not what it used to be. You're refugees, are you not? You've jumped ship?"

(Bite the bullet. But be ready to duck.) "Yes. We are."

"Of course. About half the jumpers wind up first with us. Well, according to this morning's wireless you'll need to hide out at least three days. You're welcome here and we enjoy visitors. Of course you are entitled to go straight to the transient barracks; the ship authorities can't touch you there. But they can make you miserable with their endless lawyer arguments. You can decide after dinner. Right now, would you like a nice cup of tea?"

"Yes!" I agreed.

"Good. *Malcolm!* Oh, Malcooom!"

"What, Mum?"

"Put the kettle on!"

"*What?*"

"The *billy!*" Mrs. Dundas added, to Tilly, "Child, what have you done to your foot?"

"I think I sprained it, ma'am."

"You certainly did! You—Friday is your name?—go find Malcolm, tell him I want the biggest dishpan filled with cracked ice. Then you can fetch tea, if you will, while Malcolm cracks ice. And you, sir—Mr. Roberts—you can help me out of this chair because there are more things we'll need for this poor child's foot. Must strap it after we get the swelling down. And you—Matilda—are you allergic to aspirin?"

"No, ma'am."

"*Mum!* The billy's boiling!"

"You—Friday—go, dear."

I went to fetch tea, with a song in my heart.

XXXIII

It has been twenty years. Botany Bay years, that is, but the difference isn't much. Twenty *good* years. This memoir has been based on tapes I made at Pajaro Sands before Boss died, then on notes I made shortly after coming here, notes to "perpetuate the evidence" when I still thought I might have to fight extradition.

But when it became impossible to keep their schedule through using me, they lost interest in me—logical, as I was never anything but a walking incubator to them. Then the matter became academic when The First Citizen and the Dauphiness were assassinated together, that bomb planted in their coach.

Properly this memoir should end with my arrival on Botany Bay because my life stopped having any dramatic highlights at that point—after all, what does a country housewife have to write memoirs about? How many eggs we got last season? Are you interested? *I* am but you are not.

People who are busy and happy don't write diaries; they are too busy living.

But in going over the tapes and notes (and sloughing 60 percent of the words) I noticed items that, having been mentioned, should be cleared up. Janet's canceled Visa card— I was "dead" in the explosion that sank the *Skip to M'Lou*. Georges checked carefully in Vicksburg low town, was assured that there were no survivors. He then called Janet and Ian . . . when they were about to leave for

Australia, having been warned by Boss's Winnipeg agent—so of course Janet canceled her card.

The strangest thing is finding my "family." But Georges says that the strange thing is not that *they* are here but that *I* am here. All of them were browned off, disgusted with Earth—where would they go? Botany Bay is not Hobson's choice but for them it is certainly the obvious choice. It is a good planet, much like Earth of centuries back—but with up-to-date knowledge and technology. It is not as primitive as Forest, not as outrageously expensive as Halcyon or Fiddler's Green. They all lost heavily in forced liquidation but they had enough to let them go steerage class to Botany Bay, pay their contributions to company and colony, and still have starting money.

(Did you know that here on Botany Bay, nobody locks doors—many don't have locks. *Mirabile visu!*)

Georges says that the only long coincidence lies in my being in the same ship they migrated in—and it almost wasn't. They missed the *Dirac*, then barely caught the *Forward* because Janet crowded it, being dead-set on traveling with a baby in her belly rather than in her arms. But of course if they had taken a later ship or an earlier ship, I still would have met them here without planning it. Our planet is about the size of Earth but our colony is still small and almost all in one area and everyone is always interested in new chums; we were certain to meet.

But what if I had never been offered that booby-trapped job? One can always "what if—" but I think that it is at least fifty-fifty that, after shopping as I had planned, I would still have wound up on Botany Bay.

"There is a destiny that shapes our ends" and I have no complaints. I *like* being a colonial housewife in an 8-group. It's not formally an S-group here because we don't have many laws about sex and marriage. We eight and all our kids live in a big rambling house that Janet designed and we all built. (I'm no cabinetmaker but I'm a *whee!* of a rough carpenter.) Neighbors have never asked snoopy questions about parentage—and Janet would freeze them if they did. Nobody cares here, babies are welcome on Botany Bay; it will be many centuries before anyone speaks of "population pressure" or "ZeePeeGee."

This account won't be seen by neighbors because the only thing I intend to publish here is a revised edition of my cookbook—a good cookbook because I am ghost writer for two great cooks, Janet and Georges, plus some practical hints for young housewives that I owe to Goldie. So here I can discuss paternity freely. Georges married Matilda when Percival married me; I think they drew straws. Of course the baby in me fell under the old test-tube-and-knife saying—a saying I have not heard even once on Botany Bay. Maybe Wendy derives some or most of her ancestry from a former royal house on The Realm. But I have never let her suspect it and officially Percival is her father. All I really know is that Wendy is free of exhibited congenital defects and Freddie and Georges say that she doesn't carry any nasty recessives either. As a youngster she was no meaner than any of the others and the usual moderate ration of spankings was enough to straighten her out. I think that she is quite a nice person, which pleases me as she is the only child of my body even though she is no relation to me.

"The only . . ." When I got her out of the oven, I asked Georges to reverse my sterility. He and Freddie examined me and told me that I could get it done . . . on Earth. Not in New Brisbane. Not for years and years. That settled that—and I found that I was somewhat relieved. I've done it once; I don't really need to do it again. We have babies and dogs and kittens underfoot; the babies don't have to be from my body any more than the kittens do. A baby is a baby and Tilly makes good ones and so does Janet and so does Betty.

And so does Wendy. Were it not impossible I would guess that she gets her horniness from her mother—me, I mean. She had not yet turned fourteen the first time she came home and said, "Mum, I guess I'm pregnant." I told her, "Don't guess about it, dear. Go see Uncle Freddie and get a mouse test."

She announced the result at dinner, which turned it into a party because, by long custom, in our family whenever a female is officially pregnant is occasion for rejoicing and merriment. So Wendy had her first pregnancy party at fourteen—and her next one at sixteen—and her next one at eighteen—and her latest one just last week. I'm glad she spaced them because I reared them, all but the newest one; she got married for that one. So I have never been short of babies to pet, even if we didn't have four—now five—no, six—mothers in this household.

Matilda's first baby has a number-one father—excellent stock. Dr. Jerry Madsen. So she tells me. So I believe. Like this: Her former master had just had her sterility reversed, intending to breed her, when he got this chance to sell her services for a high-pay four-months' job. So she became "Shizuko" with the shy smile and the modest bow and chaperoned me—but conversely *I* chaperoned *her* without intending to. Oh, had she tried, she might have found a little night life in the daytime . . . but the fact was that she spent almost twenty-four hours of each day in cabin BB to be sure to be there whenever I came back.

So when? The only time that it could happen. While I was huddled under that turbogenerator, half frozen, with Percival, my "maid" was in my bed with my doctor. So that young man has fine parents! Joke: Jerry now lives in New Brisbane with his sweet wife, Dian—but Tilly has not let him suspect that he has a son in our household. Is this another "startling coincidence"? I don't think so. "Medical doctor" is one of the contribution-free professions here; Jerry wanted to get married and stop spacing—and why would anyone choose to settle down on Earth when he has had opportunity to shop the colonies?

Most of our family go to Jerry now; he's a good doctor. Yes, we have two M.D.s in our family but they have never practiced; they used to be gene surgeons, experimental biologists, genetic engineers—and now they are farmers.

Janet knows who are the fathers of her first child, too—both her husbands of that time, Ian and Georges. Why both? Because she wanted it that way and Janet has a whim of steel. I've heard several versions but it is my belief that she would not choose between them for her first child.

Betty's first one is almost certainly not a knife job and may be legitimate. But Betty is such a slashing outlaw that she would rather have you believe that she caught that child at a gang bang during a masquerade ball. New Brisbane is a very quiet place but no household that has Betty Frances in it can ever be dull.

You may know more about the return of the Black Death than I do. Gloria credits my warning with having saved Luna City but it is more nearly correct to credit it to Boss—my short career as soothsayer was as Trilby to his Svengali.

Plague did not get off Earth; that was surely Boss's doing . . . although once, at the critical time, New Brisbane signaled that a landing boat could not land unless it was first exposed to vacuum, then repressurized. Sure enough, this treatment killed some rats and mice—and fleas. Its captain stopped talking about charging the drill to the colony after this showed up.

Contributions: Mail between Botany Bay and Earth/Luna takes four to eight months, round-trip—not bad for a hundred and forty light-years. (I once heard a tourist lady ask *why* didn't we use radio mail?) Gloria paid my contribution to the colony with all possible speed and was lavish in setting me up with capital—Boss's will gave her leeway. She didn't send gold here; these were bookkeeping entries in the colony's account in Luna City, under which farm implements or anything can be shipped to Botany Bay.

But Pete had little on Earth to draw on and Tilly, a quasi-slave, had nothing. I still had a piece left of that lottery windfall and all of my final paycheck and even a few shares of stock. This got my fellow jumpers out of hock—our colony never turns back a jumper . . . but it may take him years to pay his share in the colony.

They both fussed. I fussed right back and worse. Not only is it all in the family but without the help of *both* Percival and Matilda I almost certainly would have been caught, then wound up on The Realm—dead. But they still insisted on paying me.

We compromised. Their payments and some from the rest of us started the Asa Hunter Bread-Upon-the-Waters Revolving Fund, used to help jumpers or any new chum.

I no longer think about my odd and sometime shameful origin. "It takes a human mother to bear a human baby." Georges told me that long ago. It's true and I have Wendy to prove it. I'm human and *I belong!*

I think that's all anybody wants. To belong. To be "people."

My word, do I belong! Last week I was trying to figure out why I was so short on time. I'm secretary of the Town Council. I'm program chairman of the Parents-Teachers Association. I'm troop mistress of the New Toowoomba Girl Scouts. I'm a past president of the Garden Club, and I'm on the planning committee of the community college we're starting. Yes, I belong.

It's a warm and happy feeling.

About the Author

ROBERT ANSON HEINLEIN was born in Butler, Missouri, in 1907. A graduate of the U.S. Naval Academy, he was retired, disabled, in 1934. He studied mathematics and physics at the graduate school of the University of California and owned a silver mine before beginning to write science fiction in 1939. In 1947 his first book of fiction, *Rocket Ship Galileo,* was published. His novels include *Double Star* (1956), *Starship Troopers* (1959), *Stranger In a Strange Land* (1961), and *The Moon Is a Harsh Mistress* (1966), all winners of the Hugo Award. Heinlein was guest commentator for the Apollo 11 first lunar landing. In 1975 he received the Grand Master Nebula Award for lifetime achievement. Mr. Heinlein died in 1988.